TAME HIS BEAST

A Devil's Highwaymen Story
The Complete Duet

By
USA Today Bestselling Author
Claire C. Riley

Claire C. Riley

Music plays a huge part of my books. I listen while I plot. While I write. And then long afterwards.

Here's the playlist I made while writing Beast & Belle's story. Enjoy

Tame his Beast part 1 & 2 playlist

Part 1:

The River – The Darcys
The Dying of the Light – Noel Galllagher's High Flying Birds
Kyoto – Feeder
Broken - Lund
Leave it Alone – Broken Bells
True Love – WILDES
Painkiller – Ruel
The Breach – Dustin Tebbutt
Grounds for Divorce – Elbow
Cowboy Song – Thin Lizzy
Run Through the Jungle – Creedance Clearwater Revival
Closer – The Chainsmokers feat. Halsey
Lemonade – Hannah Jane Lewis
Alewife – Clairo
Unholy War – Jacob Banks

Part 2:

Promise – Ben Howard
Crazy – Nothing But Thieves

Praise You – Hannah Grace
Leave Out all the Rest – Linkin Park
Shallows - Daughter
Shimmer – JFDR
Better Love – Hozier
Smoke Signals – Phoebe Bridges
Gone Away – Five Finger Death Punch
War Pigs/Luke's Wall – Black Sabbath
My Hero – Foo Fighters
Hundred Mile High City – Ocean Colour Scene
Ready for the Devil (No Mercy) – Vision Vision
Unsteady – X Ambassadors

You can find the playlist on Apple Music!
Enjoy!

TAME his BEAST

A Devil's Highwaymen Story
The complete duet

'Remember, the Devil was once an angel too'

Beast, an enforcer for the Devil's Highwaymen MC, wakes up months after being captured and tortured by another club and discovers brutal and ugly scars covering over half his body.

Once a beautiful man, able to woo any woman into his bed, now his face and body are their own horror story. Though the torture has stopped, Beast continues to relive the agony. He can't tell anyone about the nightmares he keeps having or about the fear and depression that are tearing him apart inside. He's the club's weapon, and he can't show weakness. With no one to trust and nowhere to go, his fear slowly dissolves into rage.

Belle is working as a trainee nurse at Emory Saint Joseph's Hospital when Beast is brought in. She's at first fearful of the dark-eyed man, and the MC behind him, but refuses to let anyone see that.

Brought up by her godmother, she's been taught to trust her instincts and always see the beauty in people…even if at first you only see the ugly.

He's full of *loneliness and anger.*
She's full of *hope and love.*
Can Belle see behind the beast and thaw his heart before his rage engulfs him? Or will the broken monster destroy her right alongside himself?
* 'Tame his Beast' is a standalone MC romance and connected to my Devil's Highwaymen Series *

TAME HIS BEAST

A Devil's Highwaymen Story
The Complete Duet

By
USA Today Bestselling Author
Claire C. Riley

Chapter One
~ BEAST ~

The tortured screams of Angel rang out, echoing off the beaten-up barn walls and breaking the stillness of the cool November air.

"...Please..."

Breathing heavily, I hooked my thumbs into the belt loops at my waist and took a couple of steps closer to him, my gaze on his bloody features. Angel's eyes were rolling in his head and I was no doubt looking blurry to him.

I nodded toward Echo and he dragged Angel back up to his unsteady feet for me. Angel's body was broken and bloody. Man didn't have much left in him, but the fucker was still holding on, no doubt wishing I'd just get on with it and send him to ground. But Hardy had made it clear: the Silverbacks needed to know who was in charge around here.

No one took on the Highwaymen and walked away.

Their prez should have known better.

He would now.

"...Please, brother, please..." Angel tried to look at me. But his eye sockets were smashed, the swelling so bad his eyes were almost completely closed. "Please..." he pleaded.

Any other man would be mistaken for thinking that Angel was begging for his life. But not me. I knew better. No, Angel knew it was too late for that. It had been too late for that over an hour ago, but I'd kept the pain raining down on him and then bringing him back when it all got too much. Keeping him there, on the edge of death but not letting him fall over into the abyss of it.

No, Angel was begging me to kill him, not save him.

His chin trembled, blood and saliva dribbling from his lips as he pleaded again. I snarled, angry with him. He should have more pride in himself and his club. A man should never beg. It showed weakness to you and your club. It showed others what you were really made of.

If I was ever going to let him live, I wouldn't now.

I gripped the metal chains in the palm of my hand, enjoying their heat and heaviness, the smoothness of the shiny, bloodied metal digging into my skin and leaving an imprint. And then I swung my arm back with a grunt, relishing the feel of the heavy metal hitting Angel's ribs, the following ricochet threading back up my arms. Angel dropped back down to his knees with another final guttural cry, the chains holding his arms up above him jangling noisily as his body went limp on them.

Echo looked across to me, waiting for his order, and I nodded again. He moved toward Angel, gripping his hair in his hand and lifting his head up, unconcerned with the bloody saliva trailing from the other man's slack mouth. Echo's gaze raised to meet mine as he let go of Angel.

"It's done," he grunted.

Death. It got us all in the end.

No matter how much we ran from it or tried to hide from it. Death was inevitable. I dropped the chains to the ground and swiped my sweaty hands down my jeans before reaching into the pocket of my cut and pulling out my hipflask of whiskey and taking a long swallow of it. Damn, it tasted good.

I looked across at the silent horses standing in their stalls, their judgmental gazes staring back at me. The barn belonged to a friend of the club, and I wondered how much death these horses had witnessed.

Echo took out his knife and knelt in front of Angel's dead body, carving the message we'd been told to deliver into his chest. When he was finished, he stood up and we both stepped back to admire his handiwork.

The words bled red pain down his chest and stomach. A warning to anyone else that tried to fuck with our club.

"Ready to bounce?" Echo asked, his cigarette dangling from between his lips.

"Yeah," I grunted, my jaw ticking as my gaze moved around the barn.

"'Sup?" he asked, watching me cautiously.

I listened carefully for anything out of place. The silence of the night hung heavy in the air. Crickets chirped in the distance, and an owl hooted from a perch somewhere in the boughs of the building, but there was nothing else. It was all normal...all just as it should be. Yet something still felt off with the whole thing. I scowled harder and shook my head.

"I'm not sure, brother." I narrowed my eyes. "Just a feeling, I guess."

Echo automatically pulled his gun from the back of his jeans and flicked off the safety. I'd been training him for the past year, and he'd learned to trust my instincts. When I got a feeling about something being off, I was usually right. I'd been an enforcer for the Devil's Highwaymen for the better part of ten years, and I was damn good at my job. Maybe even too good, because I didn't flinch anymore. Not for anything. Or anyone.

I pulled my own gun out, flicking off the safety, and we made our way toward the barn doors cautiously, listening for any sound that might have been out of place. I closed my eyes and took a deep breath while I listened, but after several minutes of nothing but silence I opened my eyes back up.

"You gettin' paranoid, brother?" Echo smirked, flicking his safety back on. "Old age creepin' up on you making you not work right?"

I gave him the middle finger. "That's not what your mama said," I drolled.

"Yeah?"

"Fuck yeah." I smirked back.

"What'd she say then?"

Kid was a quick learner, with a black heart that matched my own. In another life we would have been blood brothers. As it was, we were club brothers, and the bond was just as strong. He was younger than me by a good fifteen years, easily, and he liked to remind me of that fact on a daily basis.

"She said she liked me creepin' up on her pussy while you were still suckin' on her—"

"All right, all right," Echo barked out a laugh. "Show some respect for her, brother."

"What can I say? Your mama can't resist me." I laughed back and put my gun away, more than ready to go grab a beer and get laid. It had been a long-ass day dealing with traitors and ending in death. A man needed to fuck and drink away a day like today.

We pushed open the barn doors, both of us still laughing as we came out and the full moon above shone down on us like a light from heaven, when something hot sliced past my right cheek. The pain wasn't bad, but the shock of it caught me off guard and made me stumble. I reached for the gun at my waistband at the sound of more gunfire coming from the line of trees in front of the barn, watching as Echo fell backwards in slow motion, a red stain blossoming in the center of his chest as the sound of gunfire continued to explode all around me.

I dropped to the ground with a grunt as fiery pain burned through my right thigh and something heavy hit the back of my head, making my world go black.

Death—it was nothing to be feared.

Nothing to run from.

Nothing to hide from.

Death was inevitable for us all, in the end.

*

Red-hot pain tore through my body and I coughed and choked on the blood that erupted from my dry lips and spilled over my chin.

"Beg!" someone's voice roared from above me. "Beg me, motherfucker, and we'll stop!"

Laughter so mocking it set my teeth on edge more than the pain did echoed around me and I snarled up into the darkness around me.

"Nah, not really, but I'll end it quickly," the voice laughed again.

I recognized the voice.

From somewhere in the back of my head, my memory screamed at me to remember. I knew who this was. I just couldn't place them.

Pain so bad I thought my heart would give out rattled through my body. Every organ, every limb, every nerve was on fire with the agonizing ache of death at its bony fingertips. Much like Angel, my eyes refused to open. Wouldn't matter anyway. After they'd taken a knife to one of my eyes, I didn't wanna see anything else. Blackness surrounded me, but the pain was vivid, illuminating my dark world every time my body tried to shut itself down.

How much could one body take before it gave in?

Angel had lasted four hours, but I'd known men to last for days—weeks, even, depending on the punishment I gave them. I'd never wished for death before, but in that agonizing moment, I wished for death to take me. For the pain to end. I wondered if that had been the same final thoughts of every man I'd tortured and killed over the years.

I know it was what Angel had wanted.

A hot blade sliced into my side, deep enough to inflict agonizing pain but not deep enough to kill. I didn't even have the energy to call out anymore.

The horses stomped their hooves, agreeing with my death sentence. The black steeds of the horsemen waiting on me to take my final, ragged breath. I couldn't really blame them for that. Not after the things they'd seen me do over the years.

"Beg, and it ends," the voice—closer to my face now—snarled, desperation and agony in their tone. "A single bullet to the brain and it's over. It's a better end than you deserve."

He was right; it was a much better end than I deserved, and I wanted it to end.

The pain.

The darkness.

The agony.

But real men don't ever beg, and they don't give up.

I dragged my broken body up to my knees, forcing my one good eye open as much as I could so I could look this fucker in the face. I couldn't focus properly; his face swam in and out of my vision as I swayed on my knees. I was back inside the barn, the scent of blood and death and animals' fear heavy in the air. I hissed in pain as I forced myself to stand on shaky, bleeding legs, the knee of my right leg almost giving out as pain lanced through it, causing the blackness at the edge of my vision to flash with white light. I staggered backwards, and hands reached out, pushing me forward, back into the death circle that had been formed around me.

The world was hazy and jumbled, and I could barely make out the faces that surrounded me. But I lifted my chin, spat a mouthful of blood to the ground at my feet, and laughed loudly.

"Fuck you," I growled. "Fuck all of you."

"Beg," the voice said again, his footsteps crunching over the gritty barn floor as he came to stand toe to toe with me. His amber eyes bored into mine, his voice steady. Serious. Pissed off because I wouldn't back down.

"I don't beg for no one," I replied.

"I ain't no one."

I forced a smile to my face, knowing it would likely be my last. "You're no one to me."

*

The crackle of fire was close…the scorch of flames licked my skin…the screams of animals sang me dark lullabies…my body convulsed…I coughed up blood…choking on the smoke…on the pain…on the call of death that was nipping at my heels. I wished it would hurry up and put me out of this goddamned misery. I had places to be and shit to do on the other side. My brothers were waiting on me. I could hear them calling my name…

In my new world, there was nothing but blackness, the screaming of the horses and the stamping of their hooves. And heat. So much heat. Sweat poured from me, or maybe it was blood. It didn't really matter anymore.

I was a dead man regardless.

I wanted to get up, to drag my broken body away from this hellhole, but nothing worked. My mind told my body to move, but my body was already dead. It had given up hours ago; broken, battered, bloody, dead as dead can be. The Grim Reaper was waiting for me, scythe in hand, ready to drag me to wherever dead men go to pay for their sins.

And I had sinned plenty.

But my mind.

My goddamned mind would not shut off.

It would not let go.

The horses' screams grew louder, torturing me more than any knife or gun or brass knuckles ever could. The screams of those horses burning would haunt me even in death.

The heat slid along my hands, flames licking at my melting flesh, burning me from the outside in. I coughed again, the coughing never-ending as I slowly suffocated on the thick black smoke that surrounded me.

Get up! Echo screamed from somewhere. *Get the fuck up!*

But Echo was dead, wasn't he?

I'd seen him fall.

I'd seen the blood and the bullet and the emptiness in his eyes as he'd hit the ground.

Whatever it takes.

But my limbs were broken, my body already dead.

Whatever it takes, he told me again. *Now get up.*

Grief caught in my chest like a hammer and now I was choking on the misery of his loss and the pain of losing him, and not on smoke and the fire that was torturing me. He was my brother, and it was my fault he was dead. I'd sensed something was wrong but I'd dismissed it.

My mind roared in anger. At myself. At the world. At the realization that Echo was dead because of me, and now so was I.

Get up! he ordered me again.

I didn't want to get up. I wanted to lie there and let death take me. But I couldn't. I knew I couldn't. I had to try. I owed it to Echo.

So I told my burning hands to move. I told them to do something. To drag my sorry ass out of hell and back into the world. I told them I wasn't dead yet, that I wasn't done with this world, but it wasn't until I begged them that they began to move.

A man don't beg for nothing.

That's always been my mantra, but in that moment I begged every muscle in my body to work. To move and stretch and flex and drag me out of there.

The roof above me creaked before giving an almighty roar and collapsing on top of me. Wood and debris showered the ground, slamming into my back and stealing the poisoned air from my dying lungs. Flaming horses ran past me like the apocalypse had begun, their hooves kicking up dirt and flames into my bloodied face, their screams scorched into my brain for all eternity.

I clawed at the ground, roaring in agony as I dragged my dying body out from under the flaming pile of wood, the air growing thicker with smoke and death as I pulled myself along. Things cut into my body, pain slicing from my chest to my stomach. But I ignored it all and continued to pull and drag and claw myself away from the barn, toward freedom as Echo screamed in my head to keep moving. I dragged my broken and burnt body until I had nothing left in me, finally collapsing next to an old maple tree.

I rolled onto my back, groaning in pain as something sharp dug into me. My breaths crackled in my chest as I stared up at the dark starlit sky, wondering how it could still look so fucking beautiful when everything else was so fucking rotten and ugly.

Everything blurred into one. A myriad of death and destruction. Of chaos and anarchy. Of death and devastation.

"...Beast?..."

"...Echo?..."

The screaming of the horses.

The creaking of the barn.

The burning of the wood.

The scent of death.

8

The stars above me.
The ground below.
The agony of dying.
The burning pain of living.
"Whatever it takes," I groaned as a stampede came toward me.

Chapter Two
~ Belle ~

I poured my cold coffee down the sink with a heavy sigh. Gripping the edge of the metal basin, I closed my eyes and took some steadying breaths. I was exhausted. I'd been working sixteen hours straight with no end in sight, and that had been the third coffee I'd tipped away.

The sound of footsteps coming into the cramped room drew my attention, but I didn't have the energy to open my eyes. I just needed five minutes, then I'd be good to go.

"It only makes it worse," my godmother, Jenna, said from behind me before placing a gentle hand on my back.

I groaned. "How do you do this all the time?"

I'd been working here for five months and had initially thought that I'd get used to working such long hours, but it was becoming apparent that I wouldn't. Ever. Maybe nursing wasn't for me after all. I'd wanted to be just like Jenna, but it felt like I'd never be quite good enough.

Jenna chuckled. "You just get used to it."

I opened my eyes and turned around slowly, rubbing my eyes with the back of my hands. Jenna was a beautiful woman, the spitting image of my own mother, no doubt. I looked like neither woman, unfortunately. Where Jenna had blond hair and pale blue eyes, I had long, untamable brunette curls and hazel eyes. She was petite and slender, and I was five seven and curvy. And clearly I didn't have her stamina.

Jenna leaned in and placed a kiss on my cheek. "You'll get used to it," she said again soothingly. "Or you won't and you'll find your way in something else. We all have to try a few paths before we find the right one, Belle."

10

She set about making us both a coffee, and I took a huge mouthful of it when she passed it over to me. I only had a thirty-minute break, but I was determined to use as many of those as possible drinking caffeine.

There was a metal clang out in the hallway—the unmistakable sound of one of the stretchers falling over—and Jenna frowned at me before putting down her coffee and heading to the doorway. I looked longingly at my own before doing the same thing and following her to the door.

She pulled it open and we both stepped out into a warzone of shouting and scuffling.

"What on earth is going on here!" she yelled, her voice loud even above the din around us.

A hand immediately came up and wrapped around her throat, and her body was slammed back into the chest of a heavyset man who looked like he hadn't bathed in weeks. She let out a yelp of surprise, but then to my and everyone else's surprise, she reared back with her elbow and slammed it into the man's ribs. He let her go with a grunt of pain. Jenna turned around, and as the man bent over to nurse his tender ribs, she reached back and hit him in the nose with a punch that almost took him off his feet.

I gasped in surprise. I had never seen Jenna like this before. Sure, I knew she was tough and didn't take crap from anyone, but this was a whole new Jenna altogether. She gripped him by the arm and twisted it up behind his back.

"Okay, okay!" he cried out, suddenly not looking so scary after all.

"Now you listen here, Roy. You sit down, and you wait for security to get here before I break this arm of yours, okay?" she snapped fiercely.

He sat down on the floor, looking up at Jenna with his hands out placatingly, a small drip of blood coming from his now red and swollen nose.

I looked around the hallway, shock and awe all rolled up into one. Was I dreaming? Was this a hallucination because I was so tired? The sound of booted feet stomping toward us had me looking up, and I watched as three security guards helped get the man—Roy—up.

"You okay?" one of them asked Jenna as they led him away.

"Of course," she laughed, like that experience hadn't terrified her. "Belle, come and help me with this," Jenna said as she made her way to the fallen stretcher.

"First of all, what was that!" I said, still in shock. I grabbed one side of the stretcher that had been tipped over and we pulled it upright altogether. "And secondly, who was that? And who are you, for that matter!"

Jenna shook her head. "That there was Roy Milligan. Hot-headed, red-blooded, trouble-causing, no good man. That's who that was. Always ends in up in here when he's had a little too much to drink and is worse for wear. Probably got into a bar fight before passing out and waking up here."

"So he was just a drunk?" I said, dragging a hand down my tired face.

"Yes, just a drunk. A drunk that likes to take his problems out on other people when it suits him."

I let her words sink in for a moment. "But you were…" I threw my hands up in exasperation. "Who are you?" I finally laughed.

"I'm still Jenna. But here I'm *Jenna who has to deal with distasteful individuals* sometimes."

I was still staring at her, waiting for more of an explanation to the little She-Ra scene she'd just pulled on me. My godmother Jenna didn't take crap from anyone, but she was also loving and kind, gentle and giving. I had never seen her hit someone—let alone a patient—in all my life. And since she'd brought me up from the age of three, that was a long time. Sixteen years, to be precise.

Jenna chuckled and patted my arm. "Belle, sometimes, people just need to be put in their place."

"But you're a nurse. You don't go around punching your patients in the nose!" I snorted on a laugh. "He came here for help, not to get more injured."

"People like him don't get the nice treatment, Belle. They get the this-is-all-you're-getting treatment, which consists of sticking a Band-Aid on whatever he's done to himself while drunk or high and sending him on his way. Trust me, he doesn't deserve your sympathy."

"Maybe he just needs help," I suggested, ignoring the scathing look she gave me. "Everyone needs help at times."

"Not him. He's not a nice man and does not deserve your pity."

I frowned. I'd never known Jenna to be so cold about another person. I was discovering all kinds of new things today—like my godmother was a badass. A cruel badass, but a badass all the same.

"I'm just saying…" I continued.

Jenna turned to me with a scowl. "Not everyone is good, Belle, and you need to figure that out quickly. Some people are just bad through and through, right down to their bones. But we still do our job as well as we do with everyone else. We patch them up and send them on their way and we see them again the next time they hurt themselves. We just don't have to wear a smile on our faces with the assholes. Look, what I'm saying is, we don't have to like every patient—or every person, for that matter. We just have to make sure that we help make them better and send them back on their way."

We headed back into the break room, but just as we reached the doorway, Jenna's beeper went off. She checked it and sighed.

"I'm needed with a patient." She paused, giving me a thoughtful look. "Come on, you can help out too. Let me show you how pointless your pity is on some people."

A chill ran down my spine at her words, but I nodded okay. There wasn't anything she could show me that would make me believe that someone didn't deserve pity and understanding, or even respect. People could be shitty human beings—I knew that more than most—but everyone deserved a second chance, didn't they?

And just because they were bad didn't mean I had to change who I was, right?

*

13

The scent of sanitization hung heavily in the air as we passed by several closed doors until we reached one that had a man sitting outside it. He wore a leather waistcoat and blue jeans. A thick metal chain hung from the jeans and jangled noisily as he stood up. He was tall, muscular, and had a strong chiseled jaw that was getting a lot of action as he ground his back teeth together.

"They won't give him any more pain meds," he said gruffly as Jenna and I approached, his gaze going briefly over me and then back to Jenna.

"That's because I told them that he needs to cut back," Jenna replied without hesitation. "And you're not helping him by giving him your little extra medicine on the side, so you quit that right now. I won't tell you again."

"He's in agony," the man bit out, but in fairness he did look genuinely distressed about how much pain his friend was in.

"Listen here," Jenna said, pointing a gloved finger at him like she was scolding a child, "if you want him to get through this then you have to trust me, trust this hospital, and trust that we know a little more about getting him better than you do."

I wondered if this big burly man was going to reach up and snap her finger like a twig. He certainly sized her up like he was ready to. But instead, he took a step back and nodded like a scolded child.

"Yes, ma'am," he mumbled.

Jenna reached out and patted his arm. "I know it's hard…Gauge—wasn't it?" He nodded, and she continued: "but he'll get through this."

He sighed and sat back down in his seat, throwing one ankle over the other leg's knee. "Just make him stop fuckin' screamin' all day and night. I can't take it no more."

It was Jenna's turn to sigh now, and she glanced back at me and looked like she was having second thoughts about me being there.

"Listen, most of that pain he's feeling is in his head now, and no pain meds are going to take that away."

14

Gauge looked up at her, his eyes sad and round and his hair hanging around his face like curtains that he wanted to close. "So what will? 'Cause I'm not sure how much longer I can sit here listening to him screamin' like this."

"Time. Time and rest. And probably a good head doctor at the end of it all to help with the nightmares and stop him from taking his temper out on everyone around him."

He nodded, his gaze falling to me again like he'd just remembered that I was there. "Who's this?" he scowled, and I stood up straighter in a pathetic attempt at showing I was just as tough as my godmother. I wasn't, though. Not even nearly as tough as her, apparently.

Jenna turned to me with a pleased smile. "This here is my goddaughter, Belle. She's helping me out today."

Gauge was still eyeing me, his gaze flared with hunger, but there was something cold and distant there too.

"Pretty little thing like you looks like she needs to be shown a good time," he snarled, his gaze dragging up and down my body. His expression was off, like he was looking at a side salad rather than a woman he wanted to take to bed.

"That's enough of that." Jenna snapped her fingers in his face, drawing his attention back to her. "I've brought her to see that not everyone is good. That not everyone can be…saved, and that even those that can be saved, well, sometimes, no matter what we do, they just don't want to be saved."

My jaw dropped open in shock at her cruel and heartless words.

This was it.

This was the end for Jenna and me, surely.

But instead of pulling out his gun—a gun that I could see he was very obviously and shamelessly carrying—and blowing out our brains, Gauge began to laugh.

I swallowed, not sure what to say.

"Go on in, Jenna, let her see for herself." He grinned, tugging his bottom lip into his mouth and keeping his heated gaze on me. "I'll be right here ready to comfort you when you come back out, Belle."

"Come on then," Jenna said to me like this weird little exchange was nothing to worry about. "It's time you met Beast." She put her hand on the door handle, but I gripped her wrist, a tremor of fear running through me.

"Beast?" I stammered.

"Yeah, Beast," Gauge said, standing up again. "You're gonna' fuckin' love him."

Chapter Three
~ Belle ~

Inside the room was much like every other room in the hospital: white, sterile, a curtain wrapped around a bed that was against the far wall.

The walls were bare of paintings or pictures or a TV to keep people entertained—mostly because when people were in these rooms, the last thing they wanted to be was entertained.

The bed hidden behind the curtain creaked, and I crept closer to Jenna, suddenly afraid of who or what was behind it.

Beast.

That's what they had called him.

Beast by name, beast by nature? I sure hoped not.

Jenna pointed to the cart in the corner of the room filled with sterile bandages and creams, and she headed over to the bed. I grabbed the cart and pulled it forward before Jenna abruptly tugged the curtain back from around the bed.

"The fuck?" Beast roared, his fury sounding like he'd just had his most prized possession stolen from him and not the curtain around his bed pulled back.

"Oh, quit that right now," Jenna tutted.

I stood there, my knees knocking as I stared at the man on the bed with most of his body covered in bandages. And what could be seen looked purple and yellow from bruising. God, what had happened to him? A bandage was wrapped around his head, covering one of his eyes, and since I was standing on the bandaged side and he was so focused on Jenna, he didn't notice me right away—but slowly his attention slid from her to me, his one good eye focusing in like a knife. It was bloodshot and it made him look even more frightening.

"Who the fuck is this?" he growled at Jenna. "Who the fuck are you?" he snapped at me.

17

Full-on growled like some kind of rabid dog ready to attack.

In fact, I had no doubt that if he hadn't been bandaged up like an Egyptian mummy he would have dove up and tore my throat out like the bloodthirsty animal he was.

Jenna looked between me and Beast with a frown. "Watch your language," she sniped at him, and his attention moved from me to her in a split second before he began to laugh. But there was nothing humorous about his laughter.

"Watch my language? Are you fuckin' kidding me, Nurse?" he snorted out a laugh, his mouth contorting into a sadistic smile that looked all the worse for the long red scars that covered his face.

Jenna put her hands on her hips and glared down at him. "Do you like lying in your own pee, Beast? Because I'm quite happy to let you stay like this all day if you're going to speak to me like that."

His smile faltered. "Fuck you."

"No, fuck you," Jenna retorted. "Fuck you and that dirty potty mouth of yours. If you were hoping for pudding later, you're very quickly talking yourself out of it, young man."

And that was that.

Jenna busied herself filling a bowl with warm water and soaking some sponges in the sterile liquid while I stood there staring at Beast like an idiot.

He looked away, his one-eyed gaze going out the window like he was sulking. Jenna snapped her fingers and I scurried to help her.

"Okay, Beast, you know the drill," Jenna said sternly, and he turned back to glare at her.

It was weird, almost like there was a battle of wills going on between them. Who was going to be the most stubborn? The biggest asshole to the other? The meanest? I had no doubt that Beast was without a doubt the meanest, but I'd never really seen this hard side of Jenna either. We didn't really get to work together, despite working in the same hospital.

Beast looked back at us both, his one eye staring daggers at the two of us. I knew why; this was going to hurt.

"I need pain relief," he said.

Jenna checked the board at the end of his bed and sighed. "You've already had more than enough for today."

"I need some fuckin' pain relief!" he yelled.

Jenna huffed. "Afterwards."

"Bitch, I'ma get out of this bed and—"

"Oh, calm yourself down before you give yourself an aneurism. You're not getting out of this bed anytime soon. You're going to lie there and let us bathe you, and then afterwards I'll let your little friend outside give you some of his special medicine, but not before, and that's all you get until tomorrow." She placed the board back on the hook at the end of his bed and came toward him, starting to unwrap some of the bandages without waiting for his acknowledgment.

"I want some fucking pudding too," he grumbled, and I almost laughed. His one eye narrowed in on me and I quickly hid my amusement and went to help Jenna.

"I'll do the right side, you do the left," she said, all business, and I nodded.

The right side of his body was covered in raised red scars that were still trying to heal. Purple bruising still shadowed most of his body too, and I soaked a sponge and gently lifted his arm up before wiping his skin down as carefully as possible.

His hairs stood on end and goose bumps formed in the wake of the sponge. "Is the water okay?" I asked, trying to make the experience as pleasant as possible for him.

He grunted a yes and I finished off his arm and moved over his hand and in between each finger before moving back up his arm to his armpit, where the scent of sweat was coming from. It should have been gross, but it was entirely masculine and strangely attractive.

Jenna pulled the thin cotton cover back from his chest and set straight to work cleaning him, and I worked on my side. He was a big guy. Built like a bodybuilder and at one time had been covered with intricate tattoos across his chest and arms. Now it was hard to work out

19

what the designs had ever been. Between the burns and the scars and the bruises, his body was a maze of pain.

I dipped my sponge back into the water and softly wiped down his right side all the way to his hip, my eyes and hands roving over his body to make sure I cleaned him well.

"Little lower, darlin'," he grunted as my sponge paused on his hip bone, and I realized he wasn't wearing any underwear.

"Beast," Jenna warned, and I blushed harder than a hooker in church. I glanced over to her and she nodded, because yes, I needed to clean all of him. Legs, butt, man bits and all.

I reached for the cover hiding his crotch from me, ready to slide it down, when he reached over and grabbed my wrist in his hand. My gaze shot to his, my eyes going wide.

"You got a good firm grip, girl?" he asked, his chest rumbling, his gaze holding me hostage.

"I uh, I guess so." I shrugged, my knees knocking together.

"Good, because I've got a real big cock under there that could do with some attention from a sweetbutt like you," he said with a lascivious laugh.

"Beast!" Jenna snapped.

"Oh!" I said in surprise as he thrust my hand down under the sheet and wrapped it around his soft girth. I quickly jerked my hand away, my cheeks burning with humiliation.

"Beast! I warned you," Jenna tutted.

His chest rumbled with laughter and I stumbled back, not sure where to look or what to do.

"Belle, I'll finish him off," Jenna said.

"Now there's an offer, but I'd much prefer her touch, Nurse," Beast said with another sardonic laugh, even though I could see that every laugh hurt him.

"Do you see what I was telling you now?" she asked me, ignoring Beast. "Some people don't deserve the kindness. You fix them up and send them back out. Job done."

Beast stopped laughing now. "You sayin' I don't deserve your kindness? That's shitty bedside manner if you ask me."

Jenna's gaze shot to Beast. "I'm saying you're a job. And that's all some patients are. We fix you up and send you out and we'll see you again real soon."

Beast sneered. "Real soon if you're lucky, bitch."

Jenna shook her head and looked back at me. "Some men can't be saved. They don't want to be."

"Sure as hell don't need saving from some uppity bitch like you," he spat back. "Fucking clean me and get this shit over with." He looked over at me. "And get the fuck out of here. This ain't a motherfuckin' circus, bitch!"

I stumbled backwards, grasping for the handle on the door before throwing it open and getting the hell out of there. I slammed it shut behind me, feeling awful at leaving Jenna in there on her own but glad to be away from that horrible man. He was ugly both inside and out, and I didn't want to spend any more time with him.

Gauge, the man outside, began to chuckle and I glared over at him, my chest heaving with the need to shout or cry, or both.

"He's a fucking peach, ain't he?" he sneered.

"He's such an—"

"Yeah, yeah, he's that as well," Gauge cut in with a laugh. "Don't take it personal. He hates everyone, not just you."

My mouth opened and closed. "He hates me?" I stammered. I hadn't even thought of it that way. Why would he hate me? He didn't even know me.

"He hates everyone, including himself," Gauge said before turning his attention back to his cell and effectively dismissing me.

Beast hated me.

And himself.

I should hate him back for the way he treated me and the way he spoke to Jenna. But the stupid part of me didn't. All I could think about doing was trying to take away some of his pain. I just didn't know how to do that.

Chapter Four
~ BEAST~

Every part of my body hurt. With every drag of that damn sponge across my sensitive flesh, I wanted to scream. It was like dragging nails across my skin and slicing them into the muscles. At one point I would have loved being bathed by a hot-as-hell nurse. I would have seduced her and had her bent over my bed within five minutes. But now I was reduced to lashing out angrily at her so I didn't cry out in pain.

She had swiped over one of the worst scars on my stomach and all I could think about doing was rearing back and slamming my fist into that pretty face of hers. I wanted to see her cry. I wanted to see her trembling in fear, snot and tears colliding down her cheeks as she cowered beneath me. Blood running down her face as she begged for me to stop. I hated that the thought turned me on, but it did.

I'd never in my life been violent to a woman—men, yes, but not a woman. Yet the image of her stripped naked with my handprints over her pale flesh was seducing me and making the violence inside of me grow.

"Unless you want it cut off, I suggest you quit that," the nurse snapped.

I chuckled darkly and pushed all thoughts of violating the pretty Belle out of my mind. She didn't need to know that I hadn't felt a single thing from my cock since I woke up in the hospital over three months ago. Nothing, not even a twitch. I was dead from the waist down.

"You had no place bringing her in here," I said, staring up at the white ceiling as her hands moved down my thigh.

"She needed to see that not all people were good."

She spoke matter-of-factly, like I was the epitome of the Devil or some shit. Hell, I guess I was.

"Nice," I said with a shake of my head.

"She needed to take some of the emotion out of the job so she could get on with it. Every patient can't be a bleeding heart or the job will kill her." She dropped the sponge back into the bowl and dried her hands off, her gaze moving over the tender burns that were finally healing on the left side of my body.

I'd been in here months. Some of it awake, and some of it in an induced coma. I was glad for the coma, because if the pain of what I'd woken up to was anything to live by then I wouldn't have survived that first month if I'd been awake. Pain, so much pain.

"So you brought her to see me," I chuckled. "Bitch will probably quit after this little encounter. You're welcome."

Jenna pulled out the tube of cream for my burns and my body involuntarily shuddered. Fucking hated that cream. Hated new bandages. Hated sponge baths. Hated this place and this room and this damned bed. Jenna's scowl grew deeper.

"What the fuck did I say now?"

"Her name's Belle, not bitch, not sweetbutt, and most certainly not your darlin'. Belle. Nurse Belle to you. And getting her to quit was not my intention, not ever."

I held up my hands and then winced as pain lanced down both arms when the scars and burns and bruises stretched with the too-quick movement. Fuck, that hurt.

"I'd say I'm sorry, but I'm not," I said truthfully.

"I wouldn't want your apology anyway, Beast." Jenna removed the cap on the cream. "A man like you doesn't ever mean his apologies, so what would be the point."

"True," I agreed.

I gritted my teeth as she rubbed the cream into the worst burns, the pain making me feel sick. Everything hurt, all the fucking time. But the cream was like a thousand bees stinging me over and over and over and over. Little daggers of death pricking my skin and splitting me in two. Goddamn I hated the cream.

"Almost done," she said almost kindly, continuing on with her slow torture. "Just the big one to go now."

24

Great. Just the really big one that made me want to pull my own teeth out. Just fucking perfect.

I let my mind go elsewhere. To a place better than this where I didn't constantly hurt. Where my body was tattooed and sculpted to perfection, not shredded by knives and fire. Where my muscles weren't wasting away in this fucking uncomfortable bed. To a place where grown men feared me and beautiful women adored me. I let my mind go there, ignoring the way my head spun and my stomach clenched with the need to vomit because it hurt so fucking much. I was shivering with the pain of it all and willing myself to not be there.

"I'm sorry," she said, replacing the cap on the cream and placing it on the cart next to her.

I laughed bitterly, my body already covered in sweat again. "The fuck you are."

She frowned, grabbing a bandage and wrapping it around my burns and then draping the bedsheet back over me, mummifying and hiding my horrors from prying eyes.

She removed her gloves and cleared away her torture devices before coming to stand next to the bed again.

"You don't make it easy, Beast," she said, her voice softer than it usually was.

"Nothing in this life ever is," I said, my one eye gazing out the window at the dreary day outside.

Doctor Collins wasn't sure if I'd ever be able to see out of my damaged eye again. Said it needed to heal. It needed time. And maybe, just maybe, if I was real lucky…

"I am sorry. I'm a nurse; I don't like seeing people in pain."

I snorted out a laugh. "That's not what you just said."

She sighed and I looked back at her. My body felt like it was on fire all over again. Every muscle ached and burned and throbbed in angry, vibrant pain.

"Men like me, we deserve what comes to us, right?" I bit out, and I rejoiced in the sadness that crept across her features and stole the softness that had filled her eyes. "We deserve it, so fuck it. Let's bring in people and show them what happens to men like me. Ain't that right, Nurse?"

"That's not what I said," she stammered, but we both knew that was a lie.

And we both knew that she was right too.

Men like me didn't deserve a second chance. We didn't deserve kindness. We deserved a long, painful death and a one-way ticket to hell. And that was exactly what I'd gotten.

"Yeah it is. How many men have you treated that I put in here, I wonder? How many men with bodies broken and skin destroyed? Men just like me that probably deserved it too, right?" The words tasted good on my tongue, the anger and violence that writhed inside me coming to life as she frowned harder at me and shook her head. "You wanna know a secret, Nurse? I enjoyed it every single time."

She frowned in confusion at me and I smirked. I was on a roll now, ready to destroy her little bubble of self-righteousness. Cunt thought she could come in here and speak to me like I was nothing. Like I hadn't earned my place in this world. Like she had the right to judge me.

"Every man that I broke, I enjoyed it. I enjoyed the blood I spilled; their screams of pain, their cries of terror. I fucked women afterwards with their blood still on my hands and their cries inside my head."

I felt alive for the first time in months as I let it all out—every goddamned evil truth that spilled from my viper's tongue.

She swallowed and took a step back from me with a shake of her head. "I need to go." She turned away from me and headed to the door.

"I enjoyed the death I brought. The necks I snapped, the fingers I crushed, the hearts I tore apart. I enjoyed it every time. And when I leave here, I'll go back to enjoying it all over again. Maybe more so, because now I know exactly how it feels. And when I send those men to the hospital, I'll be sure to tell them to ask for you."

Jenna turned to look at me from the doorway. "You're sick, Beast. Or should I say Nathanial?"

I gritted my teeth. "That ain't my name no more. I'm Beast. Beast by name and Beast by nature."

She smiled sadly and took a long breath. "Yes, you are, aren't you."

"Keep that prissy little bitch out of my room or you'll regret it," I bellowed as she opened the door and left. "And bring me my fucking pudding!" I roared.

God, what I would have given to get up and throw something. To smash my fist through the wall. To grab that fucking torture cart and throw it out the window and hopefully crush some poor innocent people below. But as it was, I couldn't get up and move around like that because if I did I'd be in agony for hours. My scars would likely split back open and I'd be bleeding out on this godforsaken bed all over again.

One day I'd be back on my feet again. One day I'd be strong and I'd be back to doing what I did best: killing and maiming and punishing anyone I saw fit.

One day.

And then the motherfuckers who put me here were gonna pay.

They didn't know pain. But they would.

"Gauge!" I roared, fury and pain coursing through my blood.

The door swung open and he strolled in like he had all the time in the world. "'Sup?"

I glared at him, my teeth clenching so hard I was surprised they didn't shatter. "Give me something," I snarled.

"Can't. Nurse said I wasn't allowed to give you anything else. Says you don't need it and we're fuckin' you up more by givin' it you." He shrugged like that was the end of that discussion.

"Brother, get your ass over here and give me something now before I drag myself out of this bed and tear your throat out with my teeth." My hands clenched the covers.

Gauge sighed. "Just a small hit to see you through the night. But she might be right about this; it might be time to start rolling this shit back. It can't be helping with the healing much."

"Bitch don't know shit about shit," I snapped as he came closer, eager for the drugs to take me away from there.

"She must know *some* shit—otherwise she wouldn't be a nurse." He pulled out the baggie of drugs and I almost foamed at the mouth at the sight of them. Needed them so bad my fucking teeth hurt.

"Just give it to me." I reached for them, snatching them out of his hand. "She don't know nothing about me. Good-for-nothing bitch thinks men like us are all the same. That none of us are good for anything. Thinks that she's better than us."

I sniffed the drugs up in one hit, feeling the buzz at the back of my brain almost immediately.

"Fuck," Gauge sighed. "She ain't wrong about that."

"More," I snapped.

Gauge looked like he was about to argue with me but then thought better of it.

"Whether she's right or wrong isn't the point, brother. That bitch has been in and out of this room for months, dragging me through hell and back and all the while looking down her pert little nose at me."

Gauge frowned. "Not to be a dick, brother, but she's the only one that will come in this room anymore. No other doc or nurse will come near you, so maybe just reel it in a bit before you fuck it up for yourself. She's just trying to help." He pulled his cell out of his pocket and checked it. "Look, I've got one of the prospects coming to sit outside tonight. There's a meeting I've got to go to, but I'll be back in the morning to brief you."

I wasn't listening to him anymore. I was already working out what I was going to do next. That nurse thought she was so good and pure. That a man like me wasn't good enough for a woman like her or that Belle bitch she let in here. I'd show her exactly who I was, since she thought so fucking highly of me.

And once I'd stamped my impression on her, she'd be sorry she ever opened her damned mouth.

Chapter Five
~ *Belle* ~

Sleep washed over me in waves, my muscles relaxing the second I hit my bed.

I'd stripped down to just my panties and kicked off my sneakers before falling asleep on top of the covers.

Without air-conditioning, the trailer was basically a little metal oven that cooked you. The hungry ache in my belly went forgotten. Instead, I grabbed my pillow from the top of the bed and fell into a blissful sleep before my eyes were even closed.

I slept through most of the day, the roar of engines finally disturbing me. The sound infiltrated my sleepy head, invading my dreams enough to disturb me but not fully wake me and pull me from the great dream I'd been having about eating tacos and drinking tequila. I turned over, not ready to wake up just yet. Whoever or whatever it was could come back later.

However, the heavy thump on my trailer door was what finally dragged me back into the world, blinking past sleep and sitting upright. Rubbing at my gritty eyes, I stumbled to my feet angry, exhausted, and incredibly hungry.

The thumping came again and I looked around in confusion, not sure how long I'd been sleeping or what time it even was. All I knew was that I was ravenous and still incredibly tired. But at least today was my day off, so I could eat, watch some crappy TV, and then go back to sleep. It was the routine of my life right now.

Work, sleep, eat, repeat.

The thumping came again and I groaned in annoyance. I stumbled feeling foggy and disoriented, and grabbed a pair of ratty denim shorts and a white T-shirt before heading out of my room and down the short hallway toward my trailer door. I stared longingly at my empty coffee mug on the counter as I ran a hand through my thick curls and tried to tame them into something less wild.

"Hello?" I said, hesitantly as I opened the door and blinked into the brightness, confused as hell as to why I had three leather-clad bikers on my doorstep. "Did you take a wrong turn? Do you need some directions?" I asked stupidly. My trailer was set far back from the road and away from everyone else's, so being lost was the only explanation for these men to be at my door.

The tall, dark-haired one I'd met at the hospital—Gauge, I think his name had been—glanced across at the one with a shaved head.

"You seein' this, brother?" Gauge drolled.

"Fuck yeah," the other replied with a grin. "*Now* I get it." His grin could only be described as adulterous. There was just to other way to describe it, and I suddenly felt vastly underdressed and wishing that I'd grabbed my bathrobe, or at least put on a bra before answering the door. It was another hot day today and I could already feel a light sheen of sweat trailing between my breasts and no doubt making the thin cotton T-shirt cling to me.

My arms crossed in front of me to cover my chest as I looked between them all. "See what?" I snapped. I was tired, hungry, and in desperate need of a shower and so my stranger-danger alarm wasn't quite sounding off loud enough for me to hear. "I think you have the wrong trailer."

The third man, whose shoulder-length, dirty blond hair hung around his shoulders, smiled, and tired or not, my stomach fluttered. I was only human, after all.

"Ma'am," he started, and the shaved-headed biker snickered, "my name's Shooter, and I need you to come to the hospital with us." He looked me up and down before continuing.

Panic rose in me, my hands falling to my sides. "Is it Jenna? Is she okay?" I took a step down, looking between them all with worry.

"She's fine. But a brother of ours has requested your umm…assistance," he asked politely enough.

30

The shaven-headed one chuckled. "Yeah, now we get the kind of *assistance* he wants."

Shooter turned and glared at him. "Shut the fuck up, Casa." He turned back to me. "Sorry about that. He's a dick, but he's a harmless dick."

The taller one raised an eyebrow at Shooter like he didn't quite believe him. "Says who?"

"Not my old lady, that's for certain." Casa smirked.

"You need to get anything before you leave?" Shooter asked, that panty-melting smile of his making my stomach flip once again.

"Umm, my shoes, I guess," I mumbled, completely confused.

"Go get 'em then," Gauge said.

I started to turn around to go get my shoes before turning back to them. They didn't look like the sort of men you said no to, and yet I really wanted to say no. Today was my day off. I didn't want to do anything today but veg out on my sofa and sleep. Besides, I had no idea who they were even talking about. My sleep-fogged brain was clearly slow on the uptake.

"I'm sorry, who are you again?" I asked with a frown.

"That's Gauge," Shooter said, pointing to the man I'd met at the hospital. "The walking hard-on behind me is Casa, and I'm Shooter, president of the Devil's Highwaymen motorcycle club."

I frowned. "And you want me to go to the hospital to see to your friend?"

I was even more confused than ever now.

Gauge sighed. "It's not difficult to follow, darlin'. You met our brother Beast yesterday, and he wants you and only you to look after him from now on."

Beast.

That asshole.

I shook my head no.

"Wasn't really a request," Gauge added. "Seems he's taken a liking to you, and since he's been through hell and back several times

31

these past couple a' months it seems that the least we could do for him would be to bring him the pretty nurse that looked after him so well."

"He put my hand on his you know what!" I gasped, sounding like a virginal schoolgirl, no doubt.

Casa started to laugh, and his laughter was so infectious that despite my annoyance at Beast and these men turning up at my door unannounced, waking me up and ordering me back to work like they had any say over me or my life, I couldn't help but let out a small laugh too.

All four of us stood in the sunshine, heat washing over us and laughing. I dragged my hands though my hair, finally starting to wake up.

"Look, it's not funny. He's disgusting," I said, forcing my laughter away. "And I'm not going in that room again. He treats people like crap and thinks he can get away with it. And anyway, he already has a nurse."

From inside I could hear my cell phone ringing, but I ignored it in favor of bitching out these three burly men who thought they could push me around like some dainty little woman. Like I wouldn't say no to them. Which, if I hadn't been so tired, they probably would have gotten away with, because, if I was being honest, I was a complete pushover. And these men, as sexy as they were, were scary as hell.

"She's been fired," Shooter drolled, pulling out his cigarettes and lighting one.

"Jenna has been fired?" I gasped.

Shooter sighed, like he was bored of my questions. God, did everyone just jump when he told them to? My godmother was out of a job and it was all my fault. What was she going to do? I needed to call her.

"Can we hurry this along?" Shooter blew out a mouthful of smoke as he spoke.

"Didn't you quit?" Casa asked him, pointing to the cigarette dangling between his lips.

"Only when Laney is around," Shooter replied.

"She'll cut off your balls if she finds out," Gauge added.

I watched them all talking between themselves for a moment or two, smoking and chatting like they hadn't just woken me up on my day off, fired my godmother, and ordered me back to work. I was beginning to think I was delirious, or at least having a nightmare of some sort.

"I need to go," I snapped, interrupting them. I wilted a little when they all turned to glare at me. "That nurse that was fired, that's my godmother, so I need to go and call her and see what I can do to help."

I turned to head back inside, ready to slam the door on these creeps, when a large hand wrapped around my bicep and pulled me back outside. I stumbled down the steps and fell into the chest of Gauge and his hands gripped me tightly around the waist, holding me in position, the smell of leather, smoke, sweat, and possibly whiskey washing over me.

"Listen here," he snarled, his hands snaking down over my ass to cup it. "You need to get your stuff now. We wasn't asking, we was telling you."

I stared into his face, my eyes wide with fear and my mouth suddenly at a loss for words.

"Gauge, put her the fuck down!" Shooter bellowed. "It's Belle, right?"

I nodded quickly, Gauge's grip on me still tight. My hands were on his chest in a vain attempt to push him away, but it was futile. He knew it. I knew it. God himself knew it. If he'd wanted to, he could have snapped me like a twig, so the chances of wriggling out from under his grip were zero.

"Well, Belle, what I meant was, Jenna's services are no longer required by the Devil's Highwaymen for the recuperation of our brother, Beast. She still has a job at the hospital, but Beast was a side job paid for personally by the club." He took a long drag of his cigarette and let the smoke trail out before continuing. "You are now on our payroll and we need you to be Beast's personal carer. So go get your shit so we can get going."

My cell phone was still ringing inside, and I realized that it was probably Jenna calling to warn me. I hoped she wasn't too mad. She'd raised me from three years old and even now that I was a nineteen-year-old woman, she was still helping me.

I looked between the three men, fearful of each and every one of them. Could I work for these types of men—drug dealers and who knows what else they were into? The money would definitely come in handy, and I had wanted to find some way of taking away some of Beast's pain—maybe this was it. I could give some of the money straight to Jenna so she wasn't losing out, and I could prove to Beast that he wasn't the big bad monster he thought he was.

I squirmed in Gauge's grip, my breasts pushed up against his chest and his hands lightly massaging my ass like I was a piece of meat. "Could you um…"

"Gauge," Shooter snapped, "put her the fuck down."

Gauge set me back on the ground and I stumbled back from him. I was hungry, I was tired, and I was more than ready to have my day off. Yet the thought of going back into that room was definitely alluring. Especially if I was being paid for it.

"I'll need to speak to Jenna first," I said, going back up the two steps into my trailer to stand in the doorway. "I need to make sure she's okay with this."

"She's been reimbursed already so she'll be fine," Shooter replied. "Pay is good, Belle, and the hours will be in with your normal workday."

"And Doctor Collins is okay with that?" I asked with confusion, because Doctor Collins was a chauvinistic pig who worked people to the bone.

Shooter nodded and grinned. "Doctor Collins does whatever the fuck we tell him to. So yeah, you could say he's okay with it."

It was my turn to nod then, a little gleeful feeling in my belly that someone had put Doctor Collins in his place. My cell phone had stopped ringing and I had no doubt that Jenna was on her way over.

"Okay," I finally said, "I'll do it."

Gauge snorted on a laugh and lit a cigar. "You didn't really have a choice, sweetheart."

I scowled at him and looked back at Shooter, who seemed the more reasonable of the three. "Is that so?"

Shooter shrugged, his expression neutral. He threw his cigarette to the ground and stubbed it out with the heel of his big black boot.

"Get your shit and we'll take you to him," Shooter said.

I huffed out my annoyance and turned around, looking into my crappy trailer, my gaze landing on my coffee mug. I turned back to them with one hand on the trailer door, my belly doing flips.

"I'll be in tomorrow. Today is my day off," I replied sternly, and slammed the door shut.

I pressed my back against it, waiting for the thumping of fists on the cheap metal, but nothing came. My heart was slamming in my chest and fear was coursing through me, but I couldn't help but smile regardless.

I waited to see if they'd bang on the door and demand that I come in today. Order me back to work, because they could basically do whatever they wanted and clearly no one had any real say in it. But the sound of motorcycles starting up cut into my anxious thoughts and I listened as they drove away, wondering what the hell I'd just gotten myself into.

Whatever it was, it wasn't going to be enjoyable and I couldn't get out of it now. Yet no matter how stupid an idea I thought this might be, I couldn't help but be excited of the prospect of doing this.

Adventure awaits for those who answer its call, right? And caring for Beast was definitely going to be an adventure.

Chapter Six
~ BEAST ~

Day had been long as hell and twice as boring. With my evil nurse not coming in to give me my bed bath and medicine, and my new nurse not turning up, I'd only had Max—our latest prospect—and my revenge plot against the motherfuckers who put me here to keep me company. I was not in a good enough mood when Belle decided to grace me with her presence.

The door creaked open and I glared at her as she came in acting like she had no care in the world and wasn't afraid of me. But I knew better.

"Took your time," I snapped as she wheeled the cart over to the side of the bed. She didn't rise to the bait and instead smiled like I'd just given her a compliment.

My jaw ticked in annoyance as I watched her sort through all the items on the table to make sure she had everything. I knew what was coming next. I knew it was going to hurt and I knew that she had no fucks to give about that. My hands clenched into fists at my sides.

The door opened again and the prospect came in, all smiles and cocky strut as he came toward us, eyes on Belle's ass as she bent down for something on the bottom of the cart. He threw me a grin and I gave him the finger.

Belle straightened back up, her cheeks going rosy and pink as she caught the exchange between me and the prospect.

"Umm, did you have your pain meds?" she asked, putting down the bottle of cream and going to the end of the bed.

"Did you fucking give them to me?" I bit out, making her blush harder. Bitch had no idea what she was doing. Hands shaking, cream before washing…she was already fucking this up and I was already looking forward to yelling at her and making her feel like shit for her incompetence.

"Sorry, no, I umm," she stammered, her hazel eyes moving between the board in her hand and me like she couldn't hold my stare. "I'll get them now and then I'll come back to do the bath and such after I've done my morning rounds."

"Fuck it," I growled, wanting to get this shit over with. "Prospect, gimme a hit so we can get this done."

"Be my pleasure, brother," he said, coming forward.

Belle jumped straight into action like I knew she would. Her eyes went wide like saucers and she came between him and the bed, her back to me.

"No, he can't have that stuff, it's messing with his real meds," she stammered again, trying to be forceful.

"Get the fuck out of the way," I growled.

I expected her to move the fuck out of my way like I'd told her to, but instead she turned to face me, her eyes still wide but her mouth set in a hard line. Wild curls were pinned back from her face, but one had come loose and was angled in front of one of her eyes. Wanted to reach up and brush it away, but I didn't.

"No, sir, no I will not. That stuff will kill you, and I'm here to keep you alive, so no, you will not be having that today." She nodded, looking mighty pleased with herself.

The prospect smirked over her shoulder and I glared hard enough that she should have pissed herself. She shook her head at me, her mouth still tight.

I let my gaze move up and down her. That nurse's uniform was two sizes too big for her and did nothing for her figure so I couldn't work out if she was hot as hell under it or built like a child.

"No, Belle, what's likely to kill me is men like *me*. You see, men like me, we do things to other people—people we don't like. We hurt them, make them feel so much pain that they wish for death because it's a better option than staying alive. And then we go have a beer afterwards and fuck a woman. You feel me?" I said my words slowly and carefully, accentuating each one. Bitch surprised me by shaking her head no, and the prospect snorted out a laugh. I was gonna kill that kid if he didn't fuck off.

"The drugs are keeping me alive, Belle," I said darkly, "so get out of the fucking way, now."

She huffed, unsure what to do then, and I knew that it was a matter of wills. Hadn't expected her to stand up to me, but that was okay; I liked them feisty like that, and I was going to enjoy breaking her.

Belle finally stepped to one side, her shoulders slumping in defeat and her gaze slipping from mine. "Fine, but you'll only feel worse afterwards," she mumbled.

"That's my problem then, isn't it."

Prospect came forward and gave me a hit and I groaned in response, happy as a pig in shit as the dull throb of pain ebbed and flowed away. This was the only release I got. The only time I got a breather from every part of me hurting. I wasn't stupid; I knew the pain would eventually subside on its own when my body was done healing. I'd get through this like I got through everything: with my teeth gritted and my stubbornness to survive shining through. Hell, I'd made it through the darkest days, and though death was always on the horizon, it wasn't poking me like a bear in a cage anymore. But still, I wanted the hit. I wanted it to take the pain for a bit. I wanted it so I could get out of my own damned head for a bit.

"Good to go," the prospect said, and I realized that I must have zoned out for a moment. "I'll be outside, I don't need to see your junk."

I grunted in response, too fucked up from what he'd given me to reply properly. The next thing I felt was the touch of Belle's fingertips on my overly sensitized skin, picking at the bandages and peeling them away to reveal the delicate skin underneath. It felt like broken glass being dragged across my flesh, tearing open the wounds again. My stomach ached and my blood thrummed through my veins like hot lava. I kept my eyes closed, forcing my mind to go somewhere better than this, like I did every time I had to go through this shit.

I thought of being on my bike again. I tried to remember the feel of the wind on my face and in my hair. Of the rumble of the engine and the heat of the metal between my thighs and the feel of a woman's tits pressed up against my back. I could smell the scent of engine oil and a woman's sweet perfume in my nostrils, and goddamn, it was everything and more. The wind, the roar, and the scent of oil—the world stopped for a moment, and if I could have died right then, I would have. It was bliss. Pure fucking bliss.

And then the sharp sting of pain stabbed through me again and I was brought back to earth. To this place, this room, and this pain once more.

I opened my eyes, glaring over at Belle as she soaked the sponge and cleaned my arms and legs, water dripping across my chest and stomach, dripping over the ripples of muscle that was slowly wasting away and torn-up tattoos. Over scars and cuts and bruises and melted skin. My body would never be what it was again. I was trapped in this broken, fucked-up sack and there was nothing I could do about it. Woman like Belle would have batted those pretty lashes for me at one time. She would have dropped to her knees, desperate to suck my cock and spread her legs, but now…fuck, now I was nothing but a monster. I was a monster and I'd never be anything more than that to any woman.

"Stop," I growled, the pain in my head taunting me louder than the pain on my flesh ever could.

"Are you okay? I'm sorry, I was trying to be gentle," she stammered, her hand paused above my chest. Water droplets dripped from the sponge onto me before sliding down my sides.

"No, I'm not fucking okay. You ever had your flesh peeled back from your bones? Ever smelt your own skin melting?"

She shook her head, her big eyes watching me warily.

"Then what's the fucking point in asking me if I'm okay? No, I'm not okay. But that don't change shit, does it?"

I felt angry. So fucking angry. My muscles itched to break something. To hit and smash and destroy something beautiful so it was ugly like me.

"I'm sorry," she whispered, her hand on mine. "I didn't mean to be insensitive."

Insensitive? Fuck me, this bitch had no idea what she was talking about. I started to laugh, and even to my ears I didn't recognize the sound coming from me. It was almost inhuman in its bitter suffering.

"You're sorry? You're fucking sorry?" I shouted, and she stepped back from me, her hand leaving mine. "Yeah, that's right, get the fuck away from the animal before he kills you."

"I…" She looked panicked, her chest rising and falling, making her tits push up to the top of her shitty nurse's dress. The sight should have pleased me, but all it did was anger me.

"I…I…I," I mocked, and laughed again. "Shut your mouth and do your job."

She nodded and blinked before coming closer to me, and for the first time I noticed her perfume. The scent filled my lungs, reminding me of sex and women, and at another time it would have made my dick hard as nails, but now there was just nothing.

"You wanna do something to make me feel better?" I growled.

"Yes, of course," she said immediately, her frown turning to a smile at the thought of helping me.

"Really?"

"Yes, that's what I'm paid for. To help get you better and keep you out of pain," she whispered, her words getting quieter the more she spoke, like she knew she was walking into a lion's den.

I grabbed her wrist and pulled her forward so she was closer to me. "You wanna make me feel better, then suck it," I said, dragging the sheet away from my flaccid cock. "That'll make me feel much better, darlin'," I sneered.

I grabbed my cock and started to pump it, all the while she stared at me wide-eyed, her mouth hanging open in shock. Tears filled her eyes and she shook her head, finally blinking and closing her mouth like someone had just pressed play.

"You're disgusting," she said, blinking away the tears that filled her eyes. "I'm just trying to help you."

I reached out, ignoring the pain, and grabbed the back of her neck, pulling her face to mine so we were almost nose to nose. "And I told

40

you how you can help me, Belle. You wanna make me feel better, then get on with it."

I expected more tears. More trembling. More rosy cheeks. And maybe, just maybe, for her to relent and actually suck me off. A pity suck, if you will. But instead she shoved my arm away, my grip falling from her neck, and she reached out and slapped me hard across my already beaten-up face, shocking the shit out of me—and, by the look on her face, her too.

Her hand flew to her mouth and she blinked in surprise.

I stared back, feeling the angry burn of her handprint on my cheek.

Wasn't sure who was going to give in first and break the silence, her or me. And fuck me, I wasn't sure what I could say to her that wasn't threatening her with her immediate death.

Belle stepped back, her gaze moving up and down my broken body, over my flaccid cock, and back up to my scarred-as-shit, bandaged-up face, before reaching out and pulling the sheet back over my still soft cock and then picking up her sponge.

I didn't tell her that the water had cooled too much when she picked up her sponge and began cleaning me again, and I didn't complain when she put cream over my scars and the pain made my head spin and I felt like I was going to pass out.

I didn't say another word until she'd done her job and tidied everything back away, and she cleared her throat to get my attention.

"What?" I snapped, my eyes narrowed and my mouth set in a hard line. I scowled at her, enjoying the way she blew out a frustrated breath, her usually soft features tensing.

"Would you like some pudding?" she asked tenderly, and fuck me I couldn't stop a small smile from coming to my face, despite my anger and my pain. Of all the things I expected her to say, that was not one of them. This girl continued to surprise me. No matter what I did she kept on coming back for more. "I'll take that as a yes then," she said primly, and left the room to go get it.

I shook my head and dropped my smile.

Pudding. Motherfuckin' puddin', of all the things, had made me smile.

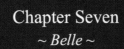

Chapter Seven
~ *Belle* ~

How is he today?" I asked Joey, the prospect sitting outside Beast's room.

I was running late that day and still tugging my wild curls into a little silver clip at the back of my head as I jogged toward Beast's room. Joey and I had gotten close since we talked every day. He warned me if Beast was in a particularly awful mood, and I brought him candy and books as payment. It was a boring job sitting outside the room all day, and we'd struck up an unlikely friendship over the past couple of weeks.

"Quiet today," he said, standing up and putting his book down. "Hey, you know Heathcliff?"

I smirked. "Not personally."

The joke was lost on him and he continued regardless.

"He's like, all broken up and shit and that Catherine bitch is—"

"Have a little respect for her," I warned.

"Sorry, well, I think she should pick Heathcliff. That Edgar dude is a dick."

I laughed and he stopped talking and looked at me with a hurt expression. "I'm sorry, I'm not laughing at you."

"Sure seems that way," he grumbled.

"No, no, I'm not. It's just Edgar is just a nice guy. How can you say he's a..." I shrugged, leaving Joey to fill in the blank because I didn't want to swear.

"A dick?"

"Yeah." I nodded.

"Because Catherine is Heathcliff's! And sure, he's a little fucked up—but most people are, and at least he has the balls to know what he wants and go after it." He stared at me, his gaze thoughtful as he waited for me to give him my thoughts on his summary.

"Wow, well, I hear what you're saying but I guess life's just not that simple."

"Nah, fuck that, it is that simple. Heathcliff was unhinged but he deserved love too. And that Edgar guy was a pussy and needed to step off. Standing in the way of true love and all that." He look so irritated by the whole thing, and I felt a motherly pride.

"I hear you out there, Belle!" Beast yelled from inside his room, and Joey rolled his eyes and swiped at his hair.

"You better get yourself in there." He sat back down and picked the book back up before looking back up to me. "Thanks for the book rec, Belle."

I smiled. "No problem."

I pushed on the door and headed inside. Beast was sitting up in bed, staring straight ahead at the small television fixed to the wall in the corner of the room. Some of his biker brothers had put it up earlier that week and he'd been glued to it ever since. He didn't really seem the sort of man to sit around watching TV all day, but I guess when you had nothing else to do…

"Took your damn time," he grumbled.

"Well, it's not like you're going anywhere so I thought why rush?" I bit out sarcastically.

His head swung in my direction. "What the fuck did you just say to me?"

I refrained from apologizing automatically and instead headed over to get my cart. I pulled out the key to the little med cupboard and unlocked it, grabbing his medicine out and locking it again.

He was still glowering at me when I turned around and I sighed. "I was joking," I said in exasperation.

"Real fucking hilarious," he bit out, turning back to the TV.

I washed him down, my gaze going to the TV a couple of times to see what he was watching. It was some old cowboy movie and I smirked and glanced over at Beast.

"I didn't know you liked cowboy movies."

"Didn't know I liked anal either but hey I guess we learn something new every day, huh," he replied without looking away.

I tutted. "You don't have to be such a jerk all the time," I mumbled, gently sponging down his thick thighs as carefully as I could.

His body was healing really well, and Doctor Collins seemed to think he was over the worst of it. There was still along way before he'd be ready to leave the hospital, but his bruises were finally fading and his skin was knitting together, leaving behind thick scars in their wake. He still refused to take off the bandage from around his head though, and despite what he said, I think he was scared that he was blind and just didn't want to know.

Sometimes it's better the devil you know. I wasn't pushing him on it—no one was. He had enough to deal with right then.

I cleared away the water and cloths and unscrewed the lid to the cream to put over his burns when he suddenly jumped.

"Fuck yeah!" he yelled.

"Oh my god, don't do that!" I yelled back, startled.

He turned to look at me, his arm snaking around my waist. "You see that, Belle? That there is John Wayne, goddamn brilliant actor."

I looked over, a small smile playing on my face. His arm around my waist felt comfortable—natural, even. His fingers played with the material as he talked, telling me about the film he was watching. I'd never seen him like this—so unleashed of his anger—and I stood there for five minutes straight while he talked about the movie.

"I'm not a fan of cowboy movies. They're all about shooting and riding and shooting some more," I said, my fingers spreading cream over his forearm. "I just don't get it."

He snorted but didn't say anything, and I stopped what I was doing and looked at him.

"What was that?" I asked.

"Women never get it."

I rolled my eyes. "Some women must."

"Is that so?"

"Yes," I said, continuing to apply cream. He hissed as I pressed against one a little harder. "Sorry."

"Whatever, just hurry the fuck up," he grumbled, his good mood evaporated.

"You don't have to be so moody all the time."

"You don't seem to get it, Belle. I am moody, and I am a jerk, and I really don't give a shit, though those are two of the lamest insults I've ever been called, but whatever." His jaw twitched as he clenched it tightly.

I pouted. "I don't believe that. Everyone wants to be liked."

He laughed, but it wasn't a good laugh. It was a laugh that said he ate bunnies and killed kittens. The kind of laugh that gave you nightmares.

"I couldn't give a fuck if people liked me or not."

I pouted harder, not ready to believe that. "Well, you're a mean, moody jerk and you should care."

He shook his head. "There you again with those bullshit insults again, Belle. You need to call me something that really gets my blood pumping if you wanna piss me off."

I finished with the cream and screwed the lid back on the tub. "Oh yeah, like what?"

"I don't know, Belle! What kind of fucking question is that?"

I shrugged. "I'm just not good at the whole calling-people-mean-names thing." I realized how pathetic that made me sound, but it was the truth.

He huffed out a breath at me. "Cock-sucking motherfucker with an ass-eating piece of shit for a mother."

I dropped the cream and it clattered noisily onto the tray.

"Jesus, Belle," Beast snapped. "Be fucking careful, will you?"

"Sorry, sorry, oh my god though, have you actually said that to someone?"

Beast stared at me, his expression shifting from thoughtful to confused and finally to amused. He shook his head and smirked. "You're something else, you know that."

46

"I'll take that as a compliment," I said, pushing the cart back across the room.

"Take it as whatever you want," he grumbled. "Now shut the fuck up and let me watch my movie in peace."

I handed him his pills and a glass of water and he took them, swallowing them down and waving me away.

"I'll be back later," I said, heading across the room.

"Belle?"

"What?" I turned back to him.

"You can stay and watch the movie if you want." His expression hadn't changed, but I could see from his sad, gray eye that he wanted me to. That he was lonely.

"Why don't you get Joey in here? I'm sure he'd like the company too if you're lonely."

His gaze narrowed on me, his expression turning dark. "You think I'm lonely?"

I realized as soon as he said it back to me that I'd said the wrong thing, but it was too late to backtrack.

"I'm not fucking lonely, bitch! Now get the fuck out of here!" he yelled.

I scurried out of the room, slamming the door shut behind me. I glanced over at Joey, who lowered the book.

"Thought it was going a little too well," he said before raising the book back up and continuing to read.

"I'll be back later," I sighed.

"I wouldn't hurry back," he replied as something in the room got thrown.

I headed back on my rounds, hoping that I could be done early enough to actually get some lunch that day. I'd barely had time to brush my teeth that morning, never mind get breakfast. The job wasn't getting any easier, and it was being made all the more difficult by working for Beast, and the fact that Jenna had barely said a word to me once I told her that I was working for the Devil's Highwaymen.

She hadn't even let me explain that I hadn't really had a choice, or that I was going to give her the money since it was her job I'd taken. Unintentionally, but I'd still taken it all the same.

I felt guilty for what I'd just said to Beast, because what I meant to say was that I got it—I was lonely too. And if my shift would have been over, I would have stayed and watched the movie with him.

Chapter Eight
~ BEAST~

"That fuckin' hurts!" I roared in anger as Belle's clumsy swipes of the cream across my sensitive skin set every nerve on edge. I wanted to dive up and tear the room apart, smash the windows, tip the bed over, tear this goddamn uncomfortable mattress in half with my bare hands and then put Belle across my knee and spank her ass until she cried.

She looked up at me in surprise. "I'm sorry," she mumbled, and then looked back down to my arm, continuing to apply the fiery cream. She rubbed a little too roughly again, like she hadn't heard the threat in my tone the first time, and a growl rose in my chest like I was an animal ready to attack. I guess I was.

"Goddamn it, what are you rubbing that shit on with? Sandpaper?" I snapped at her.

She'd been working for me for three weeks now.

Her fingers fumbled again but she didn't stop. She continued moving her hands down and over my left thigh, where the worst of the burns were. My teeth were on edge, my muscles taut, the tendons in my neck were pulled tight as I struggled to restrain myself and not backhand her across the room. I breathed heavily, gritting my teeth as she finally finished her torturous job. Pulling the cool white sheet back up, she began to neaten her little cart while I glared at her like I had lasers in my eyeballs and could burn a hole in her head with just one look. Not that she seemed to notice though. Woman was lost in her own thoughts, thinking of something other than me and the hell she'd just put me through, and it was pissing me the fuck off.

"Okay, I'll be back after the rest of my shift to check on you again," she mumbled, moving to the door, half-heartedly dragging her little cart behind her. It almost tipped over, but she seemed in such a hurry to get out of the room that she barely noticed.

"What the fuck, Belle?" I grumbled, even more pissed off then.

She didn't respond and continued walking away from me, and I lost it. I grabbed my cup of water, trying not to wince as I threw it across the room. It hit the door in front of her, bouncing back and landing at her feet while simultaneously spraying the room, and her, with water. She let out a squeal of fright and turned back to me with those big wide eyes of hers. Her hair was piled high that day, small curls tamed into a mess on top of her head like she hadn't had the time or patience to make herself presentable for me. Her cheeks flushed, water dripping down her face and onto that god-awful too-big uniform she was wearing, even though I knew she had one that fit her better. I needed Shooter to fix that shit. I couldn't stand looking at her in that for another damn day.

Woman was my nurse and I needed some goddamn eye candy to look at!

"Oh my god, Beast!" she squealed, her hands on her hips. My nostrils flared at the sight of her: furious gaze, damp chest heaving as she tried to reel in her temper and not bite my fucking head off. The look suited her well. "What? What is it that you wanted so much that you had to soak me and your room for?" she snapped, her voice rising like she'd forgotten who I was and what I was capable of.

Goddamn, it was hot.

I rearranged my junk and glared, ready to shut this shit down, but she'd crossed the line and wasn't ready to calm the fuck down yet. I knew that feeling well.

"Did you want me to fluff your pillows? Maybe give you a foot massage? Change the channel on your TV? What? What is it that was so important that you would do this to me!" she yelled, her voice rising higher with every word. "Do I not do enough for you as it is, you pig-ignorant, self-absorbed, pathetic little man?"

The door flew open and the prospect that had been assigned to keep guard came in, his gun in hand like he thought I was in danger from this little thing in front of me.

50

"Everything okay in here?" he said, his features pulled tight as he stared Belle down.

It was the sight of the gun in his hand that seemed to do the trick, finally calming her enough to drop the Wonder Woman shit and remember who I was.

Gotta say, I was disappointed. Kinda liked it when she got feisty. It was probably best for her sake, though, as the insults she'd just thrown in my direction finally got through and I decided I was going to pull out my gun and blow her brains out over the wall. Who the fuck did she think she was talking to?

"I'm sorry, this was all my fault," she stammered, looking flustered. Her gaze moved between the prospect's gun and me, and it was obvious she'd never seen a gun up close before and was ready to piss herself.

"Was it?" I growled, arching an eyebrow when she looked up at me. I liked pushing her, I realized. I liked seeing her scared. I liked the taste of her fear in the air, but mostly I liked watching her discover new parts of herself.

She nodded quickly. "Yes, I'm sorry." She glanced nervously toward the prospect again, swallowing nervously. "I'm really sorry." Her chin wobbled and she swiped at the water dripping down her cheeks.

She was verging on pathetic now, the fire gone from her eyes.

That was disappointing.

"Get the fuck out of here, both of you," I growled, pissed off that he'd interrupted her little tirade at me and even more pissed off that she'd backed down so quickly. Bitch had balls beneath that dowdy uniform; she just hadn't realized it yet.

Belle nodded quickly and turned to leave, but the prospect was still standing in her way, glancing between us both like he was trying to figure shit out. His gun was still aimed at her, and she lifted her hands in surrender like she thought he was going to shoot her.

"Did you not hear me, prospect? I said, Get. The. Fuck. Out!" I roared, wanting nothing more than to get out of that bed and punch him in his face. "And put that gun away!"

"Come on," he snapped at Belle, and they both left.

After she left I began to feel something I hadn't felt in…years. Not since I was a little boy and my mom had been gone for a week, leaving me trapped in our bullshit apartment with nothing more than two bags of Cheetos and a bottle of Mountain Dew. Or maybe it was something that I'd just tried to deny that I had been feeling for weeks now.

I was lonely.

God knows that place was isolating at times and was boring as all hell. Sitting in that damned bed, day in, day out, waiting for someone—anyone—to come in and feed me or bathe me, or speak to me. I was a strong man that hadn't depended on anyone for a long time, but at the moment I depended on everyone for everything, and I hated it.

Belle had only been gone five or ten minutes and I was already climbing the walls in loneliness, knowing that I had the full day ahead of me before she came back. My thoughts strayed to the club, wondering what was going on there. What was happening in the search for the fucks that had killed Echo and put me in here. What was happening back at the clubhouse. Had the last run gone okay? Had the shipment come in from the new suppliers? The questions swarmed my head, clouding everything but the noise, and the questions were never enough to drown out his voice.

Echo, my brother, was still calling my name, no matter how much I tried to distract myself from it. No matter how much I yelled and grumbled, shouted and pissed people off. He was still there. The pain in my body had almost killed me, but the pain of hearing him in my head was sending me insane.

The memories of that night, of that moment between life and death when everything had been okay in the world and we'd both been alive, joking about women and life, and then BOOM, the gun had gone off and he was gone. The light faded from his eyes slower when I thought about it. It set like the sun, fading behind the hills until there was only blankness.

I knew it hadn't happened like that—that it had been quick, over in an instant—but in my head, all I saw was the bubbles of death spilling from his lips and him calling my name, begging me to save him.

I grabbed at my head, wanting him to get the fuck out of it. Needing him to be quiet.

I needed drugs to dull his voice. I needed Belle to yell at. I needed her silky touch on my skin to soothe the raging in my heart. Jesus, I almost wished for death, but I couldn't let that happen—not until I'd sent the men responsible to ground.

"Prospect!" I yelled when Echo's voice got too loud and I couldn't take it anymore. "Get in here!"

The door opened and he came in, gun in hand again. Jesus Christ, this kid wasn't going to make it if he carried on like this. You can't go wielding a gun around a hospital like it's a gangland shoot out.

"Put that away!" I yelled, and he quickly tucked it back into the waistband of his jeans.

"Sorry, I was told to be on guard at all times in case they came back." As soon as the words left his mouth he regretted saying them. Knowing my brothers had been talking about that possibility with everyone but me pissed me off. I'd known there was a chance, but I hadn't realized that they all thought it was a real threat.

I reached under my mattress, my fingers finding purchase on my own gun, and I pulled it out, aiming it at the door. He was too far away to see how my arm shook under the weight of the gun, my muscles not ready for this yet.

"Any of those dumb fucks come near me and I'm sending them straight back to hell, brother. Now calm your shit down." I slid the gun back underneath, hating that I could feel the tremors moving up and down my arms, tingles in each of my fingers. Belle was supposed to massage my hands but had forgotten. I hated her in that moment. Her forgetfulness had made me feel weak.

What had gotten into her today? She was normally so attentive to everything that I wanted or needed—well, apart from my cock, that is. But she was gentle with her touch, constantly asking if I was okay, if she was being too rough or too soft. She was a regular people pleaser was Belle. But not today. Today she'd been more than distracted, and I wanted to know why.

"How did she seem to you?" I asked, curious to see if everyone was getting the same shitty treatment as me.

The prospect looked confused and shrugged. "Who?"

"The nurse, asshole!"

He frowned. "What do you mean, Beast?"

"It's not rocket science, kid. Did she seem okay to you?" I snapped impatiently.

He shrugged again. "I guess."

Man, this kid was dumber than a box of rocks. His job was to notice if something or someone was off, yet he looked like he barely knew what day of the week it was. I needed to tell Shooter to cut this kid from the club; he was no good. I was surprised he'd lasted this long.

I thought back to Echo and how shitty a prospect he'd been at first. Kid had knocked a full row of bikes over on his first week working for us. Cost hundreds of dollars' worth of damage. Back then I'd said the same thing to Hardy, our old VP—that we needed to ditch Echo because he was no good for the club. But Hardy had told me that Echo was my problem. That I was his sponsor now for being such a dick. Told me that I had to take him under my wing and make it work. Fucking hated those first few months of babying that little shit; caused me endless amounts of stress, but he'd come out the other side and had ended up one of our best prospects and eventually he'd been like a little brother to me.

God, I missed him.

"You still need me?" the prospect asked.

"No, get the fuck out," I replied, and he nodded and turned to leave. "Wait, what's your name, kid?"

He looked back at me with a frown. "Joey."

"You thought of a road name yet?" I asked.

You didn't get to pick your own road name, but all prospects tried to think of one for themselves. He shook his head, his expression remaining neutral, yet I saw something behind his eyes that told me more than he was giving away.

"What is it?" I asked, knowing he'd come up with one for himself. They were normally dumb and didn't fit them at all, but I was still curious to hear it all the same. "Go on, I know you've thought of one."

He licked his lips and smiled. "Demon."

Fucker sounded so proud of himself, not realizing he'd be laughed out of the club if he said that to anyone but me.

Hell, I wanted to laugh at him—probably would have if I could remember how to laugh. This was exactly why you didn't get to pick your own road name. Demon was a name given to an enforcer or someone who'd shown that he had a screw missing in that big old brain of his. That was not this kid in any way.

"I'm a demon in bed and a demon on the road," he continued, his grin going wider.

Jesus Christ, this kid wasn't going to make it.

Chapter Nine
~ *Belle* ~

The letter hitting my mailbox had made my good mood dissipate quicker than you could say lickety-split but when Joey had stormed into the room pointing his gun directly at my abdomen I almost peed my pants. I was a positive kind of girl, but there was just no way I could spin anything good from this. The letter, then Beast's rage at me for not being gentle or attentive enough, and then the prospect of being shot because I was clearly terrible at my job... It was just too much.

I just wanted to go home and go back to sleep. Or heck, maybe just quit this day altogether. Could I bypass Tuesday and pretend it didn't exist? Just skip straight over into Wednesday. Heck, maybe skip Wednesday too and go straight to Thursday for my day off. That would be a better option.

Making quick time on the rest of my rounds, I headed into the break room to try to grab a quick coffee before heading back to Beast's room. Seeing to him was the first thing I did in the morning and the last thing I did before I went home. I wasn't looking forward to seeing him again—not after this morning. I wasn't sure if it was because I was more afraid of him now or I just felt entirely awful that I'd hurt him when I should have been taking care of him. Either way, I felt awful and nervous and just wanted to go home and climb back into bed.

Pushing open the staff room door, my day got worse when I found Jenna sitting at the small table by the window with her own coffee in hand. She paused mid sip and I started to back away because I was too exhausted to deal with this right now. We hadn't spoken since Beast had effectively fired her and hired me in the same breath. I could understand her thinking that I'd come in and stolen her job—though honestly, she should know me better than that—but she hadn't even given me the chance to explain that I had no choice and that I was going to give her

56

all the money because I didn't want it. She'd just shut me out and refused to talk to me.

"Belle," she said on a sigh, "we should talk."

That was the last thing I wanted to do.

I was tired.

I was upset.

And I still had to go and tend to Beast one more time before I could clock out for the evening and go home and pass out. And after how I'd handled him that morning, it wasn't likely to be a walk in the park. He'd no doubt make my life hell.

I paused in the doorway, letting my gaze meet hers, and I finally realized that she looked as sad as I no doubt did, and I immediately felt ten times worse. Jenna stood up, leaving her coffee on the table, and walked toward me. Her brow furrowed when I didn't move toward her, and I saw the hurt flash across her face. I didn't want to hurt her; I didn't want to hurt anyone, but I was so tired of walking on eggshells with people. Of people assuming the worst of me. But mostly, I was tired of people taking advantage of me and thinking they could just take whatever they wanted and be damned if it hurt me.

The letter was burning a hole in my pocket telling me that I would always be used. That I was no good. That nobody really cared about me unless they could get something from me.

I lifted my chin. "What is there to talk about?"

My words came out cold and uncaring, which was exactly what I was going for, but it wasn't me, this wasn't who I was, and my shoulders immediately slumped in regret.

"I'm sorry," I said, lowering my gaze to the ground. I pushed my hands inside the front pockets of my uniform, rubbing the letter between my fingertips. "It's been a really long day."

"It's the job," she agreed.

"Look, I'm really tired, Jenna. I don't have the energy to fight with you right now, please."

"I don't want to fight with you either, Belle," Jenna said, her head cocked to one side like she was trying to work me out. "I'm just disappointed. After everything I said about men like him… you just straight up go and ignore me. I thought I'd raised you better than that."

I looked up at her sharply. "I didn't want to work for him!"

She frowned. "You didn't?"

I shook my head. "God no, but it's not like I had much of a choice. It was either me or they'd find someone else, and I didn't want you losing out on the money, so I took the job so I could still give you the money—better you have it than someone else. But then you wouldn't speak to me to let me explain that I wasn't taking your job. I promise I wasn't. And I know it was stupid, and you were right about everything; he's awful, and probably unsavable, and I'm sorry for disappointing you—"

"Go back a step. You think I care about the money?"

"Don't you? Isn't that why you're mad at me?"

Jenna scowled and came toward me before wrapping her arms around my shoulders. "No, I couldn't give a damn about the money, Belle, I care about you! Like I said, I warned you what men like him were like and then you just straight up started working for them like I hadn't said a thing. I'm mad that you've put yourself on their radar"— she paused and pulled out of the hug—"but I guess that's really my fault, huh?"

"What should I have done then?" I asked, completely confused. I'd thought I was helping her, but apparently not. I'd thought I had been backed into a corner with no other option, but I was wrong about that too.

"You should have said no. You should have sent them packing with their tails between their legs and made it clear that you can't be bought."

I felt so stupid and naïve.

My chin trembled with the need to cry, but I held it back and tried to stay strong. "I thought it was about the money," I whispered, the words lodging in my throat.

"Since when do I care about money?" Jenna shook her head at me. "I've raised you from three years old, Belle. When that good-for-nothing mom of yours up and left I decided right then that I would do everything I could to give you as many opportunities as I could. I worked my butt off, going without things for myself just to give you what I could, and you think now, all of a sudden, I give a damn about money? Girl, I haven't had a spare dollar since you came to my house." She laughed and I laughed with her, a sob bubbling in my throat and threatening to overflow.

"I'm sorry," I said, guilt eating away at me. "I haven't spent any of their money though. I was saving it to give to you."

Jenna smiled and pulled me in for another hug, her hands rubbing my back like she used to when I was little and I couldn't sleep. I started to feel better, but then the thought of the letter made me feel awful all over again.

"That's your money. I don't need it and I don't want it. Lord knows working for Beast you've more than earned it, right?"

I laughed and we pulled out of the hug so I could fan my face with my hand. I was still holding back the dam of tears as I laughed and breathed a sigh of relief.

"He's such an asshole," I said, and Jenna raised an eyebrow at me, smirking at my uncouthness. I hated swearing and never had much use for it, but working for Beast was beginning to rub off on me. Starting with calling him an asshole, though of course I would never dare say it to his face.

"That he is," she agreed, "but he'll be out of here soon enough and we can both move on with our lives and forget he ever existed. You just keep saving that money and use it toward a down payment on a decent apartment. You can't stay in that beat-up old trailer forever."

"I know, I know," I agreed, and that did seem like a better idea.

I hated the trailer, but it was mine, leaks and all. I'd moved out of Jenna's two-bedroom apartment as soon as I could. In all the years that she'd raised me, I'd never seen her with a man, so the day she brought home Gregory I knew it was serious and they needed their own space.

"You done for the day? We're going out for dinner tonight if you want to join us," Jenna asked with a smile.

59

"I still have my final round with Beast," I said with a roll of my eyes. "Besides, I wouldn't want to be a third wheel between you two."

"Nonsense! We miss you. Finish off your shift and meet us at Della Roma at nine."

My stomach rumbled at the sound of my favorite restaurant's name and we both laughed. Jenna patted my arm as she passed.

"I'll think about it. I'm really tired."

"Please come." She leaned in and kissed the side of my face. She may have been my godmother, but she was the next best thing to a mom I could have ever hoped for. If it hadn't been for her, who knows what would have happened to me. Probably dumped into the system—and then what? No one would have come to get me so I would have been stuck there until I was seventeen before being vomited out into the world and left to do my own thing.

Jenna had saved me in the best possible way; she'd given me a home, a family, love, and I would never be able to repay her for it.

"Okay, I'll come," I agreed, not feeling up to it after the day I'd had, but knowing she wouldn't let it drop unless I agreed. Besides, I could never resist Italian food.

She left and I made myself a quick coffee before pulling out the letter from my pocket. My hand smoothed over my handwritten name on the front of the envelope, the federal prison stamp shining like a beacon at me.

It was the thing I had dreaded getting my entire life: a letter from my mom. Only this was actually worse. She'd abandoned me as a toddler and I hadn't heard anything from her since, but now, after all these years, she was about to get out of prison and she needed somewhere to stay. And for some reason she'd chosen me.

I knew I was being used, but how could I say no to her?

She was mom. Not by her heart or soul, but by blood, and despite my better judgment, I couldn't ignore that.

Chapter Ten
~ BEAST ~

"Brought you a little something to keep you occupied, brother." Gauge smirked as he came into the room. Lola, one of the club's sweetbutts, tottered in on high heels, her tight little ass sashaying behind her like she owned the place. "Thought a little relief might help you to sleep better."

Sleep? Fuck, I hadn't slept properly in months. An hour here or there, but that was it. Every time I closed my eyes I watched Echo falling. I saw the blood pumping from him. I felt the fire on my skin and my flesh melting away, and I heard the horses screaming for their freedom. More than enough times I'd woken myself up by being sick all over. I'd decided it was best just to stay awake so I didn't have to dream.

But Lola, sweet-as-a-peach Lola. She had always been my favorite girl at the club and had never failed to send me off to la-la land after an epic session. She smiled as she twirled a curl around her finger, her gaze flitting between me and Gauge. I scowled, watching as she took me and all my glorious fuckedupness in.

"Pretty, ain't I," I growled with a snarl.

Her smile fell and Gauge gave her ass a tap and sent her toward me. I was still wearing a bandage around my head to cover where those fuckers had almost taken my eye. Doctors said my sight might come back to it one day, but the possibilities were slim to none. I should've just let them take the fucking thing out but I couldn't bear the thought of losing more of myself to those bastards. But I couldn't wear the bandage forever. Sooner or later I'd need to take it off and put on an eye patch like I was a fuckin' pirate or some shit. I just didn't want to. If I wore the patch it was like accepting that I'd never see with it again, and I wasn't ready for that. My depth perception was messed up and I wasn't sure if I'd ever be able to ride again, or even shoot a gun. What kind of enforcer couldn't shoot a damn gun?

Eye patch or not, there was no shying away or hiding from the fact that I was covered in thick red knife scars and half my body had been burnt to a crisp and was now bubbled and melted. And the parts that hadn't been burnt or cut into had been hacked away. Both little fingers, both little toes, and chunks randomly taken out of my body. I was a freak. A full-fledged freak. What they hadn't carved from me, they'd burnt, and what they hadn't burnt, they'd scarred. I was fit for the fucking house of horrors and it was only just really occurring to me how hideous I was to women.

Seeing Lola visibly flinch back from me made me feel sick in a whole new way, and for the first time I wasn't angry. I was destroyed.

My heart pounded in my chest and I wished it would just give up and let me die already. Because this was it for me now. This was all I had to look forward to: my brothers pitying me and women feeling sick around me. I was done.

"I'll leave you two lovebirds alone," Gauge laughed, unaware of the bombshell he'd just dropped in the room.

Lola turned and watched him leave with a horrified look on her face, and Gauge's smile fell before he winked at her, letting her know that everything was going to be okay.

This was a pity fuck.

That's what I was now—a goddamned pity fuck.

Women used to line themselves up at my door to get a piece of me and my dick, and now I was nothing but a freak.

Anger roared through me, igniting my veins and setting me on fire all over again. Only this hurt way more than just my body; this pain went down real deep.

"Get over here," I barked, more than ready to show her what she'd been missing. I may have been a freak but I could still fuck, and I'd give her the best fuck of her life and send her packing. Make sure she told every damn woman out there that I still had it. She could close her eyes and think of whatever and whoever she liked, but when I was done with her I would be the only thing she'd ever want inside of her.

Lola turned back to me, her wide eyes trying not to look *at me*. She smiled hesitantly and stumbled forward, like a baby deer learning to walk. When she reached the side of my bed, I reached out and grabbed her ass. Wearing tiny little denim hot pants didn't leave much to the imagination, and I cupped the bottom of her ass cheeks and squeezed hard enough that she squealed.

"You like that?" I growled, and she nodded and tried to smile, but it was fake, all of it. Her fake tits, her fake lips, her fake lashes and fake hair, her fake nails and now a fake fucking smile to go along with it.

The anger in me bloomed.

I threw back the sheet, revealing my body to her. "Look at it," I snarled, reaching up to the back of her neck and grabbing it before forcing her to look down at my broken fucking body.

It was like I'd been attacked by coyotes, teeth and claws taking their worth from me before chewing me up and spitting me back out. I was vile. I was hateful. I was ugly as sin and twice as dangerous.

"You like that, Lola?"

"Mmm hm," she hummed, her eyes looking back up to my face, which was just as fucked up as the rest of me. Her gaze hesitated on the bandage wrapped round my head and I knew she was wondering what was beneath it.

"Touch me," I ordered.

Her hand automatically reached out and took hold of my flaccid dick before she began running her hands up and down it. I let go of her neck and reached for her ass again, hoping to incite something inside of me to wake the fuck up. But there was nothing. Her touch was gentle yet firm, and she knew how to touch a man, but nothing happened and after several minutes she looked across at me hesitantly.

"Suck it," I snapped. "What the fuck is wrong with you? You can't even make me hard anymore!"

I laid the problem at her feet but we both knew it was me. She was doing everything right—she always did—but I couldn't let her know that. I couldn't let her know that I hadn't gotten hard in months. That I hadn't felt a single tingle of desire down there since before this happened to me. Wasn't sure if it was psychological or physical, but my dick was fucking dead.

Lola leaned over and took my dick in her mouth, pushing the floppy, useless thing between her lips and sucking while playing with my balls. I reached around and cupped her ass, pushing between her cheeks so I could feel her pussy under my fingers, and she moaned. But it was fake, just like everything else. I wondered if it had always been this way. If she'd always faked it with me. She was a sweetbutt, and she was there to service the men, but I'd always assumed she enjoyed what she did. But now I was wondering if I was wrong.

"Suck it harder!" I yelled, feeling desperate.

I needed this to work. I needed at least one part of my body to fucking work like it should. I needed her to know that I was still a man. Hell, *I* needed to know that I was still a man! But there was just nothing. Not a twitch or a tingle. Just nothing.

"Get up here and fuck me!" I yelled, and Lola looked up sharply and then back down to my limp dick. "Now!" I ordered, feeling sick. Feeling angry. Feeling desperate.

She let go of me and shimmied out of her hot pants before climbing on the bed and straddling me. The bed dipped and moved and my body hurt from it all, but I would do this. I just needed to be in a woman again and it would be all right. My dick would come alive and I'd go off like a fucking rocket and it would all be okay.

"Beast." She said my name hesitantly, confusion and disgust on her face. "You're not…"

I grabbed my soft dick in my hand and held it as straight as I could for her to lower herself down on. I just needed to be inside of her and it would all be okay. One feel of her body wrapped around me, her juices sliding down my dick, and it would all be okay. I'd be me again.

"Tits out," I ordered, and she reached up and pulled her little tank top thingy down, letting her tits out for me to see. Goddamn, fake or not, they were magnificent. They were every boy's wet dream and every man's fantasy. Lola was beautiful, perfect, but there was still nothing happening.

Lola started to lower herself down on me and I fumbled, pushing my limp dick inside of her. I was a big guy when hard—I'd almost gotten the road name "Hose" for how big I was—but right then it felt like a two-inch piece of string in my hand as I pushed and shoved to get it inside of her. Once inside, I reached around to touch her perfect tits, squeezing them in my hands, pulling on her nipples as she moved on me, rocking those little hips of hers back and forth over and over and willing my dick to come alive.

I could feel her—every muscle, every clench of her thighs; she was perfect, but the look on her face was the same: she was disgusted by me. And every thrust of her hips showed how disgusted she was as my dick flopped around in her, providing no satisfaction for either of us.

"You like that?" I growled, squeezing her tits. "Tell me you like it, Lola. Tell me."

I was desperate.

I was disgusting.

I felt sick to my stomach watching this beautiful woman bounce around on top of me, her perfect body next to my broken one. My head spun, my dick stayed soft; if anything, it shrunk in on itself even more, and my muscles ached from being so tense.

"I love it, ughhh, yeah, Beast, yeah," she cried out, bouncing up and down, rocking back and forth. Gotta give it to her, she was being a fucking trooper about it, but we both knew I was dead from the waist down and nothing she did was going to change that.

But what then?

I couldn't tell her to get off and send her away without coming; that would be even worse. Jesus Christ, I was going have to fake it. She'd know and I'd know, but we'd never talk about it again, and she'd never really be sure.

Shame, embarrassment, and repulsion rolled through me.

"Oh yeah, Beast, that's it, give it to me, baby, give it to me!" she cried out, moving faster and faster under my encouragement, my hands on her hips pushing her back and forth faster and faster.

The door opened and Belle walked in, her eyes looking up to meet mine.

"I brought you pudding!" she declared happily, spoon in one hand and pudding in the other. Her hair was down around her shoulders since her shift was over, and she'd taken off that fucking awful nurse's outfit and was wearing tight jeans and a little T-shirt that showed off a perfect flat belly.

My dick twitched at the sight of her.

Belle dropped the spoon, which clattered noisily across the floor.

Lola turned to look, a smile on her face as she continued to fuck my useless dick like she was winning this battle.

"Hey there," she said happily as my fingers dug into her hips and Belle stared wide-eyed as Lola continued to ride me. "We'll just be a minute or two, sweetheart. Y'all come back in a few minutes." Lola looked back to me. "Unless you want her to stay?"

My dick twitched again at the thought, but when I looked over, Belle was already darting out of the room, pudding and spoon in hand.

"Her loss, huh?" Lola said happily, but I could see the blankness behind her eyes. The way she wanted this over and done with. The way she was never fucking coming back in my room ever again. The way I disgusted her.

She thrust her hips roughly and my dick slipped out of her pussy and I took the opportunity to groan like I was coming. I grabbed my dick and breathed heavily before groaning again.

"That'll do, now get the hell out," I grunted, pushing her off me and grabbing the sheet to cover myself with as she climbed off of me.

She picked up her shorts and pulled them back on and I took one long, sorrowful look at her snatch because I knew I was never seeing it, or any other, ever again.

Lola patted my arm and then flinched back when she saw the burns running down it. "You good now?" she asked, almost like she gave a shit.

"Get the fuck out of here," I said, but there was no strength in my words. I turned and looked out the window, staring out at the sky as the sun began to set. "And don't come back. You don't turn me on anymore."

"What?" she said, her tone full of hurt.

I looked back. "You deaf? You're a fucking skank. You don't do it for me no more. Fake-ass tits and fake-ass lips. You're disgusting, now get the fuck out and don't come back."

Lola gritted her teeth, glancing to the door and then back to me. "Yeah, because I'm the fucking problem," she laughed, her pretense falling away.

"What the fuck did you just say to me, bitch?" I yelled, sitting up and feeling my skin stretch and muscles ache at the sudden movement. "You got a death wish talking to me like that!"

My words were angry, my tone was terrifying, but inside I was dying.

She shook her head and backed away laughing. "What are you going to do, Beast? Slap me with that useless dick of yours?" She laughed again, tottering over to the door. "The only thing frightening about you anymore is that crusty old beat-up body of yours. I need to go shower after touching it."

And then she left.

I stared after her, fury and shame and revulsion washing over me in waves. I pushed myself to get out of bed, grabbing the first thing I could, and threw it across the room. It felt good as the water jug smashed against the wall and water and glass cascaded down the walls. I spun and grabbed the hateful fucking cart that Belle had all her supplies on and started to grab everything off it, throwing them across the room too; one after another, the creams and the ointments and the pills bounced off the walls. And when it was empty I used the last of my strength to grab the cart and throw that too. But this time I threw it against the window.

Didn't expect it to break.

But it did; it smashed right through the window in a shower of glass.

Somewhere behind me I was aware that the door had opened and the prospect had come in, but I couldn't hear a damn word he was saying over the rampant beating of my own heart.

Chapter Eleven
~ *Belle* ~

Iloved Della Roma. The people, the food, even the smell was wonderful, but tonight all I could think about was Beast and that woman. My stomach turned every time I thought of it—of them, doing *it* on his bed.

I wasn't a prude—far from it. I'd had sex before—I'd even done it outside once—but seeing that woman on top of Beast, his fingers gripping her waist and the hard look on his face… I don't know what it was, but it made me feel sick to my teeth.

"You're awfully quite tonight, Belle," Gregory said, taking a sip of his wine.

He was in insurance, or something serious and important, and he was much the same. He pretty much lived in a suit or khaki pants and polo top and was always well groomed. But he was nice, polite, kind, and he was really good for Jenna. He made her smile, he looked after her, he cooked for her, and when he wasn't cooking for her he took her out to dinner. And he never, not once, made me feel like I was imposing on them. He was a good guy, he was just a little—straight, I guess. He lived in a gorgeous apartment in the center of Atlanta and had asked Jenna to move in…oh, I'd lost count of how many times, but she always said no. She liked her independence and wasn't about to give it up for anyone.

"I'm just tired. It's been a really long day at work," I sighed, but smiled. It had been a long couple of weeks in work, if I was being honest, and I was seriously wondering whether this nursing thing was right for me.

Up until recently, I'd never really given it any thought. It was what I'd been brought up on because Jenna was a nurse, and I'd always assumed that I would follow in her footsteps, but doing it and learning about it where two very different things and I'd begun to wonder whether it was me, or if I'd just assumed it was me because I loved Jenna so much.

"Maybe you need to take some time off," Gregory suggested kindly. "I've been saying the same thing to Jenna for a while now. All she does is work."

"That's just who she is." I smiled, because it was the truth. That was all I'd ever known her to do: work.

Jenna sat back down after coming back from the bathroom. "Who are we talking about?" She picked up her wine glass and took a sip from it.

"You, my dear. I was just saying to Belle that you work too hard and need to take a break." Gregory leaned in and kissed the side of her face.

Jenna pouted at him and then me. "I like to work," she said defensively. "I like to be kept busy."

"That's what I was saying," I said. "But he is right on the taking a break thing. I don't think you've had any time off in over ten years."

Jenna cocked her head to one side and tutted at me. "Says the girl coming off a fourteen-hour shift, huh?"

"Touché," I said with a smirk.

My smirk turned into a huge, unattractive yawn that felt like it was going to split my face wide open. It wasn't so much the long hours that were wearing me down, but the emotional drama that came with the long shifts. Namely, Beast. But today had just been a bad day all around and I was looking forward to Thursday when I had my day off. Jenna was covering Beast, and honestly I was so grateful to be getting some space from him. His soul was so dark that at times I felt like I was being sucked into a vortex just being around him. But I also couldn't entirely blame him. I wouldn't have been able to survive what he had. And despite what Jenna and everyone else that found out I was working for the Devil's Highwaymen said, I didn't think anyone deserved it either.

Beast was a bad man. The absolute worst. And no doubt the things he'd done in his life were horrific and would put the Devil himself to

70

shame, but pain, in any form, wasn't something that I would ever believe people deserved.

"Besides, I took a day off just last week," Jenna said. "I mean, I ended up coming in after only three hours because there was an emergency, but I tried to take it off!"

I chuckled and took a sip of my margarita. The food arrived not long after and my mouth watered at the sight of the most delicious lasagna in the world. Well, certainly in Atlanta. I was good at a cooking and loved to make food for people. It was yet another one of the down sides of living in the small trailer: the too-small oven. I'd been after the recipe for this lasagna for years but was yet to learn their secrets.

Lorenzo set the plate down in front of me with a knowing smile. "So lovely to see you tonight, Belle. It's been a while, yes?"

I nodded, inhaling the scent of the food. "It has. I started work at the hospital a couple of months back."

"It's good, yes? You're enjoying the work?" he asked, genuinely curious. He waved over some of the other servers with the rest of our order while we talked, never taking his eyes off me. Lorenzo was only a couple of years older than me, but he had been running his father's restaurant since he was seventeen, when his mother and father had retired. He was handsome in a typical way; dark hair, blue eyes, medium build, dexterous hands, and a smile that would make any girl blush.

"It is. Unfortunately it's really *really* long hours. I can barely make it to bed most nights, and the most food I get to eat is beans on toast or ramen noodles!"

"Ramen noodles!" he gasped, hand on his heart.

"I know. This is the healthiest meal I've eaten in weeks." I laughed and he laughed with me, but then a thoughtful look crossed over his face.

"Well, maybe in between those busy shifts of yours, maybe I can cook for you one night," he said, turning his body to face me and not the entire table. "I have some new recipes I've been trying and would love to try them out on someone. Barring the ramen noodles, I believe you have a very good pallet for food, yes?"

71

I started to laugh, thinking that we were still teasing, but then realized he was completely serious. Lorenzo was handsome, successful, and sweet as anything. I'd always known those things about him, but our relationship was always based on friendship and nothing more… until now. I blushed, suddenly feeling self-conscious and wishing that I would have bothered to wear something nicer before coming to dinner. I was wearing a blue denim skirt and a black blouse that had seen better days, and I thanked God that I'd at least showered and blow-dried my hair before we'd come out.

Lorenzo held his hands up and smiled. "It's okay, it's okay—you're a busy lady, like you said. I just thought…"

"She would love to," Jenna said, interrupting him before I completely blew my chances. "Just let her know when."

Lorenzo turned to look at her, his smile growing before he turned back to me. "When is best for you, Belle?"

My tongue was suddenly dry and sticking to the roof of my mouth, and my usual confidence around him had vanished at the thought of anything other than coming here for dinner with Jenna and Gregory and having some friendly chitchat with Lorenzo over food.

"Belle?" Lorenzo said my name, and for the first time I noticed how the letters played over his tongue and full lips; the slight accent he'd picked up from his father was sexy and not something I'd ever really thought about before. Until now. His blue eyes were watching me with steady confidence.

Omg answer him! I begged my subconscious.

"I have a late tomorrow but then I'm free on Thursday?" I somehow managed to squeak out. "It's my day off." I gave a small shrug.

Lorenzo smiled again. "Thursday is perfect. I'll book the night off and I'll cook only for you."

My cheeks felt hot and I had no doubt that the red was creeping down my chest and making me look all hot and bothered. Hell, I *was* hot and bothered!

"Perfect." I mirrored his words, and he winked and left our table.

I stared down at my lasagna trying to catch my breath before looking up and seeing Jenna and Gregory staring at me with grins on their faces.

"Stop that," I laughed, embarrassed but happy.

Jenna picked up her wine glass and so did Gregory, so I felt obliged to do the same. They clinked glasses with me and I felt Lorenzo staring at me from across the room. When I looked up he looked away with a small laugh and I hid my own smile behind my hand.

"New beginnings," Jenna said. "New job, new apartment on the horizon, and possibly a man in your life." She looked between Gregory and me with a happy smile. "Seems things are looking up for the two of us."

My smile dipped but I hid it by taking a sip of my margarita. "Yeah, they definitely are."

"What's this about a new apartment?" Gregory asked.

Jenna spoke for me, which was good because my mind was back on the letter in my purse. I'd brought it so I could speak to Jenna about it, but the evening was going so well and I didn't want to ruin it. And talking about my mother would definitely ruin it.

"Well, Belle has taken a second job at the hospital working on a private patient, so she's saving up for an apartment so she can get out of that trailer," Jenna said proudly. I was glad she left out the part that the private patient was actually working for a criminal gang and the patient in question was one of the most awful and dangerous people I had ever met in my life.

The image of him on the bed tonight with that woman, his gaze so dark and intense, and his hands gripping her and thrusting her back and forth on him popped into my head and I felt my blush deepen. It wasn't like they were having sex or making love. He looked angry, furious, and that poor woman must have been petrified of him. God, she was pretty though, I couldn't help but remember. Tiny waist, pert ass, and huge boobs. And despite the fact that she was on top of her boyfriend and was likely embarrassed when I came in, she had been super friendly and waved at me... omg, I realized, she wasn't his girlfriend.

I stood up sharply, bumping the table and almost knocking our drinks over. Jenna and Gregory looked at me in surprise.

"So sorry, I need to go to the bathroom," I said before darting off to the ladies' room.

Once inside I stared at myself in the mirror, feeling even more embarrassed that I'd walked in on them. It was bad when I'd thought she was his girlfriend, but realizing he'd brought a prostitute into the hospital was even worse. I mean, I was guessing that's what she was, and I held no judgment over her for it, but it was somehow still worse than walking in on them if she'd been his girlfriend. I dragged a hand down my face, feeling embarrassed and stupid at the same time. I knew so little about men and the world. Jenna had shielded me from it all, and I was so grateful, but it also left me wide open when it came to certain situations. Like walking in on your patient with a prostitute or going on a date on Thursday night with a handsome, successful man when you were nothing but a lowly nurse living in a crappy trailer and working for a criminal.

My stomach turned as I realized something else... I had never been on a proper date before. Sure, I'd been out with guys, but this was my first real, grown-up date where someone was going to cook for me.

I felt nauseous at the thought of being alone with Lorenzo. He was a seriously great guy, but I didn't know how to interact with a man like him. I lived in a trailer, for God's sake, and he had his own house and business!

I was getting more and more distressed at the thought of seeing Beast the next day, because I had no idea how to deal with the situation—and after how I'd been earlier in the morning and our argument...

And then there was still the matter of my mom's letter to deal with. At some point I was going to have to deal with it. The ten missed phone calls from her attorney proved that. She was getting out and she wanted to stay with me. Her only daughter that she had abandoned seventeen years ago…

Since when had my life gotten so complicated?

All I had done for the past few years was work and study, and I'd loved my little bubble. But now I was in the real world, dealing with real-world problems, and it was all going horribly wrong.

Chapter Twelve
~ BEAST ~

Belle spoon-fed me the pudding quietly; her thoughts were clearly elsewhere again today, which pissed me off. I was paying for her time and her attention, so I expected her goddamn time and attention to be on me 100% while she was here. She'd been exactly the same this morning, but I was about done with it now. It was the end of another long and boring day, I was aching, my skin itched, and I really needed out of this room.

She scooped some more pudding onto the spoon and directed it toward my mouth like I was a fucking child. Which, normally, I didn't really care. If anything, it was nice how attentive she was. She knew I could feed myself but that it hurt to move my arms too much, so did it for me and she seemed to enjoy making me feel better, so it was a win-win. But not today. Today her forehead was creased, her eyebrows pulled down like she was working on a fucking math problem or some shit. And she hadn't even mentioned the broken window.

When she almost missed my mouth for the second time, I snatched the spoon from her hand, making her startle and me hiss in pain.

"All right, get the fuck out of here, Belle," I growled, ignoring the pain in my shoulders from moving too fast and the sting across my knuckles from my skin stretching as I curled my hand around the spoon handle. Everything was healing—my body putting itself back together piece by piece. Skin healing, bruises fading, muscles building. I'd never be the same again, of course—not even close. Beneath the bandage wrapped around my head I only had one damn eye, and my skin was permanently scarred from the fire that had melted it, but I'd come to terms with that—mostly, at least. Women would never look at me the same; I wasn't the big alpha sex god anymore; I was literally beast by name and by looks now. But again, I'd come to terms with that. Mostly

I was getting irritable as all hell because it was happening way too slowly.

I wanted out of this place.

I wanted back on my bike.

I wanted a woman in my bed and a body at the end of my knife being made to pay for this shit. For me, for Echo, and for anything else I decided they needed paying for.

But I couldn't see any of that happening anytime soon.

Belle reached for the spoon, ignoring my comment. It was like she was in a daze or something, her thoughts elsewhere instead of where they should have been: here, on me!

"Goddamn it, get out!" I yelled.

Her wide eyes finally focused on me and her little rosebud mouth opened in shock. "I'm sorry, Beast. Please, let me keep going."

"No, fuck off, now." I spooned the pudding from the cup and aimed it for my mouth, but she reached out and tried to snatch the spoon from my hand.

"It's my job!" she said, her voice almost whiny.

"Get off the spoon," I growled, growing increasingly irritated with her behavior. Woman needed to learn her place if she was going to stick around here. Fuck, maybe it was time to let her go and get a new nurse again. Not sure where they'd find someone else though, since I'd pissed off pretty much everyone in this hospital already.

She held tight to it, even pulling a little, though for what good it would do remained to be seen because even as injured as I was I was still stronger than her.

"Belle," I warned.

"Let me help!" she said, her voice growing stronger. Angry, even.

"Bitch, get the fuck off the spoon!" I yelled loudly, startling her for the second time.

She let go so suddenly that the pink pudding flew over my chest and face. She inhaled sharply, her mouth opening in shock, her gaze dropping to my chest and back to my face six or seven times before she finally jumped into action.

"Oh my god, Beast, I'm so sorry, I'm so so sorry!" She stood up, grabbing a cloth from the little side table, and attempted to dab away the pudding while I glared at her hard enough to make my eyeballs hurt.

Cute as fuck or not, I wanted to grab her little ponytail tight with one hand and grab her by the throat with the other. Shit, maybe *because* she was cute as fuck. For the first time in months my dick twitched with real desire, and it took all my strength to not grab her and drag her onto the bed with me. Probably wouldn't have been able to do anything after that because fuck knows nothing actually worked down there anymore. The twitching stopped and my anger surged back. Belle must have sensed the warring within me, because she stopped dabbing the pudding away with a shaky hand and stared at me, her bottom lip trembling.

"Jesus, you're not gonna cry now, are you?" I growled out, snatching the cloth from her hand to wipe the pudding off my cheek. I dabbed a little too hard and hissed in pain, and Belle burst out crying.

Jesus.

Fucking.

Christ.

"What are you crying for? It was me that got hurt, not you, for fuck's sake," I grumbled.

She started to cry even harder and I threw the cloth across the room, my temper warring with my impatience and confusion.

"Just get out, Belle." I dragged a hand down my face, not able to look at her anymore, though I wasn't sure why seeing her so upset made me feel so...so goddamn mixed up. It wasn't like I'd been Prince Charming before all of this, but I'd never taken satisfaction in making a woman cry. Not unless it was in pleasure. But since the attack, all I wanted to do was hurt people. Didn't matter if they were male or female, brother or nurse. I just had so much anger inside of me that I felt like I'd burst if I didn't let it out.

Every tear, every unhappy face, just fed into my desire to make people feel as fucking awful as I did. It was like an addiction that I couldn't control, like feeding a hungry animal.

I dropped my hands to my sides and looked at her, not getting the same satisfaction I normally would. Even crying, she was pretty. Fat tears rolled down her cheeks, making them flush. Her lashes were long and thick, and when black shit didn't drip from her eyes I realized she was pretty without any makeup on. Damn.

Felt like shit for making her cry, which was the biggest surprise of all.

"I'm really sorry, Beast. Please forgive me," she sobbed.

"Calm down," I grumbled, getting more and more irritated.

She nodded quickly, swiping at her tears and trying to control her emotions. "Do you forgive me?" she asked, sounding pathetic.

I shrugged and scowled. "Sure."

She reached for the spoon again. "Can I feed it to you still?" she asked hesitantly.

I scowled. "I'm not hungry anymore, Belle. Just leave me be." I looked down, where there was pudding dripping down my bare chest. "Get me a fucking cloth before you leave, though."

She jumped up and scurried over to the cupboard to get a clean cloth, dampening it and coming back to me quick time. She leaned over to wipe at my chest when I reached out and grabbed her hand in mine, causing her to flinch. Her eyes locked with mine and I stared into those big hazel eyes of hers, getting lost for a moment in her sadness. Strangely, her sadness soothed mine instead of feeding into my need for seeing more of her pain, and I let her go.

"I'm really sorry, it's been a really long week and I've got so much going on…" She stared at me wide-eyed. "Sorry, you don't care about that, of course you don't. I'm sorry."

"Stop fucking apologizing," I growled.

"Okay, I'm sorry." She blushed when I raised an eyebrow at her.

"I've got this, just get out of here," I said, forcing the anger out of my tone, and this time she nodded and handed me the cloth before turning to leave.

"I'll see you later," she said, her voice tinged with sadness.

"Yeah, and make sure you have your head out of your ass when you come back."

She nodded. "I will. I'm just tired I think… I'll be glad for my day off tomorrow."

I cocked my head to one side. "Day off?"

"Yeah, tomorrow is my day off."

I scowled. "The fuck should I do then?"

Day off? Bitch was taking a day off? Who did she think she was? Did she think this was a part-time position or something? Did she think I'd just sit here like a good little boy waiting for her to come back?

"Jenna is coming to look after—"

"Fuck that. I don't want her here, I want you," I snapped, interrupting her. "You either be here tomorrow or you don't come back at all."

She opened and closed her mouth before nodding. Her jaw was clenched like she was holding back a tirade of abuse, and I really wanted to push that button and make her explode. Kinda liked it when she scolded me, but looking at her, she really did look tired. It didn't seem just the sort of tired you got from working hard or having late nights, either. It seemed the sort of tired you got from shit going on in your head. That kind of tired I understood. Didn't change the fact that she needed to be here tomorrow though, but it did make me curious.

"What's going on with you?" I asked, my voice hard, but I was genuinely interested.

"It's nothing," she said with a shake of her head. "I'll be in tomorrow." She turned to leave.

"I wasn't asking you, Belle. Fucking tell me!" I barked. If she was going to give me her undivided attention, then I needed to know what the fuck was going on with her.

I didn't actually care.

Hell no.

This was just self-serving curiosity.

She hesitated in the doorway, looking like she wasn't going to tell me for a moment, until I fixed her with another hard gaze.

"Belle," I growled. "Don't make me ask again."

"It's my mom," she said, her voice a whisper. "She's getting out of prison and wants to stay with me."

"So?"

She swallowed and leaned against the wall beside the door like she didn't have the energy to stand up anymore and needed the support. I scowled at her. Never took her for the judgy type, but she looked ashamed as fuck that her mom was in jail. I mean, it wasn't something to be proud of either, but her mom needed help so she should help her. It wasn't the big dilemma she was making it out to be.

"I haven't seen her since I was a baby," she said, looking down at the floor.

"She been in a long time?" I asked, my curiosity growing.

Belle shook her head. "Yeah, I don't know really. She left me on my godmother's doorstep when I was just three. I haven't seen or heard from her since then."

"She not even check up on how you were doing?"

She shook her head, her eyes going all glassy like she was going to cry again. Man, what was it with women? They fit into three categories: good old pussy, druggie and useless, or pathetic and needy.

"Shit," I said, the word slipping out before I could stop it. That was fucked up. No wonder her head had been in her ass the past couple of days. "So what are you going to do?" I asked—not that I cared or anything, but I was curious. It wasn't like I had anything else going on to entertain me just then.

She shrugged. "I don't know. I mean, I should say yes, right?" She finally looked up at me, like she was genuinely interested in my opinion, or at least wanted some advice. "I mean, she's my mom." She chewed on the inside of her cheek. "Sort of."

"What does this godmother of yours say about it? I bet she's real fucking happy about all of this."

I felt unnecessarily angry for her. This dumb bitch getting back in touch with Belle after all this time, just because she needed something... Fuck, who did she think she was? Despite me ditching

81

Jenna for Belle, I actually liked her. She was strong and didn't take shit from anyone, not even me. No doubt she wouldn't stand for this shit.

"I haven't told her yet," Belle replied, pushing away from the wall. "I don't want to hurt her, but I don't know if I can say no either. I mean, like I said…it's my mom." She shrugged. "What would you do?"

"Fuck, Belle, don't ask me that."

She cocked her head to one side. "Why not?"

"Why not? Because if I ever saw my skank of a mother again, I'd put a bullet through her brain, that's why," I growled. "You just need to ask yourself if you want her to stay with you. I mean, do you even *want* to see her?" I asked.

Not that I cared.

Couldn't give a shit what she did so long as she turned up to work and did as she was told.

"Yes and no. I mean, I'm curious to see what she's like—anyone would be, right? But Jenna *is* my family. She's loved me, raised me, cared for me, protected me… I don't really need anyone else." She sighed again.

"That's not what I asked," I said with a raised eyebrow.

She dragged a hand down her face, her expression tortured. "I just don't want to hurt anyone, and it feels like whatever I do, I'll be hurting someone." She turned to leave before looking back over her shoulder at me. "Can I go now?"

"Yeah, Belle, you can go," I replied with a grunt.

She looked so sad as she left, her chin practically on her chest, her head all confused. I hated that I wanted to help her in some way— any way—but couldn't. I could barely get out of this bed, so what good was I? Not that I cared anyway; it was purely selfish my reasons for wanting to help her. If I was going to get her undivided attention so I could get better quicker, then she needed to deal with this shit and move on.

But there was something else too. Something that was bothering me, that I hadn't realized until now—until I'd seen how cut up she was at the thought of hurting someone—anyone. She was pure. Like, her soul was the purest fucking thing I'd ever seen. How could someone be so giving? Her mom had left her on a fucking doorstep. Had never gotten in touch to see if she was okay, but now that she needed Belle she gave her a quick phone call and asked to sleep over. It was fucked up. And yet Belle was still considering it because she didn't want to hurt her.

A few months ago I would have said she was naïve. But this wasn't naivety. This was her not wanting to cause pain to another person. I let out a dark laugh because Christ, could she be any more of my exact opposite? She was like the yin to my yang.

Goddamn it, I shouldn't have had her coming in and being around me. My soul was blacker than the night. It was so dirty that it was like tar and everything good stuck to it and got sucked inside, never to be seen again. I should get someone else to look after me, especially now that she had so much shit going on. She deserved better than this—than me.

But even as I thought it, I knew that I wouldn't let her go.

When you find something that pure, the Devil inside you hungers for it more. And right then, I was hungering for Belle. I wanted her pureness. I wanted to taste it on my tongue. Feel it on my palms. And if I had to sacrifice her purity for my own selfish ways, then so be it.

Chapter Thirteen
~ Belle ~

 Jenna! What should I wear?" I whined into my cell. "We're not out because we're at his place, but we are out because I mean, this is a date, and I need to swing by the hospital before I go so it has to be appropriate for that and..." I let my words trail off as I sat down on the edge of my bed.

Clothes were strewn all over it and on the floor—piles of things that I had loved at the start of the day but now hated with a passion. Nothing looked right. Nothing felt right. I was overdressed. I was underdressed. It was too short. It wasn't short enough. I didn't want to lead him on and think we would sleep together, but I didn't want to rule it out either in case—well, in case things went really well and I wanted to.

"Do men have this problem?" I surveyed my room with dismay.

"Gregory says yes," Jenna chuckled down the phone. "He says he changed fifteen times before our first date. Oh my god, really?" Her voice got distant as she moved her mouth away from the phone to coo over Gregory.

"Jenna, focus with me!"

"Sorry, I'm back. Okay, so what about the red velvet dress? That always looks great on you."

I shook my head, staring at the offending article on the floor. "It has a stain on it. I think it's wine, but I don't even know how because I don't drink wine."

"Oh, that will be when we went out for your birthday last year and that woman bumped into you and spilled her drink. I was going to take that to be cleaned, but then you moved out."

I groaned, remembering the incident. "Ughhh, great, well now I need to drop it off to be cleaned, but it's probably ruined now."

"I'll do it. Bring it to work with you tomorrow. Okay, so what about those cute black shorts and a lacy camisole top?"

"The silk ones?"

"Yes, they would show off your legs and your shoulders, but they're not too short and the camisole isn't too low but will definitely give a good view of the girls"—she chuckled—"and it's casual but datey."

I fumbled through the clothes to find the shorts and white cami top. "I don't think 'datey' is a word," I mumbled as I pulled on the shorts. They did look cute on, I decided. "Wait a minute," I said, putting the phone down so I could pull on the silk cami top. I had to go braless in it, but it wasn't really noticeable unless I got cold.

I picked the cell back up, staring at my reflection with a satisfied smile. "This is the one, thank you!" I beamed.

"You're welcome. Have fun, sweetheart. Be safe." I could practically hear her smile.

"I will. And I'll text you when I get in." I twisted my hair up onto my head but then decided to leave it loose. The waves had come out really great after blow-drying, and it would make a change since I rarely had it down these days.

"You sure you don't want me to take care of Beast tomorrow?" she asked, but I could already hear Gregory saying something in the background.

"I've got it, but thanks. It's on the way so it's no big deal. In fact, I better go so I can do my makeup and head there or I'll be late for both men," I laughed.

"It's nearly over, sweetheart. Shooter gave me a call and said they'd be moving Beast back to the clubhouse in the next week or two. Then it's back to normal," she sighed happily. I think the whole thing had been a bigger pressure on her than me in some ways. Little did she know her happiness would be short-lived, because my mom would be coming to stay.

I really needed to tell her soon.

Tomorrow, I decided.

"Okay, I've gotta go. Thanks for the help, talk to you later. I love you."

"Love you too, Belle. And remember, own it."

I smiled at her words and hung up, and I spent the next twenty minutes applying a little makeup and putting on some heels and jewelry. I gave myself a spritz of my favorite perfume before leaving the trailer and climbing into my car, and then I headed to the hospital to give Beast his meds and apply a little cream to his skin. His needs had become less and less over the past couple of weeks, but he was still needy like a toddler at times. I really hoped he wasn't in one of those moods tonight. I found I was looking forward to my date with Lorenzo. And the more I thought about it, the more I decided we were actually a good match. We were both independent. We both loved cooking. That was probably it, but I was sure I'd find out more that we had in common tonight.

I pulled up to the hospital and headed to Beast's room. As usual, a prospect sat outside of it. He stood up when he saw me, looking me up and down with wide eyes and giving me a long whistle that made me blush.

"Nurse," he said, biting down on his bottom lip and grinning. I hated that I enjoyed the attention.

"Prospect," I replied, feeling confident.

"Where've you been hiding that sweet body of yours?"

I tried to stop my smile from growing wider at the compliment. "How's the patient tonight?"

He clapped his hands together. "Real good mood, actually. Talked about helping out at an animal sanctuary when he gets out, maybe adopting a cat."

"Wow, really?" I said, stunned.

The prospect laughed. "Fuck no. He's grumpy as shit and he's gonna be even grumpier when he sees your fine ass in that outfit. You goin' on a date or some shit?"

The prospect was only young—a kid, really—but he had the eyes of a man and the way he was looking at me told me everything I needed to know about his young mind. I felt self-conscious under his lustful stare, but then I remembered Jenna's words to own it and I forced my blush to retreat.

"I am actually—right after seeing to the big man baby in there anyway. He better not keep me too long tonight," I said with a grin.

"Nurse, I think if he sees you in that get up you're going to be there all night long. I know I wouldn't let you out of my room." He bit his bottom lip again and this time the blush won out, flushing into my cheeks.

"Well, good thing he won't be able to chase after me then, huh?" I laughed and the prospect laughed too. "I better get in there."

I turned the handle on the door and pushed it open before going inside. With my shoulders back, my head high, and Jenna's words in my head, I felt good, pretty, confident, and I was determined to own it.

He was sitting in bed, as usual, scowling at something on the TV, and didn't bother to look up as he started to yell at me for being late.

"Should have bene here twenty minutes ago, Belle. This shit ain't good enough. We pay your wages you know, you can't just fucking turn up whenever you feel like it. This isn't fuckin' Hooters," he snapped, finally tearing his eyes away from the TV as he automatically clicked it off. His mouth clamped shut when he saw me, and I felt his heated stare on my body as I strode across the room trying to act completely casual.

"Listen, first, Thursday is my day off, as you well know, and second, I wasn't going to come in tonight at all, but I did because you requested me to, so stop yelling at me or I'll just leave you here in pain," I replied as calmly as I could.

Walking to the cupboard, I used my key to unlock it and get out the meds I needed and then I loaded them onto the cart. I began to pull it over to the side of his bed, still not meeting his gaze but feeling it with every move I took. He hadn't said another word since I'd answered him back, but he also hadn't stopped staring at me, so I was taking that as a win. I refused to look him in the eye, instead focusing on putting on some gloves and opening the tub of ointment.

I peeled back the sheet to his waist. "These are looking really good, Beast," I said, scooping out some of the cream. And they were.

Like really good. The bruises had all but gone and his skin had healed really well. He was still hugely scarred, obviously, but he was definitely on the other side of healing now. He still hadn't spoken so I chanced it and finally looked at him, automatically wishing that I hadn't.

Beast was scowling, which wasn't really unusual for him, but there was something fiercer in his expression than usual. His mouth was set in a thin, hard line as I set about my business, choosing not to bait him anymore, and it seemed like he was happy enough to give me the cold shoulder too. Instead, I ignored the deafening silence in favor of applying the cream over his burns, and for once he was silent. No grumbling. No complaining. No hissing in pain. He was just silent. Watching me move around the bed, applying the cream to his various burns.

When I was done, I screwed the lid back on the cream and placed it back on the cart. It made me wonder how much of the complaining he usually did was actually real.

I cleared my throat. "Just your meds now and we're done here," I said, looking at him again.

His scowl had gone, but his eyes were still dark and stormy. "I don't need 'em tonight," he said, his voice a deep rumble in the quiet room.

"Well, you might not think you need them, but you do. It's not just for the pain, it's for the healing, Beast, and you want to get better, don't you?"

"That's a stupid fucking question," he snapped, and I rolled my eyes at him.

"There's the Beast we all know and love." I smirked and almost fell over when he smirked back. He dropped it just as quickly as it came, though. We stared at one another in silence for a moment, something passing between us that I couldn't explain. He seemed different—or maybe it was me. I hated being in that room, but there was also something comfortable and familiar about being in there too.

"You going out?" he asked, nodding toward my outfit.

I'd chosen four-inch heels to wear, which I would never normally do because I felt more comfortable in sneakers, but with the shorts, they made my legs look long and graceful and my ass look pert. I was lucky enough that I had great skin so didn't need much makeup, but I'd still gone for smoky eyes and a little lip gloss, and my hair was thick and curled around my shoulders. I felt good, and I knew that I looked good too.

I certainly looked better than when I was in the awful, too-big nurse's outfit.

"That's a stupid fucking question," I retorted playfully, raising an eyebrow at him.

His smile grew, and if I didn't know any better I would have thought that he actually wanted to laugh. Could it be that the man with the heart of stone was cracking? And all it took was a little leg and some heels?

I got his meds from the table and poured a glass of water from the jug. His eyes were on my every move as I walked around the room fetching things, and I hated that I'd turned into *that* girl, but I couldn't the extra swing of my hips I gave as I walked.

"Open up," I ordered, holding the pills in one hand and the water in the other.

He swallowed, his face growing thoughtful. "Who's the lucky guy? Or girl. No judgment from me."

I shook my head, my grin still I place as I tried to keep things light between us. I was so close to getting out of there.

"I'm serious, Belle."

I put down the water and sighed. So much for getting through this quickly. The one and only time he was in a chatty mood and I didn't have the time for him. I almost felt guilty, but then I remembered it was my day off and I was there because he'd forced me to be.

"It's a guy," I replied, putting one hand to my hip.

His eyes watched my every move, taking in every little thing I did.

"Shame," he tutted. "Could have really got behind seeing you with a girl."

"What is it with guys wanting to watch girls hook up?" I chuckled with a shake of my head.

"It's hot," he replied bluntly, his eyes cold. "All that ass and tits. All that soft pussy being licked and sucked."

My smile fell and I felt my cheeks heat at his crude words.

"Okay, we're done here," I said, all joking gone now.

"Nothing like seeing a woman with her tongue sliding up another woman's wet pussy, spreading her wide open to be sucked and fucked."

I swallowed, lost for words. I knew he was trying to bait me into something, but I couldn't find my tongue to talk my way out of it. Any other man would love to see a woman dressed up and looking sexy. They would have just enjoyed the show for a few minutes.

But not Beast.

Beast seemed almost enraged at the fact I was wearing something other than my uniform.

"You're such an asshole, Beast," I said with a shake of my head. The words barely made it past my lips in fear of what his retribution might be, but they were out and he only smiled at them like I'd walked into exactly the trap he wanted.

"You know the only thing better than watching a hot woman fuck another hot woman?" he said, watching me carefully, his stormy eyes taking in everything on my face.

Beast reached out, putting his hand on my ass and pulling me closer to him. I squealed pathetically as his strong fingers ground into me, no doubt leaving a bruise in their wake, and his intense gaze burned into mine.

"Get off me!" I snapped, but his dark smile widened further.

"The only thing hotter than watching a woman fuck another woman is fucking that woman myself. Big dick sliding inside and filling her up," he growled, his hand still kneading my ass. "Do you like to fuck, Belle? Is that what you're gonna be doing tonight?"

90

"Stop it," I said softly. My smile had completely fallen now but his had grown, like every dirty word that made me uncomfortable made him happy. I was mortified by his vulgarity, and as if sensing how I felt, he went on.

"You gonna be up all night fuckin' some guy? Then come and see me tomorrow, maybe walking with a little limp in your step because you've been fucked so good, Belle."

I shook my head. "Why? Why do you have to ruin everything?" I asked, my voice still soft but my conviction strong.

Beast sat up and leaned forward. His hand had stopped kneading my ass but it was still there, his huge palm covering it entirely, heat pouring from his palm. He stared right into my eyes, trying to intimidate me, to get me to look away, or maybe to make me cry, but for once I refused to. I wouldn't let him keep pushing me like this, I decided. Despite how awful he was making me feel and the inevitability that followed, I wasn't putting up with this anymore.

"Because, Belle," he said, moving his hand from my ass and around to my hip and gripping it, "that's all us men think about. You think whatever pretty fuckboy you're out with tonight is gonna be thinking about your smart-as-shit brain or your too-good heart? Fuck, no. He's gonna be thinking how much he wants to fuck you."

"Stop it," I said more sternly.

"He's going to think about how quickly he can get through dinner or the movie, or whatever lame-ass shit it is that pussy men like him do with their women, and he's going to be wondering how quickly he can bend you over and fuck that tight little ass of yours."

Beast slapped my ass hard and then released me. I felt cold. Cold from my toes to the tips of my nose and right through to my soul. Why was he so cruel?

"You're disgusting," I said.

"And you fuckin' love it," he said, barking out a loud laugh.

My eyes narrowed as I gritted my teeth. "Open," I snapped, my mouth set in a hard line. "It's time to take your medicine. I have a date to go on."

"Your little fuckboy boyfriend waiting for you," he growled.

"He's a businessman, actually."

"You're in for a real treat then," he laughed. "Probably only likes it with the lights out and him on top." He laughed again. "Fucking stiffs are the worst." He smiled.

"No, you're the worst!" I huffed, growing more and more frustrated. "Tick tock, I need to go have some fun in the real world. Can't stay here all night with you. I have an actual life."

"Fuck you," he growled angrily.

And then it was my turn to smile. "Not ever, Beast."

We stared at one another, seconds ticking by and turning into minutes, neither of us wanting to back down. He was even more stubborn than me, I knew that, but I was done being his emotional punching bag.

"I said, open," I said again, my eyes narrowing.

"And I said, fuck you, Belle," he drolled.

I let out a sigh of anger and frustration before slamming the meds down on the cart loudly. I pushed it back to the other side of the room and let out an angry sigh.

"Where the fuck are you going?" he yelled. "Get back here."

"You don't want to take your meds, fine. I'll leave them here for you. Take them or don't. I'm going." I pulled off the rubber gloves and dropped them into the trashcan.

"You can't go until I tell you to, bitch," he said as I stormed toward the door.

I spun to face him, fury burning through me. I was so tired of people telling me what I could and couldn't do, and acting like I was some little kid that needed looking after.

"Let's get one thing straight, Beast. I can do whatever I want. You don't own me. No one does."

"That what you believe?" he said with a shake of his head and a dry laugh.

I shook my head and smiled, feeling anger burning through me. "That's what I *know*. I'm leaving now. I'm going on my date. And yeah, maybe we'll have sex, maybe we won't and he'll just be thinking about it all night. But whatever happens it will be my choice and on my terms. Either way, I won't be stuck in here with you."

His expression darkened and I had a feeling that if he weren't restricted to that bed he would have me by the throat and up against the wall. But I didn't care anymore.

Anger coiled and writhed inside me like snakes in a pit and I finally understood why he clung to this feeling so much—why he embraced it. It felt good, especially when I saw the hurt spark behind his eyes.

After everything he'd said and done in the past weeks, I enjoyed hurting him, just a little. It served him right. I knew the night was already ruined though, because the guilt was going to eat me up as soon as I left. That wasn't me. I didn't treat people like that.

"I own you," he snarled, his expression growing harder.

"*No one* owns me. No one, and especially not you! But hey, here's something to think about: Do you want to know what women think about when they're on a date?" I paused, putting my hand on the doorknob as I forced myself to use a crude word. "We're wondering how small their dicks are in comparison to their over-inflated egos." I pulled open the door and looked back at him. "And let me tell you, Beast, nine times out of ten, it's a disappointment to us." I glanced at his loosely covered crotch area with a raised eyebrow and left. I turned and left, slamming the door shut after me.

"I'm the one motherfucker out of ten, bitch!" he yelled after me.

I pressed my back against the door, listening as he threw the cup of water across the room and yelled something unintelligible.

The prospect stood up with a grin on his face. "All good?" he asked with a chuckle. Something else crashed to the floor in the room and I winced, wondering if Joey was going to yell at me as well, but instead he laughed some more. "Fuck, guess he didn't take the sexy getup too well."

I smiled, feeling stronger than I'd felt in…god, I don't know how long. But I felt strong and it felt good. It felt good to finally answer back. To actually say what was on my mind instead of bottling it all up.

"He may need one of your extra-special hits later," I replied. Something else smashed and I winced again. "Maybe even two."

He raised an eyebrow. "And you're good with that?" he asked, sounding amused.

"He can do whatever he wants. I don't care anymore," I replied. "We really need to get a plastic jug in there too, because the rate he's going through them is absurd." I started walking away, listening to the prospect laugh again.

"I'll get right on that once he's calmed down."

"Not my problem," I called back.

And for tonight at least, it wasn't.

Chapter Fourteen
~ Belle ~

Ipulled up to Dela Roma's only thirty minutes late, which was good, all things considered. And at least I didn't appear too eager. I checked my cell, seeing that no one had called it, which I took to be another positive sign. Surely if Beast had sent out an order to kill me someone would have been in touch to warn me first.

I took a deep breath, feeling restless and frustrated, but I was determined to enjoy the night. Lorenzo was perfect, in theory, and I already knew that we got along, so there was no reason that everything shouldn't go well. Getting out of my car, I looked in through the window, seeing that the restaurant was busy as usual. I wondered if we'd actually have time to talk or if he'd get pulled away constantly with work matters. It didn't really matter; that was part of being a successful business owner.

Pushing open the door, the maître d', Aldo, greeted me with a warm embrace and one of his handsome smiles.

"Belle, so beautiful tonight. Lorenzo is a lucky man." He released me, placing his hand on my lower back as he guided me through the busy restaurant. "And you smell wonderful, what is that you are wearing? I'll need to buy some for my wife."

"You're too sweet," I said with a shy smile, knowing full well that he didn't have a wife.

When we started heading through the busy kitchens, I looked back at him in confusion. He stopped for a moment to say something in Italian to one of the chefs. They talked rapidly with lots of arm-waving and shouting and then Aldo turned back to me with a smile again.

"Come, come, he's waiting upstairs for you."

"Is everything okay here? If he's needed in the restaurant I can just tell him we need to rearrange." I really didn't want to rearrange, but

I was sympathetic to the fact the he was one of the head chefs and might be needed.

Aldo laughed. "Absolutely not, he would how you say, have my guts for garters." I stared at him in puzzlement and he laughed. "I have been studying history at night school. It is an English saying from"—he looked thoughtful for a moment—"Tudor times. It means he would not be very happy if you were to leave, Belle. Come, come."

I laughed and nodded, and when we reached the bottom of a staircase he opened the door and directed me up it as he said goodbye.

At the top of the stairs I tapped on another door and Lorenzo swore in Italian behind it before the sound of his footsteps came quickly toward me and he opened the door. He was dressed in a white shirt with the sleeves rolled up and a pair of light blue jeans. He looked handsome and he smiled widely as he took in my outfit. He wiped his hands on a dishtowel and threw it over his shoulder before dragging a hand through his hair and smiling at me.

"Belle," he said, looking me up and down appreciatively, "you look ravishing. Please, please, come in, dinner is almost done."

His living room was bigger than my entire trailer, and I looked around at the beautiful artwork on the walls and the contemporary furniture that filled his home, feeling out of my depth and a little overwhelmed by it all.

"It's not much, but it's home," he said, oblivious to the fact that I was in a state of awe. "Shit, the food." He darted off, telling me to make myself at home, and then I was alone.

I tentatively went further into the room, feeling out of place and awkward, but that was more to do with me than it was with Lorenzo or his home. The place was beautiful, tastefully decorated. It wasn't flamboyant or trashy, it was warm and welcoming, but all I could think about was what he would think when he saw where I lived. My trailer was falling apart—literally. There were holes in places, windows glued in place, the furniture wasn't second hand—it was third, maybe even fourth.

Soft music was playing in the background from some hidden speakers in the walls. I walked around the room gazing appreciatively at the art and photos everywhere. Family was clearly very important to him, and I liked that. I didn't have much in the way of family, but what I did have was everything to me.

Lorenzo came back in with two glasses of red wine. "Sorry about that, you came at a crucial point in the process of cooking." He handed me a glass and clinked his against it. "To new possibilities."

"To new possibilities," I mimicked with a smile. I was feeling completely out of my depth and all the confidence I'd felt after shouting at Beast seemed to have vanished completely. His words echoed in my head about what men think about when on a date. But when I looked at Lorenzo I just couldn't see it. He seemed too genuine for that. Surely he wouldn't have gone to all this trouble if he just wanted sex.

"Everything okay?" he asked, sensing my awkwardness.

"Yes! Just nervous, I guess." I took a sip of the wine and tried to pull myself out of the dark space that Beast had sent me. "Oh wow, this is gorgeous."

He smiled, looking more than happy with the comment. "So, I hope you don't mind but I didn't do anything fancy tonight. I made lasagna and some arancini balls and a salad. We serve a lot of the fancy stuff downstairs, but I prefer my mama's secret recipe lasagna over almost anything." He took a sip of his wine and I realized that he was obviously feeling a little nervous too.

My stomach rumbled. "That actually sounds perfect."

"Plus, I remembered that lasagna was your favorite." He grinned. "It helps to know your customers, huh?"

"Clearly," I replied with a smile.

He guided us through the apartment toward what I thought would be a small kitchen, given how big the living room was, but it was actually a huge kitchen. A large AGA cooker sat along one wall and there was a large island in the center of the kitchen, separating the kitchen from another small lounge area with a dining room table, a little sofa, and some bookshelves. A large metal rack hung from the ceiling over the island and stainless-steel pots and pans and some baskets with fruit and vegetables hung. It was every chef's dream to have a kitchen like this. No wonder he didn't need us to eat in the restaurant downstairs.

"I love your place. It's so much bigger than it looks from the outside," I gushed.

He placed his hand on my lower back and guided me to the island before pulling out a stool for me to sit on. Lorenzo smiled and looked around.

"Well, it used to be three separate apartments, but my dad bought each one of them over the years as the restaurant and his family grew. When he retired he found that he couldn't stay out of the restaurant, and so my mom made him buy a house for them far away from the restaurant and I took it as my opportunity to completely revamp the place." He ran a hand through his hair almost nervously.

"You have brothers, right?"

"Yeah, two. Mateo and Carlos. Neither of them were interested in the restaurant business though." Lorenzo fell silent, his thoughts elsewhere for a moment, and I realized that I must have hit on a touchy subject.

I put my hand on his arm. "Hey, I'm sorry if I said something wrong."

Lorenzo looked back at me and smiled, the expression vanishing. "You did nothing wrong. I just don't talk about my brothers much— none of us do." He fell silent a moment, his expression darkening. "Let's just say they chose a different path than I did."

*

The food was amazing, the wine was gorgeous, and Lorenzo's company was perfect. The evening was going just how I'd hoped, after a nervous start from us both.

"Let's go sit," he said, gesturing to the small sofa opposite the kitchen after we'd finished eating. "I'll clean up everything tomorrow."

"I don't mind helping to clean up," I offered, but he shook his head.

"Absolutely not, but I appreciate the offer."

I was feeling good. The soft music was still playing in the background, the lights were low, and I was on my third glass of wine and feeling a little fuzzy. Beast was not in my thoughts as Lorenzo and I sat next to each other on the small sofa and continued talking for a while. We talked about Jenna and his parents, about the hospital and the restaurant. There never seemed to be a lag in our conversation, and it almost seemed too good to be true. The evening had gone so well— much better than I had expected—and we'd learned that we had a lot more in common than we first realized. And I found that my little spat with Beast didn't even cross my mind.

Lorenzo took my glass from me and placed it on the coffee table in front of us before turning back to me. My heart was galloping in my chest, my blood humming through my veins as he reached out to cup my cheek in his hand.

"If you don't mind, Belle, I've been wanting to do something all night," he said, his voice soft and silky. "I'm not sure how much longer I can restrain myself." His eyes dipped to my mouth and then back up to my eyes.

I nodded, not trusting myself to speak right then, and Lorenzo leaned in and kissed me.

The kiss started off slowly, almost gentle, but slowly built until it was passionate and full of desire. My toes curled as his tongue danced with mine, and he deepened the kiss as I returned it. Lorenzo had been a gentleman all night—constantly checking that I was okay, that my glass was filled, that I was comfortable—and he was no different now as he pulled me closer, his arms reaching around me to stroke up and down my back.

"Is this okay?"

I nodded again. "Yes, definitely," I said, reaching for him greedily. My hands went to his shoulders, feeling the taut muscles underneath his expensive shirt, and he moaned into my mouth as I slid my hands down his back. Lorenzo tipped my head back, exposing my throat, and began to pepper it with soft kisses, his breath hot on my skin.

As he moved along to my shoulders, his hands slid, teasingly slow, down my arms. My nipples hardened and I was glad I hadn't worn a bra now because his nostrils flared when he noticed, and it was hot as hell. He slowly pushed down the straps of my camisole, exposing my breasts, and a rumble echoed from his chest.

He muttered something in Italian before reaching over and cupping them, the pad of his thumb rubbing over the sensitive, hardened nipple of one of them so gently that I had to clench my thighs together. He looked at me with those deep blue eyes of his, like he was asking for permission, and I panted a yes.

"You're beautiful," he said, his tongue darting out to lick his bottom lip. He leaned down and flicked his tongue against my nipple, making me groan.

I blushed and looked away, embarrassed.

"No, Belle, don't do that." He reached up and took my face in his hands again, pressing a hard, urgent kiss to my mouth before slowly laying me back on the sofa, his body covering mine.

I reached between us, unbuttoning his shirt to reveal his hard, unblemished chest underneath, my legs spreading to accommodate him between them.

"You sure?" he asked again, his breathing heavy.

I'd known Lorenzo for a long time, but it wasn't until this past week that I'd really seen him as someone other than just the owner of Dela Roma. He was handsome, considerate, sexy as hell, and successful. He was every woman's fantasy, and he was there with me.

The music finished and silence—other than our own rapid breathing and noises from the restaurant downstairs—filled the apartment as we stared into one another's eyes.

"It's okay if not," he continued. "If you want to wait." His fingers played with a curl that lay against my collarbone, and the small movement sent a shiver through my body, making my nipples harden even more and my back arch. He breathed out heavily, his hard length pulsing against my center through his jeans. "You need to decide soon, though, because I'm not sure how much longer I can wait, Belle."

I thought of Beast in the hospital, all on his own. His anger and pain burning up inside of him, ready to explode at any minute. His rage was wild and wicked, like the man it belonged to. I saw his beautiful scarred face, his eye, gray and moody, thoughtful and deep, burying everything that he could be in favor of his hatred for the world. I felt his hand on my ass, squeezing, kneading, and my pulse quickened at the thought of what his brutal touch would be like. I replayed the moment I'd walked in on him and the prostitute, his angry, almost feral expression, and the way he'd gripped her so forcefully, slamming her down onto his hard length and filling her violently. And then I thought about the way he had looked at me tonight, like he was seeing me for the first time, and I realized that he had been jealous that I was going on a date. I wasn't entirely sure if it was that I was *able* to go on a date or because he didn't want anyone else to go on a date with *me*, but jealousy had been vibrant on his face regardless.

Beast was the opposite of Lorenzo, and that was okay by me.

Lorenzo was what I needed, and Beast wasn't even an option, and that was okay too.

Curiosity played with me, and I couldn't deny that no matter how awful Beast was, a part of me was attracted to him. Was it his brutality that I found so intriguing, or was it something else?

"Belle?" Lorenzo said, his fingers tracing down the side of my face, his blue eyes searching mine for an answer.

Lorenzo was here. He was handsome, he was a good option.

Beast wasn't either of those things and he never would be.

I reached up and cupped the back of Lorenzo's head before pulling his mouth to mine. I kissed him hard, wrapping my legs around his waist, and got lost in his touch. His mouth on mine, his fingers against my skin, his body pressed against me, and everything in between.

Chapter Fifteen
~ BEAST ~

Brother, Doctor Collins says you'll be starting physio pretty soon," Shooter said.

He was leaning on the ledge by the window with Gauge, while Dom and Casa were in chairs next to my bed. I was sitting up for the first time in months, instead of lying on my back like a whore waiting to be fucked. Felt good to be upright again, like the old me was slowly returning. Shooter glanced at the boarded-up window and raised an eyebrow.

"Don't worry about it," I grumbled.

"Have we fixed this shit?" he asked, looking around at Gauge and Dom.

"Yeah, cost the club a couple of grand to set it right. The glazier's coming tomorrow to put a new window in," Gauge said with an annoyed sigh.

"I'll cover it. The club doesn't need to pay for my bullshit," I said, hoping that would put the matter to bed, because I really didn't want another fucking lecture about it.

Shooter nodded. "All right. You cover the costs, and we'll keep everyone sweet about this shit. But Beast"—he gestured toward the window, or what was left of it—"this can't happen again."

I gritted my teeth and nodded. "Understood, Prez."

"That's settled then, back to business. Doctor Collins thinks once physio starts you should be moved back to the clubhouse so we can keep you safe. Ain't much he can do to keep it under wraps that you're alive after that. You'll be seen around the hospital and the more people that see you, the more likely it is that the fuckwits that put you here—or even those that want to take a hit on the club—will come for you. It'll be too risky keeping you here." Shooter's expression was neutral but I

102

could tell he wasn't happy about the situation. Not a whole lot he could do about it though. Moving me to the clubhouse was dangerous because I wouldn't be surrounded by doctors every day and it could set my healing back, but keeping me here was too risky on everyone else in the hospital once I was out of this room.

The Highwaymen had been busy figuring out who had attacked Echo and me, and they'd finally pinned it down to a shitty little drug-dealing outfit that we'd sent to ground a couple of weeks before the attack. They'd been catering to our clients and trying to cut us out of deals, but worse, their shit was basically that—shit. Cut up so bad it was more flour and aspirin than anything else. And bad shit going around our city was a no go. I thought I'd taken them all out, but apparently not. Little punks were nothing but a bunch of lowlife crackheads that had gotten fuckin' lucky. My blood boiled with that news.

Echo was dead because of those pieces of shit. And they probably didn't even remember what they'd done. At least if it would have been another club taking a strike or the cartel it would have been a death to be proud of. But he'd been killed because I hadn't done my job right. He was rotting in the ground because I hadn't listened to my gut and had missed a couple of crackheads sneaking up on us.

The realization was eating me up and stirring up the crazy in my head.

"Fuckers were probably too high to remember what they did anyway. Which is good," I snarled, "because they'll have no idea what's coming for them."

Death.

That's what was coming for them.

A death so bloody and painful their bodies wouldn't ever be identifiable. I'd pull every tooth and nail from their body, eyes, tongue, every fucking scrap of hair from their bodies while they were wide awake before slowly peeling their skin away from their bodies to reveal the fresh meat underneath. And then I'd let them heal long enough for me to start all over again.

I was practically salivating at the thought of it.

Gauge exchanged a look with Casa and I frowned, my brows pulling in.

"Spit it the fuck out," I snapped.

"Casa doesn't think it was them," Gauge said, pulling a cigar from his pocket and sniffing it like it was a line of snow or some shit. "He's got some theory like he's…who the fuck is that detective?" He turned to look at Dom with a scowl.

"Sherlock Holmes?" Dom shrugged.

Gauge snapped his fingers. "Yeah, Casa here thinks he's Sherlock Holmes or some shit." He laughed darkly.

Casa stood up, bouncing on his heels like he always did. Brother never sat still for longer than five minutes at a time. Surprised it didn't drive his old lady mad the way he was constantly twitching and moving.

"It ain't a theory, motherfucker." Casa grinned from ear to ear, giving Gauge the middle finger before looking back at me. "And I should have been one of the motherfuckin' Hardy Boys, brother."

"Can we cut the chitchat and tell me what you have or don't have?" I bit out.

"Sorry, you got places to be?" Gauge said dryly, and I threw him a look that wiped the smug look off his face as quickly as it had come.

"Their car was broken down half a mile from the farmhouse," Casa said as he paced the room cracking his knuckles. "There were cell phones, guns, and a fuck-ton of your blood and skin covering their knives still in it, but they were gone. What kind of idiots leave that sort of shit behind?"

"High ones, dickhead," Dom said with a shrug, and Casa punched him in the arm.

"Fuck no. So they're clear-headed enough that they can catch and carve up a man like Beast, but too high to remember to take all the evidence that links it to them?" Casa shook his head. "Nah, brothers, that don't make no sense."

The room fell silent until the door opened and Belle came in. Her hair was up off her face instead of clipped back with a little silver clip like usual. I liked this look though; it was up in a high ponytail and showed off her slender neck.

"Oh, I'm sorry, I didn't know you had visitors," she mumbled.

"It's fine, we're done here anyway," Shooter said, pushing away from the window ledge.

"No, we're not. Belle, get the fuck out," I growled, making her flinch. Some days she was all feisty and hard as nails, and other days she was all jumpy and shit like this. Couldn't work her out at all, but I was asshole enough to admit that I liked it when she flinched. Though after our little encounter last night she was obviously being extra cautious.

She looked between me and Shooter anxiously, not sure who to listen to. She didn't understand the rules of club life. All she knew was that Shooter paid her wages and I made her suffer. Both of us could hurt her in different ways if we wanted to, and she knew it.

But she was dumber than the prospect if she thought she could get away with everything she'd said to me the night before and then just come back in the morning with her just-fucked hair like nothing had happened.

"I said get the fuck out!" I yelled at her again, but this time she glared back at me like I'd kicked her kitten or something. "Now, bitch."

"Jesus Christ," Gauge mumbled. "I need to get back to the clubhouse anyway. I'll be by tomorrow, brother."

"I'll come with you," Dom said standing up. "I need to speak to you about Jolie."

"Ain't that your little sister?" Casa laughed. "Better watch this old man near her fine ass or she'll be in his bed and on her back before you know it."

Dom shot Casa an angry glare and Casa laughed even more. "Watch your mouth."

"That bitch is crazy. Ain't no one—and especially not me—going near her," Gauge said as he stalked out of the room with Dom following. "Besides, she's jailbait and I don't need that kind of shit in my life."

"That's what I like to hear," Dom said as the door closed behind him.

"Give us a minute," Shooter said to Belle, and she nodded and left the room.

"She's a fuckin' snack, brother," Casa said with a smirk after she'd left. "I'd take a bite of that if it wasn't for the fine piece I have at home."

"She's not my type," I replied. I looked at Shooter, my eyebrows pulled into a scowl, though it was hindered by the bandage I still wore covering my left eye.

"Since when do you have a type?" Casa grinned. "She's got holes, right?"

"Brother," Shooter said with a heavy sigh, "can you shut the fuck up so I can speak?"

"Sorry, Prez."

Shooter looked back to me. "Look, brother, I hate to say it but I agree with what Casa said. At least, what he's saying has some merit to it."

"Fuck yeah, it does," Casa interrupted again.

Shooter sighed once more. "But we've got no leads. Nothing was left behind to point the finger at anyone else but these fucks. No clues. Nothing. Cops have scoured that place and handed everything they found over to us. Other than the car filled with evidence pointing to these crackheads, there's nothing. If it wasn't them, then whoever it was is in the wind, brother."

My teeth ground together, my jaw ticking as my anger grew like a balloon in my chest. They had nothing. Echo was dead, I was as good as, and they'd gotten nothing but a couple of crackheads.

"Get the fuck out," I snarled at him, looking toward the window. I was crossing a line speaking to him like that, but I didn't give a fuck right then.

"Brother," Shooter started, but I turned my glare on him, shutting him down.

"Get the fuck out, Prez, and don't come back until you've got someone's head I can take. If it's the two crackheads then it's them. If it's not, I'll find them when I'm back on my feet." I was trying to stay calm, but the storm raging inside me was becoming dangerously hard to control. "Tell Doctor Collins we start physio tomorrow. I need to get my life back so I can kill the fuckers that did this to me. Echo needs his revenge."

Shooter nodded, though I had no doubt he had a hundred things he wanted to say to me right then.

"You want me to bring a sweetbutt in to chill you out, brother? I heard Lola had a real good time the other night," Casa asked. Guns and pussy, that was all he ever thought about. "Got a girl at the clubhouse who has a mouth like a fucking vacuum. Not that I've sampled it for a good while now, but a man don't forget a thing like that, ya know."

"Your old lady would cut your dick off if she caught you anywhere near another woman." Shooter smiled, happy for the change in conversation. "You're under her thumb, brother."

"Because Laney is such an understanding old lady, huh?" Casa mocked. "She let you ride a fucking wave of free pussy whenever you want, huh? Nah, I didn't think so. If I'm under my old lady's thumb, then you're under an entire fucking hand, Prez." Casa laughed loudly and Shooter shook his head with a grin.

"Watch your mouth," Shooter said with a smirk, and punched Casa in the arm.

It was all too much for me. Too much talk of pussy. Too much laughing. Too much normality when my life was hardly a life at all.

"Get the fuck out, both of you!" I said, not wanting to hear about their old ladies or their sex lives. Not while I was stuck in here with no chance of any woman sharing my bed ever again. Not with a face and body torn apart like mine.

Shooter gripped my shoulder and nodded, and he and Casa left. The room was quiet, barring the hospital noises out in the corridor. I hated the silence. I needed the noise and the mania of life to keep me going, because that was all I had. This life was all I'd ever had. And now all I had was silence, broken up by the beeping of machines.

I hated it.

I hated it so much.

It was worse than the pain and the memories.

Worse than knowing I'd gotten Echo killed or that those fuckers had turned me into a monster. Carving me up and melting away the man that I was until all that was left behind was hate, revenge, and the monster underneath.

I had to get out of here.

I had to kill *them* before the hate killed *me*.

The door creaked open and Belle came back in. She headed to the machine next to my bed and checked all the numbers and lines on it, making sense of the insanity that was on them. I had no idea what any of it meant, but she seemed to, and that was good enough for me.

I hadn't realized that I was staring at her, my teeth grinding as she studied the numbers on the graph, until she looked away from it and turned to me. Her eyebrows puckered in and she sucked in her bottom lip thoughtfully before releasing it. She looked pretty today; the freshly fucked look was good on her.

"I'm guessing that wasn't good news then," she said, cocking her head to one side and ignoring what had happened between us the night before.

It was one of the things I liked so much about her; she didn't dwell. I hated dwellers, replaying arguments and shit over and over in their heads. Thinking we needed a confrontation to clear the air. Nah, fuck that. We just needed to move on. What's done is done and all that bullshit.

Well, unless I needed to kill a motherfucker, that is.

"You could say that," I replied with a heaviness to my tone that I couldn't control. Not angry for once, but frustrated and tired of it all. No one seemed to get it. How could they? They didn't live with this pain—and not just the physical pain I was constantly in, because that in some ways was good; it kept my anger fueled. But the mental pain of knowing Echo was dead because of me was what was gutting me so deeply.

"Things will get better," she insisted, her tone soothing and sympathetic. "I get that everything is awful for you right now, but I promise you, Beast, it won't always be like this."

"Won't it?" I snapped.

She was unfazed by my abruptness, letting it wash over her. "No, it won't. You'll start to get better and—"

"I'm a monster, Belle, just fucking look at me!" I gestured to my body. "This won't get better!"

"You're not," she replied, and I wasn't sure if she was the one that was blind because she even sounded like she believed it.

"What's wrong with you? Just admit it—look at me!"

She put her hands on her hips and pouted. "I am looking at you. And I don't see what you see."

I huffed out my annoyance. What was wrong with this woman?

"You want to know what I see, Beast?" she asked.

"No," I grunted.

"I see long hair that needs a good washing." She smiled, reaching out to touch the long hair around my shoulders. "I think it would look better tied up though." I thought of the scars at the bottom of my neck with a shiver. "Show off that rugged neck of yours."

I swallowed, the feel of her gentle touch on my damaged skin sending shivers down my spine.

"I see a strong, masculine man with more muscles in his left arm than I have in my whole body." She ran her fingers over my burned arm and I watched her intently. "I see beautiful, intricate tattoos over his chest," she said, running a fingertip over one of the most destroyed tattoos. "It's like tribal or something." She shrugged and then looked into my face.

My heart hammered in my chest, my pulse racing through my veins at her every word.

"I see a handsome man with a beautiful, soulful eye and a lot of pain that he's hiding inside." Her fingers ran down the side of my face.

109

"I see you, Beast. There's no point in hiding behind your anger with me. You can shout and say awful things to hide the way you're feeling"— she sighed—"but I'm going to look after you despite all of that. Maybe even because of it. And you're going to get better and you're going to realize that everything is going to be okay."

The hollow feeling in my chest turned hard, like a bullet had pierced me, as she looked into my face. There was no sympathy, no pity; there was nothing there but genuine concern in her hazel eyes.

The bandage covering my left eye was still in place, but it suddenly felt stifling to me, pressing against my skin like it was becoming a part of my body. I didn't need to wear it anymore; I chose to because I wasn't ready to let the world see exactly how fucked up I really was. I'd seen it once and once had been enough. But now…fuck, right now I wanted that bandage off. I wanted Belle to see me for who I was so that she could get out of her head any daydreams of being nice to me.

I was a monster and I wanted her to see the beast within.

"Take this off," I snapped, gesturing to the bandage around my eye. I was glad we were alone because a man didn't need to be seen as vulnerable to anyone. Vulnerable equaled weak, and weak equaled dead. Though none of that seemed to matter when I was with her. She saw through all of my bullshit no matter what I said or did. No matter how I tried to hide it.

"You want it off?" she asked stupidly.

"Are you fucking stupid? Get it the fuck off me," I growled out.

"I don't think you're supposed to, are you?" she asked, shutting her mouth as soon as I gave her a death stare. She grabbed the clipboard from the bottom of my bed, quickly reading it while I continued to stare at her.

"Get it off, me Belle," I said slowly, "or I'll do it myself."

She finished reading and looked over at me, giving me a small nod. Placing the clipboard back down, she came to my side. "Okay, let me go get Doctor Collins—"

"No, I want you to do it," I interrupted.

"Beast, you need a doctor to do this."

"No," I insisted, holding my gaze steady on hers. "I need you, Belle. Just you."

It was weak and pathetic, yet it didn't matter, because the only person that I trusted to see me vulnerable and fucked up like this was her. Because, despite not wanting her to, I really believed that she saw me. She still looked uncertain, my words not having much of an effect on her.

"Belle," I asked, no bullshit to my tone for once. "Just take it off."

Chapter Sixteen
~ BEAST~

She swallowed nervously, thinking it over, and then nodded again. "Okay, sit further up so I can get to the back."

I sat up and she came around to my left, leaning in so close that I could smell her. Not her perfume or detergent, but her. Her scent was sweet, like peaches, and it made me forget for a moment what was happening.

"I'm probably going to lose my job for this," she mumbled, but she kept on working away at the bandages like she didn't give a fuck and I knew I'd made the right decision.

I didn't trust a lot of people in my life. Not completely. A handful, at most; I could count them on one hand. And Belle, for some weird, kismet reason, had been put in my life and grouped with that handful of people, despite our blatant differences.

"You won't lose your job," I said. "I'll make sure of it."

"Keep your eyes closed," she said, her voice close to my ear as she leaned in, her fingers pulling gently on the bandages. They began to loosen and I did as she said, closing my eyes against the world and willing myself to be able to see. If I was a praying man I would have prayed, but God had left me a long time ago so instead I just hoped.

I felt the bandages begin to fall away as Belle unwrapped them and set them down. I'd never been scared in my whole life. Not as a hard-starved little kid waiting for his mom to come home. Not as a teenager in care anxious at the sound of my foster dad coming up the stairs. And not as a man waiting for death. But at that moment I felt something akin to fear as I waited to see what if I'd be able to see out of both eyes again. I needed my eyes—no, not just needed, I wanted them! And I willed them to work. To not let me down like everything else had.

Belle's hands moved over my face as she used a warm cloth to wipe my skin, and when she was satisfied, she placed her hand on top of mine and gave it a little squeeze.

"Okay, open them slowly, Beast. Try not to panic," she said softly.

I snorted out a dry laugh. "Too late," I said a little too honestly for my liking, and she squeezed my hand a little harder. What was it with this woman? She brought out a side to me that I didn't recognize and couldn't control.

"It can take a while for sight to come back after something like this. Weeks, months, even years," she rambled on, "so what happens right now might not be forever, okay? It could come back when you least expect it and surprise you, so just don't freak out or anything. And Doctor Collins said—"

"Belle," I said as calmly as I could to get her to shut the fuck up. She sounded more nervous than me, and that was saying something.

"Sorry, it's okay, Beast, we've got this."

I paused on her words, tasting them, swallowing them, devouring them whole.

We've got this.

That's what she'd just said.

We've got this. Not just me.

I'd never been a *we* before—never wanted to be either—but if it meant not facing the prospect of losing my eyesight alone, then I'd take it.

I slowly started to open my eyes, the world coming into view in my right eye, but not in my left. Panic rose like bile in my throat. I blinked and blinked, but still nothing. There was just blackness.

"I can't see anything," I said, my voice thick with worry. "Belle, I can't fucking see anything out of it."

"It's okay, just give it a minute."

She held a small light into my right eye and I blinked against it, feeling water leaking down my cheek. She wiped it away gently with a tissue before moving the light to the left. She held it there for a second

113

before lowering it. At first there was nothing but blackness, but slowly light started to filter in and a fuzzy version of the world began to show itself.

"I think I see something," I said, swallowing down the lump in my throat.

I blinked and felt tears streaming down both cheeks. Fuck, was I crying? God that was embarrassing. Belle wiped them away with a tissue, her face close to mine. She slowly came into focus, still blurry as shit, but it was livable.

"It's just eye gunk. I just put some drops to help clear it," she said as if she'd read my mind.

I grunted an okay. "I'm starting to see you," I said, and her face split into a smile that was brighter than the light she kept on shining in my eyes. The fuzziness cleared some more and now I really wasn't sure whether it was tears or eye gunk leaking down my face.

She sat on the edge of the bed and used some sterile solution or something to wipe both eyes clean, the whole time wearing a beautiful smile. Her gaze roamed over my face and she got some more cream to rub over my skin where it had gone dry under the bandages. Gently, she massaged it in, her forehead creased in concentration until she was satisfied, and then she sat back happily.

"How is it now?" she asked.

I blinked against the pain in my left eye. "A little sore."

The world focused in and out, a headache blooming at the backs of both eyes. Was it going to go now? Was that all I got? Just a glimpse at my old life before it left me?

"A little pain is to be expected; your eye hasn't been used in a really long time. You can expect a lot of headaches for a while."

There she went again, reading my damn mind.

Sensing my internal panic, she cupped my face in her hands. "You've got this. It's going to be okay, Beast."

I couldn't respond.

The words wouldn't come.

It was just too fucking much.

The men that had put me in here had taken everything from me. My life, my body, my best friend, even my dick! But to know that they hadn't taken this one thing from me meant the fucking world. My heart thundered in my chest at the realization that I wasn't as broken as I'd previously thought.

I stared at her, water streaming from my painful eyes, and I reached up and grabbed her, pressing my lips against hers and kissing her hard. It shouldn't have surprised me, but it did. I hadn't expected to kiss her. It hadn't been something that I'd planned, but as soon as our lips touched and the volts of electricity shot through us, I knew I didn't regret it and I wanted more. She tensed against me, but when one of my hands went around the back of her head, threading through her hair, she softened in my arms, her mouth opening to me as she kissed me back. I felt hungry for her, ravenous for her touch. This wasn't a pity kiss; she wanted this—wanted me.

My dick twitched and I groaned, because fuck me, she was bringing all of me back to life and I didn't know what to do about it. I'd thought I was dead from the waist down, but every time she was near it sprang to life.

"Beast," she moaned, one hand on my chest in an attempt to push me away, but instead I pulled her closer, closing the gap until we were chest to chest, our bodies heaving in unison. Because fuck that noise. I wasn't letting her go now.

I kissed Belle like I'd never kissed any other woman before. I kissed her like she was my lifeline. Like she was my savior. Like she could un-taint my dirty soul and purify me like she was a saint and I was a sinner. My dick twitched again, and it urged me on, pushing me to take more from her.

She was a saint and I was a sinner, and that was what made this all the more perfect.

My hands moved down her back to her ass, where I scooped her up and practically threw her on top of me. I ignored the pain that rained through my body as her body hit mine in favor of my dick that surged and swelled harder at her closeness, and I groaned against her mouth again, the electricity between us growing. Fuck, I wanted her. Every which way and more. I pushed the hem of her skirt up to her waist, her thighs wrapping around me as she held my face in her hands and kissed me back, the static between our lips electrifying.

Kissing Belle was like taking the biggest hit of snow I'd ever had. It was better than the first time I rode a bike, and more memorable than any fight I'd ever been in. Kissing Belle was like a magic wand that took everything else away and left me with only her.

My dick was hard against her and it wasn't going away. Almost came at the realization that they hadn't taken that either. I was a fucking man still, with both eyes and a dick fit for fucking this goddamned beautiful woman.

"Want you now," I grunted between kisses.

I gripped the sides of her panties and pulled forcefully, snapping one side of them before doing the same to the other side.

"Please," she whimpered. I wasn't sure if she was asking me to stop or asking me to continue, but until I knew which I wasn't fucking stopping.

"Wanna fuck you, Belle." I started to pull the torn panties from under her and she groaned as they slid along her pussy.

"I can't," she gasped, trying to put distance between our mouths again.

I held her tight, sucking on her tongue as my thumb went to her pussy, rubbing along the seam of it. She gasped into my mouth, panting as my thick fingers slid between her lips and I put my hand on her ass and pushed her up with my other hand so I could go deeper.

"Gonna fuck you, just like this. And you're gonna come for me," I growled against her lips.

Fuck me, she was wet and wanting, her chest heaving as I strummed her, sliding my thick finger in and out of her. Every shallow breath she took made me harder. Every soft whimper she made had me wanting her more. She was saying no, but her body and her kisses were saying yes.

"Stop, Beast," she pleaded, but her mouth was still on mine, her breath hot as our mouths moved together. She groaned, her hips rolling unbidden.

"Can't," I grunted, pushing the covers down my body to reveal my hard length. "Need you, Belle. Need inside of you right the fuck now."

I lifted her up, our mouths separating. She looked down at me, her cheeks flushed, her hair around her shoulders, and her mouth swollen from our kisses, and I almost came right there and then. All the drugs in the world couldn't make me feel like she did.

I gripped my cock in my hand, fisting it and groaning as pleasure surged through me. Felt like Frankenstein's monster—I was fucking alive! I raised her up with one hand, positioning myself at her entrance, readying to lose myself inside of her like I'd been thinking about since the day she walked into my room.

"I can't, Beast. I can't do this! I'm your nurse!" she gasped as I teased her entrance with my cock. "Beast, I'm with someone else," she said, her words coming out in a panicked rush. But she wanted it—wanted me. Her little fuckboy boyfriend needed to move over because there was a real man waiting for her now. The desire was there in her eyes, blatant as could be. I'd send her little fuckboy boyfriend to ground before I gave this up.

I shut her up by pulling her down on top of me, filling her up with my hard length until all she could do was stare at me open-mouthed and wide-eyed, gasping as I stretched her wide. I pressed the pad of my thumb against the little nub at her entrance, making her whimper loudly and throw her head back in pleasure, and then I gripped her waist and rocked her back and forth on top of me, her body squeezing around me. Unlike with the sweetbutt, I felt something—fuck, I felt everything. I was hard and pleasure was rolling through me. Belle was the best medicine I had had in months.

She put a hand over her mouth to stop herself from crying out, but the muffled calls reached my ears and urged me on. Every rock of her hips sent electricity coursing through me. Every thrust of my dick sent pleasure rolling through every damaged muscle and tendon I had, bringing my body back to life. She leaned over, pressing a kiss to my lips as I thrust my hips upwards, sliding my full length into her and finally sending her over the edge.

Belle cried out into my mouth, our tongues fucking as our bodies did the same, and I finally came so hard that my balls drew up and I thought they'd never drop back down. I grunted as she squeezed, tightening her pussy and milking every drop from me before finally releasing me with a gasp.

I'd fucked many women before.

But never in my life had I fucked like this.

Our bodies lay together—hers smooth, unblemished, and beautiful, mine disfigured and destroyed. Yet she didn't seem to care even a little. She touched me without flinching. She held me without shying away. She kissed me and wanted me like the scars weren't even there.

We were beauty and the beast as we lay on my bed together, our bodies entwined. In the back of my mind, I knew it was too good to be true. Where were the angry villagers coming to burn down my castle? They were coming, because a beast like me didn't get a happily ever after, and this fairy tale was far from over yet.

Chapter Seventeen
~ Belle ~

I need to get out of here, Belle," he said, swallowing down the lump in his throat and revealing another crack in his armor. "I need air and freedom, and the wide-open road. I need out of this room."

I lifted my head from the pillow and looked up at him, his stormy gray eyes holding my gaze as he fed me his frustrations, hoping and willing me to understand. I chewed on my bottom lip and slid out of bed, pulling my skirt back down as I thought about how I could help him, and then it came to me. I still hadn't said anything, but I looked over at the numbers on the machine next to the bed, making sure that all that excitement hadn't harmed him in any way.

My hands lifted his arms, my gaze searching his skin to make sure he was okay and that I hadn't done any damage, but after a quick search I found he was fine. His scars looked angry and red, but they were healing—he was healing—and if the way he'd looked at me only moments before was anything to go by, then he was healing from the inside too.

He closed his eyes, his chest heaving as he tried to control his frustration instead of letting it all out and yelling at me.

"I have an idea," I said, cutting though the silence. He opened his eyes and I glanced down at his nakedness, watching his body stir back to life. "But let's get you cleaned up first."

*

Beast nodded a thank you as the prospect left us alone on the roof of the hospital. At least I thought it was a thank you. It could have been anything, knowing Beast, since he never seemed to apologize or thank anyone for anything.

Joey closed the door behind him and I pushed Beast's wheelchair toward the edge of the roof so he could get a better look at the world.

119

The day was cooler than it had been in weeks. After a stifling summer, I was glad of the reprieve. We both stared off into the distance, people-watching and just enjoying the escape from the hospital. The world continued to move at a steady pace: cars honking, people walking, dogs barking, birds chirping. It was always the same, yet for some reason it seemed different being up there with him.

Maybe it was the way he looked at the world like he was simultaneously annoyed at it and in admiration of it. Like the sight of so many people living their lives unaware of everything he was going through pissed him off. And yet he was in awe of their ignorance in the same breath.

This was my special place, where I came to think when things got too much. I'd discovered it after a particularly awful encounter with Beast a few weeks earlier. Ironic to think I was here with him now.

This was the first time Beast had been outside since the night he was almost killed, and I watched him clutching at the wheelchair, his red, scarred knuckles turning white as he held tightly to it like a lifeline. I was beginning to wonder if this had been a really bad idea when he finally started to loosen his grip and come out the other side of whatever he had just gone through.

When I placed my hand on his shoulder to let him know I was there, he tensed and looked up at me sharply, but I kept my gaze out on the world below and eventually he relaxed against my touch. He needed to know, to understand, that his scars didn't define him. His scars didn't matter to me. Maybe it was because I was a nurse and had seen some of the awful things that people did to one another. Or maybe it was because I'd never seen the man he was before. Either way, I didn't care, and he needed to know that others would be the same too.

He was wearing one of the hospital nightgowns and I'd thrown a blanket over his legs to keep him warm. I'd managed to fight his hair back into a bun at the top of his head, too, and he was surprised when he didn't entirely hate the look. It was better than the greasy, lank hair that had framed his face.

He sighed heavily and I looked up at the machines, checking the numbers were still okay. He shouldn't have been out there, but I figured that a little fresh air was good for the soul. And right then, Beast really needed his soul to be cleaner—if that were possible for a man like him.

"Stop that," he grumbled, his voice gruff and throaty. "Making me feel like a damn invalid, Belle." But for once his aggression wasn't as vivid. Instead it was more of a plea. He looked up at me and he told me so much with that look.

I thought back to the night before, to our little playful back-and-forth before things had turned ugly. The memory of his hand on my ass made my body shiver as it merged with the memory of Lorenzo's tongue on my nipple. God, what was I doing? I was still in shock over having sex with one of my patients—Beast, of all men. If anyone found out, I would be fired and there would be no way Beast or the club could protect me. It was all sorts of wrong, but I hadn't been able to stop myself, and if I was being honest, I'd thought about it since I'd first met him but I'd never thought it would actually happen. And what did I do now? He was still a patient, and I was still with Lorenzo. Oh my god, that had only been last night! In the space of 24 hours I'd had sex with two different men…What was happening to me? Who was I?

The lines between right and wrong and Belle and the stranger that had apparently taken over my body were becoming very blurred, and I was struggling to understand anything. What other lines would I be tempted to cross, I wondered. Because lines didn't seem to matter to a man like Beast, and I couldn't deny that I liked that about him. Yet Lorenzo was a good man. Handsome, successful, and considerate. He was the polar opposite of Beast, and I liked being with him just as much as I liked being with Beast.

With Lorenzo, I didn't walk on eggshells. I didn't worry that I was going to get yelled at constantly. I wasn't on edge, worrying in case I did something wrong. He treated me like a princess—like I was important to him. Beast yelled at me, he made me feel like everything I did was wrong. I was constantly walking a tightrope with him.

Beast reached out and took my hand in his. It swallowed mine and I felt that same electricity surge through me that I'd felt since the day I'd met him. Being with Beast was reckless, and I worried I would be sucked into his world and would never escape, yet a part of me liked that.

"You think too much," he grumbled, and I looked down at him, forcing a smile to my face.

I cleared my throat and pushed the thoughts away. "Sorry, I forgot, you prefer your women not to think, right? To just do as they're told."

He nodded, but the corner of his mouth tipped up and told me he wasn't serious. "You get this faraway look in your eyes when you're overthinking things, and your shoulders sag like you're trying to hold up the world on them."

I sighed. "Sometimes it feels that way," I admitted.

"You ever wonder what would have happened if your mom hadn't left you?" he asked.

I frowned. "Wow, this conversation took a huge U-turn."

He looked back out at the world. "My mom used to go off for days at a time. I learned that you had to look after yourself because no one else was going to do it for you."

"And you think that's why you are the way you are?" I asked.

Beast looked back up at me. "And how am I, Belle?"

I could sense he was bristling below the surface, but I didn't care. He had asked that for a reason, and maybe that reason was because he wanted my honesty because no one else dared give it to him.

"You don't trust anyone," I began. "You don't even like most people."

"Most people are assholes," he replied.

I shook my head and laughed. "You'd be surprised...Most people are actually pretty good if you let them in."

"Do you think I'm good, Belle?"

I stared at him long and hard, thinking how to answer that question. Was he going to yell at me if I said no? Would he laugh at me

122

if I said yes? Was he asking because he wasn't sure of himself anymore, or because he was just genuinely interested in what I thought? With Beast I could never tell what he was thinking.

"I don't think anyone is intrinsically bad."

"That's a cop-out and you know it," he said with a raised brow.

I shrugged. "Okay, well, I think you're both things, actually. Both good and bad. Deep down you have a real good heart and care about people way more than you let on, but on the surface you're bad and you do bad things." I took a deep breath and waited for him to push me away and be horrible, but he just sighed and looked away.

"Fuck, it feels good to have the air on my face again." He closed his eyes but then quickly opened them, like he was afraid that if he kept them closed for too long he might never be able to see again.

I looked over at the machines, checking the numbers to make sure he was okay.

"Told you to stop doing that," he growled. "You need to stop treating me like a sick patient."

I could already sense the old Beast brimming under the surface, waiting to come out and lash out at the world again, but I wasn't ready for that man right now.

"Well, Beast," I sighed dramatically, "like it or not, you *are* a sick patient," I teased.

"Fuck you," he growled with a hard scowl.

I wagged my finger at him playfully. "Tut tut, that's no way to speak to your nurse, now, is it? Now be a good boy and sit still so I can check that you're not about to pass out or anything."

He almost choked on a laugh, his scowl falling away as easily as it had come. "A good boy? You're pushing your luck, Belle," he warned, his expression curious.

My stomach fluttered and I fought to keep the smile from my face.

Over the past few weeks, I had met many versions of Beast. From the angry and enraged, to the pained. To the ignorant and downright sexist to the horny. But this Beast was different from all of those, and he might just be my favorite of them all. Beast and I were two very different people from very different backgrounds, as far as I could tell. We had nothing in common so small talk had been awkward between us. But I had a feeling that underneath the hard-man image he liked to portray, that maybe there was someone softer there. Maybe in a different life I would have gotten to meet that version of him properly.

I continued to check the machines, ignoring his warning, and I watched him from the corner of my eye shake his head and look back out at the view in front of the hospital. We both lapsed back into comfortable silence—him, sitting in a hospital wheelchair, dressed in a hospital gown and bandages, and me, standing next to him in my ugly nurse's uniform. We looked out in silence, both of us comfortable in each other's presence for once, where usually we both walked on eggshells with one another.

I wanted to say something to make him feel better. To let him know that it would all be okay. That he'd get better and things would be different. But that wasn't true and I knew he wouldn't appreciate the lie. He would get better, but he would never be the man he used to be.

So much of him was scarred—from blades or by fire, it didn't matter. Whoever had done this had destroyed his body, carving into it like he was a log of wood. Some cuts had been so deep and had gotten so infected that chunks had been taken out, leaving dips in his muscle. His left arm bore the scars of fire, from shoulder to fingertips. And what wasn't burned on his body or carved from a knife had been broken. I'd overheard Doctor Collins say he didn't understand how Beast was still alive, and honestly, when I looked through his file, I couldn't understand it either.

There was no other way to put it: Beast should be dead.

I watched his expression as he looked out at the world, and I saw on his face that he knew he should be dead too. In fact, the more I looked, the more I saw that the only reason he was still alive was because he wanted to get revenge for what had been done. And what then, I wondered. Would he give up? Would he finally lay down and die? Would he finally have the peace that he sought? I wanted him to have peace—Lord knows that after what he'd been through, he deserved it—but I didn't want him dead.

"Grew up around here," he said, his gravelly voice breaking into my thoughts. I looked down at him but he was still staring off into the distance. "As a kid, all I could think about was getting away. Now I think I'll never escape this place."

He sounded so sad, and his pain cut into me deeper than any of those knives ever could. I reached out and placed a hand on his shoulder again and he looked up at me sternly.

"Don't need or want your sympathy, Belle," he grunted.

"Good, because I'm not giving it." I looked away. "I only give sympathy to those that are sorry for what they've done in their life, and you're not that man, are you, Beast?" I looked back down at him, watching as his brow furrowed deeper, his expression darkening.

"Ain't nothing to apologize for," he snarled.

I removed my hand with a shake of my head, feeling stupid for ever thinking that he could be anything but this beast of a man. I knew what he'd done. I'd heard a lot of stories in the past few weeks about the Devil's Highwaymen and the men that rode with them. I knew far more about him than I wanted to, and maybe he was right—maybe he didn't have anything to apologize for. But if I felt I could have asked it of him, I would have asked him to apologize anyway. People made mistakes. And people made decisions on the hand they were given. That was all he had done. He'd made a choice when he'd joined the Devil's Highwaymen, and he'd become the man he needed to to survive. Only now it had caught up with him, almost destroying him in the process.

"Probably best to go back before someone notices," I said, turning to call for Joey.

Beast reached out and grabbed my hand, and I looked back down at him. He stared up at me with his stormy gray eye full of every emotion a man could ever have: regret and guilt, shame and anger, love and hate. They all swam inside him, but his face remained impassive and closed off to me and to everyone else.

"You don't understand; I need to make them pay, Belle."

Was he asking for my permission? My acceptance? I frowned, not certain of anything anymore. Whenever I was around Beast, the world got turned on its head and left became right and up became down. Yet looking into his face right then, I wanted to understand him so much.

"It won't solve anything. It won't take anything away," I replied.

Beast swallowed. "It might take away some of the guilt."

He looked so vulnerable and lost in that moment that all I could think about doing was holding him—just climbing onto his lap and wrapping my arms around him. So I did. I sat on his lap and wrapped my arms around him, holding him as close as I could. Feeling his heart beating in his chest and his breath on my neck, and then his arms as they wrapped around me and pulled me closer. I breathed him in, every dark and awful thing that he'd done, and I tried to take his pain from him, to let him know that I cared, that I wanted better for him, that he'd get through this. I held Beast like he needed to be loved, and maybe he did, because he held me back just as tightly.

His hand moved to my hair, his fingers threading through the soft waves as he sighed. He pulled my face back from him so he could look into my eyes.

"What's happening, Belle?" he asked, searching my face for answers. "What is this?"

"I don't know," I said quietly.

"Was that it then? Back there, was that just a taste of the darkness before you go back to someone better? Someone good and wholesome?" His words were bitter, venom lacing them.

"Please, Beast, don't be like that," I begged. "I don't know what that was back there. And I don't know what I want. I don't understand any of this."

And I didn't. In many ways I detested Beast. He was an awful man.—he was the exact opposite of Lorenzo and everything that I looked for in a person—but in that moment I felt more connected to him than I had to Lorenzo the night before. But could I ever accept the things

126

that he'd done? Could I ever be with a man like Beast? Trust him with my heart and my soul?

As if getting his answer, I watched his expression harden, violence swimming behind they gray in his eyes. "I think you know what you want, you just don't want to admit it."

Maybe he was right.

Maybe I did know what I wanted, but I was too scared of wanting it.

But I didn't get chance to say any of that. Beast thought I'd already made up my mind. He pushed me from his lap and I stumbled to stand.

"You look tired, Belle. Your little fuckboy keep you up all night?" he said, his expression hardening further.

I sighed and shook my head. Why did he always do that? Why did he always ruin every nice moment between us? Between anyone?

"I'm not talking to you about this," I said, and started to walk away.

"I see you walking with a limp. Yeah, he fucked you good, didn't he?" He reached out and grabbed my arm before sucking his bottom lip into his mouth. "Or maybe it was taking two dicks in one day that's given you that limp, Belle. You know, if this nursing shit doesn't work out for you, I can get you a job over at the club servicing the boys."

I snatched my arm out from his fierce grip, sickness rolling through me at his words. He thought of me as a whore. That's what he'd reduced me to. Tears brimmed in my eyes as the hurt rolled through me in waves, from shock to despair to sadness, and finally shame.

He laughed, darkness in every chuckle he gave. "Come here, Belle, let me lick those tears away and then you can suck my cock afterwards. I'll pay you fifty bucks if you suck my balls too."

Tears streamed down my face. "Stop it," I begged, heartbroken and disgusted with him and myself.

"That's not what you were saying downstairs, and I bet that's not what you were saying last night either," he sneered. "Sure hope you fucking showered before you climbed on top of me, bitch. Don't wanna go catching some nasty skank disease from you."

I choked on a sob, praying that some part of the man I'd seen earlier would come back to me, but he was gone. I shook my head and swiped away the tears from my cheeks.

"I'll go get Joey to help you back to your room." I started to walk away from him.

"You and Joey getting close, huh? You gonna fuck him too, Belle?" he growled, sounding more like a jealous boyfriend than a fierce biker.

I swung back to face him, hands on my hips. "I'm done. I'm so done. With you, with this, with everything!" I found myself yelling by the time I got to the end of my sentence. "You can't go around hurting people like this, Beast! What is wrong with you?"

He leaned forward in his chair, his eyes cold and hard. "Don't you know, Belle, I'm a motherfuckin' beast and beasts can't be tamed." He looked me up and down like he was disgusted with himself for ever having sex with me. "Tell the prospect to bring me a hit," he growled out, disappointing me in so many ways.

"Fine," I snapped with a shake of my head as I backed away. "But you know what? I'm done. Find yourself a new nurse."

"You're not done till I tell you you're done," he snarled.

I kept on walking, ignoring his protests behind me.

"Since I pay your wages, does that make you my whore now?" he yelled out behind me, and I choked on another sob.

Joey opened the door as I got there, looking between me and Beast cautiously.

"Can you get him back to his room on your own?"

He nodded. "Yeah, no problem."

"And tell Shooter that Beast is someone else's problem now."

"You okay?" he asked, his gaze going behind me to Beast, who was still yelling, and then back to me. "He didn't hurt you, did he?" His features hardened.

"Not physically," I said, "but he's broken my heart because he doesn't have a heart himself." And then I left.

Chapter Eighteen
~ BEAST ~

The door opened and a tall blond woman walked in, her uniform cut in at all the right places, giving me a good view of her shapely ass as she sashayed across the room.

"Morning, I brought you breakfast," she said, cheery as a motherfucker, "Doctor Collins is signing off on your discharge papers this morning, so you should be out of here in a day or so. Isn't that great? I bet you can't wait after being cooped up in this little room for so long…"

She continued to drone on and on like I gave a shit what she said, and I drowned her out, wondering where the fuck Belle was but already knowing that I'd driven her away for good this time.

The chirpy little blond pulled the cart to the side of my bed. "I have your meds and your pudding. I heard you love pudding, so I made sure to bring an extra cup." She smiled and held out a Styrofoam cup filled with water in one hand and a little cup with my pills in another.

"What the fuck is this?"

"Well, your previous nurse said not to give you a glass. She said that you're very accident prone," she said, her smile faltering a little as her gaze caught sight of the broken window. "But she insisted that you get two puddings because they're your favourite."

I stared between her and the cup of water, giving a shake of my head.

She'd really just left me in the care of this nurse.

I'd known she was done with me—I'd made sure of it—yet I hadn't thought I'd actually give a shit. But now that she wasn't there I was pissed off. Pissed off that she thought she could just drop me. Pissed off that she thought she got any say in any of this. And pissed off that she'd put this bubbly little bitch in charge of looking after me. I'd be

130

gone in a day or two, but there was no way I was letting Belle get out of her duties so easily.

My gaze narrowed in on the nurse's tag and I realised that she worked in paediatrics.

Belle had gotten a child's nurse to look after me.

Anger rose inside of me, fury raging through my veins at her fucking audacity. Who the fuck did she think she was dealing with?

"Oh, now now, come on, don't get yourself all worked up, sweetie," the nurse said soothingly, like I was a fucking child.

My anger continued to grow and grow until I thought I was going to explode, but when it got to the boiling point, instead of exploding, I laughed. It bubbled out of me like vomit, so loudly and unexpectedly that the prospect stormed into the room with his gun out, and that made me laugh some more.

"Put your gun away, prospect!" I said, my booming laugh growing louder, and he flicked the safety back on and slid it into his jeans.

"Everything okay?" he asked cautiously.

I wanted to feel bad for laughing. I wanted Echo's voice in my head telling me to shut the fuck up and get back to my misery and self-pity, get back to planning my vengeance, but instead all I heard was silence.

Echo wasn't in there yelling at me, guilt-tripping me, and making me feel like the piece of shit I was. He was gone, and his silence was deafening. Even the screaming of the horses had disappeared.

I pushed the covers back from my body and slid to the side of the bed before dropping onto my feet. I felt unsteady and weak, my muscles not used to being used, but I was done with wheelchairs. I wanted to be a man again. A big-ass naked man walking across the room, but a man all the same. I wanted to walk and move and be a human being living instead of a corpse in a bed waiting to die. I hobbled over to the opposite wall where the gowns were kept, reaching for one and sliding it over my shoulders.

Joey rushed to my side. "Hey hey, hey, big man, what's going down?" He put a hand on my waist, but I shrugged him off. "Where you off to, brother?"

"Need to find her," I grunted.

"Who?"

I scowled. "Belle, asshole." I was trying to knot the little gown ties to make it go tighter around me, but no matter how hard I tied them my ass was still on show, a cold draft sliding up my back.

"What the fuck is this?" I yelled, getting irritated with it.

"They provide easy access for the doctors," Nurse fucking Chipper said helpfully.

"So my ass is going to be on show for everyone?"

"I mean, I could try and find you some clothes, but I'd need to check with Doctor Collins that it was okay first," she said, her eyes bright and cheery like it was all perfectly normal.

"Fuck it," I snapped, and stormed across the room. I'd tied it loosely, and was ignoring the aches and pains running through my body. I'd be okay once I got used to it. My body just wasn't used to moving.

When I reached the door, a dizzy spell washed over me and I clung to the wall to stop myself from falling over. The prospect tried to grab me, touching a particularly sensitive spot, and I called out in pain.

"Fuck!"

"Sorry," he said, flinching back and letting go of me. "Let me get the chair."

"No!" I barked. "I'm fucking walking down there and telling that bitch that she's fired!"

The prospect and Nurse Chipper looked between themselves, and he frowned. "Didn't she already quit?"

I glared at him. "No one fuckin' quits me."

"All right, easy, brother," Joey replied, holding his hands in the air. "Just take a breather and think about this for a minute."

"You really need to get back to bed, Mr. Beast," the nurse said, coming behind me. "Doctor Collins hasn't given you authorization to leave this room."

The prospect and I looked at each other and both started laughed. Wasn't sure what was funnier: the fact she'd called me "Mr. Beast" or the fact she thought I needed the doc's authorization to leave the room.

I threw open the door and stormed into the hallway, listening as the prospect called Gauge on his cell phone. The whole thing made me even more infuriated, like even the dumb-as-a-box-of-rocks prospect thought I needed babysitting. I was so done with this fucking place.

Every barefoot step was agony, like splinters piercing through my muscles, as I made my way through the busy hospital hallways, glaring and scowling at anyone who got in my way. Doctor Collins came out of one of the side rooms, clipboard in hand, and looked up, his eyes going wide when he saw me.

"You can't be out here!" he said, his voice filled with panic.

"Fuck off!" I barked, and continued on.

He scurried after me. "Beast, you need to get back to your room. You're putting everyone in danger by being out here. If someone sees you…"

I stopped and turned to him. Piece of shit was five foot nothing, with a head of gray hair and bronze skin from all the fucking trips to the Caribbean that being on our payroll paid for. He was a pathetic weasel of a man, long face, twitchy eyes, and I'd never liked him. Liked him even less now that he was getting all up in my space and trying to tell me what I could and couldn't do.

"Back the fuck off, Doc," I said, accentuating each word carefully so he knew I was serious and not to be argued with.

He huffed like a dog being told off. "I want you out of my hospital today," he said sternly. "I'm done treating you."

I barked out a short, sharp laugh. "You think I care?"

For a little man he had a big pair of balls on him, because he shook his head at me, his eyes narrowing. "You have one hour to get your things and leave."

"Get the fuck out of my way," I snapped, and pushed him backwards so hard that he stumbled back and fell on his ass, his little clipboard sliding along the ground.

133

I turned back around, coming face to face with Belle.

Her expression was full of surprise. Surprise at seeing me out of bed, surprise at seeing my naked white ass, or surprise at me assaulting Doctor fucking Collins, I wasn't exactly sure.

I pointed right at her, my jaw twitching as I glared. "You're fired."

Her surprise turned to confusion. "What?"

"You deaf? I said, you're fired."

She scowled at me, her pert little lips pouting. "I already quit, Beast."

"I don't accept your resignation because I was already firing you're ass," I snapped.

"You're pathetic," she said, and turned her back on me before walking away.

I stormed after her, grabbing her shoulder and turning her back to face me. "Who do you fucking think you're dealing with, Belle? You think I'm one of the good guys who lets people speak to him like that? You think you get to quit on me? Sending this fucking ray of sunshine to my room like I'm a kid with extra pudding and a Styrofoam motherfucking cup because I can't be trusted? Who the fuck do you think you're fucking with?"

I was yelling so loudly now that my head had started to hurt and I felt dizzy. Or maybe it was because I shouldn't have been on my feet. Hell, I shouldn't have been walking, or moving either. I should have been fucking dead. That's what I should have been. *Dead!* Six feet under and rotting back into the earth with Echo in a dirt grave, my cut and my gun to keep me company.

She shook her head. "I know *exactly* who you are! You're a sad little boy who pushes people away when he doesn't get what he wants!" she yelled back.

"Fuck you!" I roared.

"Fuck you too!" she screamed, stomping her foot on the ground. "I hate you! Are you happy now? You win, okay? You pushed me away and made me hate you. You sure showed me, didn't you, huh? Not everyone is good, and not everyone can be saved, I get it now. Lesson learned!"

She started to walk away again, but I wasn't done with her yet. I wanted her to care. I wanted her to argue with me. To get all feisty and backtalk the way she did sometimes. I wanted her cheeks to go red the way they did when I said something dirty to her. I didn't want her to leave me there. I wanted her to stay.

"Happy? Why would I be happy? You just up and left me like everyone else, like you weren't supposed to stay, Belle." The words were out before I could stop them and I breathed heavily, my heart and my head hurting.

The world was spinning, my body was hurting, and I felt sick.

Sick and tired of it all.

Of this fucked-up body. Of this fucked-up world. Of this fucked-up life.

"You were supposed to stay," I said, knowing how pathetic I sounded but not caring anymore.

Her hazel eyes softened a little at my words. They pierced me, consuming me entirely.

"Beast," she began, but then stopped herself before sighing.

"Belle?" A male voice said her name and we both turned to look.

"Lorenzo?" she said. "What are you doing here?"

He wasn't looking at her anymore though. He was looking at me. Glaring was more like it. Lorenzo…I knew that name from somewhere but I couldn't place it. My head was hurting too much and my body was being swallowed by dizziness. The prospect was holding me upright but I used the last of my strength to push him off me and stand straight and proud.

Lorenzo… Fuck, every time I caught the scent of where I'd heard that name before, it moved out of reach. This had to be her little fuckboy boyfriend though; maybe that was where I'd heard it. Only he wasn't a little fuckboy. Looked like a smarmy motherfucker though. All suited up, shiny shoes, hair slicked back, white shirt with a couple of buttons

135

open. His hands were tucked inside his pants pockets casually, like he had no fear of me, and I with the Devil in me screaming to break free.

"This the piece of shit you've been sleeping with?" I growled at Belle.

She turned and pouted at me, her eyes all big and wide. "This is Lorenzo, not that it's any of your business," she snapped. She turned back to him, her cheeks flaming red at the audience we had gathered. "What are you doing here?"

Lorenzo's mouth twitched into the hint of a smile. "Thought I'd come and take you out to lunch."

"I can't leave here, I'm too busy," she said impatiently before sighing. "Sorry, that sounded really ungrateful. I really appreciate the gesture, but I barely get time for a cup of coffee so lunch is out of the question."

Lorenzo nodded sagely, his hard gaze moving between me and Belle. "That's okay, my fault." He held his hands up. "Dinner tonight at my place, then."

Belle looked back to me, a small frown puckering between her brows. We shared a moment, a split second between us that was just ours. She told me so much in that look. She told me goodbye. She told me she was sorry, and good luck, but mostly she told me goodbye.

"Sure, that sounds great," she said, looking back to him.

Lorenzo pulled his hands from his pockets and my gaze roved over his hands, checking them for weapons, but there was nothing there. He was just a man coming to take his girl for lunch. And I fucking hated him with every bone in my body.

"I'll walk you back out," Belle said, moving toward him.

"Belle!" I called her name and I watched as her shoulders rounded before she turned to look back at me. "I meant what I said."

I was losing her.

Maybe I'd never even had her to begin with.

Sure as shit didn't deserve her after the way I'd treated her.

She sighed, her forehead still furrowed with tension and sadness. She glanced between Lorenzo—in his expensive suit, looking like every

136

woman's wet dream, successful business owner who could treat her right—and me, with my big white ass on show to the world, a body full of scars, a disfigured face, and a dangerous outlaw who treated her like shit and couldn't offer her anything but my fucked-up self. I already knew who she would pick, and truth be known, I couldn't blame her either.

"Stay," I practically begged as I swayed on my feet. My vision was going blurry, my head thumping so hard I wondered if my brain was trying to get out of my head. "Belle...stay."

I sounded pathetic, but I had to try. I'd fucked up—I knew it and she knew it. But I needed her. Hated the realization, but there it was, as plain as day. I needed her, but more importantly, I wanted her.

"I meant what I said too, Beast," she finally replied, and she sounded heartbroken. She chewed on the inside of her cheek and looked at the ground. I watched as Lorenzo straightened up and took a step towards me, pushing Belle behind him like he was protecting her. Like I'd ever fucking hurt her.

Lorenzo frowned. "Beast? Like Beauty and the Beast, huh?" He laughed lightly, gesturing between me and Belle. "I see it now," he chuckled.

I scowled. "What the fuck did you just say to me?" I didn't care what Belle thought; if this fucker stepped out of line again I would shoot him in the goddamned face.

Lorenzo took another step toward me, the hint of a smile on his lips. The prospect grabbed my arm as I lurched toward him, pulling me back. Lorenzo looked me up and down, a pitying look on his face. Belle reached for him but he turned to her, giving a soft shake of his head, and she released him. Who was this guy, the fucking woman whisperer, thinking he could control my girl with just a single shake of his head. And yet she'd listened to him, stepping back, and moving further away from me.

"Only this time, the beast doesn't win the girl, huh?" he continued casually, like he'd just offered me a compliment and not insulted me.

"Lorenzo!" Belle exclaimed from behind him.

"Nah, it's okay, Belle, he's right; this ain't a fairy tale, and there ain't no happy ending coming for me. You stay with your little fuckboy here." I gritted my teeth, hating the words coming out of my mouth. "But when you're fucking him, you think of me, yeah?" I laughed, a dark, bitter laugh and her mouth opened in shock. She hated me, and that was okay by me because fuck her.

Lorenzo laughed with me. "She won't have time to think of you, my friend. The places I'll take her, the things I'll show her. You're doing the right thing by not fighting this; what could a beast like you ever offer a woman like her?"

"You got a death wish?"

He chuckled, dragging a hand over his mouth and chin and looking up at me through dark lashes, that sardonic smile still on his smarmy face.

"What did you think? That she would pick you over me?" He shook his head. "It's not about the money, my friend, it's about respect. And you don't have any for her or anyone else." He looked me up and down. "You barely have any for yourself."

I grabbed my dick over the thin cotton nightgown. "I gave her all the respect she needed just yesterday," I sneered.

His smile faltered momentarily as he realized what I was suggesting, but he fixed it back in place with a shrug. "No matter, I'll just have to work twice as hard to make sure I erase any memory of you."

"Not going to happen," I snarled, staring him down. "I'm not that easy to forget."

"We'll see," he replied, and turned away from me. He took her hand and guided her away, and I stood there watching her go, my chest heaving as I tried to control myself.

From somewhere I could hear the sound of hospital security showing up and Doctor Collins ranting about getting me out of there. The prospect was arguing my corner and telling everyone to stay back, and in the distance I heard the sound of motorcycles coming as my brothers arrived to take me home. Belle looked back one last time as

138

they left the hospital. Even from there I could see the tears in her eyes, and that was my cue to walk away.

Lorenzo was right.

I hated it, and I'd never admit it to anyone, but he was right.

It was about respect.

I'd never shown her any, but I would now. I'd let her leave with him. He'd treat her right; like she deserved. Her pure soul was too good for me anyway. She deserved more than a broken-down biker like me, but that was all I'd ever be to the world.

Not all stories have a happy ending, and there was certainly no happily ever after at the end of ours. We were two different people, from two different worlds, and we would never work.

"Come on, brother," the prospect said, guiding me through the throng of people and back to my room.

Doctor Collins was stood in the doorway looking flustered. "You have 30 minutes before the cops are called and you're dragged out of here in handcuffs," he sniped. "I'm done jumping when you criminals tell me to."

I reached over and grabbed him, slamming up against the wall, my hand tightening around his throat as I pressed my forehead into his.

"You *ever* speak to me like that again and I will end you!" I roared in his face.

The prospect was pulling on my arm and trying to get me to let go but I shook him off, pain threading through my still tender skin. Doc looked like he was about to cry as I squeezed harder, his face going red. It would be so easy to squeeze the life out of him right now. Just another couple of seconds and he would be gone. His eyeballs bugged in their sockets, his hands clawing uselessly at mine.

"Beast!" the prospect roared from behind me. "Let go of him."

"When we say jump, you say how high?" I shook him, his head bouncing off the wall.

I watched the light fading in the Doc's eyes, wishing that it was me and not him. Wishing with everything I was that I could have been good enough for Belle. That I could have been someone different for her. Or at the very least, that I could have died in that barn.

It was a sick thing bringing me back from the brink, because now I had nowhere to go. I didn't know who I was anymore and I didn't know where I belonged. All I knew was that this world has chewed me up and spit me out for the last time.

I was done trying to survive it.

The next time death came knocking, I was opening the door.

I let go of the Doc's throat, letting his body drop to the floor. He gasped for air, his eyes rolling in his head and the second I stepped away a couple of nurses rushed to his side to bring him back round.

"We need to get the fuck out of here now!" the prospect said, pulling me away. "Fucking move!" he yelled.

I stumbled after him, big white ass still on show and my heart a bloody pulp in my chest, determined never to come back here ever again.

Chapter Nineteen
~ BEAST ~

Back in my room, I sat on the edge of the bed while the prospect packed up my shit. I wasn't leaving because Doctor Collins told me to—far from it. I was leaving because I hated that place and everything in it. I wanted out of there and to be back home with my club and my brothers. That place was just a constant reminder of the pain I had endured and all I had lost.

My head was spinning from the exertion of the past thirty minutes, sickness clawing at my insides and making me feel like I was going to puke, fire dousing my lungs, my muscles aching, throbbing with the constant strain of standing up, of walking and moving, of doing normal shit that normal people could do. The prospect looked over at me, his gaze filled with worry, but he didn't say anything. I swiped my hand over my forehead, feeling it slick with sweat as I struggled to stay upright.

Fuck Doctor Collins.

Fuck Belle.

Fuck this hospital.

I was goddamned fine.

Or I would be once I got out of there.

Gauge was on his way with some of my brothers to take me back home, and I couldn't wait. I was a fully working man again, and back at the club I could have all the beer and pussy I wanted, starting with Lola. I'd show that bitch how much of a man I still was and then I'd kick her out of the club for talking to me the way she had.

The door opened and Shooter, Casa, and Gauge walked in. Shooter's expression was dark, and a man like Shooter didn't look like that unless something really bad had happened. The prospect stopped what he was doing as Gauge clicked the door shut.

"You couldn't stay put for another week, huh?" Gauge grumbled, his arms crossed over his chest.

"See you got your eyes back, brother," Casa said, nodding toward me.

"Got a cage downstairs ready to take you back to the clubhouse," Shooter said, his expression hard, serious...

I looked between them all, sensing that something significant had happened. Now that I'd taken my head out of my self-pitying ass and I had the use of both eyes, I was seeing a whole lot more. And right then I was seeing that some serious shit was about to go down.

"Are any of you going to tell me what's going on or are you going to keep playing with my balls?" I snapped. "Because I'm all for foreplay, but I'd rather get it from a sweetbutt than any of you fuckers."

No one laughed.

Not even Casa, and I'd just joked about his two favorite things.

My stomach soured further.

"You found out who did it," I said, the words tasting bitter in my mouth. It was a matter of fact even before Shooter nodded. "Who?"

Gauge and Casa exchanged a look, but Shooter kept his gaze on me. Steady, calm.

"Brothers, I need to know." I took a deep breath, preparing myself for the news. Echo was back inside my head, and he was just as furious and desperate as me to know who it was that had killed him. Who it was that had almost killed me. And who it was that had lost me the woman of my dreams.

I'd always been a violent man. Violence bred violence, right? And in the end, we become what we most fear. I'd started my life unwanted and had been punished, abused, and unloved. And I'd become the outcome of those actions. Never caring enough to let anyone in. I'd never pushed someone away because I'd never let anyone get close enough to care. Not until Belle.

That one night had destroyed more than just my body. It had destroyed my mind. And I'd put myself back together as someone different. Despite what Belle thought, I wasn't good; the goodness had been cut and burned out of me until I wasn't whole anymore. And Belle deserved someone whole...someone more.

142

In a different life, we could have been good.

"You might wanna sit down for this," Shooter said, interrupting my tangled thoughts.

"Fuck that, Prez, just tell me."

He huffed out a breath and looked to Casa, whose expression was serious.

"Italian mafia," Shooter said.

I scowled. "How sure are you?"

The Italian mafia was serious.

Really fucking serious; it meant war.

"A hundred percent, brother." He looked back at Shooter. "We got the cops on the payroll to check phone records of people in the area that night, linked it up to their men. Followed them for a few days, hacked their phones, and heard talk. Realized it was connected to the new buyers we've been in talks with. Told you they were from Cali, right?"

"Yeah," I said, my scowl growing deeper.

"Big pockets, big connections, and an even bigger risk. But the payroll was worth it. Italian mafia found out and wanted in on our territory. Thought they could take out a couple of our guys and scare us off. They want our product. They want our buyers, and they want us gone." He ran a tattooed hand down his beard, his face lined with worry.

"There's more?" I asked, though I already knew the answer.

"Yeah, this is where shit starts to get fucked up." Shooter looked to Casa, who took a step closer.

"I found talk on the dark web…about that night," he began, and I froze, dread seeping into my blood and turning it to ice. "I followed some leads and traced some shit and…" Casa stopped talking, dragging a hand over his shaved head before looking at me. "It was filmed, brother," he said, his voice filled with apology and dismay.

"What was?" I asked with a heavy scowl, but then I knew, and I wished I didn't.

"That night. Everything was filmed. Echo, you…all of it." Casa cracked his knuckles and swallowed. "I've taken it down, but…" His words trailed off.

Dread hit my stomach like a lead balloon and I sat back down on the edge of my bed, feeling dizzy. Being tortured for hours was bad enough, but knowing that there were videos of it out there and people were watching it. Getting off on my pain. My screams. My nightmares…Echo's death.

"Show me," I said, my conviction weak as I looked down at the floor, shame marring every word I spoke.

"I don't think that's a good idea, brother," Gauge stepped in. "You did good. You never broke. You never gave shit away. You did yourself and the Highwaymen proud. There's no shame in it, brother."

"You watched it," I said, my words hollow.

It shouldn't have mattered, yet it did.

I'd relived that night a hundred times over, maybe more, and every time it morphed and changed into something worse, something more bloody and violent. My screams got more agonizing, the pain was more excruciating, the night darker, blacker, the fire brighter, hotter. And the screaming of the horses filled every space in between.

"Beast, you did good," Shooter said.

I looked back up. "I want to see," I growled, my tone darkening, "and then we're going to take these motherfuckers out, one by one."

"There's another…complication," Shooter said, interrupting my tirade. "The prospect says you and that nurse of yours have been gettin' close."

I scowled over at the prospect. "I fired her this morning."

"How close did you get?" Gauge asked.

"What the fuck does she have to do with anything?"

Shooter dragged his hand over his short beard again, a nervous tic that he'd developed in the past couple a years, and I knew that things were about to get even worse. "Well, seems she's been seeing someone."

"I know," I snapped. "Lorenzo or some shit. Just met him in the hallway downstairs. He's a piece of shit fancy fuckboy. What does that have to do with anything?"

Gauge and Shooter exchanged a look.

"Can someone enlighten me!" I yelled, growing more and more pissed off by the second. I didn't like being kept in the dark; it was normally my job to find out that sort of information, and being on the receiving end of it was bullshit.

"He's Lorenzo Bianchi," Shooter said, "younger brother of Mateo and Carlos Bianchi, who help run the mafia's crew in Atlanta."

The world stopped on its axis momentarily, the second turning into a minute and turning into a life sentence. My head spun at the news and everything that it meant. The splitting headache I'd woken up with grew so loud that my eyeballs throbbed.

"So, I need to ask you again, brother," Gauge said, coming forward. "How close did you get to the nurse? Because we're wondering if she might have been in on the whole thing from the start, and if so, she's going to ground just like everyone else involved."

I shook my head, stunned. Belle couldn't have been in on it, could she? Had she been playing me with her good girl act the whole time?

"Not that close," I said, my mouth dry. I thought over the past twenty-four hours; her body on mine, my hands on her...

Gauge didn't look like he believed me, but he wasn't about to call me out as a liar either.

What had I said while she was there?

Had I been as careful as I normally would be?

I didn't know. I couldn't be sure.

I'd been in constant pain the past year. My tongue had been loose, but had it been loose enough to spill club secrets?

"No, no way," the prospect said, coming forward and shaking his head. "I know her and she's not like that. Not a bad bone in her body."

"You can never really know a person, kid," Shooter said, sounding full of regret.

"Belle's not like that!" The prospect stormed toward me, his eyes full of pleading, "Beast, tell 'em she wouldn't do that!"

Belle...

Sweet, beautiful, caring Belle.

I pictured her now, that god-awful nurse's outfit, her hair piled high on her head, her face exhausted after another long shift. The way she flinched when I yelled. The way she made herself scarce when anyone came by.

I nodded. "He's right; she's not like that. She's a good girl, Shooter."

"Yeah, well let's hope so, for her sakes," Casa said, clapping his hands together, "because she's running with the wrong crew, and if she's not careful she's gonna get herself killed."

"I'll speak to her," I growled, "let her know how it is."

And she'll really hate me then, I thought. But she'd made her choice. She'd chosen him over me and she'd have to live with those consequences.

"Let me speak to her," the prospect suggested, and I turned to glare at him. He shrugged. "We became close over the past month or so. I can find out what she knows, if anything."

I felt myself filling with fury, my heartrate spiking. Close? Close? What did he mean by close? I started toward him and he held up his hands in defense.

"It's not like that, brother, I swear it's not." He backed away, his hands still in the air. "We're just friends is all."

"Maybe she's in on this. Seems like the sweet little nurse is getting it all from all over, huh?" Casa said with a smirk, enjoying the drama of it all. I knew he was winding me up but I couldn't help but rise to the bait. "Hot little nurse playing the good little girl when really she's getting dick from every brother, because, given how you're reacting right now, there ain't no way that you haven't fucked that girl. Wonder if I can get in on the action. Harlow and I have been talking about a threesome, and she's hot as they come. Wouldn't mind a taste."

146

I turned to him, pointing my finger. "I will fucking end you if you say that again!"

Casa laughed like this was the funniest shit he'd ever heard, and maybe it was, to him.

I was shaking, my arms and legs trembling with unspent rage at the thought of her fucking anyone but me while I could still feel her wrapped around my own cock like a fucking burrito. Goddammit, but she wasn't mine now. She was *his*. Lorenzo. Italian mafia. The bastards who'd killed my best friend and ruined my life...

"Casa, shut the fuck up before you give him an embolism," Shooter yelled. "Beast, I'm taking it you've gotten up close and personal with this girl." He waited for my response, but when all he got in return was a death glare, he went on. "Did it end well? You think you can talk to her? Find out what's going down with that boyfriend of hers?"

I thought about it, wondering if I could just order her not to be with Lorenzo anymore. Warn her of how dangerous he and his family were and make her see that she'd be safer with me. Or without me. Shit, she'd be safer with both of us out of her life and I knew it. But I also knew that wasn't really an option. After the way we just ended things, she'd no sooner listen to me than she would the Devil.

"Let the prospect talk to her," I said with a hard scowl, hating him for having the option of talking to her when I couldn't.

"I can do that," he replied immediately.

I looked over at him. "You fuck her?" I asked, ready to knock his damn teeth out if he said yes. Not that I gave a shit who Belle slept with. Her pussy was her pussy and I had no claim to it, but I wasn't happy about her putting out to all of my brothers, despite how I'd mocked her and taunted her about becoming a sweetbutt for the club. That shit would *never* happen.

"No, brother, we just talked about books and shit," he said.

"Books? I didn't know you could fucking read," Casa laughed, and everyone joined in, barring me. I hated the prospect in that moment. Hated that he had a connection with her that I didn't. Hated that he'd had conversations with her that I didn't know about. Hated that she was with Lorenzo right then, probably getting fucked in the back seat of his Mercedes like a high-class hooker. And yet the thought of her spread-eagled made my dick twitch again.

Fuck, what the hell had this woman done to me?

"We need to know everything about her," I said, all business. My brothers didn't need to know all the fucked-up shit going around my head right then. "Not just her address and where she works, because we know that. I want to know her friends, her family, what car she drives. Hell, I even wanna know what her lucky underwear is, brothers. I need it all, and then I'll assess the threat level she makes."

They shared a knowing look between themselves, Casa smirking like a fucking clown the entire time.

"Regular stalker," Casa snickered.

I stared him down, and though he looked away, the look remained. I turned to the prospect. "I want a list of books she recommended to you. I want to know everything you two talked about."

"Jesus, brother, let's just get you back to the clubhouse and get you a beer before we go all Special Forces on her ass," Shooter said. "I need a fucking cigarette, so get your clothes on and let's get the fuck out of here before Doctor Collins blows his top. Need to keep the good doctor onside, which, after your little stunt downstairs, is going to be hard enough."

"You mean he's going to be taking a little trip to Bali or some shit on our money pretty soon," Gauge grumbled. He hated Doctor Collins as much as I did, but Shooter was right—we needed a doctor of his reach on the payroll.

"Pretty much," Shooter said "Beast, let Gauge and Casa handle this—"

"No!" I barked, interrupting him. "I'm dealing with this."

Shooter's jaw twitched and he came toward me. "Listen, brother, I know you've been through a hell of a lot in the past year, and I've let a lot of shit slide because of that, but you need to remember your place. I think I've been patient enough, but I'm done with that now. So I'll say this one more time, as your president: leave Gauge and Casa to handle this shit for now. You keep working on getting yourself better, because you ain't fucking there yet."

Shooter held my gaze for several seconds, and I felt a rage for my president I hadn't felt before. I wanted to hit him. I wanted to lash out and hit him over and over and over, destroying that pretty fucking face of his. How dare he tell me what to do. I gritted my teeth, my jaw ticking as we stared at each other. The temperature of the room dropped and the air stilled.

"Step off before this ends badly for you," Shooter warned. "Because brother or not, I won't be undermined by you or anyone else. This is my fucking club and what I say goes. You feel me, Beast?"

I took a deep breath, staring down at him, my jaw still ticking like an alarm clock. And then I looked away, feeling all kinds of hate and guilt that I'd almost lost it on him.

Shooter patted my shoulder. "I get it; you feel things for her and this situation is messed up. But your head is all fucked up right now and I don't think you're thinking clearly. We'll keep you in the loop of what's going on and you'll be involved, but right now I need my enforcer back to a hundred and you're barely scratching forty. So get yourself right and then get yourself back to work, brother." He pulled me in for a hug and I sighed and hugged him back, slapping his back.

"Sorry, Prez. This shit with the mafia has got me all fucked up inside," I admitted—seemed safer than admitting that Belle was the one that had gotten me all fucked up, even if he already knew it. If I denied it, it wasn't happening.

Shooter sighed. "Let's get you back to the clubhouse, brother. Everyone's looking forward to seeing you again. It's been a long time and you've been missed."

I nodded, more than ready to get out of that place. Those four white walls had haunted me for the past year, and I was done with staring at them. Yet now something else was haunting me...the video of me being tortured was out there for everyone to see, and I knew I wouldn't rest until I'd watched it for myself. Even if it killed me to see.

149

Chapter Twenty
~ *Belle* ~

My shift was finally over, but I wished it wasn't. For once, I wished I still had a couple of hours to go. Tonight I was going over to tell Jenna about my mom and I was not looking forward to it.

The day had been long and hard though, and my feet were killing me, not to mention the mess inside my head. After the way Beast and I had left things, and then Lorenzo coming to my rescue... I just didn't know what to think anymore. It was all so messed up, and I wasn't sure what was happening to me. I didn't do this sort of thing; I didn't sleep with two men in less than twenty-four hours. Lorenzo hadn't said anything about it after Beast had so eloquently blurted out my misadventure with him, but he was thinking about it, that was for certain.

When we left the hospital after their argument, he took me to lunch in the park opposite. He'd packed a picnic, but neither of us ate anything. The food lay between us as he seethed over what Beast had just said and I sat there shamefaced and guilty. But he never brought it up. Never said a thing. And when my lunch was over, he let me walk away, food untouched and with barely a goodbye.

I should have been happy that it had been like that; I didn't have to talk about it. Yet I wished he would have just come out and said something, because I sure as heck didn't know how to bring it up.

I sighed and headed to my car. The air was cool but I felt like I was on fire, heat licking at my insides. The start of a headache was coming on, so I sat in the driver's seat and rummaged through my purse for some aspirin, because Lord knew it was only going to get worse. The more I thought about it, the more I was regretting saying yes to my mom. It was going to be awful for not just me, but for Jenna too. I just hoped that she didn't hate me afterwards.

Setting my purse down on the passenger side, I started the car and looked up, noticing Joey, the prospect, sitting on his motorcycle under a streetlamp. He was watching me, and the friendly face I'd come to know over the past month or so was gone, and in its place was a dark look. My blood instantly chilled and I looked away from him and headed out of the parking lot and onto the main road.

Looking back in my mirror, I saw him pull out and begin to follow me, and my heart sped up. Oh my god, had Beast ordered him to kill me? Was I going to die now? Hot tears began to roll down my face, and the more I tried to contain them, the more upset I got until I could barely see. Thankfully, Jenna lived pretty close to the hospital, and I pulled up in front of her apartment a trembling, terrified mess, but at least I hadn't crashed.

I sat there for several moments, swiping away the tears and trying to pull myself together. Joey was sitting three cars back, still on his bike, and still staring at me. I knew it was time to face this—face him. I couldn't go into Jenna's knowing he was out there waiting for me. Or worse, that he might come in to kill me and inadvertently harm Jenna and Gregory. No, I needed to face this now.

Grabbing my purse, I climbed out of my car, and with trembling knees I started to walk toward him. As I got closer, Joey pulled on his helmet, started his bike, and left without saying anything. I stared after him, wondering what had just happened.

Was this how it was going to be now? Would I always be looking over my shoulder, wondering when he was going to send someone to kill me? And why send someone to do it for him? Why not do it himself? Had I really hurt him so much that he'd chosen to have me killed but couldn't bear to do it himself? I shook my head no, realizing that I was quickly spiraling and needed to calm down. There was no way that I'd made that big of an impact on Beast. I was just another notch on his bedpost. Another woman. Another name in his little black book. I'd fallen for it—for him—and put my newfound relationship with Lorenzo in jeopardy, and for what? For a psychotic, jealous, obnoxious man who couldn't take rejection? Who didn't like to be questioned on his actions?

I stomped my foot, frustrated, upset, and annoyed at myself and at him.

Why I had even gotten involved with him, I had no idea, but I regretted it with every bone in my body. After the hospital encounter and now this—Beast was swiftly becoming the biggest mistake I'd ever made.

I was terrified of him sending someone back to finish the job, but what could I do? I had no way of contacting him and asking him to just get it over and done with or get over it. There wasn't even anyone I could tell, because I wasn't stupid enough to go to the police and I wasn't about to endanger Jenna or Lorenzo by telling either of them. No, like everything else, I was in this on my own.

Looking around the empty street, I wished that I could just go home and climb into bed, but I knew I couldn't. Regardless of what had just happened, or hadn't happened…it was time to face the music. Jenna deserved that from me, at the very least. I wasn't dead—I was just a little shaken up, and I still had to go and speak to her, and if I was about to die, then I needed to tell Jenna everything before it was too late.

After ringing Jenna's bell and her buzzing me inside, I took the stairs slowly but all too soon reached her door, which she'd left slightly ajar for me. I could hear her TV set playing and talking and I hesitated on the threshold, wanting to give her a few more seconds of blissful ignorance before I blew her world apart. My thoughts strayed to Lorenzo and his expression as we'd sat in the park in silence, Beast's bombshell of a revelation settled between us like a third wheel. I felt awful for him, and no doubt we'd have to talk about what Beast had said eventually, because if we were going to work—if he even still wanted me—then we'd need to get everything out in the open and clear the air.

A thought occurred to me that hadn't before, and it was completely and utterly selfish: if Lorenzo and I didn't work out, I wouldn't be able to go back to Dela Roma's. I sighed heavily, realizing that I was making a mess of my life from all angles.

"Are you coming in or are you going to stay out there brooding all night?" Jenna asked as she pulled the door open.

"Sorry, yeah, I was just lost in thought," I mumbled, going inside.

"Thinking about Beast?" she asked, and I swung around to face her. She gave me a knowing-but-sympathetic smile. "I heard there was a big drama at the hospital between you and him and then Doctor Collins kicked him out. I warned you about him, didn't I."

"It wasn't just between me and him," I said honestly, "it included Lorenzo too."

She tutted and headed to the kitchen. "I think we need wine for this conversation."

I followed her, watching as she put the coffee mugs away and pulled out wine glasses before pouring us both a glass of red and sliding one over to me.

"Take a long drink and go on," she instructed, and I did as she asked. Honestly, I could have downed the entire bottle with how I was feeling.

I slid onto one of her bar stools and sighed. "Beast and I..." I let my words trail off, their meaning hanging between us.

She waited patiently, my cheeks growing hot as I willed the words to come out. Slowly her expression changed and she realized what I was about to say.

"Please tell me you're not going to say what I think you're going to say, Belle!" she said, her expression souring when I winced and nodded. "Oh, Belle. What were you thinking? Kissing a patient is strictly a no-no, and you know this." She finished her glass and poured a second one, topping up mine even though I'd barely had any.

"It just sort of happened," I said, sounding utterly miserable even to my own ears.

"That sort of thing does not *sort of happen*, Belle."

"One minute I was taking the bandages off his head and the next we were kissing." I looked across at her, waiting for the other shoe to drop when she realized it had gone further than that. When the look didn't come, I knew I'd have to come clean. "And the next, he was pulling me on top of him and..." I waved my hand in the air, not ready

154

to say the words out loud, because every time I thought about it I realized how wrong it had been.

I had taken advantage of a sick man.

I mean, it had felt like a sick man had taken advantage of me at the time, though I hadn't exactly been saying no to him, but the ethics board wouldn't see it that way. They'd see it as a nurse sleeping with a patient, and I'd be fired. I wondered whether that might be the better outcome after all. The more I worked at the hospital, the more I began to wonder if this job was right for me at all.

Jenna stared at me like she didn't know who I was. Her expression was full of horror and confusion. "Jesus Christ, Belle," Jenna gasped, drinking another mouthful of her wine and nodding toward my glass. "Drink up, I think you need it."

"I'm so sorry," I whined, the tears already building in my eyes as I took a long mouthful of wine. Only now it didn't taste nice; now it tasted like vinegar souring in my belly. I sniffled. "I can't explain it, honestly I can't. Working for him has been a crazy, crazy time and everything just got so mixed up, and then I slept with Lorenzo the night before and then Beast the following day and"—I looked up at her the tears flowing—"I swear I'm not *that* girl, Jenna. I don't do this sort of thing! I don't know what came over me, I just…" The tears were full-on flowing then, shame and guilt and just shock finally hitting me at what I had done.

Jenna came around and put her arms around me, because whether she thought what I'd done was the most awful thing or not, she loved me. Yet that only made me cry even harder.

"I leave you alone with that man for a few months and this is what happens," she mumbled.

"I have something else to tell you," I sobbed, and she pulled away to look at me sternly. It was time I told her everything. I couldn't deal with her sympathy while keeping something from her.

"Please tell me you're not pregnant, Belle!"

"No, no, I'm not," I replied quickly. But then I realized that Beast and I hadn't used protection, and neither had Lorenzo and I, so I could be, and if I was…I would have no idea who the father was. My sobs got louder until I was full-on choking on a sob and gasping for breath.

"Okay, okay, breathe, Belle, just breathe. We can sort this out, I promise, we can sort this out and it will be okay."

But I didn't believe her, and by the tone of her voice, she didn't believe herself either.

I pulled myself together, taking a deep breath so I could get my words out properly. I was making a mess of this already and I hadn't even gotten to the most awful part of why I'd actually come here.

"Jenna, I'm so sorry…" I started, and she frowned as she looked at me. "My mom got in touch," I said, looking up at her with tear-stained cheeks. Her expression hardened and I almost left it at that, but I'd started now so I needed to just rip the Band-Aid off and get it done quickly. "She's in prison, but she gets out in a couple of weeks and she needed a place to say."

"Please don't say what I think you're about to say, Belle," Jenna warned, taking a step back from me. I felt cold in her absence.

"I didn't know what to say," I cried.

"You say no!" she yelled, and if looks could kill I'd be dead.

"But she's my mom and she sounded desperate and—"

"No, Belle, she's not your mom. She gave up that right when she left you on my doorstep sixteen years ago and didn't even wait for me to answer the door!" She picked up her glass and downed the remaining contents of it before filling it back up again. She didn't top mine up and I didn't blame her one bit.

"I'm sorry, I didn't know what to say and then I didn't know how to tell you," I sniffled. "I swear I wanted to tell you though. Every day I wanted to speak to you about it, but I was so worried that I would hurt you that I just chickened out. I'm so sorry!"

"How long have you known?" Jenna asked, her tone hard.

I hesitated before answering. "A week," I lied, but when she cocked her head and narrowed her eyes I came clean. "Three weeks, almost four."

156

"Jesus, Belle," she mumbled. "You know she's using you, right?" I wondered how much she knew those words would hurt me as she said them.

"I'm not stupid," I said, and she raised an eyebrow at me. But I guess I deserved that one after the bombshells I'd just dropped.

I had messed everything up without even trying; surely I should get an award or something for that.

"If Doctor Collins finds out about you and Beast, then you could lose your job, Belle." She dragged a hand through her hair. "I probably could too. I'd be guilty by association, almost. He's an asshole, but he's still the one in charge."

Jenna paced the kitchen dragging her hands through her hair. She shook her head every time she glanced in my direction, like she couldn't believe what I had just told her. I waited, not sure what to say; there was no way to make any of it better, for her or me. I had well and truly messed everything up and there seemed only one way out of at least some of it.

"I'm going to quit the hospital," I said, my voice a whisper, like I couldn't quite believe that I was saying it myself. But I knew as soon as the words left my lips that it was the right thing to do. A weight lifted from my chest. "If I leave, then he can't fire me and my record will stay intact and your job will be safe too."

"Have you lost your damn mind?" she gasped. "And how will you pay for things? How will you pay your bills? For food? For gas?" She threw her hands up in the air.

"I've been saving the money the MC paid me. I was going to give it all to you since it was your job to start with. But I can live on that for a month or so while I find a new job." I nodded at myself as I spoke, a plan coming together.

"Belle, you can't just quit your job like that. It's irresponsible." She raised an eyebrow and tutted. "But then so was sleeping with a patient too, but that didn't stop you."

I looked into my lap, knowing I deserved that. But also knowing that now that I had said it out loud, I had a hundred percent made my mind up. This job had been taking over my life more and more, and if I was at least honest with myself I had to admit that I didn't really enjoy it. I did it for Jenna—to make her proud, because she'd always wanted me to work there. It had been her dream and not mine, but now, since I'd messed everything up, maybe it was time to find out what I wanted.

"I'll speak to Doctor Collins. I'll find out what he knows."

"Jenna…"

She shook her head at me. "We worked so damn hard to get you to where you are. Sacrificed so much. You are not going to throw it all away."

"Jenna," I said hesitantly. "I *want* to quit"—I looked back up at her—"this job." I shook my head. "It was always you and not me. I think it's time I find out what I want from my life."

"What?" Jenna stopped pacing the room and stared at me, her expression full of shock and anger and sadness, and I felt the crushing weight of each and every one of those feelings, the burden heavy on my heart.

We stared at one another in silence, the room swimming with heavy emotions.

"I think you should leave," she finally said. She took the glasses off the counter and took them to the sink to wash. She rinsed them under the hot water and placed them on the draining board before turning around and putting the wine away.

"Jenna," I began, but she was right. What was left for me to say? I'd told her about sleeping with a patient—a dangerous criminal, no less. About my mom getting in touch and her coming to stay with me, and now I was quitting my job—something I hadn't foreseen me saying, but knew was what I really wanted.

"I need you to leave, Belle. I need to think."

I nodded and slid off the stool before leaving. I wondered briefly if she would try to stop me. If she would call to me or get angry and then we could argue it out, but she never did. Jenna let me leave and I didn't blame her one bit. I'd tried so hard to please everyone and not hurt those I loved, but in the end I'd ended up hurting everyone.

Chapter Twenty-One
~ BEAST ~

The party was in full swing, the club heaving with brothers from all over the country. Everyone had come out to welcome me back home. Brothers and families from all over had taken the time out to come and see me. People I hadn't seen in years and people I'd ridden with every day before the attack...they were all there for me, yet I was sitting completely alone.

How did that work?

Being in a room full of people—friends and family—all of them celebrating me being alive and being home, yet I was completely alone. I'd been back a week and it had felt like this every single day and night. The sense of belonging I usually had there was gone, shattered into oblivion, and I didn't know why.

I looked around at all the familiar faces—people I'd grown up with, ridden with, killed with. And yet all I could think was I wished I was back in the hospital, waiting for Belle to come in and spoon-feed me pudding. It was the pathetic truth of the matter that I would never admit to anyone. I missed the familiarity of her scent as she washed my body, and the sounds from the machines next to my bed. I missed the rituals Belle and I had gotten into and the fights that usually accompanied our meetings. I didn't miss her though; prim little bitch that thought she was too good for me. No, fuck that; I just missed the familiarity of everything. This place, the clubhouse, felt foreign to me now.

It was a second home to me, and I'd always felt comfortable there, surrounded by those men and women, but right then all I could think about was going home—to my actual home. Because yeah, of course I fucking had more than just a room in a dilapidated clubhouse. I had a house with a white picket fence and three bedrooms, a bathroom, and even an overgrown garden with colorful flowers and shit in it. I just didn't go there very often.

A group of sweetbutts had been slowly making their way around the room, servicing brothers and being the eye candy for the party. I'd seen Lola with them all, and every once in a while she'd look over at me and whisper to the little skanks she was with and then they'd all laugh between themselves. I wanted to shoot every fucking one of them, but decided to make a point of showing her that what had happened at the hospital was a one-time thing. I'd fuck her till she was bowlegged and then kick her skinny ass out of the club for good.

The more I watched her, the angrier I became. Her face mocking me from across the room. Laughing at me. My dick shriveled up in my jeans, refusing to come out no matter how many dirty thoughts I tried to think of to get it hard.

Lola had killed my dick—she was a dick killer. Fuck.

"You doin' okay, brother?" asked Battle, one of the nomads, sitting down next to me.

He and Fighter, another nomad, had traveled across the country to come visit me at the hospital and were surprised that I was actually out. We'd ridden together a few years back, did a couple of hits on some fucks who had sticky fingers and thought they could make a mockery of the club name. We'd put them to ground and pissed on their graves afterwards before going out and getting so drunk we'd woken up naked in a different state. Loved those guys. They were as sick and as dark as I was.

He gestured over to Fighter, who made quick work of grabbing three bottles of beer before heading over to us.

"I'm alive, right?" I replied, taking a bottle from Fighter.

He sat down opposite, his cold eyes and hard expression on me as he nodded. I took a swig of beer, savoring the taste of it as it slid down my parched throat.

I was tired.

Bone fucking tired.

I'd barely slept since I'd been back, each night waking up to the stamping of hooves on the floor and the smell of fire in the air. The sizzle and pop of my hair and flesh melting away… The nightmares had

161

eased off for a few months, but they were back with a vengeance since being back home.

"Don't mean a whole lot though, does it? Being alive. Take a whole lot more to kill you, brother, but that don't mean you're alive where it matters," Battle replied, taking a swig of his beer.

"Jesus, you're like the Dalai Lama or some shit. Calm yourself, brother, I'm doing just fine," I grumbled.

He snickered and popped the top off his beer, and I took another long pull from my own bottle. I shouldn't really have been drinking, but it'd been too long since I'd tasted beer or whiskey and I'd been making up for all the lost alcohol while I was in hospital. Besides, it was my party after all. Last night, and the night before that, and the night before that…well, that was just catching up.

"Heard you had a thing with your nurse. She not here tonight?" he continued.

Belle.

Motherfucking Belle.

The memory of her was stalking me, haunting my every move.

I gritted my teeth at the thought of her, anger sparking to life inside of me. Hadn't heard a damn thing since she'd walked off with that Lorenzo guy. Bitch hadn't even thought to check on me. Like, she'd had my money and her job was done now.

"Fucked her, doesn't mean there was anything else in it," I drolled, my gaze moving around the room again until it landed on Lola once more. My dick *still* refused to cooperate and she was *still* whispering between her friends and looking over. I was going to kill her if she kept that shit up.

Battle grinned. "That's the Beast we know. Heard word that you were going soft on us, but it seems they were mistaken."

My gaze flicked back to Battle and fury rose up in me like a phoenix from the ashes, the spark turning to a flame. I slammed my beer down on the wooden table in front of me and glared at him, watching as his expression changed from amusement to confusion before hardening.

"What the fuck did you just say to me?" I bit out.

162

"Calm down, brother," he scowled, sensing my darkening mood. "What's got into you?"

Battle and I were evenly matched in weight and strength and we both had a dark side that made us perfect for the jobs we had. I wasn't sure who would win in a fight between us both under normal circumstances, but right now, it was obvious he'd be able to take me out with one punch. Not to mention he had Fighter on side, and Fighter was one man I'd never wanted to mess with. Fucker had a heart as black and shriveled as the Devil's, and then some. Yet I still couldn't taper down my anger.

Had Lola been talking? Spreading shit around the club about me? Bitch like her walking around and mouthing off about my useless fucking dick and my repulsive fucking body.

I stood up, fury driving me onward. "I said, *what the fuck did you just say to me*? Who've you been talking to?" I yelled, causing the room to fall silent and turn toward the commotion.

I could hear Lola laughing.

Her little high-pitched cackle at my flaccid dick.

Her heels tottering over the hard floor of the clubhouse as she walked away from me.

Sickness rose up in me and dizziness began to blur my vision.

"I haven't been talking to anyone," Battle tried to placate me, but I was already too far gone. "Drink your beer and chill out."

"Brother, sit down," Fighter growled, always by Battle's side.

Fighter… Fuck, now he was one scary motherfucker, even to a man like me. You wanted him onside, and not any other way, because for him, there were no limits to who he'd cut down and how he'd do it.

I took a long breath and glared at him, staring into his cold, dead eyes, and he must have seen something inside me because he stood up, beer still in hand.

"I suggest you take a seat," he said calmly, before drinking the entire bottle of beer in one swig and slamming it down on the table.

Lola was still laughing.

The room of people were still watching.

All of 'em, staring at the beast that I had become. Burned to fuck, cut up, shredded, diced… every inch represented the evil within me. Fuck Belle, I didn't have soulful eyes or a rugged neck, my tattoos didn't look tribal and I certainly wasn't fucking strong anymore. I was a flaccid-dicked, torn-up, ugly bastard who'd put more men in the ground than all of these fuckers put together. She thought there was good in me, but she was wrong. I wasn't just going to hell when I died, I was going to lord over it and put the Devil to shame.

I shoved Fighter hard in the chest and he stumbled back a step. "I suggest you watch your tone with me," I snarled in response, fury burning through my unused muscles. "Remember who you're talking to."

"Beast!" Prez shouted my name across the room before storming toward me. "The fuck are you doing, brother?"

I was still eyeballing Fighter, who looked unfazed by my warning. He didn't scare easily—or at all. It was one of the reasons we got along so well, and yet right then I needed him to either lay me on my ass or back the hell down, because my vanity needed it. But this was Fighter and he did neither. He just stood and waited for me to make my move.

"Fighter, I've got this," Battle said, trying to calm the situation.

I shook my head, still glaring at Fighter. "Nah, brother, you don't got this. This motherfucker has come into my clubhouse and disrespected me for the last time," I ground out.

"I won't tell you again," Fighter drolled, hands in his pockets like he was talking to his mama and not a lion that had just been released from its cage. "Sit the fuck down, brother."

Gauge had come over at some point, and he placed a hand on my shoulder. Pain throbbed under his grip and the ache began to loosen the threads of insanity that were gripping me.

"Beast, this ain't right. These are your brothers, you know that. We've all got your back," Gauge tried to placate.

Shooter had reached us, and he must have realized right away that there was no calming this situation. That neither Fighter or I were about to back down anytime soon. He pulled out his gun, released the safety, and aimed it at the ceiling before letting off a single shot. Women screamed and dust rained down, but neither Fighter nor I flinched or looked away.

"I will shoot *both* of you motherfuckers if you don't step down," he ordered.

"This ends now," Shooter roared. "I'm your president and neither of you motherfuckers will disrespect *me* in *my* Goddamn clubhouse, now back the fuck down!" he ordered.

I finally took a breath, the air scorching my lungs, and nodded, and Fighter did the same, though we were still toe to toe. Lola was still laughing, the sound grating through my mind, and I shrugged out from under Gauge's grip, and before I could think it through I was storming across the clubhouse, ignoring the protests from Shooter and Gauge from behind me and heading toward her. Her eyes went wide as I got closer, and I pulled out my gun and placed the barrel against her forehead. She began to cry immediately, and the group of women she was with screamed at the sight of the gun so close to them, before backing away.

"You laughin' at me, bitch?" I growled, and she shook her head, tears flooding her cheeks.

I couldn't hear anything but the beating of my own heart. I was trapped in my own bubble, oblivious to everyone and everything around me.

"I'm not, Beast, I'm not!" she pleaded, hands raised.

I pressed the barrel harder into her head, more than ready to squeeze the trigger and blow her brains all over the wall. Teach all of these bitches not to laugh at me ever again.

"Beast, you don't want to do this." Casa's voice cut through the darkness, a gentle warning. "Come on, brother. Let's go get your dick sucked and give you a bump and all will be right in the world again."

Lola was full-on sobbing, black makeup smeared down her face. Pretty sure I smelled piss on her now too.

"Come on, brother," Casa said from next to me. "She's just a sweetbutt, you don't wanna do this."

But I did. I wanted to shoot her.

No...I wanted to shoot someone, anyone.

Casa put a hand on my shoulder. "Come on, brother."

I slowly pulled my gun away from her head, noting the circle from the barrel imprinted on her skin, and she sagged in relief but stayed frozen to the spot, her hands raised at her chest like she could stop the bullet from penetrating her.

Casa reached over and took the gun from my hand, and Lola used the moment to make a run for the door, heading out before anyone could stop her. Pretty sure she wouldn't be back around for a while, if she knew what was good for her.

"Easy, brother," he soothed. "Chill out, okay?"

I turned back to the room, noting the stares and the judgment from them all. They all thought I'd lost it, that I was done. And maybe they were right. I might have been back at the clubhouse and out of that godforsaken hospital. I might have been alive after fighting off death, but I'd never left that barn alive.

In my head, I was still trapped inside, and the horses were still screaming at me and I was still dying.

I was still burning.

I was still bleeding and broken.

Cut up, sliced and diced...and the cameras were still rolling.

Filming every inch of my misery. My death. Echo's death.

Clutching my hands to my head, I groaned. My breaths were coming out ragged like I was breathing poison, and every breath was setting my insides on fire. I was inhaling the smoke and the flames, the black stench of death curling inside me like a pit of vipers in my stomach, waiting to strike.

I didn't know I was dropping to my knees until they hit the hard ground with a heavy slam that ricocheted through my body. Didn't know I was calling out until my throat burned from the exertion. Didn't know I was passing out until the world went black and took me with it.

Chapter Twenty-Two
~ Belle ~

The thumping on my trailer door woke me from my sleep. It took a moment for me to grasp what was happening as I lay on my back and stared up at the dark ceiling, the perspiration hot on my face and neck. The trailer was like an oven and I was boiling alive inside, nicely marinated by tequila. The thumping came again and I rubbed at my eyes and sat up, grabbing the clock from my bedside cabinet to read the time.

"Three a.m.?" I groaned. Who the hell could that be at three a.m.?

After leaving Jenna's, I'd gone and gotten a bottle of tequila before coming back home and finishing most of it off. Now I felt sick to my stomach, still slightly drunk, and my mouth tasted like feet. I vaguely remembered demolishing a huge bag of Cheetos by myself too and my stomach roiled.

That would explain the feet taste.

The thumping came again, so loud the whole trailer shook, and I slid out of bed and stumbled out of my room and into the kitchen diner before heading toward the door. I hoped it wasn't Jenna because the place was a mess and no doubt she'd call me out for living like such a pig. But then why would Jenna turn up here at three a.m.? She wouldn't. She wouldn't... She wanted nothing more to do with me. Sadness gripped me and I swayed on my feet, wishing I could drink the last of the tequila and fall back to sleep, but the last remnants of sleep slunk away as I reached the door and hesitated. Who would be thumping on my door at three a.m.? The sound came again, the knocking so hard that the door rattled, and I whimpered as I realized that this might be it.

This might be the people sent to kill me.

Do killers knock?

Was this it now?

Was I about to die?

I looked around my shitty trailer—my home, my nothing. I'd achieved nothing in my short life. I was working a job I didn't like. I had no family. No friends. I looked over at my dead cactus on the windowsill—I couldn't even keep a cactus alive. Maybe this was for the best.

Tears filled my eyes at the thought of dying, and yet it was such sweet relief too—to know that it was over. That I didn't have to do this anymore. That I didn't have to pretend to be strong.

The knocking came again.

Was I ready to say goodbye to the world?

There was so much I hadn't done.

So much that I wanted to do. Places I wanted to go.

I hoped that people would remember the good about me when I was gone.

Taking a deep breath, I opened the door. Headlights filled the doorway and I was momentarily blind as the dark night evaporated into brightness. I held a hand up to my eyes to shield them, but it was still too bright so I closed them and said a silent prayer. I'd rather not see who killed me anyway.

"Belle." A deep voice said my name and I sobbed at the sound on his lips. "Belle, look at me… Turn those fucking lights down, brother! Belle!"

The lights dipped but I still didn't open my eyes. I didn't want to see. I didn't want to know. I just wanted it to be over with. Life was hard and I was soft. Too soft for it. I just went around hurting people.

"What the fuck is wrong with her?" Another voice, even deeper than the first.

"Is she fuckin' sleepwalkin'?" Another voice, sounding slightly hyper. "You can't wake her if she is, brother. You can give her a heart attack or some shit if you wake someone when they're sleepwalkin'."

"So what do I do?" the gravelly voice closest to me said.

I was tempted to look.

Tempted to see the faces of my killers.

"Just pick her up and bring her with us," the deeper voice said.

169

"And how is she supposed to stay on the bike, motherfucker? Bitch will just slide right off the seat. Maybe we could use a belt."

"A belt?"

"Yeah!" the hyper voice said. "You ever seen the mark from a belt to the ass? It's fucking beautiful."

"Will you shut the fuck up!"

"Yeah, you know, like wrap it around your waist and then around hers to keep her on it." A deeper voice now.

"Oh, oh, she might even think she's ridin' the bike in her sleep and just hold on automatically!" the hyper voice said, sounding even more hyper at his awful idea.

"I don't think that'll work…"

"Oh, so you're a sleep expert now are you?"

"And you are?.."

"Well, not to brag or anything, fuckface, but my grandma, she put me in for this sleep program when I was a teenager because I was like just *on* all the fuckin' time and wasn't sleepin' 'cause my mind was going constantly like a set of drums in my brain, a million thoughts an hour, da da dum, da da dum, da da dum…"

"And what did they find out? That you're a moron?" the deeper voice asked.

"Nah, motherfucker! They said I was taking too many drugs!" He broke into raucous laughter. "Fuckin' grandma kicked my ass when she got the results through."

"Can we get back to the problem at hand?"

"You got beat up by an old lady?" the deeper voice asked, amusement in his tone.

"Hey, you ever been hit with a walkin' stick? That shit fuckin' hurts worse than being kicked in the balls!"

I was confused as hell as to what was happening. Why weren't they just killing me? Why did they want to take me somewhere? Oh my god, were they going to torture me and then kill me? My knees trembled as I opened my eyes, my fear taking flight. I was ready to run back inside and lock the door. I could call the cops and hope they got there in time before they broke in, maybe.

"I'm not asleep," I said as I stared into the handsome face of Shooter.

He was rugged, his jaw hard and defined, his hair long around his shoulders. Lines appeared around his deep blue eyes as he scowled.

"Make it quick," I begged on a whisper.

He scowled harder and I realized both the other voices had stopped. Shooter held me captive in his gaze to the point that I couldn't break away to look somewhere else.

"Did she say make it quick?" the hyper voice from behind said on a laugh. "Ain't no woman ever said that to me before. It's normally take it slow, make it last, fuck me good." He laughed again.

"I'ma kill you if you don't shut the fuck up, Casa," the deeper voice sounded out, and I realized that was Gauge.

"I'm just sayin', maybe Beast didn't do as good a job on her as he thought. She's askin' for it to be quick an all."

"What's going on with you?" Shooter asked, his tone faking concern. He reached for me and I began to cry. "Jesus, Belle, what happened? Are you okay?"

"We're fucked," Gauge said, and I saw the flash of a lighter as he lit a cigar.

"Has someone hurt you?" Shooter asked, his scowl deepening, but all that did was make me cry harder. "Tell me," he ordered.

I sagged against the door, confused, scared, and lonely. I was going to die alone, and no one would care. Not my mom, not my godmother, no one. I cried harder.

"This is your fault," Gauge said, punching Casa in the arm.

"Why the fuck is it my fault?" he asked, punching Gauge back.

"Because you were talking about sex with Beast."

Casa laughed even harder and then Gauge joined in, but Shooter, he just stood there putting the pieces together and filling in the blanks, his calm exterior slowly soothing me.

"We're not here to kill you, Belle," he finally said.

171

"You're not?"

He shook his head. "Fuck no. Why would we kill you? We need your help."

I cried even harder at that. I was so confused, still slightly drunk, and still absolutely terrified. I thought I could stare death in the face and tell it I didn't care, but I couldn't. I couldn't even do this right. I was utterly useless.

"Jesus, this is why I don't have an old lady. Fucking women are too emotional for my liking."

"Yeah, that's the reason you're single," Casa snorted on a laugh.

"Fuck off, it's true. You ever been around Laney when it's her time of the month? That bitch is crazy! I don't want a lifetime of shit like that. Fuck that," Gauge growled.

"Laney is a psychopath when it comes to you no matter what the time of the month it is," Casa retorted.

"Ain't that the fucking truth."

"Can you two shut the fuck up," Shooter's voice boomed as he turned to glare at them. "Can't hear myself think because of all your bullshit going on behind me. Now shut up before I shut you the fuck up."

"Sorry," Casa said, sounding insincere.

"And remember that may be your kid, Gauge, but that's my old lady and you'd do well to remember that," Shooter growled. He turned back to me. "Gonna need you to come with me, Belle."

My crying had all but stopped as I'd listened to Gauge and Casa talk, so I took a shaky breath and nodded. "Okay, I'll go get some clothes on." I swiped at my cheeks to get rid of the tears. I was so tired of this world. So confused with these people. And so damn lost that I'd do anything at the moment.

"No time, just grab a jacket. I need you to come now," he ordered, reaching out to take my hand.

I snatched my arm back from his grip. "Will you at least tell me where you're taking me?"

"It's Beast, he needs you," he replied, like it was the most obvious thing in the world.

Beast…needed me… I reached out and took Shooter's hand, closing my door on the way out.

This was a bad idea, and yet I had to make sure he was okay, regardless.

Chapter Twenty-Three
~ BEAST ~

I woke to the sound of silence.
Silence and pain.
My whole body ached and shook.

My insides felt like they were trying to get outside, and my outsides felt like they were trying to get inside. I was trembling from head to toe, my teeth knocking together and my hands curled up into fists.

I was lying on my back in my room at the clubhouse in so much pain I couldn't even speak to ask for help. If I had my gun then I'd have shot myself in the head just to end it.

I'd been in this amount of pain once before.

I'd barely lived through it.

I wouldn't survive it twice.

My eyes were closed, but a noise across the room had me opening them so I could beg for help. Beg for pain relief. Beg for a gun, if need be. But when I opened my eyes and looked across, each movement in my muscles feeling like razor blades, I didn't see any of my brothers there; instead I saw Belle.

She was curled up in my big armchair in the corner, her arms inside one of my favorite leather jackets. Her long dark hair was tied back from her face so I could see every angle of her face. She looked sad as hell, pale as shit, and she kept whimpering in her sleep. A bucket was next to her on the floor, and if I hadn't been in so much pain, if every muscle twitch hadn't made me feel like I was on fire, then I would have frowned, because I was confused as hell.

I didn't for one minute think I was going to heaven after the crimes I'd committed. Lord knew there was only one place I was going when I died, and it was a one-way ticket to somewhere hot, but for a moment—just one brief moment—I thought I might have been in heaven.

Why else would she be there?

I wanted to say her name and wake her up, to beg for her to help me because I needed something to make all of the pain stop. But instead, I watched her sleep, wishing that I could hold her in my arms and take that sad look off her face.

Sweat poured from me, and my body shook harder.

Moments ticked by and I felt myself going dizzy, my mind fazing in and out. But every time I opened my eyes, she was there. Sleeping. Keeping me company while I slowly died.

*

I woke to the sound of humming.

It was annoying as fuck.

Like a fly buzzing around your face that you couldn't quite catch, it buzzed into my mind while I slept, and just as I thought I remembered what song it was, it stopped.

I decided, if and when I woke up, I was going to smack the shit out of whoever was humming. They sounded happy, and happiness had no place in my room. Not in my clubhouse. Not in my world. Not in my heaven or hell.

Happiness was the epitome of lies.

Happiness only existed to show us what we should feel. How things could be. And exactly what you were never going to have.

Even other people's happiness was fake.

All of us were wearing our smiles like crowns, trying to prove to the person in the mirror that everything was going to be okay. That the life we were living was in fact worth living. It was all lies, and nothing but trickery from the Devil.

Happiness didn't exist.

*

Cold.
I was so cold.

I wondered briefly why someone had thought to take all my clothes away. It wasn't like there was much to see beneath the heavy folds of material anymore. Just a busted-down, burnt-up, torn-to-shit body. Even my muscles had wasted away. I looked like a ninety-year-old man and I felt like one too.

So why take my clothes?

And my covers.

And all the heat from the room.

Why make me freeze? Was it just another form of torture? Was it just another punishment from the Devil? Another way of making me suffer…

Was I dead now?

Could I finally rest?

I blinked, watching as Belle slept. She was in a different position now and her hair was tied in a knot on the top of her head. She still looked sad though.

*

Hot.

So hot I wasn't sure why my bones hadn't turned to molten lava, liquefying and dripping onto the floor. I felt like maybe I already had. Like I was a volcano and I had finally erupted. All the months of anger and hate had finally spewed out of me until all I was was melted bones and ash clouds.

The humming was back, but this time I recognized the song because it was accompanied by it playing on the radio or something similar. It was a song by Michael Kiwanuka called "Love & Hate." I recognized it right away, and through the ebb and flow of the blood running through my veins and the pounding in my head, I remembered where I had first heard it. The memory wasn't a good one, and it was one I'd tried to keep buried. Not because I was ashamed, but because I didn't want to remember that part of my life.

It was a long time ago, just after I'd patched in with the club and I was just a smartass looking for a place to fit in in the world. I'd finally found my people—my family. I'd never belonged before. I'd never had a place that was mine or that I could call home. A place that made me feel safe. Until I'd found the Devil's Highwaymen it had just been me against the world.

After I'd patched in with them, everything made sense in my life, but I still felt empty inside. One day I'd walked into a bar and that song had been playing in the background. I'd drunk my beer in silence, letting the song wash over me and thinking about where I was going to ride to next.

I'd saved up and gotten my first bike a couple a months earlier, and I'd been traveling up and down the country for the past week or so doing jobs for my president, Rider. For the first time in a long time, maybe in forever, I was happy. Or something similar to it. I'd just wanted to ride and see where the road took me. I'd never felt so free and so blessed in all my life.

And then I'd seen her—my mom. She looked almost the same, barring she'd aged to look almost ninety.

She recognized me right away, despite the fact that I'd filled out and grown taller. Tattoos ran up and down my arms and across my neck, and my long hair was loose around my shoulders. I was a man now, not the little boy that had run away from home, but she still knew it was me. She was drunk, as usual, and she stumbled over, hazy eyes pinned on me, skinny arms reaching until she gripped the muscles on my forearm, her eyes widening in appreciation.

"Son," she'd slurred, a drunken smile on her wretched face, "where've you been? I've been waiting for you."

Waiting for me?

I almost laughed in her face.

That bitch hadn't been waiting for me. Not once, not ever.

That bitch had left me.

Continuously.

She'd abandoned me every night. Locking me in our shitty apartment with no food and no heating, so she could go and get drunk. The last time I'd seen her I was twelve, and I'd managed to break a window and crawl down the fire escape after being locked inside for

177

five days with nothing to eat. I was hungry, dizzy, cold as shit, and lonely as fuck.

I'd gone in search of her, out of my mind with worry that she might actually be dead that time. Instead of finding her dead, I'd found her drunk and on her knees, sucking off a guy behind his car for twenty bucks.

That was the day I left.

I'd lived on the streets until I was old enough to get a job and rent a place to call my own. But it wasn't a home. It was a room with walls, a floor, and a ceiling. But it wasn't a *home.*

Now she draped an arm around me and placed her head on my shoulder, the stench of alcohol coming from her and making me nauseous. "I've missed you, little man," she slurred, like fifteen years hadn't passed and I was still her little boy, desperate for her to love me.

I shrugged her off me and she stumbled back, her sloppy smile slipping from her mouth.

"Not your little man," I growled.

"Son," she whimpered, sadness engulfing her features.

"Not your son," I snarled. I threw some money on the counter, watching how her eyes hovered over the crumpled bills in eagerness. Leaving the rest of my beer, I turned and left the bar before I lost my shit and did something I regretted.

Outside I was about to climb back on my bike, anger, resentment, and hate burning through me and more than ready to leave that town and never come back, when she called my name. Hadn't heard my name on her lips for so long I felt a stabbing in my heart.

I hated her.

I despised her.

I pitied her.

"Please, Jacob, don't be like that. I'm your momma. I've missed you," she slurred, stumbling toward me in her too-short skirt and high heels. She looked disgusting, like a crack whore with no soul, and my hate for her increased.

She missed me…

178

The words rattled around inside my empty heart.

I straddled my bike, watching how her eyes lit up at the sight of it, and I knew right away what she was thinking. She thought I had money. She thought I'd had it easy, that maybe I'd landed on my feet. She saw me as a way to fund her pathetic existence.

What she didn't see was the devil I'd become.

She stood next to me, a hand on my shoulder. "I've missed you, Jacob, come back home and let me cook you something to eat."

I turned to glare. "Get the fuck away from me."

Her eyes narrowed, the soft look on her face turning to anger. I remembered that look too well, and I knew what came afterwards. But I wasn't a little boy anymore. I wasn't there to take her beatings. I wasn't there to be punished for her shitty life and bad choices. I was a man now and I hadn't had a mother for a long time. Maybe not ever.

Her hand reared back and she slapped me across my cheek as hard as she could, which wasn't hard in the least. Years of drinking had wasted her muscles away to nothing. I was more than three times her size and not afraid of her—or anything—anymore. She'd hardened me to the world, to life. It was the only thing I had to thank her for.

I reached into my jacket and pulled out my gun, pressing the barrel to her forehead. She squealed in fear but had the good sense not to move. I pressed it harder, enjoying how the skin puckered around the barrel.

"I said, get the fuck away from me," I growled.

Her eyes were wide, filled with fear, sadness and guilt. "I'm sorry," she whimpered, and that was the last thing I wanted to hear. Her apology meant nothing to me. It didn't excuse the starvation or the beatings or the nights when she brought men home and they'd had their fill of her but weren't sated so she allowed them into my room.

It didn't excuse any of it.

Nothing ever would.

"I love you, son," she slurred sadly, and if I'd had a heart it would have shattered. As it were, my heart was a dead, hollow thing in my chest already. "You're still my little boy."

179

Even after all the years since, whenever I thought back to that moment in time, I still couldn't remember the exact point in which I decided to pull the trigger. I don't remember anything but riding away from her and not looking back. I remembered the feel of the trigger under my finger and the sound of her body hitting the ground, but nothing more.

But as the humming of the song filled the room, I finally remembered her body on the ground and I saw the life drain from my mother's eyes. I watched the light go out and I breathed a sigh of relief.

Twenty-Four
~ BEAST ~

How's he doing?" Shooter said, waking me from my dark dreams, but he wasn't talking to me. He was talking to someone else in the room.

I was still groggy. Still waking up from whatever dark memories my mind had brought forth and decided was a good time to show me—now, of all times. Stupid mind was as useless as my stupid body.

"Better," *her* voice replied, cutting through my woozy thoughts. "I think he's through the worst of it."

I sighed internally.

Belle.

Things must have been real bad if Shooter had brought her here.

And they must have been really bad for her to agree to come here at all.

"Need you to stick around for a couple more days, make sure he's definitely on the other side of this, Belle."

It was her turn to sigh now. "I have a life, Shooter. I can't just put it all on hold and stay here. I don't even have a change of clothes, and I'm pretty sure the toothbrush you gave me wasn't new like you promised."

"I'll get you some clothes," he replied calmly. "And another toothbrush. And of course you'll be paid well and compensated."

"It's not about the clothes and the money, and you know that. I have to get back to my life. I've been here for four days now. I need to go home," she whined, and the sleepiness fell from me as my irritation clawed its way up my throat.

Four days I'd been out, and all she cared about was going back home to her man?

"He could have died, Belle," Shooter growled in annoyance, all softness falling away from him.

"I know, and I got him through it, didn't I? But I have a family and a life I have to get back to," she retorted.

"That's my brother, my enforcer, and a valued member of *my* family. You're staying and you're keeping him alive until I say so. You feel me?"

She fell silent, hearing the warning in Shooter's tone.

"I'm not dead yet," I grumbled, my words coming out throaty and cracked as I broke the silence. Probably not a moment too soon, knowing Belle, because if there was one thing I'd learned from being around her so much, it was that there was only so much shit she'd take from a man before she came out fighting. And Shooter was backing her into a corner that she didn't want to be in.

I opened my eyes, seeing Shooter and Belle looking down on me, their tired expressions mirroring each other.

"Jesus Christ, you look like you've seen a ghost," I complained, embarrassed by their staring. But if how I looked was even half as bad as how I was feeling, then they had a good reason to be staring at me like that.

My head throbbed, my body ached, my muscles were contracting and protesting, desperate to move and stretch. My stomach felt empty to the point of hollowness and it roared in hunger, breaking the uneasy silence. What had she said? I'd been out for four days? God, I'd kill for some chocolate pudding.

"Where's Doctor Collins?" I asked, eyeing Belle, who shifted her gaze from me.

Shooter chuckled. "That fuck wouldn't come near the place, not even when we threatened his family."

"He don't have any family. Just a string of women who he fucks for money," I replied.

"Yeah, figured that out real quick."

"You threaten his credibility?" I asked seriously, because that was the route I would have gone down with someone if they didn't have family.

Shooter chuckled again. "Yeah. He took off after that and no one has seen him since."

My throat was hurting, and Belle must have sensed it because she reached for a glass of water on the small side table next to my bed. It had a small straw in it and she brought it to my lips. I sucked greedily, my gaze on her the entire time, but no matter how much I stared, she wouldn't look at me. Her gaze was on the water, the straw, her hands, even the wall. But never on me. She finally pulled the straw away even though I wasn't done.

"You'll be sick if you have too much," she explained as I protested.

I turned my attention back to Shooter. "So, no idea where he's gone then?"

He shrugged. "Last we heard, he boarded a flight to Bali or some shit."

"So he cut and run rather than fix me up?" I sighed. "I'm offended."

We both laughed at that, and I watched Belle look confused as hell before turning away to busy herself with something in the corner.

Shooter, ever the thoughtful man, dragged a hand down his beard, turning the mood somber. "Thought you were gone for sure, brother," he said. "Thought we'd lost you."

"Take more than whatever that was to kill me off," I replied.

The world had been blurry in my damaged eye since I'd woken up, but things got even worse, to the point I could barely see. I blinked repeatedly to try to clear it, but it wasn't going anywhere and it had shifted to both eyes now.

"Why's he doin' that?" Shooter asked with worry, looking over at Belle.

My blurry gaze moved to her. Her expression was soft, as usual, but there was something else there too: a sadness I was growing to know so well.

"What's she even doin' here?" I asked, hating the way I'd spat those words out. Hadn't meant them to sound so hateful, but they were out now and she looked away, embarrassed.

"*She* saved your life," Shooter replied. "Now have some fucking respect."

I let out a heavy breath, not used to being spoken to like that. Not happy about it either, but Shooter was my prez, and if she'd saved my life then I surmised he was right. "Guess I should thank you then."

Her mouth pouted and she shook her head. "It's fine. I didn't exactly have a choice anyway."

She turned away, moving out of my line of sight, and Shooter glared at me, giving a small shake of his head.

I was still blinking repeatedly, and when I lifted my arms to rub at my eyes I found that my arms felt too heavy, like someone had filled my bones with lead and chained them to the bed. I could feel tears sliding down the side of my face from the repeated blinking, and I hated that I was beginning to panic. Something wasn't right. I couldn't see properly and the edges of my vision were turning darker. My body was heavy and it felt like I was sinking beneath the ocean.

"Belle?" Shooter growled. "What the fuck is happening?"

She leaned over me, her sweet flower smell mixed with the leather from my leather jacket she was wearing making everything in my body come alive. If I would have been stronger I wouldn't have been able to hold back from grabbing her and throwing her down on my bed before taking her body. She held a little light up to my eyes, flashing it quickly in one eye and then the next before pouting.

"Just needs drops," she mumbled, retrieving a small bottle from her pocket and holding my eye open while she dripped it in. I was about to tell her to back the fuck off when the world started to clear and her face transformed from blurry to perfect in front of my hazy gaze. "Is that better? she asked, her warm breath washing over me, the panic in me subsiding.

I wanted to stay like that for longer—her leaning over me, our bodies close together and our scents entwined. If I would have had any

184

strength I would have reached out and cupped her face in my hand and pulled her mouth to mine.

"Beast." She said my name, a look of worry washing through her features. "Is that better? Can you see me?" She peered into my face, her head lowering so we were even closer. Every breath of hers I inhaled, I felt cleaner, purer. Like her air was just better than any air in the world. It filled my lungs and purified them. Tasted better too. Kinda like the sweetest pie. I wanted her. Wanted her so bad that it made the pain coming from every muscle in my body pale in comparison.

But she wasn't mine.

I swallowed.

She'd chosen him.

I grunted a yes and she stood back up, moving away from me.

"We've been through hell and back, brother," Shooter said to me, oblivious to my turmoil.

"It's clearly been a walk in the park for me," I bit out, shifting my gaze back to my prez.

"What, just lying there trying not to die?" he retorted darkly. "I haven't slept in four days, brother. Haven't screwed my wife in that time or even touched a drop of beer."

"Awww, you been holding my hand while I slept, Prez?" I grinned. Or tried to. The muscles in my face seemed stiff and unused. In fact, my whole body felt like that. Everything ached and felt weak, like my muscles had been stripped away from my bones.

"You fuckin' wish!" he chuckled before his expression turned serious again. "No more drugs. No more beer. No more doing nothing until you're properly healed this time."

"Yeah yeah," I grumbled.

"I'm serious!" he said, leaning down over me. "You almost died. Almost killed a sweetbutt and started a fight with two of the craziest motherfuckers in the Highwaymen too, but that's to discuss another day." He sighed and stood back up, dragging a hand down his beard. "For now you lie there, you take your meds, you rest, and you do as you're goddamned told, you hear me? Because that's a fucking order."

185

Anyone else would have had their ass handed to them on a silver platter for talking to me like that, but he was my prez and I also had vague memories of putting a gun to the sweetbutt's head and arguing with Battle and Fighter. Wasn't scared of either of those men, but they were my brothers—they were Highwaymen—and that was just wrong.

Besides, in all honesty, at the moment all I could think about doing was sleeping anyway.

"Sure, Prez, whatever makes your dick hard," I grunted.

He shook his head. "My wife makes my dick hard, and that's where I'm going now. I expect to find you still in this bed when I get back." He took my hand in his, and I was about to call him out on being such a pussy but I saw the worry lines on his face and knew that shit must have been serious. Especially if he'd brought Belle there to take care of me. Knowing who her boyfriend was had to have made that decision a whole lot harder for him.

Shooter glanced over to the corner of the room to Belle, who was now fucking around with some equipment I was attached to. It was like being back in the hospital, but in the comfort of my own room and minus the connection we'd had previously. Whatever had been there was gone now, and all I felt from her was a coldness.

Shooter jerked his head toward the hallway when she looked his way, and she nodded and put down whatever it was she had been doing.

"No drugs, no alcohol, Beast." He turned and headed out the door and Belle followed him out.

She was dressed in tiny bed shorts and my leather jacket and my dick twitched at the sight of her. God, what I would have done to see her dressed like that every single day. Wearing my jacket and being in my bed. The smell of leather surrounding us both, her hair soft on my chest, her long legs wrapped around mine.

Fuck, what was wrong with me? I was turning into some kind of... well, whatever it was was stopping now. Belle chose *him*...our enemy. Besides, I didn't come second for anyone. I was putting what we'd shared down to a pity fuck, for both of us, and that's all it was. She'd pitied me and my fucked-up body, and I'd pitied her and her pathetic existence. And that was fine by me. It had gotten things working for me again. My dick was well and truly alive once more, and I was raring for a woman to sit on it. Any woman other than Belle.

Because Belle…she was nothing but a memory now.

Chapter Twenty-Five
~ Belle ~

Shooter had asked Joey, the prospect I'd become friends with at the hospital, to bring me home so I could get some of my stuff. He was adamant about me staying at the clubhouse until Beast was well and truly in the clear. I couldn't really blame him; Beast had undone all his hard work at the hospital in a matter of days. The drugs, the drink, the adrenaline…it had all sent his body into shock. It couldn't fight him as well as itself, so something had had to give.

Joey hadn't said more than three words to me the entire time, and I couldn't help but be hurt by his cold shoulder toward me. I thought we'd become close, but I'd obviously done something to annoy him. I decided to not overthink it and just add it to the train wreck that was my life.

I got undressed and climbed into my small shower, washing the stench of the clubhouse from my body. I hated that place. Every single part of it. The smell, which was a combination of alcohol, oil, and sex. The people, who were all bossy, overbearing, and aggressive. And everything it stood for…violence, crime, and family. I hadn't heard or seen from anyone since Shooter had practically thrown me into a van and taken me there four days earlier to care for Beast since Doctor Collins had hightailed it to Bali.

Bali, of all places!

I hated him most of all.

Because he had the money to escape.

I scrubbed until my skin turned red and sore. Until I wasn't sure what I was washing off my body anymore. Was it the clubhouse, my guilt, or was it my desire for Beast? I was losing my sense of right and wrong the longer I was around him. I no longer knew who I was and everything I had once had was now gone.

Jenna.

My career.

My sense of worth.

He'd taken it all with one touch of his calloused hands on my traitorous body.

I squeezed my eyes closed, trying hard not to cry. It was pitiful, and I knew I was blaming the wrong person, really. This wasn't him, this was me. I had let him do this. I had stepped over to the darkness to be with him without thinking it through. We were two different people from two different worlds, and we could never have worked.

The tears came hot and heavy until I was clutching a hand to my chest and practically hyperventilating. But just as soon as it came, it went. I took one last shuddering breath and decided that enough was enough. I wasn't going to be bullied anymore, by the Highwaymen or by my own guilt. Or by anyone else, for that matter. I had made my bed and I would lie in it, but I'd do it with pride and confidence. I'd do it without shame, because what was done was done.

Beast had gotten what he wanted and so had I. Now I needed to deal with the consequences of my actions and get on with my life. Despite Jenna's shock at my revelation that I was quitting the hospital, I knew it was the right thing to do. The more I'd thought about it, spinning the idea around and around in my head, the more certain I was of it. I wasn't sure what I wanted to do with my life yet, but working there wasn't it.

I stepped out of the shower and wrapped a towel around my body with a new determination. I had money saved up from caring for Beast at the hospital—enough to put a deposit down on a decent apartment—and then my mom could take the trailer, because if there was one thing I was certain of, it was that I couldn't live with her. She was a stranger to me; a stranger that had abandoned me, no less. She would be out in a couple of weeks, and now that her probation officer had checked out the trailer and deemed it okay for her to stay in, that's what we'd do. I'd leave some things there so it looked like I was still living there, and I'd come by when I knew the probation officer was coming to check up on her, but I wasn't staying there with her. Absolutely not.

I'd originally intended to give all the money from caring for Beast to Jenna as a gift. It was, after all, her job that I had taken, but since she wasn't currently speaking to me and I had no idea if she ever would again, I figured it was necessary that I spent it on getting out of there as soon as I could.

I brushed my teeth with my own toothbrush, enjoying the clean, tingly feeling in my mouth. I dried myself and put on some moisturizer before heading out of the tiny bathroom and going to my bedroom, but as I turned left, something drew my attention right.

Holding the towel tighter to my body, I stepped farther along, going into the small kitchen that led to the even smaller living room, if it could be called that, and found two men sitting on my little beat-up sofa. Smartly dressed in expensive suits, hair slicked back, and shoes so shiny I could see my face in them, I recognized them instantly.

These were Lorenzo's brothers—Carlos and Mateo. There was no denying that because of how similar Lorenzo looked to them both. But where his face was kind and full of warmth, theirs held a look I had come to recognize all too well while caring for Beast. It was a look of something dark and dangerous. Something deadly that said they didn't just cross boundaries but left those boundaries a smoking ruin in their wake.

"Belle, right?" the one on the left asked, his face a picture of calm restraint. I wasn't sure which brother was which—not that it should have mattered…yet it did, somehow. I nodded and he stood, buttoning his jacket back up. The other brother followed suit, and it took everything I had to stop my knees from knocking. "I hear we have a similar enemy."

Enemy…enemy?

I didn't have any enemies, did I?

"I…I don't know what you mean," I stuttered. "What do you want?"

The towel was pulled so tight around me that it was practically cutting off the blood flow, and yet it still didn't feel tight enough under their watchful gazes.

190

The brothers exchanged a glance, and the one on the left sighed and turned his attention back to me, and something in that look made my heart skip a beat. I turned on my heel and ran toward my bedroom, intending to slam the door closed and lock it. I could call the police. No, no, I could call Shooter!

I ran, my feet pounding over the filthy floor of the trailer, but somehow I was too slow, or they were too fast, and before I knew it, arms were wrapping around my middle. I screamed and kicked, determined to be free at any cost. I had no idea what they wanted with me, but given the dark looks on their faces, it couldn't have been anything good.

I felt my towel coming loose and then I was thrown on the bed, face first, my neck jerking violently and making me call out. But still I thrashed out, scurrying up the bed, naked and trembling.

The two brothers stood in the doorway, their hard gazes roaming over parts of me they shouldn't have been allowed to, and I grabbed the covers to hide my nakedness from them.

"Enough," one of them said, his voice commanding my attention.

I gripped tightly to the covers, my gaze never leaving them, watching every slight move they made. Would they rape me? Beat me? Steal from me? I had nothing. I was nothing! A nobody. Lorenzo had said his brothers had chosen a different path from him, but I hadn't thought this. I hadn't thought it would put me in danger.

"The Highwaymen," the other brother said, and my rapidly tumbling thoughts stopped mid tumble. "We need information and you will get it for us."

I shook my head. "I don't know anything."

"You're staying there…at their clubhouse, yes?"

I nodded. "Just for a couple of days."

"To care for the one they call Beast."

I nodded again. "I…" I shrugged, not sure where this was going. "He's been sick."

Should I have been telling them that? Would that get me in trouble with the Highwaymen? Would it get me killed?

191

"While you're there, I want you to gather information for me," the one on the left said.

"About what?" I asked, my fingers going numb from holding the covers so tightly. "I'm in his room all the time. I don't go anywhere else."

"Find a way. I don't care how," he replied.

I stared, dumbfounded and terrified. If the Highwaymen found out, they'd shoot me without asking questions. If I didn't… I shuddered, wondering if my fate would be worse or the same with these men. I was stuck choosing between two very dark worlds with no way out and wondering how I'd even gotten to this place.

"But…" I started, my voice shaking as it left my lips.

"This isn't a request, Belle. It's an order, and trust me when I tell you that you don't want to disobey me."

My chin quivered. "What do you need to know?"

A smile flickered across both of their faces. "Everything."

I was horrified by the situation and horrified by myself, but what was I supposed to do? I didn't want to die. Certainly not like this. Could I tell Lorenzo about his brothers? Would he do something to make them stop? Would he even care? They were his family, not me, regardless of the bad blood running between them.

The taller brother came closer to the bed and I automatically pulled my knees up to my chest and pulled the cover higher, gripping it between my hands like my life depended upon it.

"What's under there doesn't interest me, Belle." He glanced toward his brother and then back to me. "Mateo, though, now he has a thing for pretty women covered in their own blood, so you'd do well to mind yourself around him."

My gaze flicked to Mateo in the doorway and I whimpered at the devious look on his face. It made the dark look Beast had seem like child's play. Mateo's eyes shone with pure evil delight. Staring into his eyes was like looking at evil incarnate, and I looked away before I burst out crying. Carlos reached out and gripped my chin in his hand, squeezing so hard I whimpered in pain and looked back at him.

"Security, jobs, money, people—I need to know it *all*," he demanded, his voice cold and calculating, "and don't bother going to Lorenzo. He's not the good little boy you think he is. And if you think those pathetic bikers can help you…think again. They don't trust you and they'll cut you down before you can finish telling them."

Tears spilled from my eyes, but I didn't dare blink or rub them away.

I was too afraid to move.

Too afraid to speak.

I had been betrayed on all angles and backed into a corner, and now I had nowhere to go and no one to turn to. I was alone in this, and as if Carlos knew, he smiled, his eyes glinting as he hit the the final nail in my coffin.

"And when the time comes, Belle, you'll kill the Beast."

He let go of me and walked away, leaving me alone in my bedroom with only Mateo. He smiled, a cruel smile that showed his teeth and reminded me of a wolf that was hunting its prey, and I whimpered. Tears continued to spill down my face as he took a step toward me.

"I almost want you to fail," he said, his voice light, almost gentle. "That way I get to play with you."

He winked like he'd just paid me a compliment and then turned and left the room. As soon as I heard the door open and close and the start of an engine outside, I dove out of bed and ran down the hallway to my front door, locking it and leaning my naked back against it. I wasn't sure how they'd gotten in—the lock wasn't broken, and I was almost certain that I'd locked it when I came in—but it didn't matter. The fact was, they *had* gotten in. They had threatened my life. Threatened my everything. They wanted me to do something incredibly dangerous that they knew would likely get me killed in the end, and they didn't care.

One way or another, I realized with dread as ice filled my veins, I wasn't making it out of this situation alive. And neither was Beast.

Chapter Twenty-Six
~ BEAST ~

Belle was subdued as she moved about the machines around my bed.
Machines for fluid.
Machines to check my heart.

Machines that just beeped a fuckload at random times and stopped me from sleeping.

I watched her with an impatient eye, curious as to what had gotten up her ass that day. I knew she didn't want to be there, but she wasn't the sort of woman to be a bitch about it.

Each day I was feeling better and better—stronger and more like my old self. My vision in my left eye still wasn't a hundred percent, but Belle had warned me of that, and honestly, I was just so glad that it had come back at all so I wasn't about to complain. I would be able to ride again, and that was the most important thing.

My body was healing, my eyesight was getting better, my muscles strengthening, but the ugly scars covering my face, hands, and body were still there, constant reminders of what I'd gone through. I'd like to say that I saw them as warrior marks, representing what I'd been through, and that they made me stronger inside, but they didn't. Every time I looked at them I felt anger inside me, bubbling up and threatening to explode out of my chest. Every time I looked in a mirror and saw my torn-up face, scars littering my skin like dirt on the sidewalk, I felt fire burning within me.

Memories of how each one was made haunted me.

Each cut.

Each burn.

Each blow with a hammer. A nail gun. A hunting knife.

I spent long hours staring at myself in a mirror, lost in those memories, my head getting even more messed up at the prospect of living like this forever.

While my body healed, my mind fractured, turning darker and more violent with each passing hour until it wasn't just a hateful rage I had within me, but something worse. Something I couldn't explain.

Belle emptied my meds into a little white cup, counting them silently in her head, her forehead screwed up as she checked and double-checked them. I scowled as I watched her, wanting to know what was eating her up inside. Wanting to demand that she tell me. But there seemed little point; she wouldn't tell me anything. We weren't those people from the hospital anymore. I wasn't the same man and she wasn't the same woman. We'd both grown a little darker and a little more lost as each day passed, it seemed—to the point I barely recognized her or me anymore.

I was sitting up, my TV on in the corner of my room. Goddamn, I was sick of watching TV. It was all I seemed to do these days. Watch TV, eat, sleep, shit, and take pills served by Nurse Cheerful over here. She didn't even have any pudding to soothe me with anymore. She just came, did the bare minimum to make me comfortable, made an excuse to leave the room, and if she couldn't she just sat silently in the corner with a book. A book she'd been reading for two weeks now. A book which she hadn't turned a damn page on. She couldn't even bear to look at me anymore, that was how much she hated me and hated being there. My heart grew a little harder at that realization.

Outside in the clubhouse I could hear laughing and talking. Brothers going about their day. Harleys starting with loud, throaty roars outside. Doors opening and closing. Cries of pleasure coming from different rooms. I'd become accustomed to listening in to the club life I wasn't a part of at the moment and recognizing footsteps and bikes and which door was which. Made a little game for myself that I was getting too damn good at.

One thing was for sure: after all of this, I'd be the most feared enforcer the Highwaymen had ever seen because I'd know every person just by how they walked or closed a door.

"Open up," Belle mumbled, the little white cup shaking in her trembling hand. I scowled up at her, seeing the dark rings under her eyes.

"What's up your ass?" I asked, snatching the cup from her. Hated that Shooter had made her stay. Why couldn't he just get one of the sweetbutts to take care of me for a week or two? Or better yet, blackmail another doctor from the hospital? Having to see Belle every day was eating me up inside and feeding my anger. No one had mentioned anything about her feeding club secrets to Lorenzo since that day in the hospital, so I was guessing that the theory had died out quickly. It didn't surprise me. Belle didn't have a bad bone in her body.

"Nothing," she replied, grabbing my water from the table.

"Something is."

She shook her head, her gaze not meeting mine. It had been like that for days, and it was getting worse. She could barely look at me. Sure, she'd put on my cream and feed me pills until I rattled, wash my body down, but she didn't look at me anymore. It was like she was in physical pain every time she tried to.

I grabbed at her hand, forcing her to drop the cup of water onto the floor. She let out a small yelp of pain as I squeezed just hard enough to get her damn attention. And when I did, when her eyes finally reached mine, tears were brimming in them and a whole world of pain was overflowing. I let go of her hand immediately and she scuttled away as quickly as she could, leaving the room before I could attempt to apologize. The door slammed behind her and I was left with just the scent of her shampoo and the feeling that something wasn't right with her.

Not my problem though, I told myself.

It was her little fuckboy boyfriends.

Whatever she did now was nothing to do with me…

I swallowed, wishing she'd come back so I could apologize for scaring her.

Hadn't meant to grab her so hard.

Hadn't meant to frighten her and make her run from me.

197

Hadn't meant to do an awful lot of things, but it seemed I was destined to keep fucking up wherever Belle was concerned.

I switched my attention back to the TV, my mind going elsewhere while the pictures moved before my eyes. I was back at the barn. Echo and I were laughing and joking, and then he was gone. A puff of dark smoke and his body was dust on the ground, and I was staring down at him wondering what had just happened.

Squeezing my eyes closed, I listened to the voices that surrounded me. Feeling the ropes around my wrists, the knives jutting painfully out of various parts of my body. One in the top of my thigh, just above the artery. One in my side, missing my vital organs. Nails were being pulled from my fingers. A blowtorch to my chest, melting my tattoos away from my skin. The prickles of barbed wire as it was scraped down my back.

My breathing became heavy. I sucked in breath after breath, needing air but not finding any. All I could taste, all I could smell, was fire and animals burning alive. Skin melted, hair sizzling. I clutched at my chest, hearing horses screaming at me to move.

But I couldn't move.

I was trapped in this moment.

Trapped in this place.

I wasn't sure I'd ever escape this hell.

I might have still been alive, but I'd died that day, and the man that filled my bones wasn't a man at all anymore.

Chapter Twenty-Seven
~ *Belle* ~

I scurried over to the bathroom, slamming the door closed behind me and placing my back against it. Tears threatened to spill down my face, but I swiped them away as quickly as I could. This was what I had become now. This was what I had turned into. I hated my life so much and there was nothing I could do about it. Nothing I could do to change a single thing.

I was trapped between helping Beast heal and knowing that I would have to kill him.

Carlos and Mateo had come to my trailer again the previous night, wanting to know information. But I had nothing—absolutely nothing to give them. All I'd done the past two weeks was look after Beast and think. I wasn't really allowed out into the clubhouse, and Beast and I didn't talk, so there was just no way for me to tell them any of the things they wanted to know.

But I'd have to give them something soon or they were going to hurt me. That much I knew. And I didn't just mean by bruising my skin. That, they'd already done. They would hurt my heart. They'd threatened Jenna and Gregory, and even though she didn't want anything to do with me at the moment, I still loved her and wanted to keep her safe, even if it meant getting myself killed.

I pulled up my top, revealing the dark bruise that was forming on my stomach from where Mateo had hit me. I hadn't been able to eat a thing since because the dull ache made me feel sick constantly. Thank God that Beast and I didn't talk anymore, because I wasn't sure how many words I could get out without the pain in my voice being obvious.

Pushing my top back down, I splashed water on my exhausted face, dreading going back out there and seeing Beast. I hated looking at him, knowing that I knew who had done this to him. Knowing that I would be the one to deliver the final blow. It was hell to me. Not the pain, not just the fear, but the betrayal. I'd been betrayed my whole life, and now I was doing it to someone else.

I was worse than pond scum.

I'd thought several times about trying to speak to Shooter or Beast and tell them what was going on, but I backed down every time. The way Beast looked at me, filled with hate and anger, I wasn't sure that he'd believe me. And if he did…he might think Lorenzo had something to do with it and kill him. It would be another thing on my already overflowing conscience.

I pouted at my reflection, pulling my hair up into a high bun and wincing as I stretched and my stomach muscles cried out in pain. Tears filled my eyes again, but I refused to let them fall. I didn't deserve to cry. I wasn't worthy of those tears, because I was the villain in the story now.

Leaving the bathroom, I headed back to Beast's room. With my hand on the handle, I turned when I heard my name being called. Looking around, I saw one of the women that always hung around the club standing at the makeshift bar area, waving to me.

It was the same woman that I'd seen having sex with Beast that night, and I felt something akin to pain and jealousy combined in my heart. She waved me over and I sighed, not wanting to talk to her or anyone but already knowing that it might be my way to get information. If I befriended her then I'd have a reason to be out there more often. If I had a reason to be out there more often…

I plastered on a fake smile and walked toward her, trying to mask the pain I felt running through my stomach with every painful step.

"Hey, girl!" she said, pulling me into a painful hug. I winced and she let me go with a worried look. "Sorry, I'm a hugger," she laughed. "Fragile little thing aren't you? You okay?"

I smiled back. "I have a tummy ache, sorry. I'm fine."

"I'm Lola," she said, holding out a hand this time, and I shook it.

"Belle," I replied. "I think we've met once before actually."

She cocked her head. "We have? I don't remember, and I'm normally pretty good with faces."

I felt the blush rise to my cheeks. "I walked in on you and Beast at the hospital," I admitted sheepishly.

Lola didn't seem like the sort of woman to be shy or blush, but she looked away, her smile faltering momentarily. "Yeah, umm, sorry about that."

I put a hand on her arm. "Oh no, it's fine. I should have knocked. Totally my fault."

"How's he doing in there?" she asked, a strange look on her face.

"He's okay. He's healing." I shrugged. I needed to give her more. I needed to open up the conversation, but I wasn't sure how. A secret spy I was not.

"That's good. That man has been through so much." She twirled her straw around in her drink thoughtfully. "You heard what happened to him, right?"

I nodded. "Yeah,"

"Of course you did! You're his nurse." She giggled like she was a schoolgirl, and I envied that laugh—how carefree it sounded. "It was awful. So awful. He and Echo were like brothers. I mean, they were in terms of the brotherhood an' all, but I mean, Beast really saw him as his brother. Not to mention all the torturing they did to Beast, but I think that's the thing that hurts him the most: the loss of Echo."

"I didn't know that, actually. I thought it had just been Beast that had gotten hurt."

Lola shook her head, a sad smile coming to her face, and fresh guilt blossomed at how I was using her. "No, Echo was shot and killed right away. That meant that Beast got everything that was intended for the both of them." She leaned in. "Truth is, I don't think anyone expected Beast to survive. I heard that there were over three hundred cuts and burns on his body alone." She looked back to her drink. "How does someone survive that?"

Three hundred.

The number danced around my head like a taunt.

I'd seen his body. The cuts and the bruises. The burns, slices, the broken ribs. But I'd never counted and I'd never thought to think too hard on how he'd gotten them. Jenna had trained me to see past the story and go directly to the person so I could help them. And that's what I'd done.

I thought about Beast and the sort of man he was. All the anger and hate he carried with him. He was trapped in a pit of vipers ready to attack, but the vipers weren't snakes at all, they were his memories of that night. All his rage and anger suddenly made so much more sense.

"They don't," I replied. "I guess they have to become someone else to survive it."

Lola nodded sadly. "It's quiet around here today, maybe you could keep me company," she said. "I'm supposed to keep the men company, but they're all super busy." Her gaze went wistful. "They always seem to be super busy these days."

My mouth went dry, my tongue flaccid in my mouth as I willed it to move so I could get my words out and ask some questions. Knowing more about what had happened to Beast didn't help me. In fact, it only served to terrify me even more than I already was. But the more I tried to talk, to get my tongue to move, the more it refused to budge. I coughed, and then coughed some more, startling Lola into action. She slid off her stool and headed behind the bar quickly, popping the lid off a bottle of beer with the edge of the bar and handing it to me. I took it, drinking greedily.

"Thank you," I finally gasped, wiping the back of my hand across my damp lips. "I needed that." And I did. I longed to drink myself into oblivion so I could forget about the awful situation I was currently in. So I didn't have to think about how there was no escaping my fate, or Beast's—only delaying it.

I'd drunk practically the whole bottle in one go, but I hadn't eaten right in days and it would go straight to my head if I wasn't careful, and I couldn't afford to get drunk. If I got drunk, something might slip out about what was happening, and that would put Jenna in danger.

"I need to get back," I mumbled.

I put the bottle back down and turned to leave. I couldn't do this. Guilt and fear were warring in me. Shame at what I was doing was eating away at my insides and liquefying them.

"Send him my love," Lola called as I stumbled away.

I threw a backward glance at her and nodded.

"They're close to catching the guys that did this," she said.

I stopped walking and turned to face her, a smile touching the edges of my mouth.

"Really?" I said, the word barely a breath on my lips.

"Oh yeah, I heard Casa and Gauge talking earlier. They know who it was, they're just setting it all up to bring them down now." She looked pleased with herself. Pleased that she'd finally piqued my interest with something.

Lola came toward me, and my heart rattled in my chest, fear and excitement bubbling through me. Excitement because if they knew who it was they could catch them before I had to do anything. But fear because they might find out about me and kill me anyway.

"I heard you and Beast hooked up at the hospital," she said, her gaze drifting over my shoulder toward Beast's door.

My cheeks flamed in embarrassment. "I'm so sorry," I said, realizing that she actually might be pissed off at me because she was already sleeping with him. "It just sort of happened, but he's all yours. I wasn't trying to come between you two."

My blush deepened.

I couldn't believe I'd just said that.

Lola was stunning. Curvy, tall, long flowing hair, big boobs—she could have any man she wanted. Of course he was all hers. He was never mine to begin with.

Lola laughed. "Oh, that's okay. Beast and I aren't an item or anything. I was just wondering if it was any good is all."

"Any good?"

"The sex."

My cheeks were going to self-combust at this rate.

"Umm."

"Beast always had the best dick around here," she said wistfully. "If there was any man that was going to bring me to orgasm in thirty seconds flat, it was him. It was like magic or something." She giggled like a little girl again. "Like a magic dick!"

I was mortified at the conversation, but I got where she was going with it. Beast had been the perfect man in bed. He'd satisfied me repeatedly without even trying. His look alone had almost brought me to my knees.

I forced a small, shy laugh. "Yeah, that sounds about right."

"So, he's all good now then?" she said, a hungry look on her face. "And you two, you're not a thing?"

I finally got where the conversation was going, my heart stuttering in my chest.

I looked back toward Beast's door, thinking of how I'd washed his chest earlier. Ran my hands through his hair as I combed it and tied it back. Applied cream to his skin, my hands moving over his body and his barely concealed erection at my every touch. But he wasn't mine. He was never mine. And maybe a little time with Lola would actually help him.

Despite my jealousy, I shook my head. "He's all good down there," I said, the words barely making it past my lips. "You should go check on him."

Her face lit up like the Fourth of July. "Oh my god, thank you! We had a little thing a couple of weeks ago, and he was pissed at me and I just want to show him that there's no hard feelings between us. Ya know?"

"Go right ahead. I'll wait out here," I mumbled.

Lola squealed and hugged me again before sauntering off toward Beast's room. I slid onto her stool, watching as she cracked the door open and gave a little wave to him before she stepped inside. I picked up my beer bottle and finished the contents, but one beer was never going to be enough. I walked around the bar, my thoughts on Mateo and the devilish look he'd had on his face the night before as I grabbed another bottle from the fridge. He'd pinned me to the bed and thumped

204

me so hard in the stomach that I thought I'd be coughing up blood. The look on his face was something out of a movie. The more I cried, the more satisfied he looked and the hungrier and turned on he'd appeared for more of them.

My hand went instinctively to my stomach again; the pain was awful. Every move I made sent pain through me. I couldn't eat. I couldn't stretch. I couldn't walk without the pain threading through my spine. My gaze dropped to the bottle in my hands and I wondered how much pain he'd put Beast through to make him so hard. I'd seen the scars, I'd tended to his wounds, but the pain...God, the pain must have been incredible, and yet he was still here. He just got on with it. He just dealt with it. I was spineless and pathetic, I realized. A couple of threats and a punch to the stomach and I was ready to turn on him.

I looked over at his door, wishing that I could be strong like him, but knowing that I'd never be as good as him.

Chapter Twenty-Eight
~ Belle ~

"I haven't seen you in two weeks, Belle," Lorenzo complained, his usually soft expression now hard and unforgiving.

I'd gotten home and he'd been parked outside in a sleek black car I hadn't seen before. It was all I could do to not have a heart attack at him being there. If his brothers turned up... God, what would they do to him? They'd warned me not to get him involved.

Lorenzo had asked to come inside, but there was no way that was happening. Besides, my trailer was a sty because I'd barely been there since having to work over at the clubhouse every day, and when I was there, I was sleeping. Lorenzo had offered to take me for a drive in his car so we could talk, and now there we were, parked up at Ridgemont Crest and looking over the city like a couple of kids on a first date. It was so far away from where we were now.

"I know, I'm sorry. I'm just busy," I said apologetically.

He looked at me strangely. A hard expression in his eyes only softened by the way his hand reached for mine and his thumb stroked across it. "I know you're still working for them, Belle. Please don't lie to me and treat me like an idiot."

I closed my eyes, the guilt too much. I hadn't exactly lied to him, but I had hidden the truth. It was a sort of gray lie, I guess. Not quite white through and through.

"I just didn't want you to be mad, Lorenzo." I opened my eyes and looked at him. "I needed the money and they needed a nurse; it's nothing more than that."

"It is if you're still fucking him," he bit out, harsher than I'd ever heard him speak before.

"I'm not!" I replied quickly to reassure him.

"But you were," he said almost too calmly. I'd wondered when this would come up. After Beast let it slip at the hospital, every phone

206

call with Lorenzo had been awkward as I waited for him to say something, but he hadn't, and I'd hoped that he never would.

I swallowed. "It was just the once."

"The night after I fucked you." His eyes narrowed, the warmth gone from his usually soft features.

I looked away sharply, not liking the tone to his voice. I wanted to pull my hand out from under his but didn't want to provoke him further, and he must have sensed that because he tightened his grip on me.

"I'm sorry, Belle, that was crude of me. I'm just a man, though, and it's been eating me up inside thinking of you with him, especially after how special our night had been." He reached out and touched the side of my face, pulling gently on my chin to make me look at him. His eyes searched mine for something and he sighed, obviously not finding it. "You can't really blame me for being angry, can you? You understand that at least?"

"I'm so sorry," I said, already knowing the words were pitiful and not enough to make up for what I'd done. "It wasn't planned; it just sort of happened. But I promise it hasn't happened since and it won't. Not ever again."

Something flickered in his eyes. Jealousy or anger, perhaps. Or maybe both. I couldn't even blame him. If things had been reversed, I would have felt the same way. It didn't matter that we hadn't declared ourselves an item; I'd still betrayed him.

"I thought we had something special," he said, frowning.

"We do!" I insisted, my eyes pleading with him to believe me.

"Really?"

I nodded, desperate for him to know how sorry I was and how much I cared for him. His hand dropped from my chin and he leaned in, and at first I thought he was going to spit in my face or say something awful to me. The look of menace was so rich in his eyes that it frightened me, and I pulled away. Lorenzo reached for me again, his hand cupping around the back of my head as he brought his mouth to mine, kissing me hard and surprising the hell out of me. Our teeth clashed as I kissed him back, desperate for his forgiveness. Desperate for his love.

"You are mine, Belle," he said between kisses, and I paused, suddenly unsure of where this was going.

His kisses were deep and passionate and full of longing, but all I could give back was half-hearted attempts that in no way made up for what I'd done. How had my life come to this? How had I managed to disappoint everyone and mess everything up so badly? It was suddenly too much, and I felt the salty tears sliding out of my eyes and down my cheeks. The tears mingled with our kisses and spurred Lorenzo on, making him seem almost famished for more.

Muttering in Italian, he pulled out of the kiss, his eyes straying over my wet cheeks and his tongue darting across his lips.

"Come here, Belle, come here," he coaxed gently as his hands moved to unbuckle his suit pants.

But I didn't want to have sex—not right then, not like that. I wanted to go home and sleep. I wanted to drink until I passed out. I wanted to drive to the ocean and lie on my back, floating in the cool waves until my head felt clearer and all the stuff that was hurting me just drifted away.

"Belle," he said, his voice more forceful. "Show me how sorry you truly are."

I swallowed thickly, my body frozen to the spot. I owed him this, didn't I? I owed it to him to show him how sorry I was, and how I was his and not Beast's. How I wouldn't let him down again. I had no one left, but here was Lorenzo after everything I'd done to mess up our relationship, and he still wanted me.

He pushed his pants down and pulled his hard length out, his hand sliding up and down the shaft as he slid his seat back in one swift movement.

His unwavering gaze was on me, hard, brutal. "Take it," he said, his voice thick with authority. "Take it and apologize for embarrassing me."

I didn't want to.

I didn't want to do this.

But how could I say no to him?

How could I tell him that I didn't feel in the mood to have sex or to touch him. That I just wanted to be left alone. Because then I would be completely alone. So so alone. And maybe he'd get angry with me too, and then what? Maybe he'd tell Jenna she couldn't eat in his restaurant anymore, and when she asked why, he'd tell her and she'd hate me even more. The scenes spiraled through my mind on fast-forward, and I found more tears sliding down my cheeks as I slid forward in my seat, searching his eyes for something, anything.

"Take it and show me you're truly sorry," he growled.

Lorenzo reached for the back of my head, pushing it down toward his crotch roughly. I opened my mouth, realizing that he didn't want sex. At least not yet.

"Yes, yes, Belle, take it," he grunted, impaling my mouth with his hard length.

This felt too intimate and dirty, more so than sex. His hands wound their way into the back of my hair, clasping my long lengths in his fists, as my tongue swirled half-heartedly around his length. I didn't want to do this. I didn't want to be here. But once again, I'd found myself in an impossible situation that I couldn't get out of.

He thrust up with his hips, his rock hard length reaching to the back of my throat and making me gag, but his hand in my hair kept my head down and forced me to take all of him and not pull away. Tears bled from my eyes as I choked around his hardness. His hips bucked, thrusting himself savagely into my mouth over and over as I gagged and cried and tried to cough, my throat instinctively trying to close and stop him from entering it. But it was no good.

He was too strong, I was too weak.

He was too hard, and I was too soft.

"Yes, yes, take me, Belle," he groaned. "Take me and earn my forgiveness." And I couldn't deny that I felt better at hearing those words. That maybe I could make everything right if I could just do this one thing for him. If I could just hold on for a few more minutes without falling apart completely.

"Remember that this mouth is mine now, not *his*, not anyone's, but mine," he gritted, sounding angry with me as he slammed his way into my mouth over and over.

My jaw ached, saliva dribbled from the corners of my mouth, and still he pumped into me. Still his hand clutched painfully at my hair, holding my head in place, not giving me even an inch to breathe, grinding his way into my throat as I tasted his precum.

His words frightened me—his actions even more so. But at least I wasn't alone. At least I was being forgiven by someone. And right then, all I wanted was for someone to accept me. For someone to know that I was truly truly sorry and that I never intended for any of this to happen.

So I took Lorenzo. I opened my throat up to accept him even though it hurt. I sucked and tightened my lips around him and sheathed my teeth, and created a stronger suction as he pushed into me over and over, demanding an apology from my mouth.

Gone was the gentle lover I'd had, replaced by this brutish man as he fucked my mouth viciously, claiming my apology for himself from my swollen lips until finally he was coming in long, hot spurts across my tongue and down the back of my throat. He shouted incoherently in Italian as he ground himself into my mouth, his hands pulling at my hair painfully as he choked me with his hard length. I thought I would suffocate, as he held himself in me, his hips thrust up so high that the tip of him was blocking my airway as he made sure I took every last inch of him and swallowed every last drop of his semen.

I started to panic, struggling and pushing against him as I sought air. My eyes streamed, hot tears dropping onto his crotch that seemed to spur him on and demand more from me.

"Yes, Belle," he yelled loudly as his throbbing cock began to finally soften.

Lorenzo finally let go of me with a sigh of deep satisfaction, and I released him from my mouth with a loud pop from my lips. I sat up gasping for air, my mouth feeling bruised from his brutality, and I stared at him for long moments in silence, confused, broken, and lost. I didn't know this man—this monster, this maniac—and right then I didn't seem to know myself either. We were strangers in that car, becoming people that neither of us recognized.

My lungs burned as I breathed fresh air into them, the taste of his salty cum still in my mouth as I stared at him in horror.

His face was expressionless, his eyes swimming with darkness, until finally he spoke. "You're forgiven, Belle," he said calmly, like it was the most logical thing for him to say then, after what he'd just done.

I was forgiven.

I gasped, not sure what to say to that, and he smiled at my silence, reaching out to stroke away the spittle at the side of my mouth.

"Once can be forgiven, Belle," he warned, his thumb rubbing over my bottom lip. "But once only. Do you understand?"

I nodded, but I didn't, not really. Had he just punished me? Was that not affection but revenge he'd just inflicted upon my mouth with such viciousness that my jaw throbbed and my throat burned? A punishment to stake his claim and a warning not to do it again or worse would happen?

A sickness began to grow in my gut, worry growing deep inside me. What had I done?

"Good," he said with a smile, and the darkness I'd seen in his eyes disappeared. Once again he was the handsome Lorenzo, restaurant owner, businessman, and tentative lover, but I'd seen behind his veil now, and what I'd seen frightened me. "Let's get you home, shall we? You must be tired," he said, pushing his now flaccid length back into his pants and buttoning himself back up. I watched as he pulled some of my long hair from between his fingers, opened a window and dropped them out of it, and I realized how sore the back of my head was where he'd pulled my hair.

Lorenzo slid his seat forward and started the engine, and I realized as we pulled away from the secluded crest that this hadn't been a chance decision to go there. He'd brought me there for that purpose. I'd thought

I had sought his forgiveness so that things would be better in my life, so that Lorenzo could be the one good thing I had. But instead, I realized with sinking dread, I'd just made my situation ten times worse.

Chapter Twenty-Nine
~ BEAST ~

"Your sexy nurse said you can start doing some light exercises, brother," Gauge said around a mouthful of cigar smoke. "No drinking and no drugs, but at least you can get your ass out of that bed and get moving again."

Casa snickered from the corner. He had a cigarette dangling between his lips as he painted something on my wall. I'd given up asking him what it was.

"What the fuck are you laughing at?" I growled.

Casa looked over his shoulder. "Heard you had a workout yesterday with the lovely luscious Lola."

Lola. Fucking Lola.

Bitch couldn't keep her mouth shut, but at least she was bending the truth for both of our sakes.

"That's what she's here for, ain't it?" I grunted, throwing the sheet back and dropping my feet to the floor.

"Thought you and that nurse were a thing," Gauge said, his dark eyebrows pulled in.

"Nah, brother, she picked the fucking Italian, remember? You goin' senile or something?" Casa said without looking, his hand wrapped around a paintbrush and moving swiftly over the wall.

"Fuck off," I bit out.

"I know what happened. Just thought with her being in here all the time she would have changed her mind." Gauge threw Casa a dirty look. Brother was getting real touchy about his age. It wasn't like he was actually getting old or anything—no older than the rest of us, really—but the more it irritated him, the more Casa liked to push on that button just to piss him off more.

"Yeah, well, you're wrong." I stood up, a wave of dizziness washing over me. I stumbled, and Gauge reached for me but I shoved

213

him off with a snarl. "Get off me. I've got it. I just stood up too quick is all."

He stood back, his hands in the air. "Fine, fall the fuck over then, see if I care."

The dizziness faded and I dragged a hand down my face. I couldn't mess this up again. I had to get my shit sorted out. Things were coming to a head and I wanted to be a part of it. But for that I needed to be strong. I needed to be able to walk without getting dizzy. To be able to see other people without losing my temper. I needed to be able to ride my bike and hold a gun if I was going to hunt them down and shoot them. But most importantly, I needed to be able to wield a knife so I could cut my pound of flesh out of the men that ruined my life and took away my brother.

"Throw me my jeans," I said, taking a deep breath as I tried to cope with the sickness that was clawing its way up my stomach. I'd been lying down for too long. I'd let my muscles waste to practically nothing. I'd become weak and feeble and thin. My hip bones jutted out, my collarbones were sharp. I'd been so consumed with my own rage and desire for vengeance that I'd stopped eating properly and my body was paying the price for it.

I watched Gauge look my thin, weak, broken body over before looking away, embarrassed. I was glad that he didn't say anything about it.

Gauge grabbed my jeans from the chair in the corner and threw them over to me. "I'll meet you out there. I don't need to see your junk," he grumbled, and left the room.

Sitting down on the edge of the bed, I shoved my feet through my jeans before pulling them on. The material felt rough, almost like splinters of glass being dragged against my skin. My flesh had become overly sensitive to everything. But it also felt good to be wearing clothes again. The familiar scent of denim, and soon leather when I put my cut back on was like a dream come true. It was damn sight better than the smell of burn cream and sanitizer, that was for sure.

214

I turned, realizing that Casa was still there painting whatever it was on to my wall. "You stayin' to see my junk?"

He snickered but didn't say anything, continuing to paint, and I shook my head and grabbed a T-shirt from the floor before pulling it over my head. It was cotton and should have felt soft, but again it felt rough as jagged ice, and I winced. I refused to take it off though. Sooner or later I had to get used to this. Sooner or later the pain would subside and this would just be the new norm.

I shoved my feet into my boots—the soles of my feet where nails had been driven into them were only a little painful to walk on—and then I turned to leave. I threw a backward glance to Casa, scowling as his hands moved quickly. He was lost in whatever world he went to when he painted, cigarette ash falling at his feet as he worked his magic.

"Don't fuck around with any of my shit," I grumbled, and left the room. "And that better not be a picture of your grandma's pussy. Can't be jacking off to that every night."

He laughed again but continued to ignore me, and I stepped out into the hallway, slamming my door shut behind me. This wasn't my actual home, just my room at the clubhouse, and I suddenly realized that I hadn't been home in over a year. My worries washed around me. Thoughts of bills, of cleaning and cooking, of living on my own again. It was strange how you got used to things. My pulse spiked at the thought of being in my own home, away from my brothers or Belle.

Just alone.

Like I'd always wanted.

Yet now the thought made me uncomfortable.

I scowled and told myself to get my shit together.

Heading down into the main clubhouse, I took my steps slowly at first, letting the scent of stale beer and motor oil invade my senses. As I turned the corner a huge round of applause broke out, and I automatically reached for the gun at the waistband of my jeans, but of course it wasn't there.

215

And thank fuck too, because it took me a moment to get my bearings, but once I did I realized it was just my brothers, my friends—my family—welcoming me back into their fold. Again.

Shooter stepped forward and handed me a bottle of water. "Sorry it's not something a little stronger, but your nurse was pretty adamant on the no alcohol and drugs front for a while, and after the shit show last time, I'm inclined to do as I'm told when it comes from her." He smirked and I twisted off the cap and took a huge swallow of water before lifting my now half empty bottle into the air.

"Cheers, fuckers!" I called, and everyone lifted their glasses in the air and cheered.

Can't lie. It felt good. Better than the first time around, after leaving the hospital. I pulled my cigarettes from my jeans and lit one, inhaling the smoke deep into my lungs and giving a small cough.

Shooter patted me gently on the shoulder. "Got something else to show you."

"A surprise? For me?" I batted my eyelashes at him. "You shouldn't have."

He chuckled and started walking. "Come on, asshole."

I followed him outside, noting that Gauge, Rider, and Dom were also following us. I passed Lola and a couple of the other sweetbutts and she smiled almost shyly. I swallowed and ignored her, following Shooter outside and around the side of the building.

"So, your nurse said—"

"Can we stop calling her that?" I grumbled.

"Your nurse?" Shooter said, looking over his shoulder.

"Yeah." I shrugged, wincing as the cotton rubbed against my sensitive skin. "She's just Belle or the nurse. Not *my* nurse, you got me?"

Shooter frowned but nodded. "Anyway, so Belle said we had to start helping you build up your muscle again, but slowly."

"Right, because my granny is stronger than you now, and she's six feet under," Rider laughed from behind.

I glared. "I can still aim a gun, asshole."

Rider smirked and Dom patted him on the shoulder. "Better watch him, you know how he gets with his temper."

"Can we focus for five minutes?" Shooter snapped as we turned the final corner that led to the back of the clubhouse.

It was normally overgrown with weeds and crap piled up that the club didn't use anymore. Even the little kids didn't play back there because who knew how many snakes were hiding in the long grass. But that was all gone now. The grass was cut short, right up to the perimeter, and gym equipment was set out. A large canopy was overhead, keeping it all in the shade, and even a water fountain had been installed to the back of the clubhouse.

Benches, bars, weights—it was all there, and as I let my gaze look over it all I noticed that there was a running track laid out too, which seemed to go around to the way we had just come and came back on itself from the other side.

I didn't know what to say.

I just stood there and stared at it.

Grateful that I had these men to call a family but equally sad that Echo wasn't there to recuperate with me. He'd been my gym buddy for years, but now he was gone and he'd never train with me again.

Gauge walked past me and pointed to a couple of wooden benches, like the ones you saw in parks. "Got our fallen brothers' names carved here so that they're always with us training in spirit," he said, pointing to the gold plaques fitted across the tops of the benches. "And some trees and shit, in their memory too." He pointed to the trees growing by the fence.

"Are they fruit trees?" I asked, my words sticking in my throat.

Gauge turned and smiled, a big, shit-eating smile. He didn't smile often, so when he did you knew it was because of something good. "Yeah, that was Laney's idea, actually. She said we could pick the fruit when it grew and they would feed the club's kids and stuff." He shrugged. "Like, our brothers were still providing for our families, even in their death."

217

I looked over at Shooter, who was smiling, a cigarette hanging between his lips. "Something fucking poetic, ain't it?"

I threw my cigarette to the ground and walked forward slowly, my eyes taking in everything the men had done for me. Everything they had given me and continued to give me. That was what family was: providing for, protecting, loving, helping, respecting. Family gave and took in equal measures, and you all loved infinitely.

I stared down at the benches with our fallen brothers' names imprinted onto small gold plaques.

Fester.

Gash.

Dice

Nasty.

48.

Axle.

Echo.

Those men lived in our hearts. In the club's hearts. They'd sacrificed their lives for us at one time or another. They were *our* fallen heroes. All of our names would go onto these benches one day. I wondered when the day would be for me to follow in their footsteps.

"You okay, brother?" Dom asked, coming to stand next to me.

Shooter put a hand on my shoulder and pain emanated from my skin, reminding me that I was very nearly one of these names.

"He would have fucking hated this," Shooter chuckled, and I knew he was talking about Echo.

"Yeah, he would have," I agreed, swiping a hand down my face.

Echo.

My brother.

My *fallen* brother.

It was all suddenly too much. I couldn't breathe. My throat was too tight, the air was too thick. I dropped to a crouch as I tried to suck the air in to my lungs, vaguely aware that people were talking to me, but it wasn't until my hands came away from my face wet that I realized that I was crying.

"Jesus," I mumbled, trying to stop the tears from falling. I'd never cried in my life. Not when my mother left me to starve night after night, not when she brought boyfriends home to taunt and tease me, not when I killed her sorry ass, not when I was being tortured, and not even when I was lying in that hospital in agony and I remembered that Echo was dead. But I cried now, and once I started, I couldn't stop.

The tears flowed hot down my face, and the more I tried to stop them the faster they flowed. Arms wrapped around my shoulders, the smell of leather and cigarette smoke and whispered agreements enclosing me in their safe embrace.

This was family.

This was *my* family.

And I wasn't going to let anything hurt it ever again.

Because anything or anyone that tried to…I was going to kill.

Chapter Thirty
~ *Belle* ~

I *was a wreck.*

A total, complete 110% wreck.

I ached between my thighs and it hurt to walk. I'd gotten home and found Lorenzo parked outside again, waiting for me. I'd already known, from his dark expression, that there was no point in arguing that I was too tired to go out. He'd taken me back to his restaurant and it had started off nice. We'd eaten, we'd drunk some wine. It was relaxed and I'd begun to think the monster he'd been in the car last week had been a one-off. But then we'd gone upstairs and everything had changed.

As soon as the door had shut, his hands were on me. He was brutal and unforgiving, my whimpers and pleads turning him on more. I should have said no, but I didn't. And looking back now, I wasn't sure why I hadn't said no.

Maybe it was because I was afraid of what would happen if he had stopped. What other type of punishment he would find to take out on me.

Instead, I'd let him use my body as his plaything and I'd woken up sore and alone, with a note on his nightstand to grab an Uber home because he had a business meeting.

So I had…only to find Mateo and Carlos at my trailer, wanting more information. They'd threatened Beast. They'd threatened me. And then they'd threatened Jenna. I couldn't let anything happen to her. I squeezed my eyes closed, thinking about it…thinking about the things that I'd had to tell them.

I just needed to get through today.

Through the next thirty minutes.

Pack my stuff and get the hell out of here.

My hands were shaking. My knees were knocking. And my teeth were chattering.

They were going to know it was me, and when they did, they would kill me.

For the first time I'd given actual information to Mateo and Carlos. All the other stuff I'd given them was useless knowledge, or general knowledge around town. But this last time wasn't. This last time it was real information about a drop they had coming up. I'd regretted it as soon as the words had left my lips, but I'd been terrified!

Mateo had one hand on my throat, another on my hip, and my body pinned to the bed with his. There was only one way that was going to end. So I'd snitched and they'd left and I'd hated myself since.

And now I had to go, because when Shooter and Beast found out, I was dead anyway.

I began to pack my equipment away, putting all the little creams and pills back into the box as neatly as my shaking hands would let me. Shooter had asked for a list of stuff that I needed when he'd brought me there, and somehow he'd procured it all. I wasn't sure what I should do with it all now. The pills Beast would still need for a few months, the creams even more so, but the IV drips and bandages, and all the other hospital equipment, not so much.

"You done, nurse?" one of the bikers asked me.

He was tall, broad, with a shaved head and a cocky smile that said he could talk any woman into bed. I vaguely remembered his name as something like Cara or Casta. In his arms were paint pots and brushes, and I was guessing that he was the one that had been painting something on Beast's wall for the past week. Right now it was covered with a blanket that had been pinned up to hide it.

"Yeah," I managed to squeak out between heaving breaths.

"So we won't see you around here no more, huh?" He set his paints and brushes down with as much finesse as a bull in a china shop. "Not gonna lie, we're all gonna miss seeing your fine ass."

I didn't reply. I couldn't. I was still too terrified to speak, a ball of vomit wedged in my gut that was making my mouth water and my head dizzy.

"Of course, we're all going to miss all your good doctor shit too. Got a real hand for caring for people, huh?" he continued, oblivious to the panic attack I was having.

If he would just leave.

If he would just give me five minutes to sit down and catch my breath, I'd be okay. Though this situation would never be okay, but at least I'd survive the next hour. After that it was anyone's bet, but my money was on a bullet to the head. At least I hoped. After all, I'd seen what these kinds of men did to one another when they were angry, and I feared that I would be the one in bed covered in scars and burns and terrified that I might not be able to see again.

Casa—that was his name—came behind me and placed a hand on my shoulder, startling me so much that I screamed and dropped all the bottles in my hand. I spun to him, my eyes wide and fearful, and he lifted his hands in innocence and smirked.

"It's okay, it's just me," he said, sounding amused, but his gaze was watchful—wary, almost.

The door opened and Beast and the man I recalled as Dom charged in. Beast's eyes went to Casa and then me, with the bottles littered around my feet and the terrified look on my face.

"What the fuck did you just do?" he snarled, charging toward Casa.

"I'm innocent!" Casa laughed, without a shred of fear in his eyes.

"Innocent? Now that's the funniest shit I've heard all year," Dom replied. He looked over at me. "You good?"

I nodded quickly, not wanting anyone to get into trouble because of me. That was ironic, considering what I'd done would probably end up with some of these men dying.

Dizziness washed over me again, blackness pulling at the edges of my vision. "I just startled," I mumbled.

"Why didn't you believe *me*? I told you I didn't do nothin'," Casa continued to protest, sounding more than a little pissed off that they didn't believe him. "I've got my old lady now, I don't go near other women unless she says I can."

222

Dom's gaze slid from me to Casa with a grin. "You under your bitch's thumb?"

Casa pointed a finger at him. "She fuckin' hates being called that, brother, so unless you wanna find your own dick rammed down your throat, I suggest you shut your mouth."

Dom was full-on laughing now, a loud, booming sound that filled the small room and echoed off each of the walls. But Beast, Beast was watching me. His careful gaze capturing my every movement as I stood, trembling, dizzy, and feeling sick.

I needed to go.

But I didn't want to.

I needed to get out of there and away from him.

But the only place I wanted to be was in his arms.

Yet I knew I couldn't stay.

"I'll be back for my stuff," I said quietly, knowing my voice wasn't going to be heard over Casa and Dom's quarreling.

I left all my things strewn across the floor and began to walk across the room, intent on getting out of there as quickly as I could, but then the world began to tilt and the floor rose up to greet me. Before I landed face-first, a set of strong arms and the scent of leather wrapped itself around me.

I stared up into Beast's handsome face, blinking rapidly to ward of the darkness that was beginning to suffocate me. A single lightbulb was hanging from the ceiling, just behind his head, and gave him a weird kind of halo as he stared down at me, his dark eyes focusing on mine. He was talking, but I couldn't hear a thing over the rampant beating of my own heart and the whooshing of blood in my ears. His hair was longer now, hanging around his face in damp curtains from his earlier shower, and he continued to stare down at me, his large, muscular arms holding my trembling body tightly in his embrace. My god, this was the first time I'd felt safe in months. And yet it was probably the most dangerous place I could be.

The blackness pulled at me harder and I whimpered, my thoughts spiraling with all the things I longed to say.

Please forgive me, I didn't want to do this. I didn't have a choice. If not for my life, then I had to protect Jenna's. She was innocent and I was stupid. But I had to protect her at any cost. Even if it cost me my life.

I blinked up at Beast, watching as his lips continued to move as he spoke, but no words found me. The light behind him suddenly went out, casting his face in dark shadows, and I whimpered louder as his handsome face was plunged into darkness. The curve of each jagged scar across his forehead and around his eyes, and the burned skin on his cheeks, all made him look like something from my nightmares. He shook me a little; I felt my body being jolted as my eyes began to close.

"Are you the Devil?" I whispered as he scowled down at me, his expression growing fiercer by the second, but something in his eyes softened and looked hurt by my words. "I'm so sorry. Please don't hurt me," I said, clinging to him as I passed out, succumbing to the blackness.

*

I was on a rollercoaster, with darkness surrounding me, and on every bend and every dip it felt blacker and even more oppressive.

Sitting in a small cart at the top of a huge dip, I was waiting for the ride to plunge down to the other side, but it was frozen. I felt suffocated in the darkness, entombed by its strength as it held me there, invading my lungs and stopping me from moving. I was trapped and frightened, but then a familiar scent came to me, one of leather and sandalwood, and my heart loosened a little in my chest. I looked for it—for *him*—but couldn't see him, but I knew he was there, here, somewhere.

A spark of light caught my attention from the bottom of the frame, and when I looked down I saw orange and yellow flames slowly crawling toward me. Lazy licks of fire stretching across and burning away the frame of the rollercoaster. The crackle and hiss as the wood began to pop and burn away and the creak and tremble of the ride as it became unstable. I needed to get out of the little cart before the fire reached me or the ride collapsed, but I was too terrified to move.

I cried, staring around at the suffocating blackness and knowing I was going to die because I was too scared to get myself to climb out of the cart. I screamed into the abyss, but my voice was gone and no sound came out, and the flames grew stronger still as I tried to speak, the fire leaping toward me every time I opened my mouth.

And then, trembling and clutching onto the silver bar in front of me, I heard the most terrifying sound of all: the unmistakable sound of horses screaming. Every time I opened my mouth to scream or yell, the screaming echoed loudly around me.

The horses were burning, and so was I. Somehow, from deep down in my gut, I knew that the horses weren't going to hurt me—that they were frightened too. And just like me, they had a secret they couldn't tell.

I pushed at the bar, intent on freeing myself.

I wasn't going to die here, not like this.

I wasn't!

But the bar wouldn't move. It was stuck. I was stuck. I pushed and pulled and kicked out, wanting to escape the ride and the fires that grew hotter, but I was trapped there in the little wooden cart with the screaming of the horses surrounding me.

Together, the horses and I were going to burn, taking our secrets to the grave with us.

*

I woke with a start and a gasp.

I was so hot I thought I might actually be on fire, but when I tried to sit up to pat out the flames, I found I was trapped and unable to move.

I cried out, thrashing to be free, my hair wild around my face.

"All right, all right, fuckin' hell, Belle!" Beast roared, and I turned with a start to stare at him, my eyes wide with confusion.

We were lying in his bed, the covers over us both and his arms locked around me. He frowned at me, a hard expression on his face, as usual. Sweat glistened on his forehead and I realized the heat—the fire—had been us. Our bodies entwined under the covers as we both slept, creating a fever in us both.

"What happened?" I mumbled, realizing that I was fully dressed barring my shoes, and I had been lying in his arms. He released me and I sat up, the covers coming away to reveal his hard chest and abs. He was still wearing his jeans, but his top was off and I had the sudden urge to lie back down with him and go back to sleep. My head on his chest, my arm wrapped around his middle. Our hearts beating in unison. That sounded perfect right about now.

"You passed right the fuck out." He stretched his arms up before putting them under his head, his muscles stretching beautifully with every movement. He looked like he didn't have a care in the world, yet his dark eyes were still roving my face for what had just happened. His strength was coming back, his body contouring back to what it must have once been like—maybe even better. I'd been so unobservant the past few weeks I'd barely noticed anything. When I wasn't there I'd been with Lorenzo, and when I wasn't with Lorenzo, Mateo and Carlos had been paying me surprise visits. Between the monster that Lorenzo had become—his jealousy spurring him on to be more and more brutal with my body—and Mateo and Carlos's constant threats, I'd been completely distracted and lost within my own head.

But I noticed Beast now, and he looked *beautiful*.

There was just no other word for it.

His body looked like it was carved from marble; each muscle was defined, his stomach a wall of hardness, and his chest a steel plate. Beast stared up at me, his hands behind his head as he lay there, his arms and shoulders defined by layers of muscles as his stormy eyes continued to watch me.

I realized in that moment how much I'd missed him. At the hospital we had talked a lot, and in between his temper tantrums we'd gotten to know each other. I missed those talks. I missed his arms around me. I missed the safety that he promised without having to use words. I missed Beast and all his beautiful, brutal glory.

"You keep lookin' at me like that and I'm going to have to do something about it, Belle," he said, his words a low growl.

A threat or a promise...I wasn't sure, but I didn't care.

226

I was as close to death as I had ever been. Threats coming at me from all sides. Men wanting to kill me. Harm me. Torture me. Men pushing me to do things I didn't want to do. But this, Beast, he was just Beast. The same man that he'd been all along, only maybe softer somehow. Gentler, even if his eyes spoke deadly volumes.

It wasn't just his body that turned me on; it was that despite everything I felt both safe and terrified around him, a delicious combination of desire pooling in my belly that mixed with the fear in my heart.

Beast was the definition of a man.

He was the dark and brooding man that you were warned about as a girl, so dangerous and deadly you knew one wrong move would get you killed. He was the epitome of masculinity both because of and in spite of his scars. I stared and stared, wishing for something that I couldn't put words to, my body calling out for him to hold me, to touch me in that dark and delicious way only he could, even as my heart told me to run from him.

Beast was dangerous.

A caged animal waiting to be set free.

He was feral and savage, and completely unrestrained. He did what he wanted and he took no prisoners. He cared deeply but he hated even deeper. And all I wanted was for him to touch me. To want me. To love me.

Beast rolled his shoulders and took a deep breath as he pulled his arms out from behind his head. His heated gaze roved over every inch of me and I might as well have been naked already for how he saw me, because he *saw* every inch of me.

"Warnin' you, Belle," he said with a throaty growl. "Can't look at a man like that and not expect him to do somethin' about it." His drawl became lazier, his eyes growing darker.

I had to go.

I had to get out of there before it was too late.

Before he found out what I had done and killed me.

But I needed Beast in every possible way. I needed him to touch me, to make me feel safe, and I wanted one last time. I needed him to make me believe that it was all going to be okay. So I didn't think, I just reacted to my body's wants. I moved on instinct.

I reached down to the hem of my T-shirt and pulled it up and over my head, and his nostrils flared as my breasts came into view. It was wrong of me to take this from him, given that I was a traitor. It was selfish of me, but I needed him. I needed someone's touch. I need to feel alive again if I was going to die. I needed Beast one more time. His rough hands on every inch of my naked flesh. His tongue and teeth nipping at me. I needed to feel him deep inside me, taking from me, giving to me, burning my insides to dust.

In that moment, I needed Beast like I needed air. Maybe more so, because I could hold my breath yet I couldn't go another moment without his touch.

This wasn't me.

This wasn't the sort of woman I was; I didn't jump into bed with men like this, and yet it was the only thing I desired right now.

Beast.

This brutal and perfect man.

The man who was going to be my undoing.

I needed him to make me feel alive one last time before I died.

"I need you," I said, my words soft but firm, and I meant them to the very edge of my being. I needed him so bad it made me hurt. "Touch me," I begged him, terrified of his rejection but desperate for his touch. I reached for his hand and placed it on my breast. "Please."

Chapter Thirty-One
~ BEAST ~

Touch me," Belle begged, her eyes so round and wide that she looked like she was high. She took my hands and placed them on her breasts, and my hands moved of their own accord, squeezing gently on them. I noticed some faded bruises on her stomach and frowned, but she moaned and placed her hands on top of mine as we both kneaded her breasts. I didn't need to be asked twice, despite everything that had happened and was going to happen. Despite what I knew now and what had to happen next.

I sat up, tugging her into my lap and wrapping my arms around the back of her before pulling her closer so I could take her soft, pink nipple into my mouth. I sucked at the hard pebble, drawing circles around the end and blowing on it to make it harder. Belle writhed against me, my dick hardening in my jeans with every squirm and moan she made.

Her body was perfect: firm and tight, tiny in my arms with curves and an ass and tits that fit in my hands. She was the perfect woman, if only she hadn't been a damned traitor.

Belle closed her eyes, moaning as I sucked harder on her hard nipple, my hands reaching around under her skirt to her ass. I was taking my time this time around, no fucking and running off. No leaving with another man. No fucking for redemption because I was a broken man.

This time I was taking everything I wanted from her body before it was too late. Until the end justified the means and I could move on. I was going to fuck Belle out of my system before I sent her to ground.

I pushed her gently sideways, laying her down, my mouth still moving over her tits, to suck and bite my way down her body. I reached the waistband of her skirt, my hands gripping it and pulling it down her thighs slowly, taking my damn time. She shivered, goose bumps breaking out all over her skin as I slid the material down her thighs, over her knees, and off the ends of her feet. Her silk panties were already soaked through and I hungrily pushed her thighs apart and buried my face against her lips, sucking at her throbbing clit through the material.

Belle called out, bucking at the sudden frenzy against her pussy, her hands finding their way to my hair to tug on it as she called out something unintelligible into the air. I slipped a thick finger beneath the material, spreading her wide as I slipped it between her folds. She opened her mouth, groaning as she tilted her hips up to meet the slide and drag of my finger as I pushed into her and then back out before pushing a second finger in, widening her ready for me.

My heart was hammering in my chest, my dick so hard it could split steel, and all I wanted to do was fuck her until she passed out again so I could see that look of peacefulness on her face.

I slid my fingers in and out of her, my mouth clamped around her pussy, sucking at her juices. She was a fountain, her juices the elixir I needed to live, and I was fuckin' thirsty. I lapped at her, sliding a third finger inside. Her pussy clenched around me, tight and perfect, the throbbing vibrating through my skin. She spread her legs wider and I lapped harder, taking long strokes along her seam as she tightened around my fingers, her body shuddering at the start of an orgasm that was going to rip through her and tear her apart. But I wasn't done yet.

I slid my fingers out and sat up, and Belle looked at me sharply, her eyes wide, silently begging me for more.

I climbed off the bed and unbuttoned my jeans before sliding them off and kicking them and my underwear to one side. Her eyes were wide as she studied my cock, taking in its length and thickness, her tongue darting out to dampen those fat lips of hers as her chest heaved. Belle lay there naked and brazen, her fingers dipping between her legs as she touched herself, looking at me with her eyes all big and round and her mouth open, wishing it were me between her legs.

Fuck me, she was beautiful. Like an angel sent from heaven or some shit. Her fingers stroked and teased, her nipples hard, and the whole time she looked at me.

"Stop," I ordered, my voice hard and commanding, and like a good girl, she stopped automatically. "Turn over," I bit out, my eyes still locked on hers as I ran my hand down my length, fisting my cock tightly.

She blinked and then slowly turned over, and her ass... goddamn, I almost came as I looked down at it, long, hot sprays of my cum right across that perfect fucking peach of an ass. I climbed back onto the bed, gripping her panties in one hand and tugging at them roughly with the other. She whimpered as they snapped, the material digging into her skin before falling away. I threw them into the corner and stroked her ass cheeks, the pink flesh smooth and supple under my palm. I kneaded it with one hand, the other stroking my own cock, before taking my pre-cum and pressing it against her asshole.

Her body clenched as I pushed my juices into her tight hole with my thick finger, and she turned her head to look back at me over her shoulder, her eyes panicked. I grabbed my dick, taking the pre-cum on my fingers and wiping it over her asshole again as I slowly pushed my thumb inside once more.

Belle tightened around me and we both groaned—her because of the intrusion and me because I would have given just about anything for that to be my dick in there. I moved my thumb around, widening her, reading her as she slowly loosened, her muscles relaxing as the sharp intrusion became something enjoyable.

I pulled my thumb out, laying my dick between her ass cheeks and putting a hand in the middle of her lower back.

"You trust me?" I asked her, more pre-cum dripping onto her waiting hole. She swallowed thickly before bobbing her head up and down.

Scooping her up, my hand under her stomach, I lifted her ass higher and ran my cock up and down her seam, from pussy to ass, letting our juices mix and spread before slowly pressing the head of my cock against her tight, wet hole.

She whimpered as she slowly stretched to accommodate my size, her body clinging to the head of my cock as I pushed into her, a little at a time, letting her widen and stretch around me. And the whole time, her eyes stayed locked on mine. I rubbed her back with one hand, calming her, and held the base of my cock with the other, guiding it slowly into her.

Inch by thick, delicious inch I slipped inside her, until my balls touched her pussy and her body clung to my dick like I was her life raft and she was scared of drifting away. She was tight, almost too tight, and I lay inside of her for a moment, feeling her muscles contract and her body get used to me being in there.

Impaled by my cock, her ass high in the air, she finally tore her gaze away from mine and grunted into the pillow as I slowly started to slide back out of her. When I was an inch or two out, I pushed back in, her tight ring gripping me and making me hiss between my teeth.

"Relax," I soothed, stroking her back again.

I did it again; slowly easing myself out an inch or two before sliding back in, my balls slapping heavily against her damn pussy. With each thrust she loosened more. With each thrust she groaned deeper, a guttural sound that was primal and raw. With each slice of my cock driving deep inside her ass, her muscles grabbed at me, throbbing around me so hard I could see stars.

We didn't speak. Neither of us could right then even if we'd wanted to, the salacious need intoxicating us both to the point of delirium. I fucked her ass slowly, grinding myself into her until my balls began to tighten and my cock began to swell.

Belle groaned as I widened her and I reached between us to touch her clit. I scooped her up higher, pulling her entire body to mine, her back to my chest as I thrust into her slowly, firmly, one hand kneading her breasts, tweaking and flicking her hard nipples, the other on her pussy, thick fingers sliding into her. It was natural and intimate, and like animals we were wild and reckless as we fucked. I bit her shoulder as my balls tightened and I swelled inside of her again.

It all must have been too much because she tried to pull away from me, a whimper on her lips, but I held her tight to my chest, my arms wrapping around her and holding her tightly. Fucking her, needing her, loving her, saying goodbye.

I fucked her until she fell apart around me, her body splintering into a thousand pieces as she called out my name a hundred times, and each time was more perfect than the last. She looked over her shoulder, her hand reaching for my head and pulling my mouth to hers where our tongues collided and rolled over one another as I came in a long, hard spurts inside her. Her ass milked every drop from me as I clung to her, keeping her beautiful, soft body tight against my ugly, hard one.

We were yin and yang.

We were black and white.

We were beauty and the beast.

We were life and death and the ugly truth of it all.

"Beast," she mewled into my mouth, and I sucked my name off her traitorous tongue, her body still holding onto me like she didn't want to let me go, not now, not ever.

We stayed like that for several minutes, our mouths moving, our bodies still connected, our combined juices running down her smooth thighs as we both let the euphoria slip away and reality slide back in like a thief, stealing our happiness.

Belle kissed me like she never wanted to stop, and I kissed her back because I didn't want it to end. I wanted Belle like I'd never wanted anything or anyone in my life. She was family, she was home, she was safety. She was the arms I needed at the end of every day. She was the blood that made my heart pump. She was the air my lungs needed, and she was what I'd been searching for my entire miserable life.

Eventually my cock softened, and her ass relaxed enough that I slipped out of her. She gave another whimper as I left her body and we lay down together, side by side, her back to my front as I wrapped my arms around her, holding her in a protective embrace like I could stop what was coming next from harming her. But I couldn't.

"Go back to sleep, Belle," I whispered, holding her tightly, never wanting to let her go.

"Beast?" she whispered back, sounding exhausted.

"What?"

"I think I love you," she said, sounding heartbroken.

And I was too.

Devastated and heartbroken that the one woman I finally gave my cold, rotten heart to had turned out to be a traitor.

"Go to sleep," I said instead of returning the sentiment, my stomach feeling sick, and my head and my heart pounding in unison.

"I'm sorry," she whispered.

"So am I," I replied, and squeezed her harder. "You have no idea."

I kissed her shoulder where I'd bitten her, marking her perfect skin, inhaling her scent and listening for when her breathing became even and she fell back to sleep, and then I climbed out of bed.

Chapter Thirty-Two
~ BEAST ~

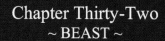You know what she did," Rider said, leaning forward in his chair.

I nodded solemnly, because it was true, did. There was no denying it.

"Then you know the club can't let it go, brother. She has to pay in blood for her treachery. It's the way of the club," Rider added.

"Club law," Gauge agreed with a growl.

I swallowed thickly, my hands steepled in front of me. I was trying to keep my calm instead of losing my shit like I normally did, but I could feel the anger and rage bubbling and churning in my gut.

"I get that it hurts," Dom said, his eyebrows pulled in deep, "but you have to see beyond that. You have to see the damage she could have caused. The men she could have gotten killed."

I looked at him sharply. "You think I don't? You think I don't see how fucked up this is? Because I do. This isn't how it was supposed to go down..." I dragged a hand through my hair and sighed. "I can't help how I feel, brothers."

And there it was.

I was Beast, the Enforcer, the most brutal man in the club's history. I had no limits, no restrictions on what I would or wouldn't do. No shame. No fear of retribution. No hard line... and right now I was talking about motherfuckin' feelings. I shook my head. What the hell was happening to me?

"This is fucked up," Casa said from his seat, and I could hear his foot tapping on the floor as his leg bounced. "Seriously fuckin' fucked up."

He was disappointed in Belle, as ridiculous as that sounded. He was hurt—maybe even more hurt than me. Casa trusted too easily, and he never saw Belle as a traitor. Maybe he was more disappointed in himself than her.

"It is," Rider agreed.

"I mean, it's Belle." Casa shrugged like it was the most obvious thing in the world. "Belle wouldn't hurt a fly. She takes care of us. The new prospect read *Little* motherfuckin' *Women* and *Pride and* motherfuckin' *Prejudice* because of her, and then he convinced me to read it. She lectured me on Mr. Darcy, and what his true intentions were and why Elizabeth couldn't be with him, she—"

"We get it!" Gauge snapped, placing his cigar into the ashtray, a long curl of smoke snaking up like a tendril. "We get it, Casa. I don't need to be schooled on books to get how fucked up this situation is."

Casa looked down to his hands like he'd been scolded by his father, and for the first time in a long time he didn't come back with some witty remark. He stayed silent, mourning Belle.

"We warned you what would happen, brother. At the hospital, we said she'd have to go to ground if she was with them," Gauge said on a deep sigh, like the air was thick and vile in his mouth and lungs and he didn't want to have to breathe it in and had been holding his breath for too long. "And we saw it for ourselves. There ain't no way that shipment could have been hijacked unless she told them. That information was privy to only us in this room and her. She made her bed, brother."

I nodded again. Because I knew. I remembered. I just didn't like it. I didn't want it to be true. Not after last night. No, that wasn't true. It went further back than that. I just hadn't truly seen it until last night. And yet here I was, nodding like one of those plastic dogs you saw on dashboards that nods every time the car goes over a bump in the road. Agreeing when I didn't want to.

We'd made sure the delivery we planned was a fake. We'd set her up once and for all to test her loyalty, and she'd failed. Gauge was right: she'd made her bed and now it was time to go to ground for it…yet I couldn't let go.

I looked over at Shooter, who hadn't said a damn word since we'd sat down in church to have this meeting. He was sitting back in his chair, a cigarette hanging from his lips as he listened to everything we all had to say, his gaze moving from each of us, taking in everyone's pain and anger.

"She needs to go to ground," Gauge said simply. "Ain't no way around it. She turned on the club." He spread his hands wide, like that was the end of the discussion, and I had the sudden urge to stand up and punch him in his face. And then keep on punching until there was nothing left of his mouth so he couldn't say those words again. "You knew when you went in there that that was the plan, brother. Just 'cause you dipped your dick in her perfect pussy don't mean anything's changed."

Despite the situation, Casa snickered, and I glared over at him. "Kinda ironic though, ain't it."

I knew what he was saying...where he was going, and I agreed. Because yeah, it was ironic that the only woman I'd ever cared about had turned out to be a traitor.

"Maybe there was a reason," Rider suggested, grasping at straws.

"Don't change the fact," Gauge replied coldly. "She turned on the club."

Shooter sat up straight, pulling the cigarette from between his lips and stubbing it out in the ashtray. He gave a long sigh, finally coming to his decision. He'd heard enough, and Belle's fate was practically signed, sealed, and delivered.

"So we use her to bait the Italians and then they all go to ground," he said, and he sounded as disappointed about it as I was. "*All of them.*"

And there I was nodding again.

Wanted to rip my own damn head off.

"Let's vote," Shooter said, his face expressionless.

Around the table, I watched my brothers' hands going up, sealing Belle's fate, a sick feeling growing in my gut like fungus. I couldn't help but feel responsible for the outcome of the situation. I'd asked for her to be my nurse. Demanded she be the one to look after me at the hospital. If I hadn't, she wouldn't have gotten herself wrapped up in all of this.

Or maybe I was just bitter because I wished I'd never met her.

Never touched her.

Never tasted her.

This was my fault.

Her death would be on my hands. Her cries would join the chorus of other screams in my head. Her tears and blood would lay at my feet, slowly drowning me.

All eyes landed on me as they waited on my decision. Nothing could be decided unless we all agreed, but how could I agree to this? I pulled my cigarettes out and lit one, inhaling the smoke deep into my lungs and holding it there for several moments before slowly releasing it. Taking my time, mulling everything over. My dick was still aching from where her body had held it tight within it. The scent of her wrapped around me, letting me know that she wasn't just a hit, she was a woman, a civilian, an innocent…only she wasn't, not really. She'd been working with the Italians, telling them club secrets. The whole time she'd been caring for me, she'd been whispering what she'd heard to them.

Belle was beautiful, but she was far from innocent.

The burden was hers to share.

And then there was Echo.

He was gone because of those Italians.

And she had been helping them.

How many more of my brothers had to die because of her?

I lifted my hand in the air, sealing her fate, hating myself. Hating Belle. Hating my brothers. This club. The Italians. This life.

"It's decided then," Shooter said. "I'll be the one to do it." And he looked me in the eye when he said it, knowing how much it would kill me to do it, but he didn't understand; I *had* to do it. It had to be me. The burden had to be shared between me and Belle, and no one else.

"I've got it," I said, my voice thick with steel.

"Brother—" Gauge started, but I held a hand up to him, my hard gaze meeting his.

"I said I've got it."

He nodded and Shooter slammed the gavel down, the finality of it a nail in both Belle's and my coffins. I took another drag on the cigarette as my brothers began to file out of the room, but I stayed where I was, my legs unwilling to hold me up, my muscles feeling like jelly. I felt weaker now than I ever had in that hospital bed.

Everyone left but Rider and Shooter. Both of them sat there watching me, waiting for me to say something, but the words wouldn't come. The silence went on and on, and they let me sit there, stewing in my own dark thoughts and wishing for something, anything else but this.

But I knew the rules.

I knew what had to happen.

Yet no matter how much I wanted to hate her, I found I couldn't.

I'd been angry at the world for a long damn time, hating and killing, violence and blood calling to my heart, but now it was Belle calling to it and I knew I'd never be the same after this. Her death was one I'd never recover from.

"If it's any consolation," Shooter finally said, "I'm sorry it had to come to this. I trusted her too, and I don't do that often."

I looked over at him, my face expressionless as a thousand emotions worked themselves into a frenzy inside of me.

Rider stood up and grabbed some glasses and a bottle of Jack from the sideboard. He poured us all a shot and slid one over to me.

"Belle said I'm not supposed to drink," I said, the words slipping out before I could stop them.

Rider raised an eyebrow at me, and I lifted my glass and threw the whiskey to the back of my throat. The past year had been hell. I'd lost my brother, my friend, I'd lost myself. My body, what little was left of my soul, and at times I'd lost my mind, succumbing to the pain and the rage I'd felt. But I'd come back. I wasn't the same man I once had been. I don't think anyone ever could ever be the same after that, but my priorities hadn't changed—the club was my life, my family, yet I desperately wanted Belle to be a part of that. Yet no matter how much I tried, I couldn't see how she could ever be a part of this world.

She'd never be forgiven.

She'd never be trusted.

She'd always be in danger.

But I still wanted it. I still wanted her. The dream. The life I'd seen my brothers have. I wanted it even though I knew I couldn't have it, and that pill wasn't just bitter to swallow, it was impossible. It was a cement block trying to squeeze down my scorched throat. It was acid poured over my favorite food. It was poison in my whiskey. It was a knife to the back and a kiss on the lips.

I wanted the alternative life I should have had with Belle—the one where we fuck every day and night and I take her for rides on my bike. I'd come home from work and find her baking muffins or some shit in the kitchen, my kid growing in her round belly. I'd put my hand there, feeling those tiny kicks of life within her, and then I'd kiss her, hard and deep, giving her all of me because that would be enough.

But that was just a dream—a fantasy. A fucking mirage, because I knew I wouldn't ever get the chance to have that life. And I knew that there would be no saving my soul after this, just like there was no saving Belle.

Chapter Thirty-Three
~ *Belle* ~

I woke up tired and sore, like I hadn't slept for hours and like I hadn't had the best sex of my entire life.

Beast wasn't in the bed, but the scent of him was, and for the first time in weeks I felt safe again. I curled my naked body into a ball and pulled the covers over my head, stewing over Mateo and Carlos and what they'd asked me to do. So far I'd given them as little information as I could—just enough to keep me alive and keep them away from Jenna—but they were getting impatient and I was getting desperate.

I'd never waivered though, sticking to only giving them useless information that wouldn't harm Beast or the club and didn't give anything away. That was until I'd come home yesterday and found a mutilated dog on my doorstep, its head missing entirely, and then I'd fallen apart. Hot tears burned my eyes, and for the first time since all of this began I felt angry. I didn't deserve this. I hadn't done anything wrong, yet I was being punished and tormented, threatened, hurt… it just wasn't fair.

So yesterday, after overhearing some of the men talking about a drop earlier in the day, I'd told Mateo and Carlos about it. I knew no one would get hurt because Shooter had said, as I'd listened from around the corner, that the truck was to be parked up and left behind the warehouse. It was being collected later in the day.

I'd told Mateo and Carlos this, leaving out the information on the truck having no Highwaymen in it. I'm not sure why I omitted that part. Maybe it was because I knew more than anything all Mateo and Carlos really cared about was hurting more of the club's bikers, and that was something I couldn't stand the thought of.

Despite what the club did—drugs and guns, violence and bloodshed—I found myself loving each and every Highwayman. They

241

were, at heart, good men. They just wanted a family. They wanted to belong. And they had found that within that club.

But none of that mattered now. Things were accelerating with Mateo and Carlos. They weren't satisfied with just the drop. They wanted more. They wanted blood. There was only one thing I could think to do now. One thing that would likely get me killed regardless, but it was the only chance I had of ending this once and for all. One big leap and one small chance that I might actually get out of this alive.

I had to finally tell the club.

I trusted Beast with all my heart, and I knew he'd know what to do.

He could protect me and Jenna and make all of this go away.

I smiled, thinking of him—my beautiful Beast. He didn't think he had a soul. He thought his heart was black and empty, but it wasn't. There was so much love in him, and slowly, inch by inch, I'd been peeling back the layers to reveal him. I hadn't meant to fall for Beast, but I knew there was no coming back from it—from him.

When everything else was stripped away, when the worry and the fear and the tears were gone, there was only Beast and the life we could have together. And after last night, despite him not telling me he loved me back, I knew deep down that he felt the same way. I just needed to strip back some more layers and show him the life we could have. One where we would make love all night and I'd cook his dinner when he came home from the club. He'd take me out on his bike and we'd watch the sunset together with a cold beer in our hands. He'd come to dinner with Jenna and Gregory, and she'd hate him and he'd hate her, and they'd argue and bicker but deep down they'd love each other really because they had to because they both loved me.

That was the life we were supposed to have, not this one.

I sighed, staring up at the white cotton sheet, the scent of Beast keeping me warm. Yes, I needed to tell him everything, and now, before it was too late. Because if he found out from someone else, he'd never trust me again. And I couldn't lose him, not now that I'd found him.

I chewed on my bottom lip, thinking of Lorenzo and how mad he was going to be. He'd changed into someone I didn't recognize in the past week. Someone I didn't like, at all. He treated me like an object. He made me feel useless. He looked at me like he owned me, and I had to really think about how much he knew of his brothers. He said that he didn't have anything to do with them anymore, but his actions and theirs spoke loudly to me.

Lorenzo and I were over, no matter what happened. I needed Beast and no one else.

I realized that knowing I was going to tell Beast meant I wasn't afraid anymore, and for the first time in weeks I felt the heavy burden of secrets shift from off of my chest so I could breathe again. God, it felt good. Like the air had been tainted with poisonous lies for so long, and now it was clean and fresh.

The sound of the bedroom door opening had me crawling out from under the covers with a smile on my face. I pushed my hair back from my eyes as Beast sat in the chair opposite, his hands steepled in front of him as he rested his elbows on his knees.

"Beast," I said, his name a sigh of relief on my lips. "Where were you?"

Beast was my savior, my protector.

"Get dressed," he said, his voice hard and clipped, like he didn't know me as intimately as he did.

My smile fell. He looked so sad and broken. So lost, like he had in the hospital. "I need to talk to you," I said, mustering all the courage I could. It was now or never. "It's really important."

His gaze was cold, disciplined, and I frowned as he sat back, lifting his leg so that his ankle rested on his knee. "No, I need you to get dressed," he said simply. Beast pulled his cigarettes out of the top pocket of his cut and put one between his lips before lighting it.

I watched him carefully, a small frown pulling between my eyebrows. "What's going on, Beast? You're scaring me."

He took a drag on his cigarette, exhaling like he was putting a lot of thought into it. His face was expressionless, devoid of everything I

243

knew and loved about him, but he couldn't hide the emotions from his eyes. Everything I needed to see was in those eyes of his, and what I saw frightened me. "Just need you to put some clothes on, Belle."

My clothes were on the other side of the room, and I wished that I had thought to get dressed before he came back. I suddenly felt completely self-conscious, like he could see more than just my skin but all the way to my soul.

I shimmied to the edge of the bed, wrapping the sheet around my naked body as I stood, and walked to my clothes. His eyes were cold and hard and watching my every move, and I swallowed, suddenly terrified of what was happening.

I grabbed my clothes and walked back to the bed, my knees knocking in fear. He was still watching me, his hard gaze not giving me even a second of reprieve. I threaded my arms through my bra, trying to put it on without flashing him, but the bed sheet was slipping and I couldn't get it under my boobs. I was getting flustered and panicked and sweating, the sheet sticking to me, the bra suddenly feeling too small, my hands trembling, and the air slowly being sucked out of the room breath by my frantic breath.

And the whole time he sat there, smoking and staring, like he didn't have a care in the world.

"Oh my god, can you at least turn around for a moment so I can get dressed without you staring at me!" I snapped, my chin trembling as tears filled my eyes.

Beast sucked in his lower lip before releasing it with a heavy sigh. He swallowed and I watched mesmerized as his Adam's apple bobbed in his throat like he was thinking it over. He dropped his leg from his knee and leaned forward, his elbows back on his knees so that when he looked up at me it was through his thick, dark lashes. And honestly, he'd never looked so beautiful or so dangerous.

"I'm not getting dressed while you stare at me like some kind of sociopath!" I yelled, my fear growing by the second. What was happening? How had we gotten to this place?

Beast scowled and stood up, his shoulders rolling. Sitting on his bed looking up at him, he seemed even bigger—like twelve feet tall and easily able to squash me under his foot. And by the look on his face right then, I didn't doubt that he would. I wished that his bed was sinking sand and it would suck me under. I wouldn't even fight it; I'd just let it take me down into its murky depths because I had no idea who I could trust anymore. Everyone I loved turned their back on me.

"Please," I begged. "Let me get dressed without you staring."

He swallowed again before turning around, and as he did I caught a glimpse of the gun tucked into the waistband of his jeans. It was a good thing that I was sitting down, because my legs turned to jelly and my body seemed to pool into a terrified puddle next to the bed.

This was it. I realized with absolute certainty that Beast was there to kill me.

I didn't know how he *knew*, but he knew. The cold look, the heavy sighs—it all made sense now.

"You done yet?" he said, his voice gravelly and cold.

I stood up, my knees almost buckling as I tried once again to put my bra on. "I don't want to die, Beast," I admitted softly, the soft material limp in my hands.

He sighed again but didn't say anything, and hot tears burned down my face. I realized that everything in the clubhouse had gone quiet. There was none of the usual laughter or chatter, no music playing, no engines roaring or doors slamming. Everyone in the clubhouse knew about me, and they were all just out there waiting for Beast to bring me out and kill me.

I suddenly couldn't breathe, the world spun and I clutched at my chest as I started to fall, the sheet pooling at my feet. Dizziness gripped me, the terror and fear ready to knock me unconscious, but then Beast's arms were around me, hauling me upright and dragging me against his hard body, and I clung to him, sobbing.

"Please don't kill me, please," I sobbed, and I felt his arms stiffen, his fingers digging into me almost painfully as I held on to him. "I don't want to die," I sobbed.

His arms were around me, my face buried in his chest as I cried, soaking his T-shirt with my misery. The safety I'd felt in his arms earlier was gone and I was suddenly petrified of him; this beautiful, brutal man who hours ago had worshipped my body with his was now the epitome of evil, ready to take my life. He gripped me tighter as I tried to pull away, his large, rough hands trying to soothe me as they stroked down my back.

"It's gonna be okay," he growled.

But it wasn't.

It wasn't going to be okay.

He was going to *kill* me.

"I can explain, Beast."

I sobbed even harder and continued to pull away, but the more I pulled the harder he gripped, holding me against him no matter how much I thrashed in his arms. I looked up at him, my tear-stained face pleading with him to let me explain, but his face showed nothing. It was empty, hollow, a shell that had been cracked open and the insides tipped out.

Beast reached down and hooked my face in his hand before leaning down and kissing my salty tears away.

"It's gonna be okay," he said again, kissing each tear away, but I saw it in his eyes that he didn't mean it. That he knew it was just lies he was telling us both. He didn't want to do this, but he still would. It wasn't going to be okay, not even a little bit.

When he pulled back, his lips glistened with my tears—their misery and sadness, their fear and shame—and I saw that he felt those things too. I sobbed as I stood on my tiptoes and kissed his lips, reclaiming my tears back from him, because if he was going to kill me then he couldn't have them—they were *my* tears. But as my lips touched his, his mouth opened and his tongue came out, pushing its way into mine so he could kiss me brutally.

I was still fighting against him, still crying and pushing him away even as I kissed him back, our mouths colliding in a nuclear collision of lips and teeth and tongue. I was desperate for him to listen to me, to

246

know me, to love me, and understand that I hadn't meant to betray him. That I would never ever want to hurt him, but even as I kissed him, I knew it was too late.

Beast had made up his mind.

The club had made up their mind.

It was over.

Chapter Thirty-Four
~ BEAST~

Belle pulled away so suddenly she stumbled backwards, and this time I let her go. The look in her eyes was one I knew well. I'd seen it on many a man's face once they realized that their time was up. That their brief moment on this earth had come to an end. She stared at me, naked, chest heaving, hair wild, cheeks damp, and I thought that she was going to crack—to break down and start begging.

There were two things in this world that I hated more than anything: cowards that begged for their life, and traitors. She'd checked off one of those boxes, and I was just waiting for the other. But she didn't. Belle smoothed back her hair and reached for her clothes, putting those beautiful tits away behind her lacy bra. She pulled on her T-shirt and slipped on her skirt, all the while her eyes darting between me and the door.

I'd seen that look too, and I already knew she was going to try to run, but she wouldn't get far.

Belle sat down on the edge of my bed, reaching for her sandals that had slid under it. As she pushed her foot into one, I noted how pretty her feet were. Small, like really small, perfect pink nail polish, and a small ankle chain, and as ridiculous as it sounds, I thought to myself how sad it was that she wouldn't ever get to use those pretty feet to walk on a beach again. Or to let the sea wash over her toes. Or how she wouldn't paint those toenails any other color. They'd just be pink, forever, until those toes rotted away.

"I'm ready," Belle said, suddenly standing in front of me, looking up into my face. She seemed smaller than normal. Her shoulders rounded, her back hunched, like she was trying to curl in on herself. She'd wrapped her hair up in a knot thingy on top of her head, and I thought about how I'd never wrap it around my hand again. I'd never feel how soft it was against my chest or move it from her neck so I could kiss a path to her collarbone.

I turned to the door, pushing all of those thoughts away. It didn't matter—none of it mattered.

She was a traitor to the club, and to me. None of this was real. I'd been played because I'd been weak, but that would *never* happen again.

"What happens next?" she asked, her voice so soft it sounded like a whisper in my head. I turned back to her.

"We're just going to talk," I said, my words devoid of emotion.

To her credit, she didn't cry, even though she knew I was lying. She knew what was coming and she was trying to make peace with it. Fuck, I hadn't realized how strong she was. I'd had grown men on their knees begging for their lives by this point. But I could see by the look on her face that she was done crying, and she was not going to beg.

"Beast." She said my name, and I realized that I'd been looking over her shoulder instead of at her. "Look at me," she said, so I did.

I looked at Belle, summoning the man I used to be. The enforcer. The human weapon. The Devil's best friend. I summoned him to help me through this as I looked down at Belle, and then she did something I hadn't expected.

She fucking smiled at me.

Not an *aha, fuck you* kind of smile either, but a smile that said she understood.

"Don't do that," I growled, hating her for smiling. Hating her for not begging. Hating her for putting me in this position in the first place. "Why the fuck did you get yourself mixed up in all of this, Belle? Why couldn't you just do your job, get me healthy, and then go back to your life?"

I felt the rage that had lived inside of me for the past year crawl out of its hole, breathing new life into me. She stared up at me helplessly, her eyes wide, her smile falling, and I just wanted to fucking shake her. Hit her. Slap her. Fuck her. I wanted her to know what a fucking waste her life had been because of all of this. How she'd screwed everything up for herself. Everything that could have been, and everything that should have been.

The anger grew and grew, wrapping tendrils of fury around my heart with every breath I took until I couldn't look at her anymore, I had to get away, but the moment I stepped outside that door it was over, so I just stood there, burning away in a vat of boiling rage as she stared up at me, looking fucking perfect.

"It's not how it seems, Beast," she replied, a frown pulling between her eyebrows. She shrugged and looked away. "It's not always so black and white."

I grabbed her then, one hand on either arm, and I shook her, my fury bursting at the seams. "It is always black and fuckin' white, Belle. Always!" I roared, infuriated by her naivety. "The fact that you can't see that is exactly how you got yourself in this position in the first place."

I shoved her away from me, her skin under my hands feeling like fire. Like I was being burned alive all over again. My body itched and ached, my muscles throbbed and my head pounded. And the gun in my waistband felt like molten lava as it touched my skin.

She was fucking stupid. So motherfucking stupid.

"Beast," she started, but I glared back at her and her jaw snapped shut.

"We need to go," I bit out, hating her for making me do this.

I wished she would beg so I could hate her some more.

I wished she would plead with me so I could tell her no.

I wished she would cry so I could laugh in her face.

I wanted her to hate me like I hated her right now.

But she didn't do any of those things, despite the fact that I could see her jaw was clenched as she tried to stop her teeth from chattering and I could see that her knees were knocking together as she tried her best to contain the tremble in them. No, Belle took a deep breath and looked down at the ground and I turned from her and opened the door, ready to take her to meet her maker.

Out in the clubhouse, my brothers were sitting, waiting.

There was no anger or resentment with them. If anything, there was sadness in all of them. None of them liked this outcome any more than I did, but it was the way of our world and it had to be done. Traitors had to pay.

Shooter stood up when he saw us, and Gauge and Rider and Dom all did the same. They had beers open in front of them, but no one had been drinking. The sweetbutts and the old ladies had been sent home and told not to come back, and most of my brothers were out on jobs. So it was just us and Belle and no way out.

I heard her stop momentarily and I thought, *This is it. This is where she freaks out and tries to run, tries to fight back. She'll start begging and crying and pleading. She'll try to explain her way out of this, but there's no explaining. She's a fucking traitor and she's going to get what's coming to her.*

Death.

It comes for us all in the end.

Death was inevitable.

Belle started to walk again, passing me and heading toward Shooter. Gauge watched her, his dark eyes full of the same coldness I no doubt held in mine.

"So," Belle said to Shooter, "what happens now?"

Shooter looked at her calmly before taking a deep breath and sighing. He glanced over her shoulder at me, holding my gaze momentarily before looking back at Belle.

"We need you to call Lorenzo," he said. "Tell him to meet you at an address at a certain time."

"And then?" she pressed.

"Then we'll make it quick."

Belle turned and looked at me. "You mean *he'll* make it quick." She looked back at Shooter and he nodded simply. "I don't want it to be him," she said defiantly.

"This ain't a democracy, Belle," I snarled.

"Fuck you," she snapped, throwing me a hurt look, and as ridiculous as it sounds, I was shocked by her uncouthness. Belle didn't

251

swear, like ever, and I had the sudden urge to laugh. "I want it to be *anyone* but him," she continued.

Shooter frowned. "I don't think you understand what's happening here, darlin'."

"I do. You're going to kill me for betraying your trust. I get that, I'm not stupid, Shooter. I knew this would happen. And I get that you don't even care that I didn't really have a choice, but—"

"You did have a fucking choice, Belle!" I yelled, interrupting her. "That's the goddamn point. You had a choice and you made the wrong one and now you're going to ground."

"Brother, calm down," Rider said, taking a step toward me.

"Fine," Shooter interrupted, "I'll do it."

"No, that's not what we agreed!" I said, storming forward. "I do it."

Shooter looked between me and Belle, giving a shake of his head. He grabbed his beer off the bar and took`a long swallow before slamming it back down. "Jesus fucking Christ, I can't believe I'm even having this discussion."

"Well believe it, Prez," I bit out. "She dies by my hand and no one else's. That's what we agreed."

I couldn't look at her. I didn't want to see the hurt on her face. The disbelief and hurt that I wanted to kill her. The resentment because this had been my deal, my *only* objection. I was a monster, and now she really did know it. Beast by name, beast by nature.

Shooter looked over at Belle. "Just need you to call him and tell him to meet you," he placated as calmly as he could.

"Then promise me it won't be Beast. I'll call him and I'll take you, I'll take the scary huge guy over there," she said, pointing to Gauge. "I'll even take the aging wannabe male model over there, but I won't do anything if you don't promise me that Beast won't be the one to kill me."

All eyes turned to Rider.

The *aging wannabe male model*.

And then Casa's booming laugh erupted through the clubhouse, and no matter how much Gauge told him to shut the fuck up, Casa just laughed and laughed and laughed. I wasn't sure if he was high or if he'd gone insane, but he just kept on laughing.

"Enough!" Shooter eventually yelled, loud enough to make him shut up.

"Sorry, Prez," Casa said, still snickering, his gaze on Rider, and I knew that in years to come, Belle would be haunting me because Casa would never let that shit drop. He'd bring it up at every party. He'd bring it up at every meet. Every argument would end in Casa laughing at Rider and his wannabe male model ways. Belle was going to be around in the club long after she was dead.

"You know, we have ways of making you talk," Shooter said, and Belle looked like she was about to piss herself because she'd seen on my body the ways men like us used to make people talk, but she lifted her chin and held her ground. "Fine," Shooter finally agreed, and when I opened my mouth to argue with him, he glared at me. "This has to happen, Beast. We need to finish this today, so learn to deal with it, for the sake of the club."

For the sake of the club…

His words cut and burned me worse than the bastards that had tortured me for hours.

I'd lost everything for the sake of this club. My body, my mind, and now my woman. All for this fucking club. I gritted my teeth and bit my tongue, holding in my anger, because once I let it go I wouldn't be able to stop. I'd rip and tear and kill anyone and anything in my path.

"Phone," Shooter said to me, and I pulled out Belle's cellphone from my cut. He took it and handed it to her along with a scrap of paper with an address on it. "Call Lorenzo. Tell him to meet you here."

She nodded, her hand shaking as she took the phone and paper. I watched her swallow, her face paling, her body trembling, before she finally looked up at Shooter with a small frown.

"What now?" he barked, growing impatient—which was unusual for Shooter, because ironically he had the patience of a saint, but this shit was wearing on us all. We all liked Belle and no one really wanted her to have to die, but it was what it was.

"Why do you want me to call Lorenzo?" she asked, and she genuinely looked confused as shit about it. The sort of confused you couldn't fake.

Shooter glanced between Gauge and Rider, his face expressionless. "Because this is all on him, Belle," he said, looking back at her. "And we're going to make him pay for it."

Belle's face paled further and she stumbled back. I moved forward quickly, catching her so she didn't fall, but she shrugged out of my grip like she'd been burned.

"Don't touch me!" she yelled, glaring before turning back to Shooter. "No, no it can't be." She shook her head. "I've never told him anything."

Shooter frowned even further.

Belle glanced between us all. "I never told Lorenzo *anything* and he never asked anything. He was awful to me—treated me like…like…" Her hand went to her mouth, rubbing her bottom lip subconsciously. "But this has nothing to do with him."

"Shooter," I warned, because if they'd gotten this wrong and I'd lost her because of it, heads were gonna roll.

"So who have you been talking to?" Rider asked.

Belle swallowed

"It's his brothers, Mateo and Carlos," she said, looking like she was going to be sick just by saying their names. Like saying their names might bring them forth, kinda like saying *Candyman* in the mirror five times. "They came to me, threatened me." Her hand went to her stomach. "Beat me." Her gaze dropped to her feet. "They said they'd kill my godmother Jenna if I didn't do what they said."

"Fuck, I thought those two had moved back to Italy," Gauge said.

"Looks like they're back," Rider replied.

"Don't change anything," Shooter said. "She's still a traitor to the club."

"I hate to say it, brother, but the prez is right," Casa said to me, because we all knew that this wouldn't even have been a conversation if it weren't for me.

"They left a mutilated dog in my bed!" Belle cried, like she'd been holding everything in for so long and now she just needed to get it all out. "They chopped off its head and left it in my car!" She grabbed them hem of her T-shirt and lifted it to show the faded bruise on her stomach, which I'd seen earlier. "They hit me, threatened to rape and torture me." Belle was sobbing now, her cheeks flushed red as tears streamed down them. She looked between us all. "They said they had someone watching me, that if I told anyone what was going on that they'd have Jenna and I tortured for days before they killed us. I was terrified!"

Rider stood next to Shooter. "Prez."

"I know," Shooter said sharply.

"This changes everything," he continued.

"I know," Shooter said again.

"And believe me or don't, it doesn't really matter anymore, but when I told them about that drop, I knew none of you were going to be there." She looked between us all. "I heard you say that it was a drop and go, or something to that extent. I would never put any of you in danger—not because I'm scared of you, but because I care about you all."

Silence descended like a lead balloon and we all stood there with our tails between our legs. We'd fucked up, bad. We'd been in such a hurry to finish this shit and find someone to blame that we hadn't looked into it properly, and it had nearly gotten her killed. Belle was far from innocent, and what she'd done was still wrong, but we should have helped her. We should have spoken to her. Let her know in no uncertain terms that we would protect her from anything and anyone.

Belle scrubbed at the tears on her cheeks and finally turned to glare at me, her eyes connecting with mine and burning with pain and anger and resentment. "This is all your fault, Beast. You dragged me into your world, and these monsters came for me because of it."

255

And she was right.

Every last word of what she was saying was right.

This was all my fault.

Chapter Thirty-Five
~ *Belle* ~

"You should have told Beast. He would have protected you," Joey was talking, but I wasn't really listening.

How could I? Thirty minutes ago I'd been a dead woman walking, my final breaths ready to be breathed before Beast put a bullet in my head. My future was still hazy and uncertain, and death was still in the cards, but for the time being I was alive.

"The club would have protected you, girl," Joey continued. "Hell, *I* would have protected you." He shook his head, sounding less like the Joey I'd come to know and more like a stranger. He even sounded sad.

"I shouldn't have ever been put in this situation," I finally said, still refusing to look at him. "This wasn't my fight, yet I've been dragged into it, terrorized and then told I was going to be killed…by Beast, no less." My voice cracked on his name, the disbelief that he had wanted to be the one to kill me still squeezing my heart in a vise. "He wanted to *kill* me."

Despite him having all the charm and sophistication of an alley cat, Joey suddenly dropped to one knee in front of me and took my hand in his.

"You're an innocent, Belle, and a friend of the club. We would have protected you until our last breaths. You have to fuckin' know that. And Beast…shit, bitch, he was punishing *himself* by killing you. In his eyes, this was his cross to bear."

I looked up then, my gaze meeting his, and I felt even worse because it was unwavering. I should have told one of them. I could see it in his eyes that he meant every last word of what he was saying. Joey would have died protecting me. He would have given his life to save mine if need be. I wasn't sure about the others—I hadn't looked into their eyes—but despite everything that had happened, I trusted Joey enough to know that he wouldn't lie to me.

257

"I don't know this world," I whimpered, wanting to be strong but feeling so weak. "All I know is that I was asked to nurse a man back to health, and in doing so I've been beaten, had my family threatened, terrorized, and then almost killed."

I stated it as simply as I could in the hopes that he could understand; black and white, good versus evil. Beseeching him to appreciate where I was coming from.

Joey leaned over and pulled me into his arms, and I didn't fight him. All my fight was gone. The only thing left was a puddle of despair and worry. I'd been agonizing over this stuff for weeks, and to have it all out in the open was like breathing fresh air. Joey held me and I sobbed quietly, hating how pathetic I was, but glad to be able to let it all out. Glad to be able to confide in someone.

The door to the Church, or whatever it was called, suddenly opened and Beast stepped out first, his eyes flaring in annoyance when he saw Joey holding me.

"What the fuck is this?" he yelled, storming forward.

Joey let me go and jumped back up to his feet. "Sorry, just comforting her."

Beast stormed forward and grabbed Joey by the front of his scruffy black tee so quickly I barely saw him move. He slammed him against the wall hard, so much so that I felt the vibrations through my feet.

"Oh yeah, comfortin' her? You keeping her real happy, prospect? You making sure she's well looked after?"

The murderous intentions on Beast's face were obvious to anyone who looked. Anyone but Joey.

"Yeah, for sure, Beast. I've been looking after her for weeks!" he said innocently, and it seemed I wasn't the only one that wasn't cut out for this life.

Beast slammed Joey against the wall harder and I jumped to my feet. I grabbed Beast's arm and pulled, but his muscles had solidified and turned to stone.

"Get off of him!" I practically screamed. Beast slowly turned his gaze on me and my eyes narrowed. God, I hated him so much. "What is wrong with you? You're unhinged!" I tugged on his arm again, but he still wouldn't budge.

"You letting the prospect keep you cozy now, Belle? First the Italian, then me, and now him? You working your way through a lot of men."

I glared at him before reaching back and slapping the side of his face so hard my hand stung and I yelped in pain. But I wasn't done. I wasn't even nearly done. I hit him again, and again, slapping and kicking and growing more infuriated by his lack of response.

"How dare you!" I screamed.

"Beast!" Shooter yelled as the rest of the men came out of the little room. "Let the fucking prospect go! Gauge, grab the bitch before she hurts herself."

I could feel the anger emanating from Beast. It was like the beams of the sun—heat and radiation vibrating from him and burning everything it touched—but he made no move to stop me from hitting him, or to hit me back. He just glared and took my anger.

Gauge stormed toward me. He grabbed me around the waist and dragged me away from Beast even as I continued to yell and scream, all self-preservation out the window.

"I was crying, okay!" I shouted. "I was crying because *you* wanted to kill me, Beast, and Joey was hugging me and telling me I was an idiot for not coming to the club about this. He was telling me that he would have protected me—that *you* would have protected me!"

Beast's nostrils flared like a bull ready for a fight. His gaze never left mine and I let out a shaky breath. I was so done with all of this. It was too much. How did they live with this every day of their lives? How did they survive this drama? This heartache? This fear?

Beast suddenly let go of the prospect. He looked Joey up and down, his jaw twitching so violently I wasn't sure why something hadn't broken in it. The room had fallen into silence; a tense standoff between me and Beast. Gauge was still holding onto me, his arms locked around my waist. I was breathing hard, practically panting in equal parts fear as anger, and Beast looked like he was having the same problem too. His chest was heaving, his nostrils flared. I wasn't sure if he wanted to kill me, beat me, or fuck me. But the look on his face said that it was maybe all three.

"Who the fuck is Joey?" Casa said, cutting the tension like a chainsaw through butter: messy and completely unnecessary.

"The prospect," Rider said.

"No fuckin' shit!" he returned with a grin. "Well, Joey, prospect, kid that almost got his ass whooped into oblivion, I suggest you go do some errands before Beast breaks out of whatever fuckin' stupor he's in and decides to tear you motherfuckin' apart."

"I was just trying to help. She looked sad," Joey tried to explain.

Beast broke our fickle bond to glower at Joey, and the poor kid paled before moving quickly out of his reach.

"Fill the bikes up," Rider said as Joey left without another word. He turned to me. "Shit's about to get real dark, darlin'."

My heart stuttered in my chest.

This was it.

They were still going to kill me, despite everything I'd said.

I braced myself for his wrath, yet welcomed the end.

"Just get it over with," I said, gritting my teeth.

"Belle," Beast uttered my name, sounding pained as he took a step toward me.

I moved away from him as if he were a virus and I could catch him.

"You don't get to say my name ever again," I replied without looking at him.

"Belle—"

"Never!" I yelled, finally looking at him.

His expression caught me off guard; it was somewhere between grief and shame, and I swallowed and looked away, knowing I'd back down if I looked at him any longer.

"So what happens now?" I asked, my gaze going between Shooter, Rider, Gauge, Casa…anyone but Beast.

Shooter sighed and I felt his weary sigh all the way to my bones. "Not entirely sure anymore," he admitted, running a hand down his beard. He shook his head. "Seems this fuckhead here is in love with you and doesn't want you to die, the person we thought you'd been talking to you haven't, and the people we thought were long gone are anything but. I need a fuckin' beer."

He stormed toward the bar and headed behind it, and we all followed him with our eyes as he pulled out a cold bottle and popped the lid before downing it, his previous half-drunk one now forgotten. When he finished that beer he set the empty bottle on the bar and pulled out a glass before pouring himself a neat whiskey. He pulled out his cigarettes, lit one, and then went and sat back on his bar stool, glass of whiskey in one hand, cigarette in the other, and his eyes closed in deep contemplation.

I looked around at the bikers in the room, all looking as confused as I was. I wanted to go home and crawl into bed. I wanted to sleep for a year. I wanted to call Jenna and explain everything to her. There were a lot of things that I wanted in that moment, but all I could think about was that Shooter had said Beast was in love with me.

I hated him—Beast—with every fiber of my being, and yet a part of me still longed for him. A part of me, despite hating him, loved him too. Why does that happen? Why do you always want what is so bad for you? Why do we surround ourselves with narcissists and bullies, users and abusers, the people that if we saw our friends in a relationship with we'd drag them away… and yet when it was our turn, we still fell in love with them.

What was it about these people that could capture a heart as easily as a butterfly?

Was it those glimpses of good that tormented us? The taunts of what could be that kept us there letting them hurt us? Or was it that we were just gluttons for punishment, because deep down we had some deep-rooted dislike of ourselves?

I headed to Shooter and picked up the bottle from the bar. He raised an eyebrow but handed me a glass regardless, and I poured myself a whiskey. Taking a sip, I winced as it burned all the way down into my stomach and lay there warming my insides. And then I went and sat next to Shooter—the man who had wanted me dead thirty minutes earlier—and we sat in silence together.

Eventually the other men came over too, smoking and drinking, all of us in deep contemplation. But Beast, he just stared and watched, and I could see the misery and torture on his face more blatant than the scars that ran down it. I refused to put him out of his misery though, despite what Shooter had just said and despite what I felt. After what we'd shared last night, he'd still intended to kill me. I let that sink in, hoping that would be enough to cut him out of my heart, but it didn't.

When I finished my whiskey, I chanced a glance at Shooter. His eyes were open now and he was staring down into his glass. He was so deep in thought I could practically hear the cogs working in his brain like he was putting a puzzle together.

He threw the rest of his whiskey to the back of his throat and rolled his shoulders before standing up. "How do Mateo and Carlos contact you?" he said to me, and the whole room froze as they listened.

"They just turn up." I shrugged. "Once it was the middle of the night and I was sleeping. I woke up to find Carlos standing in the doorway and Mateo on top of me, his hand over my mouth."

A low growl like an animal rose up from Beast, and I chanced a look at him. He looked furious, like he wanted to tear something apart. The irony had me shaking my head.

"Another time," I continued, "I got home after being here all day and they were waiting for me inside. Another time they grabbed me while I was grocery shopping and threw me in the back of their van. They drove me to the woods. They had me strip naked and told me they were going to rape me and then cut off my head before leaving it on Jenna's doorstep."

Another growl from Beast.

He started to pace the room, his hard stomps echoing through the clubhouse.

"I think they just enjoyed terrorizing me," I said, my voice low so as not to infuriate Beast any further. "They wanted me to be too scared to say anything."

"And Lorenzo," Rider asked, coming closer. "You said he treated you badly?"

I looked away, my cheeks flaming with shame. "Yes, but I don't want to talk about it. It was probably just me being overly sensitive."

"Need to know, Belle," Shooter said, sounding regretful. "Not to be a dick, but you don't seem the best judge of character. He was supposed to have cut all ties with his family years ago—it's the only reason we've allowed him to operate here. His business, his home, it's all been left alone because he said he had nothing to do with his family."

"Has he hurt you?" Casa asked, coming closer.

I looked up, noticing that all of them were close now, like they wanted to protect me. Only Beast remained outside of the little circle they had formed, pacing and glaring, his hands clenching and unclenching.

I swallowed. "He...he forced me to do things." I shook my head, feeling ridiculous.

"He raped you?" Gauge asked, sounding furious.

I shook my head no. "No, not really. I mean, I didn't want to, but he made me feel like I couldn't say no. And it was different—"

"Different?" Shooter asked.

"Aggressive. Violent. Forceful." As soon as I said the words, I felt sick. The memories of Lorenzo and the way he'd treated me, the things he'd made me do.

Beast lost it.

He just lost it.

He picked up a heavy armchair and threw it against the wall. It smashed with such force as he roared and picked up the coffee table and threw that. Anything within arm's reach he grabbed and threw, roaring through his anger. Violence surging through him as he lost control.

Gauge and Casa ran to him, grabbing him in an attempt to control him, and I stared on in total shock.

Shooter nodded thoughtfully. "We need protection on you at all times then. Gonna need someone staying with you so you're not unprotected."

"Protection?" I frowned. "I thought you were going to kill me."

"We'll deal with that shit later. Right now I need you to help me get the fucks that did this to my boy over there. Our brother Echo still needs revenge, and I have no doubt that you have a little anger broiling over for all the torment they've put you through, huh?" he said matter-of-factly.

"I'm not killing anyone," I replied quickly. "I can't do that! I'm not like all of you." I looked between them all, my eyes frantic.

Casa looked over and smirked like I'd just paid him a compliment. "We've got your back on the killing shit, nurse."

"Just need you to go on as normal. Wait for them to come to you, and when they do, we'll be waiting. That's your job—your role in all of this—and maybe, just maybe you'll come out of this unscathed," Shooter continued.

Unscathed! I blinked, relief and anger twisting inside of me. How could they think I would come out of this unscathed? I was already scarred to my core from these men and this club and all their drama.

"I won't be unscathed, Shooter. I've already been broken, by them and by this club. But fine, I'll do it, if nothing else but too be free of all of this—all of you."

"Whatever helps you sleep at night," he drolled.

Casa snickered and I turned and glared at him.

"What? What's so funny?" My hands were on my hips and I knew I needed to calm down. This was good, and I should have at least been a little grateful for the fact that I wasn't dead yet. Beast had shrugged Gauge and Casa off and was staring at me, his nostrils flared, an indecisive look on his face like he was being tormented.

Casa lit a cigarette, taking his sweet time before replying to me. "That you think you'll ever be done with *any* of this. Any of us, nurse."

"I will be." My eyes narrowed at him but he continued to smirk around his cigarette, smoke trailing up past his face.

"Shut the fuck up, Casa," Beast growled.

Casa shook his head. "Nah, girl, this club is in your blood now. Besides, you really think *he's* about to let you walk out of his life for good?" He nodded toward Beast and I frowned.

"*He* won't have a choice," I bit out.

"Belle," Beast warned, turning his attention back to me.

"I told you not to say my name," I gritted. "We're done. And when this is all over I want you out of my life for good. In fact, from now on I don't want you anywhere near me." I turned back to Shooter. "So who's going to be my protection?"

It was his turn to smirk now, a coy smile that lit up his face, and I knew automatically who he planned to keep with me.

"You've got to be kidding," I groaned, feeling even more annoyed.

"We wanna draw them out quick, get this shit over with. And the two of you together—you'll be the best bait there ever could be," he drawled, his eyebrows pulling in as he thought it over some more. "Yeah, Beast needs to be on you twenty-four/seven until this shit is done."

I glared at Beast and he scowled right back, his look telling me that this wasn't over. That we weren't done. Little did he know that he didn't get a say in the matter anymore. Because carved into my heart or not, I was done with Beast and this club, once and for all.

Chapter Thirty-Six
~ BEAST ~

Belle's trailer was the absolute worst.

I mean, I'd stayed in some shitty places before, but this thing was the next best thing to a tent.

It was drafty as hell, it creaked and rocked, the windows were busted and held together by tape, the floor felt like it was rotten and I was about to go through it at any minute…yet I kinda loved being there. Belle was all around it. Her floral scent clinging to the furniture and walls, her little knickknacks on the shelves and walls. She'd repurposed some wood for a table and it was sturdier than most of the stuff you could buy in IKEA.

I was staring down at the smallest double bed I'd ever seen in my life—I mean, it was the next best thing to a child's bed—and wondering if she'd fucked Lorenzo in it, when she cleared her throat behind me. I spun around to find her glaring at me—that seemed to be her typical expression since that morning.

"You're not sleeping in here," she bit out like I'd just pissed on her pillow.

"Need to stay real close to you, Belle, in case they turn up," I replied, even though I hadn't planned on sleeping in that bed anyway, but fucking with her and trying to win her back around was becoming my number one priority. Especially since her pissed-off expression was particularly sexy.

Her eyes narrowed on me. "You can't stay here with me." And with that, she stormed off in the opposite direction. I snickered to myself, but the happiness faded real quick as I stared back at that piece-of-shit bed.

"I mean it!" she yelled like an old fish wife from the other end of the trailer.

I followed the sound of her angry muttering, having to bow my head to accommodate my height. God, I fucking hated this trailer.

266

Needed to get her somewhere better than this. Death was still in play for her in the club's eyes, but I'd already come to the conclusion that this bitch was going to be mine now. I'd stared at the back of her head, imagining a bullet going in her skull and the feel of the ricochet from the gun going up my arm, and I didn't like it. Traitor or not, I wasn't letting her go to ground, and I'd told Shooter and Rider as much. From everything she'd told us, what information she had given to Carlos and Mateo had been bullshit anyway, and it had been under duress. Sure, she should have told us still, but we should have kept a better eye on things.

She should have been under our protection in the first place—so that was on us.

I had one last chance to save her life from the club, and I had to give it everything I had. Unfortunately, she hated my guts.

"You cooking us dinner?" I asked to irritate her. Because I wasn't going to win her around with charm, so my next best bet was to let her work through her hatred for me and hopefully come back around to something better. I moved to sit opposite her on the piece-of-shit sofa. It groaned under my weight and I braced myself to go through it.

Belle stared at me aghast. "Are you kidding me?"

My cold expression told her I wasn't, and she spluttered and tried to stand up quickly, as if I was a virus she needed to get away from, but I grabbed her wrist and stopped that shit real quick.

"Calm yourself, Belle, I was kidding." I scowled at her. "But I am hungry, so let's go eat."

She opened her mouth to respond and I let out a heavy sigh, already tired of her backtalk. Perhaps this hadn't been such a good idea of mine.

"You go eat, Beast! On your own. Away from me!" she snapped, looking away. I could tell she had more to say but was holding it back, and that was good because her fierce tongue was going to get her in all kinds of trouble if she weren't careful.

267

"Belle, it's just food, not a proposal," I gritted. My body was starting to ache, my skin feeling tight across my burns, but I ignored it in favor of our little back-and-forth argument.

"My mom comes home later and I need to get everything ready, so no, Beast, no thank you. I don't want to go eat with you, now or ever." And with that she snatched her wrist out from my grip and scooted her way off the sofa.

"She can't stay here," I growled after her.

Belle turned back. "She has nowhere else to go."

"You want her dead? Because that's what will happen if she's here." I crossed my arms over my chest and waited for her to reply. Fuck me, this woman was infuriating. Hadn't been this annoying at the hospital or when she was at the clubhouse, but now it was all coming out. Maybe I should rethink my plan, because there was only so much of this shit I could put up with.

"Well in that case, surely I'm going to end up dead if I stay here," she said.

I stood up and stalked toward her. "No, Belle, you're going to be just fuckin' fine. I won't let anything happen to you. But that bitch mom of yours—if you can even call her that—she won't be, because I won't do anything to save her ass if Mateo and Carlos come here. She's on her own."

Her eyes widened, and I thought she was going to thank me for keeping her safe but instead she shook her head and took a step back from me.

"So it was okay for you to kill me this morning but no one else? You do the killing because you're this big, masculine killing machine, huh? But no one else gets to do that. God, what is wrong with you?" She looked at me with such hatred that I wondered if there was any way of coming back from it. I wondered if maybe it was too late and there was nothing left in her that had anything but hate for me. I couldn't blame her either, but I also couldn't give up.

"And she has nowhere to go, Beast," she continued. "She has to come here, and you have to protect her if anything happens."

I stared down at her, feeling like a giant asshole in this piece-of-shit trailer she called a home, and she stared up at me, her eyes filled with so much hurt and anger, her body practically vibrating with it, and I felt it again—the connection we had, like a small current of electricity running between us. It was still there, but it was faint. I didn't believe in fate or any of that shit, but if I did then I'd believe she was my fate, my destiny, or whatever the hell else you wanted to call it.

Our lives were threaded, even if she didn't want them to be anymore.

She'd never understand why it had to be me to pull the trigger, and I wouldn't ever try to explain it to her, but she had to know that it was all about me and nothing to do with her, and fuck me but I was trying to fix that shit.

"Promise me that you won't let her get hurt," she said, her tone softening and expression pleading.

"Why is this woman so important to you? You have Jenna, right? She raised you, she gave you everything you needed, so why bring this bitch that abandoned you into your life? You don't owe her anything." I reached for her and she didn't pull away. I placed a hand on either bicep and she stayed fixed in place, a firm resolve in her expression. I wanted to pull her in and kiss her, then fuck her so hard the trailer would fall apart around us, turning to nothing but broken pieces and dust—which actually wouldn't take an awful lot, given its current condition.

"She's not important," she said, her voice quieter and her eyes shimmering. "I hate her."

I frowned. "If you hate her then why are you letting her come here?"

Her chin trembled and it was obvious even to a dumbass like me that she regretted her decision to let her stay and didn't want to go through with it, but something was holding her back. Something was making her do this. Fuck me, how many secrets did she have?

Belle took a deep breath and then, as if realizing that I was touching her, she shrugged out of my grip. "Don't touch me, Beast," she said, turning away. "Don't ever touch me again."

269

"Belle—" But I didn't know what to say after that. "I'll drive you, when you're ready to go," I said instead of saying what I really wanted to.

She looked back at me and nodded before heading back to her room and closing the door behind her. Everything was starting to hurt: my chest my arms, my legs, even my face. I headed out to my bike to grab my painkillers and the lotion that I used to put on my burns. Every step was beginning to feel like glass was being dragged through my muscles, and I winced with every movement. I was parked at the back of the trailer where a ton of old crap had been left abandoned for who knows how long. I'd thrown some tarp over the whole pile to hide what was under it, and now it resembled a pile of junk instead of my most prized position. But it had to be done so Mateo and Carlos wouldn't know I was there.

The club had also put Dom and one of the prospects in the trailer opposite so that we were constantly watched. I looked up at it now, watching as the blinds twitched, and I gave a subtle nod in their direction as I lifted the tarp and rooted through my saddlebags for my meds. I shook out two pills onto my tongue, swallowing them quickly and wishing for something stronger, but knowing I needed to keep a clear head. Besides, going back in there high would only further infuriate Belle and I'd already done that enough today.

Heading back inside, I clasped the tub of burn cream tightly in my hand. Belle was still in her room, no doubt pacing back and forth and figuring out ways to kill me without rousing suspicion. I shrugged out of my cut and pulled my T-shirt over my head, every movement painful, like I was back at the barn and flames were licking at my skin again.

I unscrewed the lid and dipped my hand in before smoothing the cold cream over my skin. It stung like a motherfucker at first, but the pain began to ease as it soaked in, and the tightness to my skin lessened, making it so I could move more freely. It was like my skin had shrunk and was way too small for the body it was trying to contain. The weights I'd been lifting probably didn't help with that though, because with all traces of fat having wasted away this past year and then working out like a maniac the past couple of weeks, I was now just pure muscle. I was large before, broad shouldered, my chest hard and defined and tapering down to a thick band of muscle around my stomach and hips, but that was nothing compared to now. The only way I'd been able to control my temper and not fall apart had been to work out. I'd been lifting heavier and heavier weights, building and defining each muscle as I stared at the names of my fallen brothers on the benches outside the clubhouse. The ache and burn in my muscles from exercising took away from the pain inside my head and the need to lash out at anyone and everything that got in my way. I wasn't a beautiful man by any means though, and I wasn't trying to be. I was ugly as sin, both inside and out, broken, torn apart, but still breathing. No matter how much I wished I wasn't.

I smothered the cream over my arms and chest, focusing on blocking out the pain as my calloused hands smoothed over the ridges of my muscles, but there was no way to reach my back. I glanced over at Belle's closed door and considered knocking on it and asking her to help, but I had a feeling she'd only have two words for me, the second one of them being the word *off.*

I chuckled as I remembered her telling me to fuck off back at the clubhouse.

Sitting back down, I breathed a sigh of relief as the burning pain I felt daily dampened to a low throb and I got a brief respite. A lot had happened in twenty-four hours and I didn't know what the next twenty-four held for Belle or for me, but one thing I was sure on more than anything else was that we were close to catching Echo's killers. So close that I could practically feel their blood growing cold under my fingertips, the screams lingering in my ears as I showed them what real pain was. What real torture was.

271

Chapter Thirty-Seven
~ Belle ~

My cell buzzed and vibrated against my leg and I fished it out of my pocket, vaguely recognizing the number on the screen. This number had called me so many times over the past couple of months, and each time I dreaded answering it. The voice on the other end was a stranger wearing a cotton candy smile, telling me all the things that I wanted to hear and yet knew weren't true—no matter how much I wanted them to be.

I sighed and hit the accept button, putting it to my ear. "Hello?"

A robotic voice spoke on the other end. "An inmate from Emanuel Women's Facility is trying to contact you. Will you accept the charges?"

"I'll accept," I replied numbly.

Mom. If she could really be called that.

My heart sagged right along with my shoulders.

"Sweetheart!" her overly happy voice filtered out of the earpiece, carving another piece out of my already damaged heart. "It's me, your mama."

As usual, whenever she said those words, my skin crawled and my stomach tumbled over and over like I was going to be sick.

"Hey," I replied sullenly.

I could hear shouting and arguing in the background, the familiar chatter of women, and doors opening and closing, but she raised her voice to speak over them. "I'll be ready to leave here in a couple of hours. Don't be late to pick me up, okay? I want to get as far away from here as quickly as I can. Do you have everything ready for me?"

Staring down at my feet, I felt the familiar sense of longing and dread roll into one. I wasn't stupid; I knew that this was all fake. I knew she was using me. But my heart wanted it to be real so much that I was willing to put myself through the misery anyway.

"Yeah, everything's ready."

She squealed loudly down the phone. "I can't wait to see you! My little girl, all grown up! I bet you're beautiful and successful. You know you get that from me, right? Your daddy was a good-for-nothing bum who couldn't hold down a job, but I was destined for great things!"

My daddy.

Yeah, I'd wondered about him too, but I hadn't dared ask her who he was, yet. Who my daddy was was the greatest mystery of them all. She hadn't told anyone and his name had been left blank on the birth certificate. I was determined to find out though. I wanted to know my roots—who I was, where my blood came from. Even if he was as big a disappointment as she promised he was.

"So, if you can pick me up at four and then maybe tomorrow we can head down to my old storage unit to pick up some of my stuff. You remembered to get the tequila, right? Your mama loves tequila, and I deserve it after the hell I've been through in here!" She was babbling, conversing with herself rather than me. It was the one thing I'd realized pretty quickly about the woman that had birthed and abandoned me: she loved the sound of her own voice more than anyone else's.

"Yes, that's fine. I'll be there," I replied, feeling numb, feeling lost, feeling scared, but mostly feeling like a little girl adrift in the ocean with no one to save her.

"All right then, well, I'll see you soon, sweetheart." And with that, she hung up.

I sat down on the edge of my bed. The bed that she'd been sleeping in tonight. In the room that she'd be filling with her things. In the trailer that I called home. It was hard to believe that it was finally happening now. That she was almost here. I'd seen a couple of photographs of her through the years, but I'd never met her. Never seen her, or touched her hair. Never been able to smell her perfume or hear her voice in person. In all the years since she'd abandoned me, I'd never heard from her, not once. Yet every birthday I'd waited by the mailbox hoping that a card would come from her. At my graduation I still prayed that she would come to see me. At every special occasion in my life I had hoped she would show some compassion—some love for me—and come to see me. To meet me, and maybe tell me she loved me. But she never had. And now she was going to be here, under my roof, eating my food and sleeping in my bed because she needed me.

And I realized, with absolute clarity, that for the first time since I could remember thinking of her…I really really didn't actually want her here. She didn't know me and she didn't really want to know me, and that was okay by me. If I let her into my heart, I'd be letting her break it forever, and I had to stop that from happening. It was the only thing left that I could control.

They say curiosity killed the cat, and that's what I felt like now: a cat that was curious about who she really was and where she came from, but the thing was, I already knew that. My mother wasn't a part of me. Sure, I'd come from her; her flesh and bones and her DNA, but a person was so much more than that. They were the good in their hearts, the sadness in their souls, the intelligence in their heads, and I already knew that part about myself.

Jenna had raised me with every ounce of good in the world. She'd filled me to the brim with love and laughter, with the brains to do whatever I wanted in life.

I suddenly realized why Jenna was so upset with me, and it wasn't because I wanted to meet my mom. It was because she thought that she hadn't been enough—that she hadn't given me enough, when we both knew that she had given me everything.

I leaned over and put my head in my hands, pressing my palms into my eyes sockets to stem the tears. I'd cried so many times over my mother's absence through the years and I swore she wouldn't get any more of my tears, yet there I was, terrified of her rejection still, seeking her approval and trying not to cry.

How many times was I going to let other people hurt me before I said enough?

Beast was moving around on the other side of the door; I could hear his heavy footsteps walking around, the creak and groan of my trailer floor. And I hated that too. Beast and my mom were going to be

274

living in my house. *My home*. Two mafia men were going to come in and try to kill me. My boyfriend was a narcissistic jerk. A motorcycle club was using me as bait. I had quit my job—a job I had trained really hard for and worked toward my entire life but didn't really want.

How had this become my life?

I'd ruined everything.

But that wasn't the worst of it. The worst of it was that Jenna and I weren't talking. That she hated me, and I had hurt her.

I had to fix this. I had to fix everything before it was too late.

Standing up, I pulled out some clothes to change into. The ones I'd been wearing held the scent of Beast, and even though I found it strangely comforting, I wanted him off of me. I opened my closet, seeing the box with all the cash inside of it that I'd been paid while looking after Beast, and hoped that I got to put it to good use someday.

Pulling out a dusty blue summer dress with thin spaghetti straps, I stripped quickly, kicking my underwear off and putting on clean ones. Fully dressed, I looked at my face in the mirror, seeing how puffy it was from all the crying I'd been doing. I hated crying, but who could blame me?

I had almost been killed today… I let that settle into my soul for a moment before staring into my own eyes and seeing the sadness there. Beast had intended to kill me this morning. We'd made love last night and I'd given him my heart…and he'd rejected me. He'd practically begged Shooter to let him put a bullet in my head, and all for what? Because I'd been a traitor to the club? He hadn't even let me explain. I shook my head, the sadness mingling with regret.

After applying some fresh makeup, I pulled my hair up off my face and into a high ponytail, realizing that I looked almost normal again, like I hadn't gone through hell in the past twenty-four hours. That I hadn't had my heart broken and my life shattered over and over.

It was time to take account of my actions and make some things right. Because if Mateo and Carlos did kill me, I needed Jenna to know that none of this was her fault. That I loved her more than anything or anyone else, and that she was more than enough. If I could have picked anyone to be my mom, it would always be her.

I picked up my purse and opened my bedroom door, passing through the small kitchen to find Beast sitting topless, his burn cream soaking into his skin. He looked like he was in pain, and the nurse in me wanted to ask him if he was okay, but I couldn't—not if I wanted to keep my self-respect.

He looked up at me as I got close, his eyes widening as he looked me up and down. His tongue darted out to lick his lips and I watched his chest heave on a deep sigh.

"You calmed down now?" he asked, raising an eyebrow at me.

I ignored his comment, because it was only said to irritate me further and I was sick of his games. Sick of him, even as my heart longed for him. That was the thing with love: even when you knew it was bad for you, that it would likely be the death of you, you couldn't help but feel it. Love wasn't something you could turn on and off like a tap. It was a broken dam that wouldn't stop flowing. It burst its banks and touched every part of you, destroying parts of you in its path.

"I need to go see Jenna," I replied coolly.

"Thought we were going to get your mom from the slammer." He scowled.

"We are, but first I need to see Jenna. You can stay here if you want, I don't care."

I did care.

And I hated him even more for that.

Beast stood and picked up his T-shirt and cut, pulling his tee over his head and then sliding his cut over his shoulders. I watched him wince with every movement.

"Not that I care because you are an awful human being, but have you taken your meds today?" I popped a hand on my hip and feigned indifference.

"Trying to cut back on them," he grunted, picking up his bike keys.

I pointed a finger in his direction. "First, I'm not getting on that bike of yours—we're taking my car, and second, that's the stupidest thing I've ever heard. Your body is still healing and you're still in pain, so take your painkillers."

Beast stood there staring at me like I had not one head or two, but maybe a whole orgy of heads just popping up out of my shoulders. He stared at me like he didn't quite know who I was, and I didn't blame him because I hardly recognized her either. But that's the thing when you have nothing left to lose: you become someone else.

"If I need medical advice, I'll go ask a doctor or nurse," he replied curtly after a long moment of silence.

Ouch, that hurt.

I glared at him and he glared right back, neither of us willing to back down. It was like we both had so much to say but neither wanted to be the first to say it. There was a line between love and hate and once you stepped over it, it was hard to recover from that pain. That's where I felt I was now, and yet with that biting comment I realized that Beast still had the ability to hurt me. The threat of him putting a bullet in my head hadn't turned it all the way off, but his mean comments brought me closer. It was ridiculously messed up.

"Whatever, are you coming or not?" I asked as I opened my trailer door and stepped outside.

I heard and felt Beast stand up and come toward me, the trailer rocking and creaking as he walked to the door and down the steps. He slammed the door and barged past me and I locked the door—not that it seemed to keep anyone out these days—and headed to the driver's side of my car. Beast was standing there, leaning on the hood like he owned it.

"Keys," he barked.

"I'm driving," I snapped back.

"Like hell you are. I'm not being driven around like some little fucking husband, now give me the damn keys, Belle, before I come and get them from you." He glared at me over the roof of the car and I stared at him with resentment and hate in my eyes before throwing them to him. I purposefully threw them wide of his position, but his long arms had him still easily catch them and I glowered at him harder before getting in the car and sitting down.

Beast sat down and started the engine. "You throw like a girl," he chuckled nastily.

"I *am* a girl, idiot."

His smile widened. "No, you throw like a little girl. Like a child. Now put your seatbelt on and sit quietly."

My mouth gaped and my vision blurred with anger. Is this what people felt like when they said they saw red? When their world throbbed with anger? Beast chuckled and pulled away from my trailer and I turned away to glare out the window because it was obvious that whatever I said would only encourage him further.

"You need to take the next left," I said, directing him to Jenna's apartment.

"You think I don't already know where she lives? That the club doesn't know everything about you?" he drolled, like that was perfectly normal.

"You realize that you and that club of yours is super weird and stalkery," I replied, still staring out the window, because maybe if I didn't look at him he would just disappear.

"You realize that my little club isn't filled with the most lawful of society and that we make it our business to know everything about our enemies, right?" he retorted, like I was as dumb as a box of rocks.

I finally turned to glare at him. "So I'm your enemy now?"

For some reason, that hurt more than anything he'd said previously.

All those months ago, I'd wanted to save Beast, and now it turned out that all I'd done was make myself a target and become the enemy of a notorious motorcycle club. It was stupid, really, to even think that I could save him; I couldn't even save myself.

"When you decided to spill club secrets to our biggest rival and the men that put my brother in the ground, to the men that tortured me to the brink of death but never let me fall over it, then yeah, you became

278

an enemy, Belle." He said it like it was the most obvious thing in the world—and it was. But it also wasn't.

"It wasn't like that and you know it," I mumbled.

"So tell me, what was it like then? Because I'm real fuckin' confused how little mousy Belle could have turned into such a hardass bitch that would willingly risk other people's lives! People that would have done anything to look after and protect her!" he yelled, his anger and resentment getting the better of him.

I stared at him in shock, not sure if he was done and not sure, even if he *was* done, what I could say to that. We drove in silence, my gaze on the side of his face, watching his jaw ticking and his teeth grinding, his knuckles going white on the steering wheel as he gripped it tighter than necessary.

I realized, with sudden shame, that I owed him an apology too. Him and Shooter. Hell, the whole damn club. They had trusted me—he had trusted me—and I'd abused that trust. It didn't matter that I had been scared or threatened; in their world, trust was godly and I had blown that trust into a thousand pieces.

Beast slammed on the brakes with sudden sharpness, the squeal of tires pulling us to an abrupt stop in front of Jenna's apartment building. He was glaring out the window, refusing to look at me, and I finally saw something more than just his anger.

He was hurt.

He felt betrayed.

He felt just like I did.

"I'm sorry, Beast," I said, my voice soft. His jaw ground harder and I swallowed, my hands wringing the strap of my purse like it might be able to save me. "I'm really sorry. I never meant to hurt you."

He scoffed and finally turned to look at me, and I saw the hurt in his eyes that he tried to hide from me. My guilt and shame flooded me, from the top of my head right down to the tips of my toes. I felt my shame at hurting him like I was under a magnifying glass. It burned like the rays of the sun were scorching my skin.

I reached out and placed my hand on his arm, and my heart hurt like I'd been stabbed in it as he bristled under my touch.

"Beast…" I said his name, needing him to look at me so he could see how sorry I really was, but he was still refusing to. I sighed and pulled my hand back. "I was scared. Really scared," I admitted.

"I would have protected you. The club would have," he finally replied.

"I know that now. But that's the thing about hindsight, right?"

He finally turned and looked at me, and staring into his eyes was like looking into two dark chasms of pain. It was obvious now that he'd been hurt in the past, and my betrayal had made that ten times worse.

"You should have known I wouldn't have let anything hurt you, Belle."

And maybe I should have.

I stared harder at him, our gazes colliding in a mixture of pain and guilt and shame and hurt, and I felt tears prickle at the backs of my eyes.

"I didn't mean to hurt anyone. I honestly tried not to. I was just trying to protect my family," I said, my tone pleading with him to understand. "Jenna is all I have, and they threatened her. I was scared for me, but I was terrified for her. And I did everything I could to keep you all safe, because believe it or not, I care a lot about your family too."

We sat in silence for several moments and I decided he wasn't going to say anything else so I unclipped my seatbelt and opened my door.

"Belle." Beast called my name and I turned to look at him. He sighed before speaking. "I'll speak to Shooter. I can't promise anything though."

I nodded and sighed. "Thank you," I said, which seemed like the two most pathetic words in existence.

Thank you for trying to save my life.

Thank you for not killing me yet.

Thank you for not hating me entirely.

It seemed absurd to be thanking him for not killing me, but there it was. This was what my life had been reduced to. And I deserved every part of it.

Thank you wasn't even nearly good enough for how much I'd betrayed and hurt him, but it was all I had. Now if only he could say sorry to me too.

Chapter Thirty-Eight
~ BEAST ~

I wanted to tell her that nothing—not even God himself—was going to harm a hair on her head, because if he tried I'd bring forth so much wrath that even the Devil himself would be terrified of me. But then the irony of that statement, given that I'd intended to kill her only a few hours before, taunted me and I kept my mouth shut.

This morning had been different.

This morning I'd been hurt and angry.

Now I was hurt and angry but for different reasons.

Jesus fucking Christ, when did I turn into this guy—the one that had feelings? I'd cut off that side of me the day I'd killed my own mom, and I hadn't missed him.

I slammed my hand on the steering wheel. "This is bullshit!" I yelled to no one, growing more and more frustrated.

And it was.

Total bullshit.

Belle didn't deserve to die, even if the code said she did.

Shooter and the club had given her her life back while we waded through the shitstorm she'd helped create, but that didn't mean they'd let her off. Despite the fear she'd felt, she'd still betrayed us—betrayed me. But maybe if she could redeem herself in their eyes.

I pulled out my cell and dialed Shooter, who picked up almost immediately.

"She cut loose already?" he asked.

Yeah, we'd all expected her to try to run. People in her situation tended to have the same two responses: fight or flight. So far she hadn't done either of them, and maybe that was what was confusing me. Fuck, this whole thing with Belle had been confusing, right from day one.

"No, she's gone to visit her godmother Jenna," I replied, looking up at the window I knew Jenna occupied.

"What's up then?"

"You spanked that bitch already?" Casa yelled in the background.

"Will you shut the fuck up?" Shooter grumbled. He was irritable. He was always irritable these days. Life at home wasn't getting any better, and every day I saw more and more of his father in him with the way he spoke to everyone. Shooter's dad Hardy had been the worst and best thing to ever happen to the club. He'd made all of us so much money and opened up so many channels for business, but then he'd gotten greedy. Life had run him through the mill until he'd turned his back on everything we ever stood for. When all this was over I needed to speak to Rider and Gauge and try and sort this shit out.

"She wants to make it right with the club," I said bluntly, ignoring Casa.

Shooter sighed. "It don't work like that, Beast, you know that."

I pulled my cigarettes out of my cut and tapped one out with one hand before popping it between my lips, but then thought better of it. This wasn't my car and she'd have a shit fit if I smoked in it. She was clearly proud of it, because it might have been a piece of shit but it was immaculate: not a piece of paper or a coffee cup, not even a smudge on the window. I unclipped my seatbelt and climbed out, and leaning back against the door I lit the cigarette and blew out a mouthful of smoke.

"It needs to work like that," I replied as calmly as I could. Because it did. He needed to make it work or I would. No one was going to hurt her, I didn't care what our code said. "She's willing to do whatever it takes, Prez. She knows she fucked up and I'm backing her a hundred percent."

Shooter sighed again and I realized that everything had gone quiet behind him. I looked up and down the street, and then back up to Jenna's window. I'd been in these apartments before and knew they were nice inside, so it didn't make any sense that Belle was living in such a shitty trailer while Jenna lived here. I scowled and took another drag of my cigarette, feeling pissed off for Belle all over again.

I was slowly figuring out what it was about Belle that had me all messed up: she reminded me of myself ten years ago.

"Well?" I prompted, trying to tame the attitude in my tone so as not to piss off Shooter, because that wouldn't help Belle at all. But it was hard, because inside I was a mass of anger and frustration. "Don't make me choose between her or the club, Prez."

I hated saying those words to him, because we both knew what they meant. It meant if it came to a choice between her or the club…I'd pick her.

"I'll put it to the club today, but don't get your hopes up," he replied.

"Why would I get my hopes up? I don't care about her, I just think everyone deserves a second chance," I lied, the lie transparent.

I threw my cigarette to the ground, watching as Belle came out of the apartment building. She walked with her shoulders slumped and her eyes on the ground, and I swallowed at how beautiful her misery was.

"Beast, you're all fucked up over this girl, and I get why, but it can't affect the club. You know the rules. And you know what happens to traitors."

"But she isn't!" I yelled, my gaze still on Belle. She looked up when I raised my voice, a frown puckering between her eyebrows. I held up a hand, telling her to stay away for a moment, and she nodded and stepped over to the sidewalk behind the car. I lowered my tone when I spoke next. "We brought her into this without telling her the rules. Brother, she never stood a chance and that's on us—that's on you and me, not her."

"You're right, it is," Shooter agreed. "We should have warned her."

I breathed a sigh of relief that he was at least listening to me, and I dragged a hand down my face as he continued.

"I'll set up a meeting today. We'll figure something out," Shooter said. "I need to go, Casa thinks he might have figured out where those two bastards are hiding out."

A smile crept up my face. "You make sure you give me that address, Prez."

"Your revenge will be purifying, brother," he replied, and clicked off the call.

I took another long breath, letting the early afternoon air fill my lungs for what felt like the first time in two days. Belle cleared her throat as she came closer, and I nodded that it was okay to do so.

Standing next to me, she looked up into my face, the sunlight dancing off her dark hair like vibrant rays. She looked goddamn beautiful. Innocent, pure, everything I wasn't. The hurt was still fierce within my heart and we had a long way to go before shit would be right between us—for one, I'd intended to put a bullet in her head this morning, so that was going to take some figuring out on her part. We'd both hurt each other—sometimes without thinking, other times despite it, but the stupid thing was, neither of us had wanted that…any of it.

Somewhere in the darkness, Belle had found me and brought me back from that barn, and no matter what she'd done or not done, there were no words to describe how grateful I was for that. I just hadn't realized it until this moment.

Without thinking, I reached out to cup her cheek in my hand, and she leaned into my touch.

"Beast," she said, my name a murmur on her lips.

I leaned in and pressed my mouth to hers, kissing her, needing her, wanting her.

I kissed Belle with every apology in my heart, already knowing that it wasn't enough, but trying to prove it to her anyway.

When we pulled out of the kiss, her lips were red and swollen and her eyes full of need and desire, and if today hadn't already been a pile of shit then I would have grabbed her, sat her down on my lap and fucked her right here in this piece-of-shit car, but I couldn't.

Things were moving out of our control. Chess pieces were moving into position, readying themselves for battle, and I needed to be on the front line of that.

"Need to get going," I said, and she nodded, her needy gaze still locked on mine. "Everything go okay with Jenna?"

285

She nodded again, the name of her godmother drawing her back to reality. "Yeah, I mean, we have some stuff to work through, but she loves me and she only wants the best for me."

"We still going to get your mom?" I asked. Already hated the bitch and I hadn't even met her. But I didn't need to. I knew her kind— popping babies out and then leaving them to raise themselves with barely any concept of what it was to have a family, to have love.

Belle looked away, her gaze going out the window. I hated that; I wanted her eyes locked on mine again.

"Yeah, I don't really have a choice. They won't let her out without somewhere to go." She sighed, like she knew she'd made the second biggest mistake of her life.

I reached over and pressed my rough palm against her cheek again and she turned to look back at me, her eyes looking so sad that it made my chest hurt.

"Hey, what have I said about letting me help you? I've got your back, Belle."

"Even after…"

"Even after all that other bullshit," I agreed, cutting her off. "I don't know what this thing is with you and me. I don't know whether we can make it work. I don't know if the club will forgive you, and even if they do, I don't know whether they will ever accept you—fuck, I don't even know if you really want in on my world…"

"I do!" she replied quickly, cutting me off this time.

"Well, all that being said, I've still got your back. You fucked up, big time. There's no getting away from that. But that was the club's fault too, for not showing you how shit was handled. All I know for certain is that we've both made a fucking mess of this thing, but that ends now." I let go of her face and looked out the window. Things were so messed up, and it felt like everything was set in our path to keep us apart, but for as long as I could, I'd fight to keep her. I knew that more than I knew anything else right then.

She shook her head. "I don't know what to do about my mom. I don't need or want her in my life. I thought I did. I thought I needed her to find out who I really was. I wanted to know more about me, about who I was and where I came from. I have this bunch of freckles on my inner thigh," she said.

"I know the ones," I interrupted, my hand going to her leg, and she smiled properly for the first time in too damn long.

"Those stupid freckles are what started this whole thing. Because I was wondering where I got them from—*who* I got them from. No one knows who my daddy was. Mom never told anyone and never put his name on my birth certificate. It was spiteful and mean, but I guess that's just who she is. Anyway, I saw those freckles and I wondered who I got them from, my mom or my dad. And it makes you wonder: all the little things that make a person up, where did they come from? Do I have my mom's temper? My dad's fondness for spicy food? Are these his freckles, or hers? And then as if by fate, I got her letter and it just seemed sort of kismet." She sighed like she'd just spilled her heart out to me.

"Belle, none of those things make up you. The only thing that makes up you is you. It's the history we have, the people we meet, the choices we make, the paths we choose. Those are what makes us who we are. Not moms or dads, but people and life. Trust me on this one."

She nodded like she understood, but I wasn't sure she did, so I pressed further to make my point drive home.

"I grew up in a tiny one-bed apartment that was infested with roaches and had mold on the walls. My mom was never home, and when she was, she wasn't really there. We never had food in the house, and she couldn't have cared less if I lived or died. So I left. I got out and never looked back. And it was then that I started to live. It was then that I started to become the man I wanted to be. *Without her.*" I squeezed her thigh. "The person you are is because of you, Belle, not from your mom or dad. It's just you."

"And the freckles?" she asked.

I chuckled. "The freckles are all yours, babe. Doesn't matter who they came from, they're yours."

She smiled as I pushed the hem of her skirt up to reveal the little bunch of freckles that looked like an astrological cluster at the top of her thigh. I pointed to one and looked at her.

"Apart from this one right here," I said. "This one here is all mine." I smirked and she did a weird laughing-crying thing and hiccupped, and I hated that it was cute as fuck, but there was no denying that it was cute as fuck either.

"I never want to hurt you again, Belle, but I can't promise you I won't." I held her gaze as I spoke the truest words of my life. "But I promise that I'll try to be the man you need if you'll have me."

Chapter Thirty-Nine
~ *Belle* ~

We drove to the prison to pick up my mom, because despite what Beast said, I couldn't leave her in there. If I hadn't replied to her letter or if this hadn't already been arranged, then maybe I could have walked away from her, but as it was, I couldn't. I had to see it through.

After meeting with Warden Hoole and signing all the necessary paperwork, we were instructed to wait outside and that they would send her out to us. I was leaning against the side of my car, feeling sick with nerves, when Beast came over to stand in front of me. He reached out and I leaned into his arms, feeling safe and protected in his embrace. I leaned my head on his chest as his body held me steady, and I breathed in his aura, hoping that it might give me a little more strength.

"It'll be all right, Belle," he said, and I nodded in agreement, even though I wasn't sure I believed him. "I'll make sure of it."

My chest tightened, my body flooding with affection for him. He really meant what he'd said earlier about having my back, and it brought tears to my eyes because of how close I'd come to ruining this. Beast and I had nothing in common, nothing but what we felt for each other. I had no idea if this could work between us, and at the moment I didn't care. All I cared about was living each moment with him. Because if caring for him in the hospital had taught me anything, it was that things could change in a heartbeat. Nothing was safe from the finality of death. It could all be taken away in a moment's notice.

"Belle?" A woman's voice called out my name and I took a deep, calming breath of Beast before standing up. The moment his arms left me I wanted them back, so I reached over to take his hand. I glanced down at our joined hands, realizing how comical it looked—my tiny one swallowed by his huge one.

I finally looked up, my gaze meeting my mother's—or at least the woman that called herself my mom. She was tall and lithe, with bony shoulders and hip bones that jutted out—but not because she was skinny, but because she'd been blessed with a flat stomach and large hips. I didn't get my figure from her, that much was obvious.

Her hair was long and blond. Not even fake blond, but real blond. Like the sun had kissed the top of her head. And God, she was pretty. I wanted her to be ugly and awful, so her outsides would match her insides, but they didn't. She was tall and blond and beautiful and I looked nothing like her at all.

She smiled widely and came toward me, a paper bag hanging limply in her grip. "Baby!" she said as she got closer and opened her arms for me to fall into. But instead of going to her, I stepped back, pulling Beast with me.

"You okay?" he asked, and I nodded yes, but I wasn't. I wasn't okay at all.

This woman was a stranger to me in every way, and every part of me from my head to my toes was telling me to get away from her. She stopped walking and scowled.

"Well, that's no way to greet your mom now, is it?" She popped her hip as she put a hand on it, dropping the paper bag of her things at her feet. "Clearly you get your manners from your dad," she bit out nastily.

I opened my mouth to say something, but I wasn't sure what, so I was glad when her gaze finally turned on Beast. Not so glad when her eyes lit up at the sight of him.

"My little Belle, seems like you got yourself a naughty biker boyfriend." She stepped closer to Beast, taking in every tattooed, scarred inch of him with a discerning eye. "Shame you picked the ugly one, but at least you know he'll never leave you," she laughed, dismissing him and looking back at me. I felt Beast's grip tighten on mine.

"Don't speak about him like that," I said, my voice quiet, almost shy. Beast didn't need me to defend him, and he certainly wouldn't want me to, but I couldn't stand there and not say anything. Especially when she was so wrong.

Beast was the most beautiful man I'd ever seen, with or without the scars, and I'd be damned if I let anyone say any different about him.

She rolled her eyes. "Whatever, we're all into our own kinky stuff. You obviously have a hero complex. It's fine, at least you know no one will try and steal him away from you." She snickered. "Can we go now? I'm starving and I've been stuck in that hellhole for four years."

My mom moved toward the back seat of my car, and as she opened the door I reached out and slammed it closed again, making her jump. My hand slipped from Beast's as I glared at her. Suddenly, I wasn't a lost little girl needing her mother's love anymore. I was Beast's woman, and no one spoke about my man like that. Not even this awful woman.

"A hero complex?" I said, my voice hard.

She turned to me, her gaze going briefly to Beast, who hadn't moved from his spot. I wasn't sure if it was because he was hurt, angry, or because he thought that I could handle this situation on my own, but either way I was angry and embarrassed that she'd treated him like that, but mostly I was hurt for him.

Mom rolled her eyes. "Sweetheart, it's okay, I'm not judging. Some people just like to be the hero of their own story. Me, I prefer to be the damsel in distress. It's all okay."

But it wasn't okay.

Every word she said made her pretty mask slip further and further until all I could see was the ugly underneath her skin. The vileness in her soul. She thought I was with Beast because I had a hero complex, and maybe that had been true at one point. I wanted to save him, not because of his scars, but in spite of them. But the real hero here was Beast. He'd saved me over and over. The fact that she couldn't see past his scars and burns told me everything I needed to know about me as a person and who I was.

"Who's my dad?" I asked bluntly.

Her expression changed from sardonic to blank in a split second. "It doesn't matter who he was. You're my daughter, not his."

I gritted my teeth, hating her for making me ask. Hating her for not putting his name on the birth certificate. Hating her because I was nothing like her, and despite what Beast said about the person you really were having nothing to do with your parents, I hated her because I still wanted to know.

"But I'm not, am I? I'm his daughter." I waved a hand between us. "Look at us. I'm nothing like you."

She rolled her eyes again. "You certainly get your dramatic flair from him."

"Tell me," I pressed, almost pleading.

"No." Her gaze hit mine and I knew she wasn't going to budge on this. She wasn't ever going to tell me, and I would never know who he was.

"Please," I begged, "just tell me who my dad is and then we can leave."

She opened the door to the car again, and this time Beast banged his hand against it, slamming it closed and making her jump. Her gaze met his with steely determination and she shook her head.

"No. You don't need to know who he is. He was a one-night stand. He was a nomad in the wind. He was a man I met in a bar. I don't know his name. He said he wanted nothing to do with you... Which excuse do you want, Belle? You can take your pick, because I'm not telling you who he was!" Her voice remained calm as she spoke, but I saw the wildness in her eyes and the resentment she felt every time she looked at me.

We stayed that way for a moment, my mom and I staring at one another in defiance. And I knew she was never ever going to tell me. I'd never know who he was. I'd never know where my hair color came from, or my obsession with sushi. Or even the freckles on my thigh.

I wondered if she even knew who he was.

I stepped away from her, pulling Beast with me, and she opened the door and got inside. I looked up at Beast and could see the frustration and anger rolling through him, but not for himself because of the awful things she'd said, but for me.

"Are you driving, or am I?" I asked, knowing that would get him to move into action.

He snorted out a laugh and pulled open my door for me.

I swallowed some of the hurt and the pain in my chest and climbed in the car. "Such a gentleman," I said, looking up at him, and he smirked and closed my door before walking around the car to the driver's side.

"A man like that has to be," my mom chuckled from the back seat.

I turned in my seat to glare at her, but she wasn't looking at me. Instead she was opening her window and lighting a cigarette that she'd fished out from her paper bag.

"Did you get the tequila and smokes for me?" she asked, oblivious or just indifferent to how she was making everyone feel.

Beast opened the door, the whole car rocking as his heavy frame climbed inside. He started the engine and we pulled away from the prison. Mom looked back at it, and when she turned her gaze back to the front I finally saw something more human in her. I saw her fear.

"Yeah," I replied, and the fear disappeared as she forced a smile to her face.

"Good, me and you are going to party tonight. We need to get to know each other, don't you think?" She was trying to be nice—I think—but I didn't want to get to know her, I already knew everything about her that I needed to, and I didn't like any part of her.

Back at my trailer she walked around, her critical gaze taking in my home and my things. She looked out the window at Beast, who was on the phone to the club, and then back to me.

"There's not enough room for all three of us here," she stated matter-of-factly. "I'm guessing he has somewhere else he can be."

"No, he's staying here," I replied.

She scoffed. "Even dogs have other places they can go when they get kicked out, Belle. Someone will take pity on him."

"Oh my God, will you just stop!" I yelled, anger and resentment uncurling inside me. "Do you even know who he is?"

293

"I don't need to. I know his type."

"His type?" I scowled. "What does that even mean?"

"He's latched on to a pretty, successful girl who took pity on him, and he won't give you up without a fight. You need to kick him to the curb. You're a beautiful girl, Belle, and you can do so much better than that." She rolled her eyes like what she was saying made sense, and I guess in her head it did.

Everything she cared about in the world was superficial.

She looked at Beast and all she saw was his outsides, his thick red scars, his pink burns, his damaged eye. She didn't see the beauty of who he was underneath all of that. She just saw that he was different.

"Get out!" I said, calmly, meaning it. I didn't want her near me or Beast if that was how she was going to be.

Hurt flashed across her face before she pulled her smile back in place. "Fine, I'm sorry, okay. If you want to be with him, then be with him. All I'm saying is you can do better. You're a beautiful girl, Belle. Maybe you don't see that, or maybe no one has told you that enough. That's Jenna's fault. I thought she would have done a better job with you, but clearly I was wrong."

She grabbed the tequila from the kitchen counter and unscrewed the lid before taking a long swallow of it and then offering the bottle to me.

"Come on, drink with your momma. We're celebrating my homecoming, sweetheart." She shook the bottle, trying to temp me.

"I'm not sure there's anything to celebrate," I replied coldly before heading outside to Beast.

The door slammed closed behind me and Beast looked up, his eyes meeting mine. He said something into his phone before hanging up and slipping it into his cut, and then I was in his arms, right where I belonged.

"You good?" he asked.

I listened to his steady heartbeat in his chest, his scent wrapping around me as tight as his arms were, and I nodded.

"I am now," I replied.

Chapter Forty
~ BEAST ~

Belle's mom was a bitch.

A grade A, top-of-her-class, deserved-everything-coming-to-her bitch.

Not because of what she'd said to me; I couldn't give a shit about that. I was a big boy and I knew how to handle myself. Besides, I knew that everything she said was right—I was a monster, both inside and out, and Belle deserved so much better than me. What I hated about her mom was the way she treated Belle. The way she spoke to her. The way she looked at her. The way she was clearly using her because she needed a place to stay so she could get back on her feet.

She had no desire to get to know Belle, and she wasn't even trying that hard to hide the fact. She was just selfish to the bone.

Between Belle and I we'd been in and out of the trailer more times than a cat in heat. Every time I thought I could just about stand to be around the bitch without wanting to put a bullet in her head, her mouth opened and something cruel came out.

"What are you cooking for your mama tonight, Belle?" she called from the bedroom where she'd been lying for the past couple of hours watching TV and eating all of Belle's snacks. We'd gotten in and she'd sunk almost the entire bottle of tequila in an hour before turning the radio on loud and dancing around the trailer until she'd thrown up. I'd carried her to Belle's bed, where she'd passed out for an hour before waking up and demanding to watch *Sex and the City* reruns, more tequila, and food.

Belle glanced over at me before looking away quickly. She was embarrassed, but I couldn't work out if she was embarrassed because of the way her mom treated her or just because of the way her mom was. Either way, she had nothing to be embarrassed about. I'd had one of these types of moms too and I knew how they thought, how they worked, and I knew that unless you cut them off like a leech, they drained you of everything.

That was what Belle needed to do with her mom—cut her off and kick her out—but she was never going to do that. She was too good and too kind to do that. It was what I both loved and hated about her, because it made her an easy target for people to take advantage of.

I rolled my shoulders as I stood up and Belle looked over again. She was standing in the little kitchenette opening and closing the cupboard doors and trying to figure out what she could make to eat.

"Heading out for a cigarette," I grumbled. The truth was, being stuck in there with Belle's mom was like having the air sucked out of your lungs. She was a syphon that sucked all the joy out of a room. "Don't cook. I'll order us takeout."

Belle's cheeks were flushed. "I don't mind cooking."

"And I don't mind buying somethin'." I leaned in and kissed her forehead before heading outside, leaving no room for argument.

The air was warm that night—sticky, almost—and my skin was already clammy from being cooped up in her little tin can of a home. I pulled out my cigarettes and lit one before calling Shooter for an update. He didn't sound too happy about Belle's mom being there, and I couldn't blame him, but what could I do?

"We hit the warehouse we had intel on, but they weren't there," he said, changing the subject and moving back on to Mateo and Carlos.

I hadn't thought about either of them in a couple of hours, I'd been so caught up with all the drama going on and making sure that Belle was okay that I'd practically forgotten that the reason I was stuck there was because of those two bastards.

I realized with surprise that this had been the longest I'd gone without thinking of revenge in over a year. The longest without thinking about who had killed Echo and how I was going to make them pay. We were so close to catching them, and yet all I could think about was Belle and her goddamned crappy mom.

I sighed, trying to get my head back in the conversation. "At some point they'll have to make contact with Belle, and when they do, I'll be here," I said, not sure what else I could do right then. "And if they call, she'll let me know."

I was walking around the back of the trailer, trying to keep out of sight as much as I could. I lifted the tarp that was covering my bike, checking that it was still there and okay.

"Well, we've got her cell tapped now, so if they call her we'll know about it anyway.

"She'd tell you," I insisted, and he sighed.

"We're voting tonight."

Voting on her life. Fuck.

I wanted to be there for it, but I couldn't leave her alone. Besides, it might not be a good idea given that I'd want to put a bullet in the brain of anyone who voted for her death.

"Whatever happens, Beast, you know I trust you and I trust your instincts, brother," he said, and now it was my time to sigh.

"Appreciate that, Prez."

It was going to take a lot for them to trust her ever again. Maybe they never would. The thought made my stomach tumble a little, which was pathetic of me. I'd never wanted or needed anyone's approval before, but getting my brothers' and my prez's approval on Belle seemed like the second most important thing right now. I wanted—no, needed—her in my life, and for that to happen they needed to accept her. But we all had trust issues and Belle had broken the number one rule. If it had been any of my other brothers I wouldn't have backed down, so as much as I hated it, I understood their reluctance.

I just wasn't sure how I'd move past it if they voted the wrong way.

In truth, I wouldn't let them harm her no matter what they voted, and Shooter knew that without me having to say it. I wasn't sure what this thing with Belle and I was.

Inexplicable

Unpredictable.

Complicated.

298

It was all of those things and so much more, and I wanted more of it.

If it came to it, I'd put her on my bike and we'd leave together.

My heart thudded heavily in my chest as I realized the certainty of that decision in my head. I'd leave my brothers, my home—my family for her, and I wouldn't regret it.

"Hey," she said, and I turned to see her standing right there looking at me, like all I'd had to do was think about her and she'd appeared. The sun was going down behind her and making it look like she was glowing, and she practically stole the air from my lungs.

"Gotta go," I said to Shooter and hung up. "Hey," I said to her and she took a step forward, her hands clasped in front of her, her left wringing out the right. "You okay?"

She nodded. "Yeah, she's fallen back to sleep." She jerked her head in the direction of the trailer. "I just wanted to say thank you for today, for helping me with my mom, for…" She looked away as she thought over her words.

"For not killing you." I filled in the blanks and she nodded as she looked back at me. "You going to be able to get past that?" I asked her bluntly, because one of us needed to address it before it turned into a festering, weeping wound and ruined whatever was happening between us before it even started.

Yes, I was going to kill her that morning.

Yes, I would have done it.

Yes, I probably would have followed right after too, because her death was one I wouldn't be able to get over. I'd killed hundreds of men and even a handful of women—hell, I'd killed my own mom and not felt anything but a passing thought about it—but Belle's murder was something that would have destroyed me. And that was why it'd had to be me to do it.

"If you can get past the things I did, then yeah," she said, but I could see it in her eyes that she was trying to convince herself as much as me. She had questions, and I already knew what they were.

299

"Ask me," I prompted, and she frowned a little, playing coy. "Just ask me, Belle. It's okay." I sighed my chest feeling heavy.

I watched her swallow as she came closer, looking up at me with those big Disney eyes of hers. Sometimes it felt like she could see right into my black soul. Maybe if she looked hard enough she'd find the man that was worthy of her, because I sure as hell wasn't.

"Why?" she asked, the single word sounding shaking on her tongue, and I knew what she was asking. She wasn't asking why her death was the only option. Or why life was so unfair. She was asking why I had insisted that it be me to kill her.

I threw my cigarette to the ground and dragged a hand across the back of my neck as I thought of a way to verbalize my answer to her.

"These men," I started, "they're my family."

She nodded like she understood, but she didn't.

"They're more than family, they're a part of me…I'm nothing without them…I'm a bad man…they don't judge…" I sighed, the words coming out all jumbled and fucked up.

"It's okay, it doesn't matter," she said, trying to save me from my own stupid mouth.

I stepped closer to her, hooking a hand to her cheek and tilting her face up to look at me. "It actually does," I said with insistence. And I meant it. It mattered that she understood, that someone knew all of me instead of just a part of me.

"So tell me, I won't judge you," she replied, and I smiled down at her. Fuck, but she was perfect, and she didn't even know it.

I took a deep breath. "I didn't know what love was before this club. I'd never had that before. My mom, well, she was kinda like yours actually, but unlike you, I didn't have any other family. It was just me and her, and she was never there. Or if she was, she was drunk. I was always hungry, always cold, always lonely. By some miracle, I made it to my teens. No idea how, given the hell she put me through. The people she brought into our lives, the things they did to both of us…the things she allowed to happen." I shook my head, trying to banish the images that haunted me. "I broke out of our apartment one day and left. I had nothing but a pair of shoes two sizes too small and a backpack with a pair of jeans, a sweatshirt, a change of underwear, and a beaten-up copy of *Huckleberry Finn* in it." I laughed dryly at that, remembering how I'd packed that bag, realizing that I had nothing but threadbare clothes and a single book to my name. How it hadn't hurt, because at that point I was numb to everything. I felt nothing. Not physical pain, not sadness. I didn't even feel hunger anymore because I was so used to feeling empty that it was just part of who I was by then.

Belle reached out and placed a hand on my chest, but by the furious look on her face it wasn't because she pitied me.

I chuckled. "It's all good, woman."

"It's not though, is it." She shook her head, her feather-soft hair brushing around her face. "People like that don't deserve to have children and they shouldn't be allowed to get away with being so cruel."

"Babe." I wrapped my arms around her and pulled her against my chest. Just feeling her body next to mine made me feel a hundred times better than any of the medicine the doctors at the hospital gave me. "The thing is with women like that, is that everyone knows one, and everyone turns a blind eye to it."

"That just makes me madder," she mumbled against my chest, and I chuckled again.

"Yeah, me too." I sighed. "But none of that tells you why it had to be me, so let me finish." I swallowed thickly, my hands running up and down her back, needing her closer to me. "I left, and I never looked back. I was dull to everything. The world was gray and muted and I was just still just trying to survive. Just trying to get through each day and each night. No one sees these kids on the street as anything but a menace or an inconvenience. They turn away so they don't have to see the ugly truth. But then I met Shooter." I laughed. "Actually, I tried to steal his bike, but I was too skinny and weak to be able to ride it so I got barely five feet away and me and the bike fell sideways, trapping me under it. Thought I was going to die. Thought him and his friend were going to kill me there and then, but they didn't. They took me back to the

301

clubhouse and introduced me to his dad, Hardy, who insisted that I had to pay for the damage to the bike."

"But you had no money!" she said, pulling back from me to look in my face.

I smirked. "Yeah, and he knew that. So I had to stay at the clubhouse and pay off my debt. Didn't really understand it at the time, but I was prospecting for them without even knowing it. I was still in the mentality that no one in this world was to be trusted and I was surviving day to day, but as time went by, I bulked up, I made friends, they became my family, and the day they voted for me to patch in was, and is, the proudest day of my life."

Belle chewed the side of her cheek. "I think I get it. I feel even worse now."

I shook my head. "You don't get it, and I haven't finished yet. A few months later I was on a run for the club, and I walked into a bar and saw my mom. She looked the same but older and sadder, and in her eyes I was still the same little boy she'd locked in the apartment every night while she went out drinking. The same starving kid she'd let her friends spend time with for twenty bucks and a bottle of vodka. There was no love there, no sadness that she'd missed me, no guilt about what she'd done to me."

Belle's face contorted in anger and sadness and back to anger and I leaned down and pressed a kiss to her lips to thank her for giving a shit. It would have been easy to keep kissing her and pretend that was the end of the story, but I wanted to get it all out in the open. I wanted her to understand.

"I killed my mom that day, Belle. Put a bullet in her brain and I didn't feel a goddamn thing about it. Not anger, not guilt, not shame. Nothing. I didn't even kill her because I was angry, I just wanted her gone from this world like she'd never existed."

I felt her muscles tense at my words, but I kept on going regardless. She knew what I did for the club, so she knew I wasn't a saint, but finding out that I'd felt no remorse at killing my own mom, I

302

guess that hit a nerve for her. Still, I had to finish my story no matter what.

"I was picked up by the police for her murder a couple of days later and it wasn't looking good for me. Thought I'd get the death penalty or at the very least life imprisonment, but then it all just went away. All of it. When I left prison, the club was outside waiting with my bike. We didn't ever talk about how or why. Later found out that the cops had no real evidence and thankfully Hardy had someone on the payroll to make all of the circumstantial shit just disappear. They couldn't prove anything even if they knew it was me. They had my back then and they've had it every other time since. I trust them with my life and they trust me with theirs. When I found out you'd been telling club secrets to those fuckers, I hated you, Belle. I hated you because for some inexplicable reason you had come into my life and I'd looked at you like family, and then you'd gone ahead and betrayed me and I finally felt something."

"I'm so sorry," she whispered, with tears in her eyes. I silenced her with another kiss.

"I know you are, but that's not the point of me telling you all of this." I stroked her hair back from her face. "Belle, as much as I hated it, it had to be me to kill you because you didn't just make me feel something, you made me feel *everything*, and if you were to die I knew I'd never feel anything ever again once you were gone. I had to be the one to kill you because if any of those men laid a hand on you I'd send them to ground, and just the thought of that..." I shook my head. "I was tortured to the brink of death, but I still didn't fall over the edge, and yet you...you could kill me so easily. You are the beginning and ending of me, Belle. You're everything."

Chapter Forty-One
~ *Belle* ~

People may have thought I was stupid to so easily forgive Beast, and maybe I was. But I didn't care what anyone else thought. All that mattered was him and me and the stuff in between. All that mattered was proving myself to his family so that they accepted me, because I couldn't imagine my life being anywhere but next to his.

Love made us foolish, but it also gave us strength. And at the moment I felt stronger than I'd ever felt before. Like I could take on the club, Mateo and Carlos, and even my mom. When I was with Beast, I could take on the world.

"I'll do whatever it takes to show you that you can trust me again, Beast," I promised.

"An' I'll do whatever it takes to show you I'll always protect you, Belle," he returned.

He reached for me, pulling me against his chest, and I sagged with relief as the scent of him—of leather and smoke, of sandalwood and sweat and all things Beast—wrapped itself around me and finally I felt safe. Despite the awful woman currently asleep in my bed, despite the two men who would show up soon and try to kill me, despite Beast's club hating me and probably still wanting to kill me too…I felt safe. There in Beast's arms, I had hope.

The slam of a door startled me, and Beast quickly shoved me behind his back and pulled out a gun from inside his cut. I gasped at the sight of it, a tremble starting in my belly and working its way around my body.

This was it.

This was actually happening.

They were finally here for me.

We crept to the trailer, pressing our backs against it before Beast began moving around the side of it. I'd never seen that look on his face before, and it scared me. Gone was the man I had fallen in love with—the vulnerable, beautiful man—and in his place was a cold-blooded killer. I could see it in his eyes, in his stance, in the way his jaw ticked. I felt safe but terrified of him all at the same time.

The sound of an engine coming to life brought my thoughts back to the present, and Beast looked back at me with a scowl. We moved quicker, heading around to the front of the trailer, gun raised, just in time to see my mom taking off in my car.

Dirt and gravel flew up behind her as she tried to get out of there before she had to face me, and I gasped as I put the pieces together. The car was loaded with boxes on the back seat, and without thinking I ran from around the back of Beast and up the steps of my trailer.

Inside was a mess. Every cupboard door was open, the small sofa was in disarray, cushions scattered on to the floor, ornaments knocked over, and pictures hanging to one side.

She was looking for something…

"No!" I cried out, and ran toward my bedroom.

"Belle, wait," Beast called after me, but I was already gone, throwing open the rickety door to my room.

The room had been tipped upside down, drawers emptied, the mattress dragged up. The door to the small closet was open and its contents were spilling out: clothes, books, CDs—my life was in an unwanted heap. I dropped to my knees in front of it and began rummaging through my things, searching for the rose-scented box where I kept my savings. I breathed a sigh of relief when I found it, but it was short-lived.

The lid was off it and the contents were gone.

A sob left me and I buried my face in my hands.

"What is it?" he asked.

I glanced up briefly. "My savings…she took all of it."

Beast sat behind me on the edge of the bed, one hand rubbing my back as he let me cry out all of my disappointment and sadness. When there was nothing left in me, I rubbed at my cheeks and looked back at him, and his expression was haunting.

He knew my pain.

He'd lived it too.

The disappointment of a mother, of family, was agonizing. These were the people that were supposed to love and protect you. To keep you safe and pick you up when you fell down. They weren't supposed to hurt you. They weren't supposed to allow bad things to happen.

"How much was in there?" he asked.

"Everything," I said, my voice hoarse. "All of my savings. Everything that Shooter paid me to look after you, and everything from before then. It was all I had in the world—maybe ten grand, give or take."

"Jesus, Belle," he sighed, dragging a hand down his chin. "Why would you keep that sort of money lying around here?"

"I was saving for an apartment. I just—I wasn't sure if I could put it in the bank what with it coming from the club. I didn't want anyone asking questions in case I got you in trouble." I looked back at the empty box again, and then my eyes surveyed the mess my mother had left in her hunt for my savings. She'd torn the place apart looking for it. "I need to clean up," I said sadly, getting to my feet.

"Hey," Beast said, reaching for me, "come here."

He pulled me to him and I buried my face in his neck, swallowing down the tears that were threatening to come again.

"I can't believe she'd do this to me," I mumbled against his skin.

His hands rubbed up and down my back, soothing me. "People are shitty, Belle. It's just the way they are."

I pulled away to look at him, his sadness matching mine. God, he was actually sad for me, and for some reason that made it more bearable. He got it, he understood. He was furious for me, but mostly he was just sad for me.

Beast pushed my hair back from my face and I took a shuddering breath. "People are shitty," he said again, "but I know that there are good people out there too. And the good far outweigh the bad."

"How can you be so sure?" I said with a sniffle.

He smiled and didn't say anything, and I knew what he was saying without words, and I found myself agreeing with him. I surveyed the damage again.

"I'm never getting out of this dump, am I?" I said on a heavy breath.

"I'll sort it out," he replied, and I shook my head firmly. "Belle—"

"No, I have to do this myself."

It was his turn to look frustrated then, but he nodded all the same. "All right, if that's what you want. But maybe, when all this shit is behind us—because it will be soon—how about I put the deposit down for you and you just pay me back? Or not. Whichever."

He smirked, and I smiled at him but shook my head. "No, but when all this is over, how about I let you take me out to dinner?"

"As long as it's not Italian." He winked, and despite the awfulness of the situation, I couldn't help but smile. It quickly fell when I thought about Lorenzo, though, a frown replacing my smile.

"What's this all about?" he said, indicating my frown.

"I need to speak to Lorenzo." I looked away from Beast. "I need to end things with him."

"Fuck him, he'll know it's over when he sees you with me," he bit out, and I shook my head and looked back at him. "I'm serious, Belle, stay away from him."

"I'm serious too. I need to break up with him. He's not the man I thought he was; he's a bully, but he's *just* a man. I'm doing this, with or without your blessing." I pulled out of his grip and started picking my things back up off the floor and putting them back away.

I noted certain things were gone as I cleaned up: my favorite dress, a pair of heels, some of my makeup, jewelry. I sighed with each new thing gone, a new kind of sadness growing inside my heart.

It took us over an hour to put my trailer back together, and the whole time Beast wouldn't speak to me. I decided to take his silence as him brooding and not being mad at me, because that was easier to handle. I finally sat back down on the sofa in the small living room and

307

looked back around at my home. I'd found more and more of my things missing as I'd tidied, and I no doubt would find more as the days went on. She'd pretty much cleared me out of food, which was the most hurtful. It was like, not only was she stealing my things—my clothes, my jewelry, my money, but she also didn't care that I'd have nothing to eat, and as far as she was concerned, no money to buy food with.

I was exhausted, emotionally, physically. It had been the longest day in history, and it was barely 7 p.m. I yawned and stood up to make some coffee, but when I opened the cupboard I noted that she'd even taken my coffee.

Gripping the kitchen work surface, I leaned over and tried not to cry again. Beast came behind me and wrapped his arms around my body.

"Why don't you go get some sleep? I'll call and get a prospect to bring us some food for when you wake up," he said, his lips against my neck. My body sparked at his touch, his breath brushing over my sensitive skin, and I could have quite easily stripped naked for him and let him take my body to forget about all the awful in the world right then. I'd been through so much today already, and tomorrow didn't seem like it was going to be any better. Why not enjoy Beast while I still had him? While I was still alive? Because Lord knew everything was against him, me, and us.

But my exhaustion was like a heavy blanket, the toll of the day finally wearing me down, so I nodded and headed to my bedroom to sleep.

Chapter Forty-Two
~ BEAST ~

The prospect handed over three bags of groceries and I put them by my feet while he headed back to the truck to get the takeout I'd told him to pick up for us. I wasn't sure what Belle liked to eat and I had never really put much thought into what I ate—it was just food to fill a hole—but it mattered for some reason that I got her something she liked. Healthy groceries and Chinese food for now seemed like a good choice.

It seemed as if only Jenna had ever given a shit about her, and though Belle never complained at all, I had a feeling that it would mean something to her.

"So, they didn't have the wholegrain bread, so I got whole meal," he said, handing over the takeout bag and then pulling a scrap of paper from his cut.

"I asked for wholegrain," I snapped, and he looked up. "Why didn't you go to a different store?"

"I err…" he stammered.

"Here's a pop quiz for you, prospect: if a man asks for beer and they only have light, do you get him the light, or do you go somewhere else and buy him what he asked for?" I snarled, glaring down at him.

He cowered under my stare. "I guess, I ummm…"

I gripped him by his cut and dragged him close to my face. "You go somewhere else and get him what he goddamn asked for!" I yelled, and he nodded quickly. I dropped him and he stumbled down the little steps, almost falling on his ass. "Next time you fuck up will be your last."

I slammed the door on him and turned back to the food, happy in the knowledge that the little shit was probably pissing his pants right then. It was all part of prospecting—taking our bullshit, and doing lame-as-shit menial tasks and not being able to complain about it. We'd all done it at one point or another. If they wanted in the club, they gritted

309

their teeth and got on with it. If it was a passing phase they'd fuck off and join some Jap crap club instead. It was no great loss if they chose the latter option. The Devil's Highwaymen needed men, not pussies that couldn't follow orders.

I picked up the bag of takeout and placed it inside the little oven so it would stay warm and then I set about putting the groceries away, growing more pissed off when I realized that he had missed other stuff from my list. I'd had to go through Belle's trash to work out what food she liked to eat and had been dismayed to learn that I didn't know what half of it was. Humus…what the fuck even was humus? Belle may have been poor as shit, but she liked to eat good food and I kind of liked that about her. Her trailer was busted up but it was clean and tidy to the point of obsession, her cupboards were pretty bare but what they did hold was exotic—at least to a simple man like me, and her clothes may have been thrift store bought but she had great taste and knew what looked good on her beautiful body.

"What's all this?" Her soft voice reached me as she came out of the small bedroom yawning. She stretched her arms up high, her small tee lifting up to reveal her bronzed stomach, and my dick twitched in response to seeing just the barest bit of flesh on her.

"Nothing much. I got a prospect to bring you some food since your cunt of a mom took most of yours," I snapped like I was angry with her when it was her mom whose neck I wanted to break.

She looked up at me with those big doe eyes of hers. I'd offended her, or hurt her, or…surprised her? I wasn't sure which, so I moved on. "I got you some steaks and some healthy green shit, and I saw from your trash that you liked jelly beans, though why you don't like the apple ones is beyond me because they're the fucking best, but whatever."

Pulling open the oven door, I dragged out the bag of Chinese. "Ordered some takeout too. Wasn't sure what you'd eat, so I ordered…" I scratched at my beard, uncomfortable under her scrutiny. "…pretty much everything from the menu, apart from those prawn sesame seed things because I don't like the smell of them, and that's selfish but I'm

310

a fuckin' man so I'm allowed to be so don't start getting all mad and pissy at me."

She was still staring at me and I was feeling more and more uncomfortable. I'd tried to do something nice for her, but she was looking at me like I had two heads, ten arms, and a robotic dick. I felt stupider by the second and suddenly couldn't even remember why I'd bothered or why it had seemed like a good idea at the time. I decided right there and then never to do anything like that ever again, and that the next time I saw that fucking prospect I was going to punch him in his face for not telling me that it was a stupid idea.

"Goddamn it, Belle!" I finally yelled when I couldn't take her silence anymore. "Will you fucking say something?"

She blinked like I'd broken her out of her trance and then she threw herself at my chest, wrapping her arms around me and mumbling something against my body. Jesus Christ, women were weird. No wonder I'd never picked an old lady; I couldn't deal with this 24/7.

"What the fuck is wrong?" I snapped, still tense and irritated, but mostly confused because it sounded like she was crying and all I'd done was buy noodles and fucking humus! "Belle, damn it," I grumbled, and pulled her away from my chest to look down at her.

Belle's cheeks weren't wet from crying, but they were pink. And her mouth wasn't frowning up at me like she thought I was an idiot— she was smiling. And her eyes…those Disney character eyes of hers were staring up at me with a look I'd never seen on any woman before, and I'd seen *many* looks on women's faces. But this, this was something else. My chest felt too tight. My stomach felt full, like I'd already eaten. My body felt warm, like I'd been wrapped in a thick wool blanket all day and was about to overheat. But my head was the most fucked up of all, because the only thought that was going around in it was her name over and over and over.

Belle reached up, placing her hand on the side of my ugly-as-sin, face and I tried to pull away from it because no woman wanted to touch that shit, but she rose up on her toes and clasped my cheek again, her eyes boring into mine.

311

"Nothing is wrong, Beast," she said, and I swallowed thickly at the reverence in her tone. "Everything is right. For once…everything is right." She was smiling up at me like I was Prince Charming and this was our fairy tale. Like this was the last page of the book and it was time for our happily ever after. And I wanted that too. I wanted it for me and for her. But life was never that good. It could never be trusted that much.

"I want you to kiss me, Beast," she said, her voice breathy. "I want you to kiss me and then I want you to take me back to bed, and this time, when I wake up, everything will be just as perfect as when I went to sleep, because I'll still be with you."

The air had been sucked out of the room.

Hell, out of the whole goddamn trailer.

I wanted to tear the door off its hinges and let some in.

I wanted to punch a hole in the window before we both suffocated.

But I wanted to kiss her more.

I grabbed Belle by the waist and lifted her up, her legs automatically wrapping around me like my own personal koala bear, and then I kissed her like her life depended upon it. She groaned into my mouth and I sucked the groan off of her tongue and swallowed it, letting her groans and moans fill me up to overflowing as my hands clasped her ass and I walked us to her bedroom. I didn't know what love was, but it had to feel something like this, because I'd never felt like this before in my whole damned life. I felt a combination of nauseous and ecstatic. Terrified and overjoyed. I felt starved for her, for oxygen, for whatever it was that she kept giving me. It wasn't enough—I wanted more of it. It would never be enough but I'd stick around to keep on trying. I'd let her pump whatever this shit was right into my black veins until I ODed on it because I was addicted to *this*—to *her*—to whatever kind of drug she was.

My shins hit her bed and I laid us both down on it, my mouth momentarily leaving hers so I could pull up my T-shirt before dragging it off me. Her hands went to her own tee but I batted them away before

312

gripping either side of it and tearing it down the middle, and she giggled. Her breasts popped free and it was my turn to groan because I'd almost forgotten how fucking good they looked. I leaned down and sucked her pink nipple into my mouth, my tongue playing with the hard bud. Cupping her breasts with my hands, I pushed them together so I could slide my tongue across them both before nipping at them, making her arch her back and squeal into the air around us.

My hands went to her hips and I slid the little bed shorts she was wearing down her thighs right along with her panties, and then I stared down at her—all of her, taking in every naked perfect inch of this beautiful woman.

Her cheeks turned pink as her tongue darted out to wet her bottom lip and my chest rumbled at the sight.

"Come here, Beast," she sighed, arching a finger at me.

I unbuckled my jeans and dropped them to the ground before kicking her legs apart so I could get a good look at her.

"Fuck, Belle," I rumbled, my hand moving to my hard cock.

"Yes, fuck Belle!" she said, her cheeks going even pinker because she'd cussed.

"Love it when you talk dirty to me." I grinned and she giggled.

It was just another way that we were different. She was calm and I was hot-headed. She was patient and I had no tolerance for anyone or anything. She was prim and proper and it didn't matter how much soap you washed my mouth out with, nothing was getting it clean. Her body was smooth marble and mine was old, crumbling tree bark. I was a monster next to her and I finally embraced that, loving how different we were. Relishing in our differences.

I wanted to grab her legs and put them to my shoulders so I could fuck her while looking into her eyes, but the piece-of-shit bed was too low so I flipped her on her side and lay down behind her. My hand moved over her ass and down over her puckered hole before I found her pussy. Rubbing along its seam, I pressed two fingers inside of her and she pushed back against the intrusion. I slid an arm under her, and I pulled out my fingers and guided my cock to her entrance, teasing her with the tip of it as I rolled my hips.

"Please…Beast, please," she whimpered, writhing against me as she tried to get me to move.

I put my arm over her belly so that I was holding her in my grip, and I slowly thrust my hips forwards, filling her up and stretching her wide. Belle whimpered into the air as I grabbed her face and tilted her head to the side so I could kiss her swollen lips. Every thrust had her crying into my mouth, every roll of my hips had her mewling like an animal. I stole every sound she made with my tongue, fucking her mouth as my cock branded her insides.

We were animals, our bodies in sync with each other as we fucked and kissed and moved together, taking and giving and relishing in each other. She was wet, sloppy wet as my hips bucked and I ground into her, taking each grunt and sigh, each hiss of delicious pleasure that she released into the air around us. Mine, all mine.

"Close…" she panted. "So close, Beast."

My tongue moved over hers, sucking on it like I could taste the pleasure right on the tip of her tongue.

"I got you, Belle," I grunted, my hips slowing their rhythm.

I flipped her onto her front, and she screamed into her pillow as I wrapped an arm under her, lifting her ass into the air and slamming myself back home. I pounded into her harder and harder, my dick sliding in and out of her wet center from tip to balls and back again, each thrust hitting her core until she finally climaxed around me with a silent scream. Her pussy clenched and shuddered around my cock, drawing me closer and closer to my own climax until finally I reached the peak, tumbling over to the other side. My hands gripped her hips as I ground into her, letting her body pull every last drop of sweet satisfaction from me until my knees were almost buckling under the pressure to stay upright.

My heart was racing a million miles an hour as I slowly slid out of Belle and lay down next to her. I pulled her against my chest, our sweaty bodies sticking to each other as our hearts beat in unison.

314

"That was…" she started to say, her voice thick with emotion.

"Yeah," I agreed, kissing the top of her head. "Yeah, it was."

Forty-Three
~ BEAST ~

Hurry up, I'm starved!" Belle called from the bedroom, and I chuckled.

"It's coming," I yelled back.

"I'm wasting away here…There'll be nothing left if you don't hurry!"

I shook my head, a huge, shit-eating grin on my face as I grabbed the bag of Chinese takeout and some forks for us. Fuck the plates and all that shit—we could eat straight from the boxes. I was ass naked as I strolled back into the bedroom, food bag in one hand, forks in the other, and my huge dick hanging between my legs.

"Quit your bitchin', I'm back." I smirked.

Her eyes strayed to my dick and I raised an eyebrow, already getting hard at the thought of being back inside of her.

"Yes, you are," she said, her voice still all husky.

I climbed on the bed. "Can't believe I'm about to say this, but you need to eat—then we can fuck some more."

She pouted—full-on pouted—and I leaned over and pressed a kiss on her mouth, sucking that fucking pout right off those beautiful lips of hers. Her hand went to my hair and she gripped it tight and pulled me closer, her kisses growing hungrier with each roll of my tongue.

I'd never have enough of her kisses. This mouth, this body, this woman…I would never have enough of her. I let go of the food bag and forks finally, my hands roving over her body, one throwing the covers back and the other diving between her lips to feel how wet she was already.

"Fuck, Belle," I groaned as her hand went to my dick, sliding along it and sending shudders of pleasure rolling through me.

Her back arched as I hooked my thick finger inside of her, hitting her G-spot with surprising ease. Jesus, she was close already. I dropped to my knees, my dick slipping free of her grip, because as much as I wanted her to touch me, I wanted to taste her more.

I pushed her legs apart and clamped my mouth over her pussy, tasting her juices on my tongue as I licked her from back to front. I lapped at her, splitting her wide as I slid a thick finger in her and strummed that G-spot again.

Fuck, she tasted good.

Really good.

Like peaches and cream.

Strawberries and lemonade.

Like pussy and love.

I flicked my tongue over her clit and her body jerked to attention. She threw her head back and made some indescribable noise in the back of her throat. Belle's hands were in my hair and she tugged on it again as I blew lightly on her pussy, sliding my fingers inside of her. As I pulled them back out, I sucked on her clit. Her thighs tightened around my head as she squeezed and panted and clawed at the pillow, and then she was coming against my tongue as she screamed into the air, her body shuddering as she came apart against my mouth.

Sitting back up, I swiped my hand over my wet mouth. My dick was aching it was so hard, and I lined myself up with her entrance and gripped her thighs in my hands before sliding myself into her in one quick move. Her eyes flew open, meeting mine as my hard length filled her up.

Fucking loved that look on her face, her full mouth open as she groaned and panted, her Disney eyes owning my soul as she batted her long eyelashes. I was becoming the very definition of pathetic as I watched in total awe of her as I moved in and out, loving every little noise she made. Every pant, every mewl, every sigh. *Mine, all mine.*

I fucked her hard and quick, finding my own release within minutes. My balls drew up as she clenched around me on the brink of another orgasm, and we flew to the other side together in a wave of heaven and skin slapping against skin.

Clutching onto the headboard behind her, I ground into her pussy, letting her body milk every last drop from me, and I sucked on her lips and tongue until we were both fucking spent and exhausted. Finally, I rolled off of her and lay down, an arm thrown over my chest as I stared up at her ceiling.

"You're not busy for the next month, are you?" I drawled, looking over at her.

"What?" she giggled. "I mean, I need to find a job, but…"

"I'm going to need you to stay naked and in this bed for at least a month so I can do that every minute of the day, Belle. It's the only way this thing is going to work between us," I teased, and she giggled again.

"Is that so?" She turned on her side to face me, my gaze going to her perky tits and hard nipples.

"Fuck, I'm getting hard again just looking at you," I said seriously with a shake of my head.

"You're a machine," she replied, her own gaze going down to my hardening cock. Her eyes widened. "Oh my God, you were serious!"

"Fuck yeah, I was. I don't joke where my dick is concerned, Belle." I reached over and hooked a hand around the back of her head, pulling her close enough so I could kiss her already swollen mouth again.

I would never tire of kissing those lips. Ever.

She moaned into my mouth and I was definitely up for round three right the fuck then, but then I heard her stomach rumble loudly and I chuckled against her lips.

"Let's feed you, woman, and then we can finish this off."

She pouted, but her stomach growled again and she conceded, sitting up to pull the covers around her body. I raised an eyebrow at her, seriously not happy about her hiding that beautiful body from me.

"We'll never get to eat otherwise," she laughed, and I smirked.

I grabbed the bag of food, which had fallen on the floor. Some of the lids had come open and food had spilled out, so I picked out the ones that looked the least destroyed, found the forks I'd brought, and got back in bed.

"We have…I think chicken chow mein and whatever the fuck this one is," I said, opening a pot of noodles and vegetables. "Smells good, whatever it is."

Belle took the chow mein and I took the mystery box and we ate in silence. Every once in a while I caught her stealing glances at me, a smile on her face. I finished my food in record time and went and grabbed us two beers from the fridge. I'd had the prospect get us a pack of them, but I had no intention of drinking more than this one before I got lost in her body again.

After over a year of no happiness, no sex, and nothing good in my life, I was making up for lost time. I stood in the doorway watching her eat slowly as I drank my beer. Pretty sure she was eating slow on purpose too, but I wasn't about to let her know that she was driving me crazy. I couldn't give her all the power in this.

"That good?" I asked, nodding toward the food on her fork. She'd been eating a single long noodle off her fork for what seemed like five fucking minutes now, and it was taking all of my restraint not to throw the food to one side, lay her back down spread-eagled for me, and devour her body again.

"Uh huh," she said with a nod of her head and a grin that told me she knew exactly what she was motherfuckin' doing.

"How good?"

"Reallllly good," she said, her voice dropping an octave as she drew out the word. She sucked the noodle into her mouth and chewed slowly, making a big deal of twisting another noodle onto her fork.

My dick was already hard and ready, and she tried not to smirk as she noticed it. Both me and my dick were growing impatient and she was loving it.

"Really good, huh?" I asked.

She nodded again. "Uh huh. So good, Beast, like you wouldn't believe."

My nostrils flared as she reached for the bottle of beer I'd given her and she took a long pull on it. I watched her throat bob as it slid down her throat, a drop of it dampening her lower lip. Her tongue darted

319

out to swipe it away and I put my beer down and stepped forward, holding a hand up to her.

"Allow me."

I climbed back on the bed and crawled toward her, grabbing her by the ankles and pulling her down flat. She dropped whatever was left of the chow mein onto the floor beside her as she giggled and struggled to hold the bottle upright so it didn't spill.

My arms boxed her in, trapping her within their confines, and I leaned down and licked the beer from her lips. Fuck, she tasted good. Like beer and perfection.

Taking the bottle from her hand, I dribbled it over her tits and she gasped as the cold beer splashed over her nipples and ran down the sides of her body. Leaning down, I lapped at it, sucking it off her body as she arched her back, pressing her tits into my mouth as I moved between them.

I dribbled some more beer between her tits and it trailed down her chest and over her stomach, pooling in her belly button. I put the bottle down and sucked the beer out of her belly button, my hands slowly massaging her tits.

I trailed lower on her body, my tongue finding her clit and lapping at it as she let out a raspy moan. Her body tasted of sex and beer and I wanted to take my time with her, but her hands were already moving to my face and pulling it back up to her mouth as her legs hooked around my waist until my cock was nudging at her entrance again.

"You want this?" I asked, and she nodded emphatically. "You not hungry anymore?" I teased, and she grinned.

"I'm starved," she replied huskily before squeezing her thighs and ankles and lifting her ass up to push me inside of her.

I gripped her wrists in my hands and pressed them into the bed as I rocked my hips back and forth, fucking into her slowly.

"You like that, Belle?" I grunted, my balls slapping against her pussy with each thrust.

"Yes," she said automatically, and I chuckled as I rolled my hips and she whimpered as I hit her G-spot perfectly. "Don't stop," she groaned, her gaze never leaving mine.

"I don't intend to," I replied. "Like I said, my plan for the next month," I continued, as I slid out of her to my tip before pushing back inside, "is to stay here until you can't walk straight and you have a permanent imprint of my cock inside of you."

She groaned again, and fuck me if it wasn't the most beautiful sound I'd ever heard.

I slid back out before slamming back inside hard enough to make her gasp and clench around me.

"And what about you?" she grunted as I rolled my hips again.

"What about me?"

"It seems hardly fair that you're going to imprint my..." Her cheeks were pink from sex already, but they went even brighter.

"Your pussy," I prompted. "I'm going to fuck you so much that I imprint my cock in your pussy so it never wants anyone but me."

"Yes, that, so what about you? Does your..."

"Cock," I said, slamming into her hard enough to make the headboard bang against the wall and her whimper.

"Yes," she groaned. "What about that?"

I knelt up, lifting her ankles to my shoulders so I could reach a new angle. I was so deep inside of her then that I had to give us both a few seconds to adjust to how fucking good it felt.

"What are you asking, Belle? Will your pussy be imprinted on my cock? Is that it?"

She opened her mouth to speak but was rendered speechless as I flexed my hips and rocked into her. She nodded, her mouth open in a silent *O*, and I chuckled.

"Then yeah, if that's what you're asking, yeah, your pussy is imprinted all over my cock, my tongue, my balls, and every other part of me," I said. "Ain't no part of me that wants to be anywhere else, with anyone else."

321

I wrapped my arms around her legs, holding them tight against my chest.

"Do you mean that?" she asked, her knuckles going white as she gripped the pillow under her head.

"With everything I am, Belle," I admitted.

We stared at each other for a moment in silence, taking in each other's honesty. I felt vulnerable but not weak. I felt stronger than I'd ever felt before, and for the first time since this nightmare began I was finally glad that I'd gone through all that other shit because it had brought me here to her.

"Beast?" she asked, her voice soft, and I almost lost it right there and then.

"Yeah?"

"Will you fuck me now?" she asked, her cheeks flushing on the cussword.

I hadn't realized I'd even stopped fucking her, and I grinned down at her and began moving again.

"Absofuckinglutely, Belle," I grunted as I slammed into her harder. "And tomorrow." I slammed in again and she called out my name. "And the day after…" I thrust again. "And the day after that…" I fucked into her over and over, harder and harder until I felt my balls draw up and my cum douse her insides as her muscles clenched around me and her back arched upwards. I fucked Belle hard until there was nothing left of either of us, and then I leaned over her and pressed a rough kiss to her panting mouth. "And every day after that," I said against her lips.

Chapter Forty-Four
~ *Belle* ~

If it wasn't for the fact that Mateo and Carlos were still out there, or my mom having stolen my life savings and run off, or that I hadn't told Lorenzo that it was over…the day would have been pretty perfect.

I was lying in Beast's arms, my body tired and aching after spending most of the day in bed with him. I was sore, exhausted, but so happy. We just needed to get through the next couple of days and that would be it. We could be like this every day. This could be our life.

Me and Beast.

Beast and I.

Together.

I hadn't known that I wanted or needed a man like Beast until he'd come into my life, but now that he was in it I didn't ever want to let him go. I wasn't stupid enough to believe that he was some boy scout who helped old ladies across the street or had a five-year. That he wanted a white picket fence and a healthy retirement option. He was none of the things that I'd always sought out, and yet he was exactly what I needed.

He was currently snoring like a freight train after our sixth or seventh time having sex, and though I was exhausted too, I couldn't sleep. The prospect of the future was too exciting, and I found that every time I closed my eyes my body tingled for his attention.

I decided to get up and make some coffee because sleep clearly wasn't coming for me, and I snuck out of bed without disturbing Beast. Beast…the name still kind of threw me, and I realized that I didn't actually know his real name. I'd never asked and he'd never said, and though it should have been important, it wasn't. He was Beast and I was Belle and that was all that mattered.

Wrapped in my dressing gown, I made coffee and then opened my front door so I could sit on the steps and watch the sun coming up.

It was a favorite pastime and something that I used to do a lot when I'd first moved there, but I'd been so busy with work for the past year that I hadn't had the chance to do it.

There was something about watching the sun come up that made me feel good. Watching the birth of a new day was almost godly, and I felt blessed each and every time. I sipped my coffee, watching as the orange and yellow glow rose slowly above the trees, casting warmth on my face as it finally reached me.

I wasn't sure what was going to happen between me and Beast. Could it actually work? Would his club ever accept me after what I'd done? Would Jenna ever accept him? I didn't know the answer to any of those questions, but I was willing to try to find out. For the first time in my life, I felt complete. I'd been searching for who I really was, thinking my parents could solve the riddle for me, but the whole time the answer had been with me. Being with Beast had helped me see that. Maybe it was the way he accepted himself that helped me to do the same. Or maybe it was that he accepted me and gave me confidence I'd never had before. Either way, I felt whole. Like a jigsaw that had finally been finished.

I heard Beast's snoring stop and then the trailer creak and groan as he got up, and several moments later he came and found me.

"Everything okay?" he asked, running a hand through his loose hair and yawning. He was topless and I watched him stretch, each thick band of muscle moving beneath the skin.

"I am now," I said, worrying my bottom lip.

His sleepy expression fell into a dirty smirk as he looked down on me. "Oh yeah?"

I nodded, put my mug down on the steps, and stood up. "Much better now."

His nostrils flared as my hands went to the tie at my waist and slowly untied it. The two sides of my dressing gown slipped apart, revealing my naked body underneath, and he automatically reached out, cupping one of my breasts in one of his large hands.

"Fuck, Belle, aren't you sore?" he asked, sounding genuinely concerned even as he was pushing me back against the doorframe. His head lowered to take my nipple into his mouth and suck on the hard, pink nub, and I arched back and groaned.

"Yes, but I still want more," I sighed, my hand going to his hair as his other hand slipped between my legs, pushing them apart so he could push a thick finger inside of me. I gasped as he stretched me wide. My body was already ready for him and I fumbled at his jeans.

"I don't want to hurt you," he mumbled, his mouth working its way up from my breasts to my throat.

"So don't," I sighed, lifting a leg up to his waist to give him deeper access to my body. He knew exactly the spot that I liked, and he hooked his finger and hit it repeatedly until I was a trembling mess on the brink of an orgasm within seconds.

I'd finally gotten his jeans open and was frantically pushing them down his thighs when his cell began to ring. Beast hesitated until I gripped him in my hand and began to slide up and down his hard length. He grunted against my throat, his mouth moving up to my chin, nibbling and licking a path to my mouth where we fell into a kiss.

I hooked my leg around his back, wanting to coax him inside of me, but he was so much taller than me that it was never going to work. He realized what I was trying to do and his hands gripped my waist, lifting me up and pulling me back down onto his hard length. He filled me up as I gasped into his open mouth, my hands in his hair as he thrust slowly and deliciously into my body, setting every nerve ending on fire.

"Oh God…" I cried into his mouth, my body ready to go off like a firework already. "Beast…" I cried out as he thrust harder and harder, my entire trailer rocking dangerously. He slid in and out of me, hitting every nerve and setting them off until I was exploding around him like a Fourth of July firework.

I threw my head back and cried out into the early morning air, not caring who or what I woke up, and he continued to push into me harder and harder until the force of his thrusts made the entire trailer shake in

325

its foundations. I felt him swell inside of me before finally coming in a flurry of thrusts and *fuck me*'s' as he found his own release.

Beast pressed his forehead against mine as our breathing slowed, and then he kissed me like it was our first kiss. His tongue moving slowly, tenderly, his hips still rocking gently into me, each delicious movement turning my mind and my body to Jell-O.

His kisses were possessive, yet delicate in their own way. Raw and carnal. With Beast there was no such thing as *just a kiss*. With Beast there was only *end-of-the-world* kisses, that he gave everything he was into.

Slowly, he slid out of me and lowered me back to the ground. "Fuck, Belle," he grunted. He pushed his hands into my hair, pushing it back from my face and tipping me up to look at him. His eyes searched my face for a moment, and it felt like he could see into my soul. Like he could see every wrong or right thing I'd ever done in my life. Satisfied with what he saw, he ran a thumb across my swollen bottom lip.

"Ain't never letting you go," he finally said, his voice hoarse and his gaze burning with intensity. "Not fuckin' ever."

My face split into a smile and his thumb ran across my lip again as he smiled right back.

Beast grabbed both sides of my dressing gown and pulled them together, tying it closed, and I giggled because the realization that I'd just had sex in my doorway where anyone could have seen me was finally hitting me. What was it with this man that made me so reckless?

He pulled his jeans up and fastened them. "Any more of that coffee left?" he asked, and I nodded and grabbed my mug from the step before heading inside to make us both one.

My cupboards and fridge were full of food from what he'd bought the day before, and I fixed us up something to eat and made fresh coffee and we sat and ate it in silence, both of us chewing and watching each other before smiling.

Both of us waiting for the other to finish so we could go back to bed again.

As he swiped the last of his toast around his plate to soak up the juices, I squeezed my thighs together, more than ready for him. Watching him eat was like watching graphic porn; every bite, every chew, every swallow was filled with seduction and desire, and I was practically panting for him by the time he swallowed the last of his coffee.

He slammed his cup down and stood up, grabbing my hand. "Okay, come on then."

I laughed and let him pull me to the bedroom, more than ready for his caveman action, but the sound of motorcycles outside had us both stopping in our tracks.

His phone started to ring again as the motorcycles got louder and louder until it sounded like there were a hundred of them outside my trailer. I squeezed his hand, suddenly terrified they'd come for me. That his club hadn't accepted me and had decided to kill me instead.

"Beast?" I whispered his name, too terrified to say any other word.

"I've got this, babe. Go get dressed," he grunted, pushing me toward my bedroom as he stalked toward the door. Sunlight illuminated the trailer as he opened the door, gripping the top of the frame as he watched motorcycles pulling to a stop in front of the trailer. "Go, Belle. Put some clothes on," he ordered, all softness gone from his tone.

I skittered toward my bedroom quickly, my legs shaking as I wondered what was happening.

My bedroom was a mess, clothes and blankets, Chinese food and beer bottles scattered everywhere, and I grew increasingly upset as I struggled to find something to wear. My mom had stolen most of my nicest things, and the resentment I had for her grew in my chest like a black hole. I finally pulled out an old black T-shirt I couldn't remember ever buying and some blue denim shorts, and I dressed quickly. I could hear lots of voices talking, but no one seemed to be shouting or yelling so I took that as a good sign as I pulled my hair into a messy bun on top of my head and slipped on some sandals.

327

I made my way back down the hallway, hesitant but determined not to run away from whatever this new challenge was. I wanted Beast to know that I was strong and I would stand by him. I'd said I would do whatever it took to make his club accept me, and I meant it. Especially after the last twenty-four hours we'd just shared.

"Beast?" I said quietly as I came up behind him.

He turned, his expression hard, but softening once he saw me. He reached for me, pulling me to his chest automatically, and I fell into him, embracing the safety that he offered.

Most of his club was parked outside my trailer, or so it seemed. Men that I had seen at the club before. Men I had spoken to on many occasions, and men I hadn't seen before. But they were all part of his club. They all wore the same patch of the Devil's Highwaymen. And they all wore the same grim expression.

"What's going on?" I asked him, looking up into his face.

I watched his Adam's apple bob in his throat, his gaze still on his brothers. He took a deep breath and tore his gaze away from them to look down at me.

"Beast?" I said his name again when he still hadn't replied. "It's okay. Whatever it is, we'll get through it together. Just tell me what it is."

"They have Mateo and Carlos," he said, his voice like stone.

I frowned, surprised by his emotionless tone. I thought he would have been on his bike and out of there so he could kill them, but instead he just looked worried and frustrated.

"That's good, right?" I said, tearing my gaze away to look at his brothers. My gaze settled on Shooter. "Right?" I asked again.

"Right," Shooter replied. "It's real good news."

"Shut up," Beast barked, making me flinch. "Don't you fuckin' talk to her."

"Easy, Beast," Rider placated.

I pulled out from under Beast's arms so I could look up at him properly. "What's wrong?" I searched his face for something, anything,

328

but he gave nothing away. "Beast? You're frightening me, please tell me," I pleaded.

"You want to be accepted into the club? As his woman?" Shooter said, and I turned and nodded at him.

"Yes, more than anything."

"Prez," Beast warned.

"It's the only way we'll trust her again," said Gauge, the bigger of the men, his cold stare on me.

"You," Beast said, stepping forward and thrusting his finger out, "you shut your goddamned mouth before I shut you up permanently. She's not doing it, end of."

"Then she'll never be fully trusted, brother," Rider said, his gray-white beard looking out of place on him.

"Then I'll take her and we'll leave," Beast said, and I saw the shock on everyone's face at that.

I looked between them all, completely confused and frustrated by what was happening but determined that I wouldn't be the one to make Beast lose his family.

"I'll do it," I said, and all eyes fell on me. "Whatever it is, I'll do it."

Beast gripped my arm and spun me to him. "You don't know what you're saying, Belle. You don't even know what they're asking of you."

I shrugged out from under his grip. "I don't care. This is your family, and you're not leaving them because of me, and I'm not losing you, so whatever it is, I'll do it. I was frightened and made the biggest mistake of my life, but I'm not scared anymore—not now that I'm with you." I turned to face the men again, steeling determination in my tone as I looked them all over, my gaze finally landing on Shooter. "Tell me what I need to do."

Shooter glanced over at Gauge and they seemed to have a silent conversation between themselves before Shooter finally looked at me again.

"You have to kill someone," he said.

And the pieces clicked together.

329

"Mateo and Carlos," I said, and I felt Beast put his hand on my back. I swallowed and nodded, thinking of all the pain they'd caused Beast. The scars, the cuts, the burns, the agony, how he almost lost his sight. How he almost couldn't walk again. How he almost lost his life because of them. And I wasn't afraid. "Okay," I said with firm resolve.

"Just one of them—the other is for Beast," Shooter said almost sympathetically, and I nodded okay again.

I felt sick at the thought. I hated them, but to take someone's life... Yet I would do it. For him, I'd do it.

"Belle?" Beast said from behind me, and I turned to look at him. His expression was blank, devoid of the warmth I'd felt for the past day, and I worried that I'd just failed some test. Worried that my wrong answer meant my death, or worse. "Not just kill, babe," he said, his hand cupping my face. "Torture and kill...while they film it."

I stared at him in shock, my stomach flipping over and over and over.

Kill, I could just about do.

But torture and kill?

Could I do that?

Could I harm another person like that? Cause them pain over and over before finally putting them out of their misery?

I looked into Beast's eyes and knew that I couldn't lose him. I *wouldn't* lose him, not after everything we'd been through.

"It's okay," I said, the word barely a whisper on my lips.

He leaned down and pressed a kiss on my lips and I tried not to shake, terrified of this awful thing they were making me do.

"It's going to be okay," he promised, but I wasn't so sure it was going to be okay.

Chapter Forty-Five
~ BEAST ~

I'd never hated Shooter or Gauge or the rest of my family the way I did right then. It was almost level with my hatred for Mateo and Carlos, the two bastards that had tortured and almost killed me over a year before. The two bastards that had sent Echo to ground. The two bastards that were now strung up by their arms in the clubhouse basement, waiting for their punishment.

Belle was standing in the corner where she'd been for the past twenty-five minutes, too terrified of what she had to do to move. Both men were unconscious; every time they started to rouse I punched them back into silence, and I heard her whimper at my brutality. But it was the only way. I couldn't let her do this alone; she had to know I was by her side every step of the way, and the simplest way to do that was to be by her side while we killed both of these men together.

She took a step forward, and Gauge and Rider stood to attention. Rider was filming it—evidence if she ever tried to turn on the club again—and I hated him for being a part of this, even if I knew why they were doing it.

In theory it was really fucking smart, and I would have done the same thing if the tables had been reversed on someone else. In reality it was fucking cruel.

Belle was a civilian. She was an innocent. She was purer than snow and more gentle than a damned butterfly. This would be a stain on her heart and soul.

Shooter was sitting on a crate next to Dom behind Mateo and Carlos, smoking a cigarette, waiting patiently for her to come to terms with this, and I hated him for that. Hated him for his calmness, for his patience. For his understanding.

Belle's gaze found mine and I held a hand out to her. She walked toward me slowly, each step like it was her own death sentence. Her hand in mine, I pulled her close and kissed the top of her head, feeling her whole body trembling.

"You okay?" I asked quietly.

She was trying to be strong, for me, her eyes like steel.

"You don't have to do this. We can just leave, Belle."

This was my family, but I'd leave them for her. I'd leave everything and everyone for her.

"I have to," she whimpered, tears filling her eyes. "I have to, because I love you, Beast, and I don't want to take your family away from you."

It was like her own words solidified it for her, and she pulled away from me and headed over to Mateo. She stared at his unconscious form, hanging there, waiting for his execution, and I wanted to tell her that it would be okay, that she wouldn't be haunted by the things she did next, but that would be a lie.

She turned to look at me, her face pale. "What do I do, Beast?" she asked, the words barely audible.

I walked to the table with my tools on it and looked over them all, trying to choose the simplest, easiest, and least bloody one for her—something that would inflict pain but not be too horrific or too gory—but they were all the same; they were all *meant* to inflict the biggest amount of pain, and each scream that she tore from Mateo would kill her a little inside.

I glared across at Shooter again, my nostrils flaring in anger at him for making her do this, even though I knew it wasn't entirely his decision. It had been a club one.

But this was Belle.

Beautiful, innocent Belle.

Belle, who wanted to care for people, not cut them up.

Belle's hand reached out and she started to pick up a gutting knife. I clamped my hand down on hers and shook my head.

"Not that one, babe," I said, and she withdrew her hand quickly like she'd been burned. I looked over the knives and weapons laid out on the table and picked up a simple combat knife. "This one," I said, handing it to her.

It looked huge in her small hand and she struggled to get a good grip on it. Or maybe she struggled to hold it because everything in her was telling her to drop it and run. We were so far away from her world now, and waist deep in mine. I wanted to protect her, but there was nothing I could do. All of the things I would usually do wouldn't work here in this moment, with these people. Blood and violence and releasing the monster within me would only make this situation ten times worse. The best I could do was to stay calm and help her through this.

She stared down at the brutal weapon in her hand and swallowed so loudly I could hear it over the rampant beating of my own heart. I picked up a knife for myself, a classic Bowie instead of my favorite skinning knife. Nothing brought a man more physical pain than having his skin slowly peeling back from his body and seeing his own flesh and blood underneath.

I walked to Mateo and she followed, and I heard Rider zooming in with the camera to make sure he got everything on film. Belle must have heard it too because she started to turn her head to look, but I reached out and gently took the end of her chin in my hand and guided her back to me.

"A man has many spots that won't kill him," I began, "many places where you can hurt him and he won't die, he'll just bleed. It looks bad, but they can survive it. We're going to hit some of these, okay?" I said as gently as I could, and she nodded slowly. I pressed a hand against Mateo's stomach, just to the side, where no vital organs were. "Here," I said, and reached for her hand with the knife. I pressed the tip of the blade against his side, but I could feel her straining to pull away from it. Her grip loosened on the knife and she whimpered as the tip of it pierced his skin, a small drop of blood forming. He murmured even though he was still passed out, but he was slowly coming back around. He'd sure as hell be wide awake in a moment.

"Beast," Gauge warned as a thin line of blood trailed from the small cut, basically telling me to step away. This was something she had to do, so there was no doubt that she had done it and hadn't been forced by anyone.

Belle looked up at me again, her eyes trailing tears down her face. Her chin was trembling and I leaned down and placed a kiss on her lips.

"You don't have to do this," I whispered, pressing my forehead to hers again. "We can leave and forget all this shit."

"You'll never forgive me for making you leave them," she whispered back.

And I pulled away to look at her. "I will, Belle. You're forgiven for everything, if I am."

She glanced between Mateo and me as he stirred more, his head rolling on his shoulders and his eyes flickering open. He saw Belle and me and a sneer formed on his face when he recognized her. I would have loved nothing more than to cut his throat there and then, but she placed a hand on my arm like she knew what I wanted and then she stepped closer to him.

"The fun we could have had," he said between bloodied teeth.

Belle looked down at her knife as if contemplating his words, this man, and how her life had ended up in this moment. Tears dripped off the end of her chin, and her shoulders shook, but as I reached out to pull her away from him, she stabbed him abruptly, the knife going in to his side exactly where I'd shown her. Mateo called out in pain loud enough to make Carlos stir in his bonds, and Belle gripped the blade handle tighter and pulled it back out.

Blood dribbled from the wound, trailing down his body, and began to form a puddle at his feet, and she stared down, mesmerized by it. Rider had moved positions to catch every gory detail and she looked up, right into the camera lens, and froze. Long seconds passed before she moved and then her gaze strayed to the blood on the floor and Mateo glaring up at her.

"Babe?" I said, not wanting to use her name on camera, and she slowly turned to face me, almost like she was in a daze. "You okay?"

"Where next?" she asked firmly.

Her tears had stopped, though I could see she was still shaking. Blood splatter was down her front and up her arm from when she'd retracted the knife, and I knew she was going to lose it when she saw it on her.

Carlos had woken up, his head rolling on his shoulders as he tried to focus on everything and everyone around him. He knew his time was up once his gaze landed on me, and he froze momentarily, his fear giving way. He was muttering in Italian until he saw Belle, and then his words died on his lips and a grin cracked his face.

"Pretty girl, I warned you what my brother would do to you, didn't I?" He smirked and licked his lips. "He'll fuck you until you can't walk and then he'll kill you."

The room fell away from me and I saw red. I dropped my knife and stormed forward, my fist rearing back and slamming into his face before he could speak again, knocking the breath from his lungs and the teeth from his mouth. I raised my fist again and slammed it into his face over and over until he was coughing and choking on his own blood and Belle was screaming at me to stop. I'd waited for this moment for so long, and the scent of his blood spurred me on. I wanted to beat him to death with my bare hands and show him exactly how the next few months of his pitiful existence were going to be. And if it would have been at any other time in my life, I would have kept him chained like that for months, if not years, repeatedly beating him until there was nothing left of the man he once was but broken bone and dying flesh.

Belle tugged on my arm and screamed my name again and I turned to look at her, my fists dripping with his blood, and one look at the horror on her face had the feeling of rage dying away like the tide slipping out.

She looked terrified of me and what I was capable of, and I felt sick to my stomach that I had caused that look in her eyes. I had made her cry. Me. The monster I was. The monster I had hidden from her, but now she had seen me in all my black glory and there was no point in hiding anything from her now.

"Stop," she begged, fresh tears trailing down her face.

The world came back in, and I saw my brothers and I saw Carlos's blood and I heard Mateo yelling at me in Italian, pulling on his chains frantically to get to me, to stop me from killing his brother. It spurred me on and calmed me all at the same time.

I was panting, the blood hot on my knuckles, and I nodded at Belle. "It's okay," I said, my voice thick with barely contained rage. She let go of my arm and I turned back to Carlos. Stepping closer to him, I clasped his head in my hands, letting his blood trail between my fingers. "Remember me, motherfucker?"

He spat in my face, blood and saliva sliding down my chin. I reared my head back and slammed it into his, hearing the satisfying crunch of his nose against my skull and he called out. I let his head go and it rolled on his shoulders, his eyes swimming in and out of focus, but he was laughing hysterically a high-pitched hyena laugh that set my nerves on edge.

I raised my blade up. "Something funny?" I asked, and he spat on the ground in front of him, his gaze straying to Mateo, whose blood was still dripping slowly from his stab wound.

"You think you've won?" He laughed, blood dripping down his face and into his eyes. "That's what's so funny. You think that this is over. That it ends with us." He laughed again and I gripped my knife tight in my grip and stabbed him in the same spot that I'd just shown Belle.

Carlos grunted as I held the blade in him. I stared into his eyes and I felt like God, looking life and death in the face, deciding someone's fate with a strike of my knife. I twisted it and he grunted again, his mouth opening and blood spilling off his flaccid tongue as he tried to call out. I put a hand over his mouth to stifle his cries and glared at him.

"You're lucky I'm not going to make this last," I gritted out, "that I'm going to end this quickly for you instead of keeping you on the brink of death for the next year, just like you did to me. I'm sending you on a swift one-way journey to hell, where you can serve your time with the

336

real Devil, but you make sure to save a place for when I'm done up here…because I'll be seeing you again."

I pulled the knife out of his side, gripped the handle tighter, and stabbed it into his chest, the sharp blade cutting through bone and muscle easily. I dragged it down his chest all the way to his belly button, cutting him open like a fish and letting his screams of pain fill up my cup for bloodlust to overflowing. When I reached his belly button, I pulled the knife out as he let out a final raspy breath and his insides tumbled at his feet.

I felt, rather than saw, Belle come to stand next to me as I stared at Carlos, feeling nothing but hatred for the piece of shit who'd brought me so much pain. Belle reached over and pried the knife from my hand, and I finally tore my gaze away from Carlos to look at her. I expected fear or terror, and she did look frightened. There was no denying that. But mostly she looked determined. I'd shown her the beast that lived within me and she was still by my side. She wrapped herself around me, burying her face against my chest like she was trying to calm me, like she was trying to soothe me, and I held her back, feeling more at peace than I ever had done in my life.

"He deserved that," she said, finally pulling away. Her face was smeared with blood and her eyes looked brighter. "After everything he did to you…he deserved that."

She looked over at Mateo, who was glaring at us both. But there was no mistaking the fear in his eyes or the sadness as he saw his brother dead, his blood and guts dripping to the floor.

"You going to do that to me now, gorgeous?" he asked with a smirk, and I started toward him but she put a hand to my chest. "Pity, I had big plans for us."

"I have to do this," she said softly. "I have to do this for us." She reached up and cupped my face, running her thumb along one of the deeper gouges down my cheek. "I'll do it for you, Beast."

If I could have loved her any more than I already did, my heart would have burst out of my chest.

Belle turned away from me and stepped toward Mateo, a knife in each hand now. Mateo lifted his chin and sneered at her.

"Sweet piece of ass like you going to cut me open?" he asked, coughing and wincing at the same time. "Sounds like a good time, not punishment." He licked his lips and sneered at her.

"I hope this hurts," she said, sounding fierce as fuck, and my dick twitched.

His smile grew wider. "I'll be seeing you in hell soon enough, bitch. I'll take my punishment and when you get down there" —he side-eyed me—"I'll be waiting for both of you."

I thought she was going to cry—she was already shaking from head to toe—but she stepped right up to him, close enough for him to stick out his tongue and lick along her cheek, but she didn't flinch. Not even a millimeter.

"Are you done?" she asked, and he laughed in response. Belle looked across at me. "Show me," she said. "Where can I hurt him the most?"

My Belle.

My beautiful Belle was turning into a monster just like me.

I should have pulled her away from the darkness, but instead I helped her run toward it, directing her blade toward the places I knew that would inflict the greatest amount of pain but keep him alive through it all.

The blood flowed and Mateo released his howls of pain into the air surrounding us. Belle embraced it all, hating it, loving it, wanting to be a part of my world no matter the consequences to her own soul. And when it was over, she was bathed in his blood and her eyes were empty.

I took the knife from her grip as Mateo lay limp from his chains, his face red with his own blood, his body wilted and empty. I looked up at Shooter and he nodded okay.

I leaned in to Belle and whispered into her ear. "Finish him, baby."

She nodded, and I pointed a thick finger at where his heart was in his chest and she took a step forward, raised the knife, and delivered the final blow to his heart, killing him instantly.

Rider clicked the camera off, and Gauge and Shooter stood up, coming toward us both. Belle looked at them all, her face red with another man's blood.

"Is it done now?" she asked, her voice sounding empty. "Are we good?"

My brothers looked at Shooter and he nodded. "Score is settled, Belle. You're one of us now." He looked at me. "Take your woman and get her cleaned up. Tonight we celebrate Echo's revenge, brother, and I want you both there."

I had *killed* a man.

I had *tortured* a man.

I was covered in his blood—my hair, my face, my hands, my clothes.

We were at Beast's home and he helped me strip out of my clothes and turned on the shower. He helped me in and I stood under the hot, beating water numbly watching the blood drain away.

"Do you want me to stay?" he asked, and I shook my head. He left, hesitating momentarily in the doorway before leaving.

I needed to be alone for a little while. To comprehend what I had just done and to come to terms with it. I had killed someone. The words seemed like fantasy in my head and I couldn't get them to make any sense.

The water had finally washed away the blood and gore that had covered me. Not blood from saving someone, but blood from killing someone. My soul felt wilted and empty, like someone had sucked all the good out of me and left me nothing but an empty body. A million hours of sleep wouldn't cure me of this feeling. I wasn't sure what would. I wondered, not for the first time since I'd seen myself bathed in blood, if this was how Beast felt every day. Did he feel empty? Did he feel devoid of emotions? Is this why he held on to his rage so tightly, because it made him feel something? Would that be me now?

The door creaked open and I looked up as Beast peered around the shower curtain, finding me sat in the bath hugging my knees to my chest, the water pounding down on me, and I saw the pain in his eyes. I wanted to get up and act like this was okay. That I was fine. I didn't want him to feel guilty for this. He'd already suffered so much, I wasn't sure how much more he could take.

But I couldn't hide it.

I couldn't switch myself back on to do anything but stare blankly at him.

He pulled the curtain all the way back and stepped into the bath, his jeans and T-shirt getting soaked as he reached for me and pulled me into his arms. He turned the shower off and carried me naked and wet to his bed before laying me down in it, and then he lay next to me. Holding me. Keeping me warm. Keeping me safe. Keeping me sane.

I needed to sleep, but every time I closed my eyes, I saw the blood—so much blood. I felt the tearing of Mateo's flesh reverberating up my arm. The crack of his bone as the knife cut into it as I stabbed him. I felt sick and empty. Lost. Afloat in my own nightmare.

"It's okay, Belle," Beast murmured, and kissed the back of my head, his arms wrapping tighter around me. "I've got you. I won't let anything happen to you now."

I wanted to fall apart in his arms. I wanted to cry and scream and lash out. I wanted to come apart—to splinter into a thousand pieces so that I could attempt to put myself back together again, but every time I tried to let go, all I felt was numb.

The killing seemed to have soothed him somehow, and I took satisfaction in that at least. The beast that normally raged inside of him, tearing at the walls to get out, seemed to be sated and calm. The blood and death had mollified it, yet I wondered how quickly it would return.

*

Belle had barely said two words since I'd brought her home and left her to shower, and I wasn't sure how to deal with that, or even if I needed to. I wanted to crawl inside her head so I could hear what was going on in there, so that maybe I could help her, because she seemed broken.

She finally fell asleep on my bed, wrapped in my arms, a whimper leaving her lips every now and then, like she was reliving the horror of what she'd done over and over, and I hated myself even deeper every time she did.

This was my fault.

I had created this.

I didn't really believe in heaven and hell, and if I did, I'd made my peace a long time ago that I was going to hell, but if hell was real then Belle didn't deserve to go there. She deserved to go to heaven. She was pure and wholesome and all things good. Or at least she was until I broke her with my dark world. Until I mutilated the good inside her and turned her soul black.

This was my fault.

Her sadness, her grief, her tears. All mine.

I could have stopped this from happening. I could have said no to Shooter and took her away from all of this, and I knew I should have. No matter what she said, I wouldn't have hated her for making me leave my family behind. But I was greedy—I wanted them *and* her. I wanted the girl and the family, and so I had allowed her to kill for me—for us. To butcher another person for my own gain, and now she was broken, because of me.

I climbed out of bed, tucking my blanket around her so she wouldn't get cold; her body had dried but her hair was still wet from the shower. I headed to the bathroom and stripped out of my damp clothes and turned the shower back on. I'd washed at the sink in the kitchen so she could take the shower, but now I needed to clean myself properly. It was the first rule of murder: cover your tracks. Burn the clothes, wash your body, and that's what I'd done. Not that Mateo and Carlos's bodies would ever be found, but regardless, I always followed the same routine no matter what.

The water sprayed across my back and I leaned against the wall, letting the hard spray work out the knots in my neck. Staring down at my feet, I saw the water turn pink as it reached places I had missed to wash away the rest of the blood, and I knew I'd been right to get in here. I scrubbed my body as hard as I could stand without damaging my skin. My skin was so sensitive to things that even water stung it at times, but right now I relished that pain. It made me stop recalling the things in my head that were making me grow hard.

Belle…covered in blood.

Belle…with the knives in her hands.

Belle…cutting him open…the dagger piercing his skin and slicing him down the middle.

Belle…eyes wide, blood and gore dripping from her hair and fingertips as Mateo cried out, begging her to stop, pleading with her.

And Belle, or some version of her…smiling in satisfaction as she ordered him to apologize to me and he complied.

My hand found its way to my dick without me even thinking about it, and I found myself grunting as I slid my hand along my hard length, the images of her killing and torturing him turning me on like nothing ever had before.

Fuck, I hated myself for it, but I couldn't stop it even if I tried.

This was who I was.

And maybe, now, it was part of who she was.

It was dark and deviant and so wrong, but the animal inside me loved seeing her like that. Loved seeing her anger as he mocked the marks on my skin that he'd put there. Loved that she took vengeance for me, slicing his skin and driving the knife deep into his body.

Something had come alight inside of her that hadn't been there before, and I knew we were bonded in more ways than could ever be really spoken of.

I didn't want it to be like that, but it was, and I couldn't help that my heart and head rejoiced in it. The memory of her wielding that knife, delivering that final blow, blood gushing from him and spraying back over her, covering her face and tits and… I came in long, hard spurts against the shower wall, grunting with each one. I bathed myself in her misery as I climaxed, hating myself for it but loving it regardless. It was sick, but I loved her all the more for stepping into my world and tasting the darkness that surrounded me. Even if it meant heaven and hell existed and she would have to spend all of eternity in hell with me. Especially that.

Mateo and Carlos were dead and gone. I should have been able to rest. To finally heal my heart and mind and not just my body. Echo had been avenged, and I had gotten my revenge for what they had done to me, and yet I still felt restless. The monster inside me was sated by their deaths, but something still wasn't right and I didn't know what.

The sound of Belle crying out had me switching off the shower and climbing out quickly. I grabbed a towel as I ran to the bedroom, and she sat upright quickly when I came in, her eyes wild.

"You're okay," I said, reminding her.

"I dreamt that he wasn't dead. That Shooter made me do it again," she whispered. "And again, and again."

I wrapped the towel around my waist and stalked toward her. "You will never have to do that again."

Belle…covered in blood…wide eyes staring back at me.

"I…I'm not sorry he's dead," she said, pulling her knees up to her chest. "I need you to know that."

Belle…knives in her hands.

"He deserved it," she said, hesitantly. Her gaze strayed to my chest—to the scars and burns and destroyed tattoos—and her mouth fixed into a straight line. She had life back in her eyes again, and I breathed a sigh of relief that she was coming back to me and maybe I hadn't completely broken her.

Belle…blood dripping from her hair.

"What they did to you," she said with a shake of her head, her forehead creasing with frustration. "It was evil."

Belle…cutting him wide open…the blood spraying back onto her…gasping.

Belle slowly pushed the covers away from her body and crawled toward me. She was still naked, her hair still damp from the shower. Her eyes were fixed on the hardness that was steadily growing beneath my towel, and when she reached me, she pulled my towel open, letting it fall around my feet.

Belle…stabbing and killing…death at her fingertips.

I gritted my teeth together, my jaw set in a hard line. "Belle," I said, cautiously.

She sat on her knees and took my dick in her hand before bowing her head to it and taking it into her mouth. I groaned as she took me to

344

the back of her throat and my hands automatically went to the back of her head to steady her rhythm as she sucked her way up and down my length, letting me fuck her mouth.

"Belle," I said again, but this time it was a groan, images of her flooded me as she took me into her throat over and over, her tongue sliding up and down me.

Belle...stripped naked, blood dripping down onto her tits and belly. Blood, sliding between her thighs.

I pulled her hair, dragging her mouth away from my dick so I could stare down at her. Her mouth was swollen and pink, wet with spit and pre-cum, her eyes wide and hungry. She panted as she looked up at me.

"They were evil," I agreed, and her tongue flicked out to lick along her full bottom lip. "They were evil, but I'm no better." She needed to know the truth. She needed to know all of me.

Belle rose up to her knees and placed her cheek on my hard chest, pressing kisses along each scar and burn, trailing her tongue along each groove that had been carved into my own flesh. She reached my chin, her arms wrapping around my shoulders, and then she looked me in the eyes, her expression serious.

"I know, Beast. I saw," she whispered before swallowing. "I saw all of you today." Her hand moved to my wet hair and she threaded her fingers through it, her gaze moving over my face—my lips, my nose, my chin, my cheeks and eventually my eyes. "They say the eyes are the door to the soul, and I saw that too."

I stared at her, and for the first time in my life I was afraid; afraid of what she might say, and afraid of what she wouldn't.

"And what's my soul like, Belle?" I asked, resentful because I already knew.

"Your soul is black, like death. Red like rage. And green like cruelty," she said matter-of-factly, but without any judgment. "I love you, Beast. I love you and your multicolored soul and your strong, capable hands that can inflict so much pain, and so much love." She reached for my hands and kissed my split knuckles.

345

"But I'm a monster," I said, my tone dark.

Belle smiled up at me. "And I love your monster too. It's a part of you, and now it's a part of me too."

I reached for Belle, pulling her face to mine and kissing her. I wanted to be gentle and loving, to be tender like she deserved to be treated, but that wasn't me and never would be. So I kissed her with all of my rage and all of my desire and all of my cruelty and all of my love, all rolled into one. I kissed her so hard that one or both of us was bleeding and that turned me on even more because I could taste it on my tongue.

I lay her back on the bed, pushed her legs apart, and filled her in one quick movement. She gasped and cried out, taking every inch of me, her body clinging to mine as I filled her and fucked her and allowed my monster to be free, finally. And she took all of me—monster and man, beast and beauty combined.

We fucked until the sun set and birds went to bed. We fucked wild and calm, we fucked like animals and like man and woman, we fucked until we were both too sore to fuck anymore and then we fucked each other with our mouths. My tongue on her slit, my mouth sucking on her clit, her tongue lapping at my dick and her hands on my balls.

By the time we finished, Belle and I, our monsters combined, were exhausted and sated. Every muscle and bone in my body ached. Her skin was bruised where I'd been too rough with her, my scars tender and raw where she'd dragged her nails down my flesh, not holding back anything for once.

I lay at her side, an arm thrown over my eyes, my dick flaccid and useless between my legs, my head buzzing with energy.

"Beast," she said.

"Uh huh," I grunted back.

"Do we get to have our happily ever after now?"

I moved my arm away from my eyes and turned to look at her. Her eyes were closed, her hair wild around her head. Her naked body was pale and she'd bruised like a peach, but she was perfect in every way, bruises and all.

"I don't believe in happily ever afters, but if I did, then I'd say yes."

She opened her eyes and looked at me. "I think so too," she said with a shy smile.

I leaned over and pressed a kiss to her forehead, and her hand reached out and found my chest, sliding down to my stomach before reaching for my dick. It was sore as hell, but her touch brought it to life almost instantly.

"You're going to fuck me to death, Belle," I said, hissing and groaning at the mixture of pleasure and pain that I'd come to love so much.

"But what a way to go," she said with a smile, and I chuckled at that, my hand reaching between her legs to part them and my fingers pushing inside of her. She gasped, the spark of life in her eyes flaring brighter with every touch.

If heaven and hell didn't exist, then all that mattered was now, and right now, I couldn't have been any happier.

Chapter Forty-Seven
~ BEAST ~

The party was in full swing when we arrived. It was noisy and busy and Belle clung to me like her life depended upon it. It was sweet as hell watching her see this place with new eyes. Witnessing it as I did—as a safe place and as a home.

"Beast," Gauge said as he came close to shake my hand.

I slapped his back as we shook. "Everything okay?" I asked, and he nodded.

"We've been waiting for you to arrive. We've got a meeting in church," he replied. "Got some things that need clearing up."

I scowled. "Things?"

Belle's grip on my hand tightened, but I didn't look away from Gauge, my mood growing darker.

"Don't get your panties in a twist, brother. Just club business and shit, nothing else." He glanced down at Belle. "You good?"

She nodded.

"Hungry?"

She nodded again.

"You lost your fucking tongue?"

I snarled, the hairs on the back of my neck bristling at the way he spoke to her.

"Leave her alone, you fucking pig!" said Laney, his daughter and Shooter's soon-to-be wife, coming to a stop by Belle's side.

"You watch your fucking mouth!" Gauge yelled, and Laney laughed in his face. "Cunt."

"Sorry, Daddy," she said, rolling her eyes at him before turning back to look at Belle. "Ignore this sack of shit, he has no manners whatsoever. I think he was raised by animals or something."

"It was wolves—dangerous and sexy," Gauge snarked.

"More like warthogs. Fat and greedy." Laney laughed again. "Come on, Belle, come and help me in the kitchen."

348

Laney started to pull Belle away with her, and Belle and I reluctantly let go of each other. She glanced back briefly before Laney ushered her into the kitchen where all the other old ladies no doubt were.

"She's such a bitch," Gauge sighed with a shake of his head.

I smirked, my anger dissipating. "She gets it from you."

Gauge dragged a hand down his beard and took a swallow of his beer. "Don't I fucking know it. Come on, let's get in there."

Everyone was already sitting and waiting for me to arrive when Gauge and I walked into church, and I sat in my usual seat, looking over at Shooter with a hard scowl. I didn't like this. Something felt off, but I wasn't sure what.

My jaw ticked, my teeth grinding as a prospect shut the door from the other side and left us all alone. The club noises faded away and silence surrounded us before Shooter finally spoke.

"Firstly," he began, "I want to say thank you to Beast and his old lady for bringing vengeance for Echo. You did your club and your brothers proud today. Echo would have been happy with how that shit went down. You made 'em pay, and the club got justice. But more importantly, *you* got justice."

Every one thumped the table repeatedly, offering words of agreement, but I was still lost on his words—old lady. It hadn't occurred to me that that was what she was now. I smiled at that realization.

"I also want you to know that we all know what a huge ask it was of your old lady to do what she did, and I know that don't come easy. Whatever happened previously is forgotten. Whatever happens in the future, the club and every man around this table and out that door has her back. You feel me?"

I nodded and the table thumps began again. "Appreciate that, Prez."

"She doing okay? Can't have been easy on her," he asked, sipping at his whiskey. "Think I saw her limping when she came in—she hurt?"

I smirked. "The limping is on me—we had some stuff we needed to work out, if you feel me."

"Bedroom stuff?" Casa asked, leaning forward, eager and horny as always. "You tried anal yet?"

Gauge sighed. "What is it with you and assholes, brother?"

"You don't know what you're fuckin' missing!" Casa laughed. He glanced over at Dom. "This man knows what the fuck I'm talking about, am I right?"

Dom scowled at him and lit a cigarette. "Shut the fuck up."

Casa smirked and looked back at me. "So? Anal. I can show you where to get a big-ass strap-on dildo from, and then what you do is—"

"I'm good," I cut in, not needing or wanting to hear anymore.

"Your loss, motherfucker," Casa tutted, sitting back in his chair.

"I'll take my chances." I turned back to Shooter, ignoring the snickering around the table. "She's gonna be okay. I've got it handled. And I want you to know, Prez"—I glanced around the table—"I want all of you to know that we both appreciate the chance you've given her to prove herself and her loyalty. The shit that went down was bad, and I blame myself for some of it because I didn't show her how shit was around here—and that's on me. But it's done now, Belle is here to stay. She's my old lady now."

"Never thought I'd hear you utter those words," Rider said, a smile on his face.

"Neither did I," I agreed, and everyone laughed.

Shooter stood up and raised his glass and everyone followed suit. "To Beast and Belle," he said. "To her making a good man out of you."

Everyone laughed at that too, and for the first time in my life, my heart didn't feel empty. Maybe I didn't believe in happily ever afters, but this was as close to one as I could ever imagine.

"Okay, next order of business—the prospect," Gauge said with a scowl. "He ain't gonna cut it."

"Nah, kid's too soft for this life," Casa agreed. "He wants it, wants it real bad, but..."

"I'll handle it," I said, and Shooter raised an eyebrow at me. I held my hands out. "Need a new project anyway, so why not him?"

350

Casa chuckled and I shot a scowl at him, which only made him laugh more. "You're like Bette fucking Midler taking the kid under your wing."

A few men chuckled, and then surprisingly Gauge shook his head and frowned. "That doesn't even make sense."

"What doesn't?" I asked.

"The song is about the other woman being the wind under her wings…so that would make the prospect Bette and Beast the other woman." He said it so matter-of-factly that the room was stunned into absolute silence.

"Barbara Hershey!" Rider said, snapping his fingers. "That was the other woman's name."

The room erupted into laughter again, and even I found myself laughing right along with them.

*

Belle was sitting between my legs on the grass outside the clubhouse. The fire pit was burning brightly enough that we could make out the people moving around us, but people farther away were just dark shadows. Her head was leaning back on my chest and her hands were stroking up and down my legs and fuck me, she smelled good. Like sin and seduction. Like heaven and hell. Like peaches and pussy. Fucking delicious.

"You need anything?" I asked her for what seemed like the hundredth time that evening. She was still pretty quiet, but she was beginning to come back out of herself. It was hard not to in this place. The women were good women, even the sweetbutts, and the men all respected her after everything she'd done that day, and they made that clear to her.

"No, I'm fine." She turned her head to look up at me, the light from the fire catching in her eyes.

"You let me know when you do and I'll get you whatever," I said, not being able to tear my gaze away from hers. God, but she was pretty. So pretty it made my chest ache.

She smiled. "I'll be sure to let you know."

I reached down and cupped her face in one hand before pressing a kiss on her mouth, my tongue darting into her warmth to slide across hers. She moaned against my lips and my dick hardened in my jeans, pressing into her back. When she pulled away she was smirking at me.

I swiped my thumb across her swollen bottom lip. "You be sure to do that."

"This feels sort of…surreal," she said, looking back into the fire.

"The club? It's probably the fumes from the fire. I think Casa burned something he shouldn't have," I replied.

She giggled. "Not the fire, stupid. Just this. Being here, with you. A year ago I was working my ass off at the hospital and saving up for an apartment. I only had a handful of people in my life and only one family member."

"And now?" I asked, genuinely curious as to how she viewed things now.

"I don't know. I have you, for starters, but all my savings are gone and I'm stuck in that stupid trailer still. I have no job, no clue as to what I want to do with my life, and I tortured and killed a man today and then had sex with you while thinking about it…" Her words trailed off and I grabbed her, spinning her in my lap to face me.

I searched her face for something. Anything. But her expression was blank.

"It's going to be okay," I said.

"I know," she said, looking away from me. "It's just, I don't know. I have this weight in my chest and it just keeps pressing down on me over and over until I can't catch my breath. The only time I can breathe is…" She blushed and tried to look away, and I touched the bottom of her chin and brought her gaze back to me.

"Is when?" I frowned.

"Is when you're inside of me," she said, no humor to her voice. "When you're making me…" She swallowed, her cheeks, even in the dark, glowing red.

"When I make you cum?" I smirked, more than happy about that. "Because if that's what it takes to make you feel better, then I'm more than happy to keep on helping out for as long as it takes."

She laughed again and it was the purest thing. "Shut up, Beast." She placed her lips on mine and kissed me, her tongue licking my lips and then pushing between them. The kiss was deep and growing deeper by the second, and I wasn't sure how much longer I could go without being inside of her again. I realized that I hadn't taken my pain meds all day. I hadn't even thought about them. Being with Belle had been enough pain relief.

I reached between us, pressing my thumb down on her clit and rubbing it in slow, steady circles until she gasped into my mouth. My dick was hard enough to cut glass and I gripped her tightly as I stood up, her legs automatically wrapping around my waist as I walked us inside.

Cheering rose from around us and I felt her laugh against my mouth, but fuck them if they thought I was stopping for even a second to give them the middle finger. I walked us back into the clubhouse and straight to my old room there, pushing the door open and then kicking it closed behind me before laying her down on the bed.

She was already stripping herself out of her dress and the biker boots I'd got the prospect to drop off earlier before I'd even unbuckled my belt. Her hand dipped between her legs as I pulled my dick out, the heavy weight of desire settling into my stomach as I watched her hand move, my eyes hooded.

"Fuck, Belle," I said, my hand pulling on my dick until I couldn't take any more. I climbed onto the bed, pushing her legs apart so I could settle myself between her thighs, the tip of my dick nudging against her wet entrance.

"Fuck me, Beast," she said, and my nostrils flared at the dirty word on her lips.

I pushed inside of her, driving myself home as my balls slapped against her asshole and my dick nudged the spot inside of her that made her fall apart. She sighed into the air, her eyes closed and her head

353

thrown back as I fucked her slowly. My hips rocked me into her over and over, harder and harder, until I felt her pussy tighten around me and she called out my name loudly. And my name on her lips made my balls draw up and I swore against her lips as I ground myself into her, dousing her pussy with my cum.

I stole glances at her as she pulled her dress back on over her head and she looked around for her panties. I dangled them in front of her with a smirk before slipping them into my pocket.

"Pervert," she laughed, her cheeks still pink from her orgasm. "Fine, keep them, let's just hope there isn't a breeze out there in case my skirt rides up."

I grinned at her. "I'll take my chances on that. The less clothing you wear, the better."

She pushed up on her tiptoes and kissed me again and my hand lifted the back of her skirt up to squeeze her naked ass.

"See? It's already working in my favor."

"Beast," she said, her gaze on the painting that Casa had been working on, and I smiled and turned to look at it. She took a step forward, her fingers reaching out, wanting to touch it.

"Not sure why that little fucker decided to paint a giant-ass red rose on my wall, but there it is," I grumbled, though there was something about it that I loved.

"It's beautiful. I love it," she said, staring up at it in awe. "I wonder what it means."

I shrugged. "No clue. I have no idea what goes through that man's head."

Chapter Forty-Eight
~ *Belle* ~

Beast had gone to talk to Rider and I was sitting by myself drinking a beer at the edge of the party, watching everything and everyone.

I didn't normally like beer that much, and this was the second time in a week, but it didn't seem the sort of place that I could ask for a glass of red wine, so I went with it. I wanted to be a part of his world so much. I needed to be accepted by these people so we could survive, and I'd do anything to make sure that happened.

I wasn't sure if I'd be able to survive without Beast.

Not now that I'd learned to live with him.

My cell was buzzing in my purse, and I pulled it out thinking perhaps it was Jenna. We'd reconciled in her apartment the day before, and I'd promised to come by for dinner over the next couple of days. She was still hurt by my actions, but she understood why I'd wanted to see my mom so badly. Why it was so important that I got to know her. It was the job at the hospital that she couldn't get her mind around, and in truth, neither could I.

I'd worked for so long and for so hard to get that job, but upon getting it I realized that I didn't want it. And now…now I had no idea what I wanted to do with my life. I wasn't too concerned though. I may have lost everything, but I'd also gained everything that mattered to me too.

I didn't recognize the number on my phone, and I frowned as I answered it.

"Hello?" I couldn't hear the voice on the other end and I covered my other ear with my hand as I darted away from the party to find a quiet spot. "Hello? Sorry, it's so noisy here. Can you say that again please?"

"I said, is your new man celebrating killing my brothers?" Lorenzo's voice cut through the noise and found its way into my heart.

"Lorenzo," I stammered, looking around me, suddenly terrified that he was there.

"My place, twenty minutes, Belle."

I looked back at the party, the fire dancing across everyone's happy faces. I didn't want to worry anyone with this, but I needed their help. I needed Beast, and my eyes frantically searched the darkness for him.

"Come alone, or Jenna is dead," Lorenzo said, and though I'd found Beast finally, I knew I couldn't go to him. I couldn't risk her life.

I stepped further into the shadows, away from Beast, away from his family. I was alone in this. I had to be. I knew what Mateo and Carlos were capable of, and after getting to know Lorenzo, I feared that he would be much worse.

"Okay," I said quietly into the phone.

"Good girl," he replied, and hung up.

I dropped my cell back into my purse and walked into the clubhouse, heading straight to Beast's room. I picked up the small handgun and knife that I knew he kept under his mattress. I'd seen them there when I'd been nursing him back to health and had changed his bedding, and now I slipped them into my purse and left, heading toward the front door.

"Belle?" Laney called my name and I looked back at her, forcing myself to smile. "Where you off to?"

"Just getting some fresh air," I said like an idiot, because it was the only thing I could think of.

Laney looked back to where I'd just come from with a frown. "Okay," she said, her gaze searching mine. "I uh, I got us some vodka, and some gin," she said, giving the two bottles in her hand a little shake. "Boys drink beer. Us women deserve something a little nicer, don't you think?"

I forced another smile. "Yes, absolutely. I'll be right back if you can get me a gin ready."

I turned and left without waiting for her to reply. There were a few men out front watching the bikes. They were bikers as far as I could see, but they weren't allowed into the party. It made no sense to me, in all honesty, but I didn't question it. I had no idea how I was going to get to Lorenzo's from there. I had no car, thanks to my mom, and Beast had the keys to his truck in his pocket. I'd refused to go on the back of his bike tonight—one thing at a time, I'd told him, and he'd promised me he'd get me on the back of it tomorrow.

A promise, I realized now with dread in the pit of my stomach, that he might not be able to fulfil thanks to Lorenzo. I couldn't help but wonder, as I started walking toward town, how Lorenzo had known his brothers had been killed. He'd told me he didn't have anything to do with them, that they hadn't spoken in years, so how could he know? The problem twisted itself in my gut, maybe because it was easier to focus on that than it was to focus on the fact that I was going to be at the center of his fierce temper when I finally got there.

All the years that I'd known Lorenzo from a distance, he'd seemed such a nice man. Calm, cool, collected. A businessman with a good head on his shoulders and strong family values. Yet after that night at the Crest where he'd forced himself into my mouth, I knew there was a much darker side to him, and he'd proved himself with every meeting since. He had a wicked temper and a dark and calculating side to him. That part of him I was terrified of. Maybe even more than I had been of his brothers.

I walked for fifteen minutes and was about to call Lorenzo back and beg him to give me more time to get there when a smooth black car pulled up beside me. I remembered the car and knew instantly that it was him. The windows were tinted but when the locks unclicked, and I got in without question.

"Looking pretty tonight, Belle," he said, his accent sounding thicker as he pulled away and started to drive again.

"Where's Jenna?"

"Do you remember the last time we were in this car together?"

"Where is she?" I looked across at him, hating him in that moment more than I'd hated Mateo.

"Do you remember the fun we had?" he teased, his hand going to my thigh and stroking up it. I batted his hand away.

"Get off of me!" I snapped, and he laughed manically. He seemed almost unhinged.

"Calm yourself down. It's not like we haven't done this before anyway, what's one more time for old times' sake?" His hand slid higher, pushing my skirt further up my legs, and I pushed it back down and attempted to pry his fingers off of me but he gripped me tight enough to make me whimper.

His hand moved higher and then his head snapped to look at me, his nostrils flaring and his eyes wide. "No panties? Little whore!"

"Where is she? Where's Jenna?" I sobbed, fear and desperation making me break. I'd wanted to be strong like Beast, like the woman I had been back in the basement when I'd killed Mateo, but I couldn't find her now.

I felt weak and small.

I felt devastatingly alone.

He swore in Italian, his words no longer sounding romanticized but vile and ugly. His fingers tried desperately to reach to my most private parts but I continued to bat his hands away from me.

"Get off me!" I screamed.

Lorenzo's hand let go of my thigh and he swerved the car as he reached back and slapped my face. At the awkward angle it was less painful, but it still stunned me into submission enough to stop fighting him momentarily.

"Stop fucking fighting me, little whore. I'm not going to hurt you. At least not yet. I need you alive so I can make that piece-of-trash boyfriend of yours pay for what he's done to my brothers." He gripped the steering wheel with both hands and I whimpered, swiping away the drop of blood I could feel on my bottom lip.

It was darkness on either side of the car. Night had fallen, and out there no one was around to help me. I remembered Beast's hands on my skin, his lips on mine and the feel of him buried deep inside of me, and I gritted my teeth.

I loved him.

I loved him so much that I'd give my life for his.

"It was me," I said, quietly, my gaze out the front window.

"What did you just say?" Lorenzo replied.

I turned to look at him, seeing the amusement on his face. He didn't believe me.

"I killed them both," I said, my voice growing bolder, the lie only small. Beast had killed Carlos, but I had killed Mateo.

Lorenzo laughed harder and continued to drive. "Nice try, Belle, but you can't save that piece-of-shit biker of yours. His fate has been sealed. He'll pay for what he's done. Do you want to know how?"

"It *was* me," I said between gritted teeth, my stomach rolling in fear.

"I'm going to send pieces of you back to him. A finger. A toe. A hand. A foot. Each piece delivered daily so that he comes to dread each package." Lorenzo smirked like he was the cleverest man on the planet. "And then finally, I'll send him your fucking head."

Terror threaded its way through my muscles because I believed him. Every single word. It took everything I had to force myself to sit still and not tremble uncontrollably.

"I stabbed him in the side," I said, my voice quiet, my mind going calm as I remembered the things I had done to Mateo. "I took my knife and I sliced it down his chest all the way down to his stomach."

My voice sounded foreign to my ears, like it didn't belong to me at all but to some imposter that had taken over my body. But the voice wasn't lying; I had done those evil things, and I didn't regret any of them.

"And when he begged for me to stop, crying like a baby and pleading with me, I cut his face and made it look like he was still smiling." I turned and looked at Lorenzo, his gaze no longer on the road but on me. "I took the tip of my knife and I cut him here," I said, pointing to the right corner of my mouth, "and here."

His eyes were filled with hatred and pure, unadulterated rage. "Mateo would never beg," he said slowly, carefully, like what I was saying was starting to make sense to him.

"But he did," I replied, still looking at him. The car was beginning to swerve across the road because he wasn't looking where he was going, too intent on glaring at me. "He begged for his mom—for his *mia madre*. He didn't beg for Carlos though, because he was already dead, gutted like the pig he was."

Lorenzo suddenly lunged for me, his voice high-pitched as he screamed at me. "*Bastarda!*" If it wasn't for his seatbelt jarring him backwards, he would have had his hands wrapped around my throat already. "*Puttana, ti ucciderò!*"

My hand fumbled in my bag momentarily, seeking out the gun, but when I pulled it out and aimed it at him, squeezing the trigger without fear, nothing happened.

"*Stupida puttana!* You think you can kill me!" he roared, steering the car straight again to keep it from driving into a tree. One of his hands batted the gun from my grip and I cried out as it flew under the seat. "New plan, Belle! I'm going to fuck every hole of yours until you bleed. Until you can't walk ever again. I'm going to keep you alive, trapped as my own personal sex slave until I'm done with you. How does that sound?" He laughed with wickedness in his tone, his fury growing.

My hand was back in my purse but he was too intent on his fury at me, his sadistic plan coming together in his head as he drove faster and faster, to notice.

"I'm going to make your *sofferenza* exquisite, Belle. You've never felt pain like the kind I'm going to put you through." He laughed insanely, and I should have been frightened. I should have been terrified, but all I felt was emptiness. "Beg, princess—beg me, and maybe when the time comes I'll slit your throat quickly and be done with it."

The knife was tight in my grip as we raced through the night toward a lifetime of hell that he was planning for me, and I thought of all the things I hadn't gotten to do yet. All the plans Beast and I had, the dreams we shared. I didn't want to be a nurse anymore, but maybe I could still have worked with people. Maybe I could have become a counselor for children. And Jenna, what would she do without me? Would she be happy that she was free of my burden and she and Gregory could finally marry and travel like he wanted them to, or would she be broken by the loss of me? Would she suffer?

I couldn't let it happen.

I thought about when I'd first met Beast in the hospital. How broken he'd been. How ill. And how much he'd already survived at that point. He hadn't given up at any point. He kept on fighting, his will to live stronger than his will to die.

It would be easier if I could accept my fate and sit back and wait for whatever was coming next, but if Beast had taught me anything it was that no matter what, you never gave up fighting. You fought until your last breath, no matter the consequences.

And you never fucking begged!

I glanced across at a raging Lorenzo, his eyes wild as he continued to yell and spit all the vile things he was going to do to me. He believed me now; he knew it was me that had killed one if not both brothers.

"Lorenzo." I said his name, my voice too quiet for him to hear me over his own raging. "Lorenzo!" I suddenly yelled, cutting through his monologue of violence and forcing him to look at me.

"What?" he yelled back, and I lifted my hand and slashed it across his throat in one brutal blow.

His hands left the wheel as he fought frantically to stop the bleeding, but it was no good. He tried to speak, his words coming out as nothing but garbled, bloody nonsense, and the car began to veer quickly toward the edge of the road.

I grabbed the door handle and threw it open, giving one terrified look at the ground speeding past before I dove out of the car, hitting the ground with a thump. I rolled over and over, feeling my skin tear and bones break, and I screamed out loudly before coming to a stop in the ditch. The world was ringing and then it was ablaze as Lorenzo's car hit something in the distance and the sound of crunching metal and glass smashing had me covering my head in case something fell on me.

I wasn't sure how long I lay there, panting and too terrified to try to move, before I heard the sound of motorcycles coming toward me. They went straight past, not seeing me in a heap farther away from the wreckage. I forced myself to move and I stood on unsteady feet as several bikes came to a stop before the destroyed car.

Beast's voice found me in the darkness as he called my name, yanking open Lorenzo's door and dragging his dead body from the wreckage in search of me.

"Beast," I called for him as tears poured down my face, stinging the fresh cuts. "Beast!" I screamed for him and I watched him turn and seek me out.

He ran toward me, stopping himself as I came into view, his dark eyes washing over me, taking in all of my cuts and bruises and the way I was cradling my arm against my chest.

"I thought," he said, his arms reaching for me.

"It will take more than that to kill me," I replied, my voice hoarse from screaming. "I'm your old lady now, and you taught me never to give up."

Epilogue
~ BEAST ~

I watched her sleeping, feeling like a creeper but not caring enough to stop doing it.

When Laney had come and found me and told me Belle had left, my heart had sunk. Shame clawed at me that I'd thought that maybe she'd tricked us all. That maybe she'd been working with someone all the way along and this had all been one big fucking trick. That perhaps she hadn't loved me after all.

I'd never known real love before—not the kind between a man and a woman. Not the kind between a mother and a son. I only knew club life, and the bond between a man and his brothers, and even that I wasn't sure on sometimes. These men didn't owe me anything, yet they gave me it all. Couldn't quite get my mind around that, just like I wasn't sure that I'd ever get used to the fact that Belle really did love me.

How could it be that I, the Beast with no heart and a soul as black as the night, had found love in this unforgiving world after all?

She stirred in her sleep and I went to her, getting in bed behind her so I could cradle her small body with my own. She was so precious and so strong, and I'd almost lost her. Almost was too close, and I would never allow that to happen again.

"Beast?" she whispered, her eyes fluttering open.

"I'm here," I said, squeezing her gently.

"I thought I died…" she said quietly. "I dreamed that I died and I went to hell, and I was all alone there without you." Her shoulders shook and I kissed the back of her neck and hushed her.

Two people dead at her hand.

If there really was a heaven and hell, she was headed for the latter for sure.

"I won't let that happen. Not ever," I promised. "Where you go, I go, forever."

She looked over her shoulder at me, and the fire in her eyes was there—the little spark of Belle that made her who she was. I thought that part of her was lost after what she'd had to do to Mateo, but it was still there. Thank God it was still there.

"I love you," she said.

I leaned down and kissed her gently, even though every muscle in my body wanted to kiss her hard. I was gentle and tender and everything that I wasn't used to. I guess we both had to become something else to stay together.

"Can you really love a beast like me?" I asked. "I've caused you nothing but pain, Belle. I've destroyed everything and almost gotten you killed over and over…"

She kissed me, silencing my words for the moment, and when she pulled away her expression was vibrant. There was no other way to describe it. She was vibrant with life.

"I love you, Beast. And no matter what you think, this wasn't your fault. What I do know for certain is that after everything we've both gone through, we've still come back to each other. We've survived it all."

Fuck me.

I was done for.

I could have died right then and I would have died a happy man.

Did I deserve her love after all the evil I'd done in the world? Probably not. But was I going to grasp it with both hands and never let go? Hell yeah.

"I love you, Belle," I said, the first time those words had ever left my mouth. "I love you now and forever, and until the end of time."

She smiled up at me and I kissed her again, our tongues moving in sync. She pulled away first and looked at me, those big Disney eyes staring right into my wretched, rotten soul and accepting everything about me. Man, beast, biker. I was hers and she was mine.

"Do we get our happily ever after now, Beast?" she asked, and I smiled, the biggest smile I'd ever smiled in my whole Goddamned life, because for the first time ever I felt the truth of those words and I believed them.

"Hell yeah, we do, Belle. Hell yeah."

The End

Ready for more Highwaymen?

You can find more of your favorite Highwaymen in the following:

Ride or Die: The Devil's Highwaymen Series

The Devil's Highwaymen Nomads:
Crank #1
Sketch #2
Battle #3
Fighter #4

Coming 2021:

Last Night in Georgia Duet

Thank You.

To the Queens in Claire's Queens … thank you so much for everything. For being so passionate about my stories. For loving my tortured alphas and for wanting them to have their happily ever afters.

Thanks especially go to Julie & Emma, my Alpha readers. Sorry for dragging these poor men through hell and back for my own enjoyment. I hope it brings you as much pain as it brought me joy… hahahahaha!

Thank you to all the bloggers and bookstagrammers who helped spread the word for this book and others. The community wouldn't be what it is without your support and commitment.

Thank you to my friend and editor Amy Jackson. Thanks for always highlighting my stupid typos and laughing at me. My books would be a hell of a lot more humorous if it wasn't for you, so ummm thanks hahaha

Hugest of thanks to my fellow ginger Northerner, Sarah Barton. Thanks for organizing me and keeping me sane. You rock my socks, Queen, so pleased to call you a friend.

And finally, thank you to my best friend from across the world, Elizabeth Constantopoulos. Thank god I have you in this world full of so much madness to keep me sane.

Claire xox

ABOUT THE AUTHOR

Claire C. Riley is a *USA Today* and international bestselling author.

She's a genre-jumping book nerd who likes to write about psycho stalkers, alpha males, anti-heroes, and the end of the bloody world! She lives in the United Kingdom with her husband, three daughters, and ridiculously naughty rescue beagle.
Gryffindor. Targaryen. Zombie slayer.

Also by Claire C. Riley

MC & Mafia Romance:
Ride or Die The Devil's Highwaymen series
The Devil's Highwaymen Nomad Series:
Crank #1, Sketch #2, Battle #3, Fighter #4,
Tame His Beast duet: Beast & Belle's story – *A Devil's Highwaymen story*
Born to Darkness ~ *The Bratva Mafia twins duet* ~ co-authored with Ellie Meadows coming 2021

Post-Apocalypse Romance:

Odium: The Dead Saga series.
Odium Origins Series
Out of the Dark #1
Red Eye: The Armageddon Series – co-authored with Eli Constant
Thicker than Blood series – co-authored with Madeline Sheehan
Paranormal Romance:
Limerence (The Obsession Series)
Limerence II (The Obsession Series)

Twisted Magic Raven's Cove

Romantic Thriller/Suspense:
Beautiful Victim
Fragments of Delores

New Adult Romance:
Wrath #3 the Elite Seven Series

Horror:
Blood Claim

CONTACT LINKS:

Website: www.clairecriley.com
FB page: https://www.facebook.com/ClaireCRileyAuthor/
Amazon: http://amzn.to/1GDpF3I
Reader Group: Riley's Rebels:
https://www.facebook.com/groups/ClaireCRileyFansGroup/
Newsletter Sign-up: http://bit.ly/2xTY2bx
IG: https://www.instagram.com/redheadapocalypse/
Twitter: @ClaireCRiley